Best Kept
Secrets

Also by Shelly Ellis

Chesterton Scandal series

Lust & Loyalty
Best Kept Secrets
Bed of Lies

Gibbons Gold Digger series

Can't Stand the Heat
The Player & the Game
Another Woman's Man
The Best She Ever Had

Published by Dafina Books

Best Kept Secrets

SHELLY ELLIS

Property of
FAUQUIER COUNTY PUBLIC LIBRARY
11 Winchester Street
Warrenton, VA 20186

WITHDRAWN

Kensington Publishing Corp.
http://www.kensingtonbooks.com

To the extent that the image or images on the cover of this book depict a person or persons, such person or persons are merely models, and are not intended to portray any character or characters featured in the book.

DAFINA BOOKS are published by

Kensington Publishing Corp.
119 West 40th Street
New York, NY 10018

Copyright © 2016 by Shelly Ellis

All rights reserved. No part of this book may be reproduced in any form or by any means without the prior written consent of the Publisher, excepting brief quotes used in reviews.

If you purchased this book without a cover, you should be aware that this book is stolen property. It was reported as "unsold and destroyed" to the Publisher and neither the Author nor the Publisher has received any payment for this "stripped book."

All Kensington Titles, Imprints, and Distributed Lines are available at special quantity discounts for bulk purchases for sales promotions, premiums, fund-raising, and educational or institutional use. Special book excerpts or customized printings can also be created to fit specific needs. For details, write or phone the office of the Kensington special sales manager: Kensington Publishing Corp., 119 West 40th Street, New York, NY 10018, attn: Special Sales Department, Phone: 1-800-221-2647.

Dafina and the Dafina logo Reg. U.S. Pat. & TM Off.

ISBN-13: 978-1-61773-401-4
ISBN-10: 1-61773-401-2
First Kensington Trade Paperback Edition: September 2015
First Kensington Mass Market Edition: November 2017

eISBN-13: 978-1-61773-400-7
eISBN-10: 1-61773-400-4
First Kensington Electronic Edition: September 2015

10 9 8 7 6 5 4 3 2 1

Printed in the United States of America

To Chloe and Andrew, my heart and my home

Acknowledgments

.

If it takes a village to raise a child, it certainly takes a village to produce a book—and keep an author sane while she's writing it. In the past four years, I've written a total of eight books. (*Best Kept Secrets* is my fifth. The rest, for now, are sitting on my laptop waiting for the green light.) Though I've been the one at the keyboard, I've had plenty of help in bringing each book to fruition.

I want to thank my husband, Andrew, for his time, for lending an ear, and for watching the little one when needed so that I can hide away, write, and follow my dreams. I want to thank my mother and father for their assistance and for giving both Andrew and me a break from the wonderful though exhausting enterprise known as raising a toddler. I know that without your help writing books would be a lot more challenging.

I want to thank the wild and crazy little girl known as Chloe who makes Mommy laugh and helps me to keep things in perspective. (It's hard to be frustrated with writer's block when someone is making spitty face at you.)

As always, I want to thank my editor at Kensington, Mercedes Fernandez, for giving my writing a chance. What started out as a contract for three books after you pulled my manuscript out of the slush pile has since blossomed to a NAACP Image Award nomination, preliminary talks of television show spin-offs, and me finally landing an agent. I will always be grateful that you took a chance on me. And thanks to my new champion and agent, Barbara Poelle. I'm shocked at how much you hustle and how you're such a great advocate for your clients. Thanks for reaching out to me and pushing me to write even better.

To all my fellow authors and aspiring writers who I've connected with online and at author events: I wish I could list you all by name, but it would be the length of a novella. Thank you for all your support, love, and encouragement. I hope I reciprocate everything that I've been given.

Chapter 1

LEILA

Leila Hawkins paused as she mounted the last concrete step in front of the double doors of the First Good Samaritan Baptist Church—one of the oldest and largest churches in Chesterton, Virginia, her hometown. Nestled on Broadleaf Avenue across the street from rustic Macon Park, the house of worship had hosted many a baptism, funeral, and nuptial inside its brick walls in the one hundred and some odd years of its existence. And since 1968, a stark white sign had sat along its exterior, highlighting a Bible verse chosen by the honorable reverend, or the assistant pastor when the reverend was ill or on vacation. Leila stepped aside to let a couple pass as she squinted at that sign, which hung a foot away from the doors and several feet above her head.

A FOOL GIVES FULL VENT TO HIS ANGER, BUT A WISE MAN KEEPS HIMSELF UNDER CONTROL, the sign read in big bold letters. PROVERBS 29:11.

Her eyebrows furrowed.

What the hell . . .

Was someone reading her mind?

Who cares if they are?

She grabbed one of the church's stainless-steel door handles.

She was on a mission today and she wasn't going to be deterred from it. She was giving "full vent" to her anger, whether any celestial being liked it or not. Leila was crashing this hifalutin wedding, and only lightning bolts or locusts would keep her away!

She walked into the vestibule, then tugged a heavy wooden door open, preparing herself to be met by a hundred stares, finger pointing, and indignation the instant she stepped inside the sanctuary.

"Hey! You're not supposed to be here!" she waited for someone to shout at her.

Instead, she was greeted by a light melody played by a string quartet and the polite chatter of the two hundred and some odd guests who were taking their seats in the velvet-cushioned pews.

No one stared at her. Hell, they barely seemed to notice her!

The tenseness in her shoulders instantly relaxed. Her white-knuckled grip on her satin clutch loosened. She reminded herself that she was walking into a wedding, not a gladiator pit.

"You're here to talk to Evan," a voice in her head cautioned her. "Not to fight with him. Remember?"

That's right. I'm just here to talk to him, to have a conversation with an old friend.

And if Evan chose not to be polite or listen to her, then and *only then* would she go off on him.

She looked around her.

The sanctuary was filled with splashes of pink and lavender, which Leila remembered were the bride's favorite colors. Roses, hydrangeas, freesias, and lilacs decorated the pulpit and pews, filling the space with their alluring scent. Ribbons and ivy garland were draped over anything and everything, and free-standing candelabras were along each aisle and by the stained-glass windows.

Leila felt an overwhelming sense of déjà vu. She hadn't set foot in this church since her own wedding day ten years ago. As she gazed around her, all the memories of that day came rushing back like a tsunami: the anticipation and nervousness she had felt as she waited for the church doors to open, the happiness she had experienced when she'd seen her handsome groom waiting for her at the end of the aisle, and the overwhelming sadness that had washed over her when she had looked at the wedding guests and had not seen her then best friend, Evan, among their friendly faces.

But she had known Evan wouldn't come to her wedding. Stubborn Evan Murdoch had told her in the plainest way possible that there was no way he would stand by and pretend that he was happy about her nuptials.

"That son of a bitch is going to break your heart," Evan had warned her over the phone all those years ago when she'd made one last-ditch effort to ask him to come to the wedding. "He's going to drag you down. And when he does, don't come crying to me."

Leila wasn't sure what had made her angrier: that Evan had given her that dire, bitter prediction on the eve of her wedding—or that his prediction had come true. But today she would have to put aside all that resentment and anger if she was going to get Evan to do what she needed him to do for her mother. Her mother . . . a proud woman who had juggled multiple jobs and saved every dime she had for decades to gather the money to put Leila through school and give her a reasonably happy life. Leila had tried to repay her by purchasing her a two-bedroom bungalow in a middle-class neighborhood where they still held summer block parties, where neighbors still waved and said hello. But now Leila's mother would lose her home in a few months without Evan's help.

Leila's grip on her purse tightened again.

She'd argue. She'd beg. She'd do what she had to do to get Evan to listen to her.

For Ma's sake, she thought.

"Bride or groom?" someone asked, yanking Leila from her thoughts.

"What?" Leila asked.

She turned to find an usher leaning toward her. An officious-looking woman stood behind him with the kind of pinched face reserved for those who waited at the counter at the DMV and dentists' offices. A clipboard covered with several stacks of paper was in her hands. The woman discreetly whispered something into her headset while the usher continued to gaze at Leila expectantly.

"Are you with the bride or groom?" He gestured toward the pews. "On which side would you like to be seated?"

That was a tricky question. The bride hadn't invited Leila to the wedding; neither had the groom. But Leila certainly knew the bride better. Paulette Murdoch, Evan's sister, was someone Leila had once considered a friend—almost a little sister.

"Umm . . . uh, bride . . . I-I guess," Leila finally answered.

They noticed her hesitation and exchanged a look that Leila couldn't decipher. The woman behind the usher whispered into her headset again and waited a beat.

What? Leila thought with panic. *What did I do wrong?*

The woman stepped forward, plastering on a smile that seemed more forced than friendly.

"I'm sorry. Would you mind giving me your name?"

"Uh . . . why?"

"I just want to make sure you're seated in the proper area." The woman then pulled out a pen and pointed down at the stack of papers. Leila could see several names listed along with check marks next to each of them.

You've gotta be kidding me, Leila thought.

They actually had a guest list for the church! What did they think? Someone was going to sneak into the wedding?

"You are sneaking into Paulette's wedding!" the voice in her head chastised.

But still, this was ridiculous! Leila wondered if the guest list had been Evan's idea.

Wouldn't want the unwashed masses to wander in off the street, would we? Leila thought sarcastically. *Wouldn't want the poor people to stink up the place! Only the best and the brightest for the M&Ms!*

M&Ms or Marvelous Murdochs . . . People had been muttering and snickering over that nickname for decades around Chesterton, using it to derogatorily refer to the Murdochs—one of the most wealthy, respected, and (some said) stuck-up families in town. Of course that was better than their old nickname, the "High Yella Murdochs." That name had faded once the Murdochs became more equal opportunity and let a few darker folks like Evan's mom into the family.

"Well, my . . ." Leila paused, wondering how she was going to get out of this one. She most certainly wasn't on the list. "My name is . . . my name is, uh—"

"Leila! Leila, over here!" someone called to her. Leila turned to find her childhood friend Colleen waving wildly. Colleen sat in one of the pews toward the front of the church.

Saved by the bell!

"Come on, girl!" Colleen shouted, still grinning. "Sit by me!"

"I guess my 'proper area' is up there, then?" Leila asked.

The usher laughed while the woman with the clipboard continued to scrutinize her, not looking remotely amused.

"Go right ahead," he said, waving Leila forward.

She walked down the center aisle to Colleen. As she did so, she ran her hands across the front of her pale yellow dress. It was an old ensemble that she had thrown on at the last minute after raiding her closet. She hadn't worn it in years, certainly not since she had given birth to her daughter. It felt a little tight and she worried that it wasn't very flattering. The ill-fitting dress only added to her already heightened anxiety.

"I haven't seen you in ages, girl! I didn't know you'd be at Paulette's wedding," Colleen cried, removing her heavy leather purse from the pew and plopping it onto her ample lap. She shifted over, causing an elderly woman beside her to glance at her annoyance. Colleen then adjusted the wide brim of her sequin- and feather-decorated royal purple hat. "I saw you come in, but you didn't notice me waving at you. What were you thinking about, staring off into space like that?"

Leila pursed her lips as she took the seat nearest to

the center aisle. "Just took a little trip down memory lane, that's all."

"*Memory lane?*" Colleen frowned in confusion. Suddenly, her brown eyes widened. "Oh, I forgot! This was the church where you got married too, isn't it?"

Leila nodded.

"Ten years ago last month! Girl, I remember," Colleen continued. "It was a beautiful day, wasn't it? And you had looked so pretty in your gown." She patted Leila's hand in consolation. "I'm so sorry to hear about you and Brad, by the way."

"Don't be sorry," Leila assured.

I'm certainly not, she thought.

Not only had Brad broken her heart, like Evan had predicted, but that man also had put her through so much pain during the course of their marriage—between the lies, philandering, his get-rich-quick schemes, and his all-around bullshit—that he was lucky she hadn't thrown her wedding ring down the garbage disposal in outrage. Instead, she had pawned it to pay for a hatchback she'd purchased for her move from San Diego back to Chesterton. She'd had to get a new car after her Mercedes-Benz was repo'd thanks to Brad neglecting to mention that he hadn't made any payments in four months.

"So it *is* final then?" Colleen asked. "It's over between you two?"

"Almost. The divorce should be finalized in a few months, I guess."

Leila certainly hoped it would be. But frankly, it was no telling with Brad. He had been dragging his feet on the divorce proceedings, saying that his focus was instead on his criminal case. He faced charges for fraud and money laundering because he and his partners had bilked several wealthy clients in Southern

California out of more than twenty million dollars with some elaborate Ponzi scheme.

Thanks to Brad, his lawyer, and the California court system, Leila's life was still in limbo. She felt like she was *still* swimming her way out the whirlpool Brad kept sucking her into.

"Well, I'm glad you came back here," Colleen said. "We missed you. I know I certainly did. I'm sorry your divorce is the reason why you came, but . . . you tried your best, right?"

Leila nodded then turned away to stare at the front of the church, wishing desperately that Colleen would drop the topic. She didn't want to think about Brad right now. She had enough on her plate today.

"You put up with more than most wives would," Colleen continued, oblivious to Leila's growing discomfort. "It's a wonder you lasted as long as you did. I know I wouldn't have!"

Leila's smile tightened.

"All that lying and cheating—and now that pyramid-scheme nonsense! That man has dragged you through the mud, Leila. Right on through it!" Colleen shook her head ruefully. "Girl, I would have taken a frying pan to the back of that man's head *years* ago!"

It was bad enough to have a wreck of a marriage, to find out that you were sharing a bed every night with a liar and a hustler. But it was ten times worse knowing that everyone in town also knew—and Chesterton was a town that loved its gossip. She was sure her failed marriage and Brad's criminal charges had been gossip du jour in every beauty salon, church gathering, and coffee shop in Chesterton for months!

Of course, Evan had discovered the truth first, but he hadn't needed the town gossips to tell him. He had figured it out himself. He had seen through the varnish and spotted the shoddy workmanship underneath. He had seen the *real* Brad back when she met the smooth-talking Casanova her junior year in college. Though Brad had blinded Leila with his sweet talk, worldliness, and charm, Evan had called him on his bullshit. But she had been too naïve and lovesick at the time to listen to her then best friend. She wished now that she had. It could have spared her a lot of disappointment, agony, and heartbreak in the long run. It could have spared her from severing ties with Evan and the humiliation she was suffering today.

"The flowers are beautiful," Leila said with a false cheeriness, trying to change the subject from Brad. She looked around her again, taking it all in.

Paulette Murdoch was probably deliriously happy with how the decorations had turned out. The décor fit her to a T.

"I knew everything would be this nice though," Leila said. "Paulette's dad never spared an expense, *especially* when it came to his little girl. I've been away for a while, but even I remember that much."

Colleen shook her head and leaned toward Leila's ear. "Not her father, honey," she whispered. "All this was arranged while he was sick in the hospital and after he died seven months ago. It's Evan who dished out the money for this wedding. He controls the purse strings now!"

Of course he does, Leila thought sullenly. Evan controlled everything. He held all the cards, which was why she was here today.

The last note of the melody the string quartet had been playing ended and the violins started to play *Canon in D Major.* The chatter in the sanctuary ceased as the church doors opened. The groom and his six groomsmen strolled toward the front of the church, near the pulpit, in single-breasted tuxedos with pink calla lilies pinned to their lapels.

The groom was a handsome man. He stood at six feet, had ebony-hued skin, and wide shoulders.

Just Paulette's type, Leila thought, remembering when Evan's little sister had described her ideal man more than a decade ago as Leila painted the teen girl's toenails.

Leila watched as the bridesmaids began the processional. They were all wearing satin gowns of various designs, but in the same shade of lavender. They clutched bouquets of hydrangea, freesias, and roses. The adorable ring bearer and the flower girl made their way down the center aisle next. The little girl reminded Leila of her own daughter, Isabel.

Suddenly, the music changed again. This time it was Vivaldi's *Spring*. Everyone took their cue and rose from the pews in anticipation of the bride's entrance.

Seconds later, Paulette stood in the church doorway, and she took Leila's breath away.

Leila couldn't believe this was the same unassuming teenager she had last seen ten years ago. This woman was beautiful and regal. Her long, dark glossy hair cascaded over her bare burnt-copper-toned shoulders. Her curvy figure was accentuated by the mermaid cut of her strapless wedding gown, which was decorated with Swarovski crystals and lace. A cathedral-length veil trailed behind her dramatically.

Paulette looked so beautiful, so stunning, so absolutely—

Perfect, Leila thought as she stared at her in awe.

And holding Paulette's satin-gloved hand was Evan. Being the new family patriarch, it only seemed right that Evan would give the bride away today. Judging from the grin on his strikingly handsome face, he seemed proud and happy to play the fatherly role.

Evan hadn't aged much in the past decade, but he certainly looked more handsome and distinguished than Leila remembered. He had the same coppery skin as his sister and was even taller than the groom. The glasses he'd often worn during childhood were gone. Leila was happy to see he had finally given them up for good. She had always thought he had the most soulful dark eyes that shouldn't be hidden behind thick, plastic lenses.

As the brother and sister walked down the center aisle toward the altar, a lump formed in Leila's throat. Her heart ached a little. This was the man whom she had once called her best friend. Once, they had been so close. She had been able to turn to Evan in her darkest moments, to confess to him her worst fears. Now he wouldn't even return her emails or phone calls. He hadn't met her daughter. He had gotten married five years ago and she had found out about it months later. She hadn't even met his wife!

Leila stared at the front pew, looking at the faces of the folks who sat there, wondering if his wife was among them.

She and Evan were practically strangers now. What the hell had happened to them?

Time . . . distance . . . silence, she thought.

But they could still make it right, she told herself, filling up with the warmth of the moment. They could put the past behind them. They could make amends. The guy standing in front of her didn't seem petty or angry. Maybe she had just misunderstood him. Maybe they just misunderstood each other. Once she told Evan why she needed his help, he would listen. She knew he would!

As Paulette and Evan drew closer, Leila grinned at the bride, whose loving gaze was focused solely on her husband-to-be.

Meanwhile, Evan's eyes drifted to the wedding guests. He nodded at a few in greeting. Finally, he noticed Leila standing in the pews near the center aisle.

"Hey, Magoo," she mouthed before giving him a timid wave.

Magoo. It was the nickname she had given him back when they were kids. Whenever he hadn't worn his glasses, he had squinted like the cartoon character, Mr. Magoo. His nickname for her had been "Bugs" after Bugs Bunny, thanks to her bucked rabbit teeth, which had thankfully been corrected over time by a good set of braces.

When Leila waved at him as he walked past, Evan did a double take. Leila watched, deflated, as his broad smile disappeared. His face abruptly hardened and his jaw tightened. The dark eyes that she had once admired now snapped back toward the front of the church. Evan looked more than irritated at seeing her standing there in the church pew. He looked downright furious.

The warm, mushy feeling that had swelled inside of her abruptly dissolved. Her cheeks flushed with heat. Her heart began to thud wildly in her chest again.

"There goes that fantasy," the voice in her head scoffed.

She should have known it wouldn't be easy. Evan was obviously still cross at her and even more so now that she had sneaked into his sister's wedding.

Fine, she thought angrily. *Be that way, Evan.*

But she wasn't giving up. She was still going to find a way to talk to him today—or yell at him or plead with him, whatever was required. She would find a way to plead her mother's case.

Chapter 2
EVAN

"What the hell is Leila doing here?" Evan snarled as he stood at the bar in the hotel's immense and elegant ballroom.

"Paulette said she doesn't remember inviting her," his equally handsome brother, Terrence, replied. "Maybe there was a mix-up." The younger man adjusted the bowtie at his throat. "Hey, is this thing on straight? It feels crooked."

"There was no goddamn mix-up! I can't believe Leila had the balls to just . . . to just *show* up!"

And to think, Evan had initially balked at the idea of having a church guest list when the mother of the groom had made the request. She had explained that she wanted to make sure the VIPs, like Mayor Crisanto Weaver and his wife, were properly seated in the church, but Evan suspected that the meddling mama really wanted to make sure no undesirables made it into the wedding. Evan had thought it was not only in poor taste but outright rude to ask people to give their names as they entered the sanctuary, though now he was starting to have second thoughts about that.

The list didn't work anyway. Leila still made it in!

Terrence lowered his hands from his bowtie. "I know you're pissed, Ev. But just chill out, all right?" He shifted a shot glass toward Evan. "Here. Have my drink. Maybe it'll calm you down."

Evan highly doubted that. He was too hot with anger to be cooled down right now.

Terrence nudged the glass again with the tip of his finger, easing it closer to his older brother. "Go on."

Evan hesitated for only a few more seconds before he raised his shot glass to his lips and downed his drink in one gulp. He then slammed the shot glass down on the bar's granite countertop and grimaced. *"Ugh,* what the hell was that?"

"Tequila," Terrence answered as he sniffed the shot glass. "Why? What was wrong with it?"

"It tasted like shit!"

"No, it didn't." Terrence held up two fingers to the bartender behind the counter, silently conveying that he wanted a double. "You are such a pussy now, man! There was nothing wrong with that drink. You've just lost your taste for liquor. That's what happens when you act like a monk and stop drinking alcohol."

"You know why I don't drink," Evan said tightly, silencing his brother. "Charisse drinks enough for the both of us," he muttered.

In fact, seeing his wife, Charisse, slur and stumble her way around their home had put Evan off drinking for years. The taste of the stuff he had just imbibed told him he wasn't missing much.

"She's lucky I don't have her ass thrown out," Evan said.

"Who? Charisse?"

"No, not Charisse! Leila!"

Terrence tiredly closed his eyes, which were a shade of caramel that he had inherited from their father. "So we're back to Leila, huh? Ev, we all know how you feel about her, but Paulette said she's okay with her being here. So why don't you just—"

"But what if *I'm* not okay with it?" he asked indignantly, pointing at his chest.

"Yeah, I figured you'd say that. I told Paulette you wouldn't like it. She said . . . and I quote . . . 'It's my wedding day and Ev will just have to get over it.'"

Evan blinked in amazement. Did he hear him correctly? *"Get over it?"*

Terrence shrugged. "That's what she said."

Evan turned his menacing gaze to the parquet dance floor, where his mutinous sister and her new husband danced under the misty glow of an orange spotlight. He gritted his teeth. *Get over it?* So this was the thanks he got for the more than two-hundred thousand dollars he had spent on this little shindig?

Paulette had nearly fainted when she'd seen her Vera Wang wedding gown at the bridal shop and she'd just *had* to have it. Had Evan balked when he'd seen the fifteen-thousand-dollar bill months later? *No.*

Had he complained when the wedding guest list got as long as his arm? *No.*

Had he objected when he'd heard about the ice sculptures, four-foot chocolate fountains, performance artists, and fireworks display planned for the reception? *No!*

And why had he simply opened his checkbook and wordlessly written check after check?

Because I wanted to make my little sister happy, Evan thought irritably. Whatever Paulette wanted on her special day, he promised he would give it to her.

Even their crusty father would have done as much. But how had Paulette repaid Evan's graciousness? By siding with the one woman he had avoided for almost a decade, the one woman who had betrayed him and broken his heart.

"Look," Terrence began, reaching for his own shot glass, "Leila is one out of I don't know how many guests here tonight. I wouldn't worry about her. You probably won't run into her again anyway."

"But what if she's here to start some shit? What if she's here to ask about—"

"But what if she's not? Maybe she came because she just wanted to see Paulette get married."

Evan squinted in disbelief. "You don't really believe that, do you?"

"Yes, I do, and I'll bet you a hundred bucks that I'm right. If I'm wrong, then you get a hundred bucks and we'll have her escorted out. Until then, just forget that she's here and go enjoy yourself. Do some schmoozing." Terrence smirked. "You're a Murdoch. It's what we do best."

Evan gazed around the darkened ballroom, his expression grim. That was easier said than done. Even if he didn't see Leila, he knew she was probably out there sitting at one of the banquet tables. Feeling her presence in the room ruined his evening, though he kept telling himself that such feelings were nonsense.

"Just misplaced anger," a voice in his head said.

Maybe, he conceded.

The person he was really mad at was Charisse, who hadn't bothered to stay sober enough to at least make it through the entire wedding. She had sat bleary eyed during most of the ceremony, hiding her hangover and her bloodshot baby blues behind tinted sunglasses. After a few drinks during cocktail hour, she was back to her outgoing self, laughing and charming everyone. But, of course, she had started to go downhill by the time the bride and groom had their first dance. She had been constantly tripping over the hem of her evening gown. Her words had become more and more slurred. She had been on the verge of getting full-on drunk and making a real ass of herself when Evan had her spirited away.

His half brother, Dante, had agreed to drive Charisse home. Dante had only connected with the family less than a year ago, not too long after their father's death. He was eager to be accepted into the Murdoch fold and wanted to be helpful. Thank God he had offered to handle Charisse!

But now Evan had another headache to deal with, thanks to Leila Hawkins crashing his sister's wedding. He could feel the tenseness winding up inside him, making the muscles in his neck and shoulders rigid. His eyes darted anxiously around the darkened room, anticipating the moment when he would spot her again. Would she come up to him and tap him on the shoulder? Would she corner him and confront him in the open? It was like he was preparing for battle.

"Hey, sexy," a female voice said from over Evan's shoulder. He turned to find one of Paulette's bridesmaids smiling up at him. She laid a warm hand on his arm. "Wanna dance, baby?"

"There you go! A distraction, Ev," Terrence said. "Just what the doctor ordered! Go out there and get your groove on, boy!"

"Uh, I'm married," Evan muttered to her, holding up his ring finger and ignoring his brother. He returned his gaze to the ballroom.

"So! I'm not asking you to run away with me! I'm just asking you to dance," the bridesmaid persisted.

She wrapped an arm lazily around his shoulders. "Come on! Dance with me!"

Evan narrowed his eyes down at her.

Her name was Angie. Or was it Amy? *Something that begins with an A,* he thought.

Loose curls had fallen out of her chignon and one lock hung limply over her heavy-lidded, glazed brown eyes. One of the straps of her satin dress was hanging off her shoulder, revealing the lace bra underneath.

If he had wanted to dance with a drunken woman tonight, he would have just asked his wife for a twirl on the dance floor.

"Look, why don't I do this?" he asked, gently shifting the young woman toward the bar counter. "Instead of us dancing, why don't I get you a cup of coffee?" He then motioned to get the bartender's attention.

"I don't need a cup of coffee," the bridesmaid argued. "I said I wanna *dance!*"

She then shoved away from Evan and turned, snagging the heel of one of her stilettos in the hem of her dress. She stumbled forward with arms flailing wildly.

"Oh!" Terrence shouted. "There she goes!"

Both brothers caught her just before she tumbled.

"You got her?" Terrence asked, shifting her toward his older brother.

Evan nodded, slowly bringing her back to her feet. "Yeah, I got her."

The bridesmaid gazed up at Evan and Terrence woozily. She slumped against the older brother's broad shoulder. "I don't . . . I don't feel so well. I think I'm gonna be sick."

"*Sick?*" Terrence exclaimed. He eased back and pointed at his tuxedo. "Oh, no! Not on this! *This* is a Tom Ford."

"You're a real prince, Terry," Evan murmured sar-

castically. He then returned his attention to the bridesmaid. "Let's get you out of here. I'll get you to the
ladies' room. All right?"

She closed her eyes and weakly nodded.

Evan guided her across the crowded ballroom to the
double doors, drawing a few curious stares from wedding guests. There was nothing he hated more than
making a scene. Having a woman besides his wife
clinging to him was bound to cause some talk, but he
couldn't let her stumble drunkenly around the reception, or worse—lose her five-star dinner right there on
the parquet dance floor. Like with Charisse, it was better to spirit away the bridesmaid to a place where she
could recover privately. Terrence was obviously no
help so Evan would have to take care of this himself.

Evan stepped into the carpeted foyer with his arm
wrapped around her waist and her arm draped around
his neck.

"I'm really going to be sick," she murmured again.

"I know. I know. I'm working on it," he grumbled,
glancing frantically around him.

He struggled to remember where he had last seen a
women's bathroom. Finally, he saw a few women
streaming out of a door on the other side of the foyer's
winding staircase. He walked toward them and started
to ask if one of them could help him, but when the
women's bathroom door opened again, the words
halted in his throat.

Leila Hawkins stepped out of the tiled bathroom
into the foyer. She dropped a compact into her clutch
purse, snapped the steel clasp shut, and looked up to
find Evan staring at her. Her mouth fell open in shock.

"Evan," she whispered breathlessly.

Shit, he thought. This was the last person he wanted
to see right now!

His jaw clenched. "Leila."

As much as he hated to admit it, Leila was as gorgeous and sexy now as she had been ten years ago. The only thing that was different was her hair. It was shorter now, chin-length and cut in a fashionable bob. He also noticed that she was wearing heels, something she had never worn when they were younger because she had said she didn't know how to walk in them.

Her honey-hued skin glowed under the foyer's chandelier lights, and she looked elegant and alluring in the simple pale yellow cocktail dress that hugged every delectable curve in just the right place.

She doesn't have a right to look this good, he thought. He'd prefer for her to be a hunchbacked cyclops, or at least to have gained forty pounds or more. Then he wouldn't have to worry about reacting to her like the way his body was responding now.

"I'm glad I ran into you, Ev," Leila said as she took a step toward him. "I mean I'm glad we . . . we ran into each other. I wanted to talk to you about . . ." Her eyes shifted to the drunken bridesmaid at his side. "Is she okay?"

"No, I'm *not* okay!" the bridesmaid garbled against his shoulder.

"She's had a little too much to drink," Evan explained now that he was cornered. "I was trying to get her to the bathroom."

"I can take her," Leila volunteered. She grabbed the bridesmaid's hand. "Let's get you into one of those stalls, honey."

Evan watched as Leila guided the hapless young woman through the swinging door. He heard the loud retching and dry heaving a few seconds later and cringed. He could have left then. His intoxicated charge was now in capable hands, but he would feel bad if he didn't stick around to see if the bridesmaid survived.

The young woman and Leila emerged from the bathroom fifteen minutes later. Angie (or Amy . . . he still couldn't remember her name) looked more sober and slightly less ill, but still seemed out of sorts. Leila had an arm wrapped around her protectively.

"I think I'm going to say good-bye to Paulette and go home now," the young woman mumbled, wiping her mouth with a wet paper towel. "I've had enough fun for one night."

"I think that's a good idea," Leila said.

The bridesmaid looked at Leila, then Evan. "Thank you for your help—the both of you."

"No problem," they answered in unison. They then glanced at one another. When their eyes met, they broke gazes.

The bridesmaid walked back toward the ballroom doors, looking worn and tired.

"Do you think she'll be all right?" Leila asked, watching the bridesmaid's retreat. "Does she have a safe way to get home? I hope she's not driving."

"I'll have my driver take her home. He can come back later to get me."

Leila turned to him. "That's very nice of you."

When she beamed, something inside his chest warmed instantly. He shouldn't still be reacting to her this way.

Not after all these years. Not after what she did.

Leila had long ago proven that she couldn't be trusted.

"I'm not being nice," he answered firmly, so that there was no misunderstanding that he was a pushover anymore. He could tell from the look on her face that his tone had caught her off guard. "I don't want her driving home and getting into an accident. Something like that would end up in the paper, probably on the front page. Paulette doesn't need that type of drama around her wedding."

Leila's smile disappeared. "Yeah, Ev, because it's less important that the poor girl might plow into a tree and kill herself, than whether her accident might ruin the vibe at the wedding or"—she mockingly raised her hand to her lips and widened her eyes—"bring shame to the Murdoch name."

Sarcasm. He should have expected as much from Leila. It was a shield she had always used in the past. Well, he had a shield too—a formal blandness he reserved for business meetings and acquaintances he wanted to get rid of quickly.

"Well, thank you very much for your help earlier. It was a pleasure seeing you again," he lied, buttoning his suit jacket, then gesturing toward the double doors. "Now, if you'll excuse me, I should get back to the reception."

Just as he turned to head back to the ballroom, Leila grabbed his arm, making him pause. "Evan," she said softly. "Evan, please . . . please wait."

Her touch ignited a small spark inside him that he hadn't felt in quite a while. His pulse quickened, and his skin tingled on the spot where she touched him. He wanted to take her hand within his own, tug her toward him, and kiss her. Instead, he forced himself to pull his arm out of her grasp.

"What, Leila? Look, I'm supposed to be hosting this thing. I can't just disappear and—"

"No one's going to think you're a bad host if you disappear for a few minutes! No one's going to look down on you for taking time to talk to me . . . *me*, Ev."

She pointed at her chest. "Someone who used to be your friend!"

"The operative words are 'used to be,'" he said coldly, making her cower as if he had hit her. He began to walk away again.

"What did I do?" she asked as she trailed him, taking fast steps to match the strides of his longer legs. "What the hell did I do to you to make you . . . you cast me out like this? You treat me like I'm some leper!"

"Keep your voice down," he snapped as he turned back to her. They were drawing stares from a few of the guests who lingered in the lobby.

"No, I'm not keeping my fucking voice down! I've tried doing this quietly and privately! I've tried emailing you . . . *calling you!* But you never responded! I need your help!"

Of course she does, he thought bitterly.

Terrence owed him a hundred bucks! He knew Leila had shown up here because she wanted something, and he suspected he knew what that something was. But Leila had always needed his help. She had always needed *him*. In their friendship, he had been the one she would lean on when things went wrong: when her father walked away from her family, when her mother lost a job, or when one of Leila's boyfriends broke up with her. But Evan would be damned if he'd be the shoulder for her to cry on or the shrink for her to drone on and on to today. He wasn't that guy anymore.

"My mother is going to lose her home! Look, I fell behind on the payments. I mean . . . well, Brad *and* I fell behind. I thought he had it covered, but he didn't. Anyway, Murdoch Bank owns the mortgage now and—"

"I don't want to talk about this," he said as he neared the double doors. "Not here. Not now."

"But all we need is one word from you! If—"

"I told you that I don't want to talk about this! This is a wedding, Leila. Not now!"

"If you would just make one call—"

"What did I just say?" he boomed.

"But you don't understand!"

No, he understood perfectly well. He knew that her mother was in default of her mortgage and the bank was now taking her home. Almost more than two dozen other mortgage owners at Murdoch Bank were in the same situation.

Evan had inquired about the loans when the stories first started to appear in the local newspaper about how several homes in one neighborhood in Chesterton with mortgages all owned by Murdoch Bank had either fallen into arrears or were in foreclosure proceedings. The neighborhood also happened to be on land that a major corporation wanted to purchase to build a new shopping center in town. The reporter shared a few of the homeowners' conspiracy theories that the bank was in cahoots with the corporation to push them off the land to make way for the brand-new center.

When Evan's father, George, had told him two years ago that Murdoch Conglomerated was acquiring the local savings and loan bank, Evan had thought it odd. Banking didn't really fall under the company's portfolio. Their company focus was usually foods and retail. Why did his father want to purchase a bank? But when the news stories came out soon after George's death, all the pieces of the puzzle had fallen into place. His father wanted that shopping center so that Murdoch Conglomerated could open a new store there. The houses were an obstacle to his goal and he had found a sneaky way to get around it.

But, of course, George wasn't a stupid man. What

he did may have been unethical, but it certainly wasn't illegal. All of the homeowners were behind on their mortgages. The bank had every right to use its own discretion to try to reach some settlement or simply allow the homes to go to foreclosure. Evan had no desire to micromanage and tell Murdoch Bank what to do. He had enough to worry about with his own duties as new CEO of Murdoch Conglomerated.

"Do you want me to beg, Ev?" Leila yelled, drawing more onlookers. "Is that what you want? Because that's what I'll do if it'll mean you'll—"

Her words were cut short. This time he grabbed *her* arm. He practically dragged her across the carpeted foyer to a secluded spot near a trickling water fountain. He finally let her go with a shove.

Evan glanced over his shoulder, making sure they were no longer being watched. "Are you trying to embarrass me? Are you trying to embarrass Paulette?"

"No, I'm trying to make you listen, damn it! I can't let my mother lose her house!"

"So get your husband to take care of it. He's the big shot. Let him pay off her mortgage!"

Her face crumpled. That was a low blow and Evan knew it, but he couldn't help himself. She had cast her lot with Brad and it had turned out ugly. Now she had gone running back to Evan like he'd always known she would.

Leila crossed her arms over her chest. "If Brad had the money, believe me, I'd ask. Unlike you, I'm not too proud to humble myself to help a friend!"

He fixed her with an icy glare. "You said what you had to say. You asked the question you wanted to ask and the answer is still no. So now I'm going to ask you as politely as possible to leave."

She raised her chin in defiance. *"Or what? You're*

gonna have someone come over here and toss me out?"

"No," he said menacingly, taking another step toward her, "I'll toss you out myself."

"Yeah, right! Like you'd ever get your hands dirty, you self-entitled son of a bitch!" She shoved him aside and walked off. "Tell Paulette I said congratulations," she muttered over her shoulder.

Evan then watched Leila stomp toward the hotel's revolving doors, leaving him both stunned and furious.

Chapter 3

DANTE

"Oh, yeah! Yeah, baby! Oooo, yeeeees! Right there," she moaned, making Dante Turner roll his eyes even while he continued to lick to ecstasy the woman bucking on the white satin sheets beneath him.

He liked for a gal to be expressive in bed, to let him know she was enjoying herself, but all this moaning, groaning, and yelling was starting to get a bit tiresome—even for a guy like him who was more than eager to please, who liked to have his ego stroked as much as his dick. Not to mention the fact that she was holding his head between her smooth, pale thighs so tightly that he was starting to get a headache.

"Yes! Oooo, like that! Right there!" she shouted, squeezing her nipples as the death grip around his head tightened.

Dante shoved her thighs open, raised his mouth to take a few quick breaths, then dove in again.

He soldiered on despite the theatrics, despite the pain, because there was more at stake here than getting off the very loud and moderately drunk Charisse Murdoch. He had something to prove as he brought his sister-in-law to a fist-pounding, pillow-biting orgasm. He wanted to prove that he was a better man than his half brother, Charisse's husband, Evan Murdoch.

Because I am, he thought as Charisse continued to writhe and scream.

Too bad his late father, George, hadn't bothered to notice, or Dante would be the CEO of Murdoch Conglomerated, not his pampered pussy brother, Evan.

While Dante had had to fend for himself most of his life—dodging bullies and bullets in the rough D.C. neighborhood of his childhood, and working his way through college and law school—the little Sun King known as Evan Murdoch had grown up in a mansion high up on the hill with tennis courts, swimming pools, and nannies. And why had the two men grown up so differently? Simply because Evan, Terrence, and Paulette had been born to a woman George chose to marry, while Dante had the unfortunate luck of being born to a woman George had accidentally knocked up during a clandestine one-night stand.

In fact, Dante hadn't known who his real father was until about two years ago, when his dying mother had told him the truth on her death bed. His entire life he had thought his dad was one of her junkie live-in boyfriends, some forgettable bum that no one but his kind-hearted mother would want anything to do with. But no, instead he found out his sire was esteemed local businessman and millionaire George Murdoch. His mother had also revealed that for years George had sent her hush money to ensure she would never tell his wife or anyone else the truth.

"Your father . . . is a . . . is a very proud man," Mary Turner had said between coughs in the hospital room after pushing aside her oxygen mask so that Dante could hear her more clearly. She was in her last throes of emphysema and lung cancer at the time. The diseases had winnowed her down from her hefty two-hundred-and-ten-pound frame to a mere hundred pounds. "George thought a . . . a baby by a girl like me would ruin his . . . you know, his reputation. Plus, he was . . ." She paused to let out another chest rattling cough. She smacked her parched, blood-encrusted lips. ". . . was married at the time. He had a-a lot to lose, honey."

But even more to gain if he would have accepted me and taken me under his wing, but he was too dumb to realize that, Dante now thought bitterly.

He had turned Dante away when Dante had finally gone to see him at his office and had introduced himself. He had insisted on continuing to pretend that Dante wasn't his son long after his wife had died and no one else would care. It had been Dante's siblings who had finally acknowledged him after his father died. They had found out his name when he was mentioned in George's will—a line item where Dante was given a measly two hundred and fifty grand when, as the eldest son, Dante felt he was owed more . . . a *helluva lot* more!

Why hadn't George realized that Dante was a son cut from the same cloth, carved out of his own image? Couldn't he see that Dante was as shrewd, cunning, and ruthless as he?

"Oh, God," Charisse moaned as she flopped back against the mattress, shuddering all over. She raked her fingers through her tousled blond hair while Dante pushed himself off his elbows and sat upright at the foot of the bed.

"Damn, you're good," she whispered.

Tell me something I don't know.

He grinned. "I just love to please a beautiful woman."

"Yeah, I bet you do," she drawled.

Charisse gave a throaty laugh, then shifted onto her side to turn on a nearby crystal table lamp. She fumbled around woozily—undoubtedly still feeling the after-effects of the glasses of champagne she had downed at Paulette's wedding—and opened one of her night table drawers. She pulled out a dainty silver cigarette box that could have been made in the early last century, and accidentally dropped it to the hardwood floor. She let out a few snorts and giggles, laughing at her clumsiness. Dante reached for it and handed it to her.

"Thanks," she mumbled before pulling out a cigarette. She fished for a lighter in the same drawer, fumbling again. He sighed and found the lighter for her, then handed that to her too. When she made several attempts to light the cigarette that dangled from her lips but didn't succeed, he lit it for her.

Dante gazed at Charisse as she smoked. Usually, Charisse was a woman whose gorgeousness made men do double takes, but at this vantage point, with the harsh light of the lamp playing on the angles and planes of her face, her "cracks" were starting to show. Maybe it was the years starting to catch up with her, carving away at her youthful beauty, or the alcohol or the smoking, but she was beginning to look a bit haggard. The first signs of crow's-feet were at the corners of her baby blues, despite her monthly Botox injections. Wrinkles were around her puckered lips. Red capillaries were etched like spider webs along the edges of her nostrils and pale purple circles were under her eyes.

He wondered if it was her good looks that had

drawn Evan to her in the beginning, or maybe it was her pedigree. Charisse was the granddaughter of a former governor of Virginia and had a family history in the state that went as far back as the antebellum South. The fact that a white woman like her had married a black man such as Evan was a major coup for him and showed how far the Murdoch family had come. Of course, now that she was a sloppy drunk, Charisse wasn't quite the prize that she may have been a decade ago.

She noticed him staring at her, but mistook his gaze for admiration. A smug smile slowly crossed her collagen-plumped lips. "Want one?" she slurred, offering him the silver case.

He nodded.

The two sat and smoked in silence, gazing at the dark landscape outside of Charisse's bedroom window.

The first time Dante had fucked Charisse at her home, he had rushed the deed like he was on a stop clock, wanting to get it done before Evan came home and walked in on them. It wasn't that he was afraid of confrontation with his brother. Dante just had a few things he wanted to accomplish before Evan figured out he was boning his wife. He had to keep up the pretense of the friendly brother who was eager to please his long-lost relatives. But Charisse had later assured him that the rush wasn't necessary.

"Evan hasn't set foot in my bedroom in more than a year. He sleeps down the hall . . . when he *is* home," she had muttered, making Dante stare at her in disbelief at the time.

"What do you mean, 'when he is home'? Are you saying he doesn't come home anymore?"

She had shrugged in response. "Maybe twice a week, if that."

"He isn't fucking around on you, is he?"

She had smirked before sipping from her glass. "Yeah, with a mistress called 'Murdoch Conglomerated.' Please! Evan is a total workaholic. He wouldn't find the time to screw around on me unless his secretary typed it into his Outlook calendar for him!"

Since then, Dante took his time whenever he and Charisse hooked up. Hell, he had even gone downstairs naked to make himself a ham sandwich once—that's how bold he had gotten! He had just missed the housekeeper, who had stumbled into the kitchen to make herself a late-night snack.

He now eased back on Charisse's bed and continued to stare out the window. From this vantage point and with the help of the floodlights hanging along the mansion's brick exterior, Dante could see most of the grounds: the paved stone circular driveway, the sculpted hedges, the neatly trimmed rose bushes, and the garage that housed Evan's four cars, ranging from a Range Rover to a 2014 Maserati GranTurismo convertible.

Dante slowly took it all in, admiring it and envisioning that one day, it would all be his.

Just give me time, he told himself.

"I wonder if the fireworks have started yet," Charisse murmured as she reached for the glass of bourbon on her night table.

"What fireworks?"

"For Paulette's wedding. They're supposed to have some . . . I don't know. Some big fireworks display at the end."

Dante tried to recall his own marriage—a quick, understated ceremony with the justice of the peace. The bride had wanted to celebrate with a small reception with family and friends afterward, but Dante had thought it a waste of time and money. Instead, he had headed back to the law office where he was clerking to finish the work day. It didn't seem worth making a big deal about it. It was just a wedding, after all.

Maybe that was why they got divorced three years later.

Her priorities were obviously out of whack, he thought.

"Fireworks," he repeated, blowing smoke out of the side of the mouth. "It would have been better to set stacks of hundred-dollar bills on fire. What a waste of damn money!"

Charisse chuckled, cocking one leg and absently tugging down the bedsheets, revealing her bare breasts and pert pink nipples. "Yeah, but it's the Murdoch way. They like to do things big."

"It's because they've never had to work hard for anything. They've had everything handed to them on a silver platter so they can just throw money around like it's nothing."

"That may be true about Terrence or Princess Paulette, but not Evan." Charisse tapped the ashes of her cigarette into a glass ashtray near the lamp on the night table and stretched. "They live off their trust funds, but he doesn't. He's definitely a hard worker . . . always has been. He's just like that—all sense of obligation and what? I don't know the word . . . duty, I guess. That's how he's made."

Dante narrowed his eyes at her. "Oh, so we're sticking up for Evan now?"

She cringed with disgust. "I'm not 'sticking up' for him! I'm just saying that—"

"That's he's a hard worker. Yeah, he's a great goddamn guy. Well, if he's so great then why am *I* the one here eating you out and not him? *Huh?*"

"You are so . . . so crude," she huffed.

Crude? Dante almost laughed. Here she was pretending to be the demure socialite when she had been anything but that less than five minutes ago. He wished he had a tape to replay to show how fast she had ripped off her reception gown, reached for his pants' zipper, and had his dick in her mouth. He wished he could replay all the moaning and yelling she had done.

"Let's cut the bullshit, Charisse. I'm crude, but I'm honest, which is more than I can say for that corny-ass husband of yours."

Charisse scowled and extinguished her cigarette. She climbed off the bed, stumbling slightly before she regained her footing. She grabbed the pink silk robe that was tossed over the side of her grand oak headboard.

"I'm, uh . . . I'm getting tired," she mumbled as she started to shove her arms into the robe sleeves.

Tired?

Okay, maybe he had pushed her a bit too far with his honesty. He knew he could be a little caustic, and maybe even crass, at times and often found it hard to keep himself in check. But he wanted to woo this woman, to win her to his side, because there were sides here in the war he was waging. He wanted to use her affections in his favor in the future. He couldn't do that if he pissed her off.

"Charisse, come on, baby—"

"You should . . . you know, probably head home now," she said, stepping out of his grasp. She tied the robe belt into a bow and pushed her hair out of her face. "Evan might be heading back from the wedding soon."

Not likely, Dante thought. She was just making up excuses to get rid of him, but he wouldn't be put off that easily.

"Honey," he whispered as he stood from the bed and walked naked toward her. "I'm sorry if I upset you."

She looked away and pretended to cry, wiping at her eyes, puckering her lips. He wrapped an arm around her slender waist as she dropped her head to his shoulder.

"Evan's so mean to me, Dante," Charisse whimpered with a sniff, slurring some of her words again. "I don't . . . I don't need for you to be mean to me too."

He wondered if those fake tears worked on her husband. They certainly didn't work on him, but he was willing to play along.

"I know. I'm sorry if I hurt you." He reached for her now empty glass, grabbed a nearby decanter, and filled the glass again. "Here, have a drink. It'll make you feel better."

She hesitated before accepting his liquid peace offering. He knew her. She was never one to turn down a drink. She sipped from the glass before raising her head from his shoulder and looking up at him.

"Do you mean it?"

He nodded. "Of course, I do."

After that, she downed the rest of her glass in one gulp.

Dante reached for her robe belt and began to slowly untie it. "What do you say we have one more go around before I leave?" he asked, pulling open one of the robe panels and cupping one of her breasts. He ran his thumb over the nipple and could feel her tremble slightly under his palm. "One more before I hit the road, baby . . . before Evan comes home?"

If he comes home . . .

"I don't know, Dante," she whispered.

Then his hand descended to the moist spot between her thighs. "You sure about that?" he asked, rubbing her there. He lowered his lips to her neck and kissed her pulse then her shoulders.

She set her glass back on the night table and pushed the robe off of her shoulders, letting it fall to the hardwood floor, her tears now forgotten. "Well, okay, but we'll have to be . . . you know, quick."

"Quick, huh?" he asked before roughly shoving her back onto the bed, then flipping her over so that she was face down on the sheets.

She raised herself so that she was kneeling on all fours. "Well, not too fast," she moaned as he began to stroke her again with the tantalizing slow circular motion of his fingers, making her wetter. She balled the sheets in her fists. "We . . ." She groaned and started to pant. "We still have to enjoy ourselves, right?"

"Damn straight," he said, parting her legs further and climbing between them. He then reached for one of the unopened packets of condoms still on her night table.

Because if there was one thing he did do for Charisse, that was help her enjoy herself. He offered her booze, conversation, and "no-strings attached" sex while she played poor little rich girl in her jilted husband's mansion.

And she better remember that shit when I need a favor from her one day, he thought as he entered her and the yelling started all over again.

Chapter 4

PAULETTE

"Positive thoughts. Positive thoughts," Paulette murmured as she set the pregnancy test on the marble countertop. She gazed into the mirror, wiping at the lipstick on her teeth, finger-combing wayward strands of hair back into place. She glanced at the pregnancy test, willing the word PREGNANT to appear in the digital window. When the twirling hour glass stayed on the screen instead, she grumbled.

What the hell is taking it so long?

Unable to handle the torture of suspense any longer, she decided to cover the plastic stick with a hand towel and busy herself straightening up the master bathroom, wiping down the counter, rearranging the toothbrushes and cans of shaving cream.

She glanced at the hand towel again.

It was one of eight embroidered in Edwardian Script with the letter W. The "W" represented Williams, her new surname since tying the knot with the love of her life, Antonio Williams, five weeks ago. The hand towels had been a wedding gift—one of many that Paulette still was unearthing from the four-foot-tall piles of wrapped boxes and gift bags in their living room downstairs. She had taken a break from the great unwrapping to take her pregnancy test, and now she was questioning that decision.

I should have waited a few more days, maybe even a week, she thought. *I took it too soon.*

But she couldn't turn back now. She had peed on the stick and now she'd just have to wait for the results.

Paulette turned on the faucet and washed her hands though they weren't dirty. She was running out of ways to distract herself. Her gaze drifted back to the hand towel on the counter yet again.

The test should be finished by now. The box said less than five minutes for results.

She reached for the towel, then hesitated. What if the test said she wasn't pregnant?

She was only late by a couple of days, but her periods had always been so regular that you could practically set a clock to them. And she had prayed during her honeymoon that she and Antonio would make a baby while in Cabo San Lucas. Maybe God had heard her prayer. Wouldn't it be perfect for a little girl or boy to arrive nine months after their wedding—a little girl who had big brown eyes like Paulette or a little boy who would one day be as tall and strong as his daddy, Antonio? This baby would make everything right in their lives, and he or she could finally erase the memory of the baby Paulette had lost long ago.

"Lost? What do you mean 'lost'? The baby you killed, you mean," the shrewish voice in her head corrected, but she quickly snuffed it out.

She didn't want to think about that right now. That had happened back when she was sixteen years old.

She hadn't known any better. She wasn't that foolish girl anymore, desperate to break out of the mold of "Perfect Paulette" that had been created by her family and her father, George, in particular. Now she was a happily married woman!

Paulette pursed her lips, closed her eyes, and pulled back the hand towel. When she opened her eyes and saw the digital screen on the pregnancy test, her shoulders slumped.

NOT PREGNANT, it read.

She took a deep breath, sucking in her disappointment and pushing it like her breath to the pit of her stomach.

"Well, I've only been off the pill a couple of months," she whispered, gnawing her bottom lip. Her body probably needed time to adjust, for the plumbing to get back into the swing of things. She would get pregnant soon. She was sure of it.

"Baby," Antonio said, startling her with a knock at the bathroom door, "you've been in there for a while. Everything okay?"

"I'm fine," Paulette answered quickly, grabbing the pregnancy test, instruction leaflet, and box, and dumping them all in a grocery bag. She knotted the bag and frantically looked around her for a place to hide it. She settled for a shelf underneath her side of the bathroom counter. "I'll be right out!"

She didn't want Antonio to know she was taking the test. He didn't even know she was trying to get pregnant, that she was off the pill.

When she'd tried not long after they'd become engaged to broach the topic of having a baby, he'd said that it would probably be better for them to wait.

"What's the rush?" he had asked. "Let's get settled

first. Let's spend a few years with it being just us.
We've got *years* to have a baby."

But she couldn't wait years. She wanted a baby
now! When she got pregnant, she'd tell Antonio it was
an accident.

*I guess something went wrong with my birth control
or maybe I skipped a day,* she thought, rehearsing the
lie in her head. Besides, she knew when he found out
that he was going to be a father he'd be too elated to
ask any questions.

"Baby, seriously, are you okay in there?" Antonio
asked, knocking again.

"I'm fine . . . really!" She closed the oak cabinet and
turned off the faucet. "I'm just . . . just freshening up!"

"Well, hurry up and come out here! I've got a surprise for you."

A surprise? She paused.

Antonio was always full of surprises. He had been
since the early days when they started dating. He'd
surprise her with sweet gestures that would make most
women swoon. Of course, since they had arrived home
from their honeymoon it had been a while since he had
brought home a bouquet of roses or since she'd wan-
dered into the bathroom to find a candlelit bubble bath
waiting for her. Now Antonio was more preoccupied
with catching up with work at his consulting firm. He
hoped to move up the management ladder and maybe
become a senior VP one day. That meant long hours
and Antonio often coming home late, but Paulette sup-
ported her husband's industrial spirit. So what if it
meant she ate more and more meals alone at home and
sometimes went to bed without seeing him at all? She
was his wife and therefore, his biggest cheerleader.

"Your job as a wife is to maintain the home, your
family, and your marriage, Sweet Pea. That's what

every good woman does," Paulette's deceased mother's voice suddenly intoned, playing back from memory. The instant Paulette heard the voice, she cringed. She didn't want advice like that. She didn't want to be like her mother, ignored and taken for granted by their father—hell, taken for granted by everyone!

No, Paulette wouldn't be like Angela Murdoch. The distance she felt from her husband was only temporary. She'd carve her own path and have a happy marriage—unlike her mother.

Paulette opened the bathroom door to find her husband patiently waiting for her.

While she had been unpacking their wedding gifts, he had been in their garage, cutting the wood trim that would go in their entryway. Since about 8 a.m. neighbors could hear the sound of his buzzing table saw halfway down the block. Antonio's T-shirt and jeans were now covered with sawdust and oil. Sweat stains were on his shirt along his chest and under his arms.

He had never looked more handsome or sexy to her.

"What's the surprise?"

"It wouldn't be a surprise if I told you." He then leaned forward to kiss her.

She closed her eyes and braced herself for a warm, wet one, but instead he placed a chaste kiss on her cheek. She opened her eyes, taken aback.

"Come on," he said, grabbing her hand and dragging her down the hall toward the stairwell.

Steel pans with paint rollers, paint cans, and tarp littered the hardwood floor and leaned against the wainscoting, making their hallway a bit of a hazard zone. Antonio was still putting the last finishing touches here too.

Paulette thought all his DIY projects were sweet. She had grown up having servants doing things for her.

Having a man who insisted doing everything himself was rather charming.

"It must be a good surprise if you're this excited," she said as they walked down the stairs.

"Oh, trust me," he assured her as they stepped off the last riser. "You'll love it. Close your eyes first."

She did as he ordered, allowing him to guide her a few feet as she held out her free hand to avoid hitting a wall or stumbling on their Afghan rug.

"All right. Open your eyes," he said.

She slowly opened them, still grinning. When she saw who was standing in front of her, her smile teetered a little. It took all her willpower and upbringing to keep it in place.

"Mama's here to make us brunch, baby!" he said, rubbing Paulette's shoulders. "And she brought your favorite—sticky buns!"

His plump mother turned around from the oven, bumping the door closed with her hip. She proudly held up a steaming pan of the buns in illustration.

This was the surprise?

First of all, Paulette hated his mother's sticky buns with a passion. The melted icing would stick to the roof of her mouth. The pecans would lodge in her teeth. And she didn't know what diabolical substance was in those things that always made her constipated.

"I just warmed these up," said Reina Williams, taking off her oven mitts and setting the pan on the granite countertop. She glanced at Paulette and absently waved her toward the overhead cabinets. "Go and get some plates so I can serve this, will ya? Antonio, honey, you go and have a seat at the table."

The way Reina was acting, you would think she was standing in *her* French country kitchen and Paulette was the visitor. Paulette gritted her teeth as she walked to the cabinets, while Antonio grinned as he pulled out a chair at their kitchen table, shoved aside the pitcher filled with hydrangeas, and waited for his wife and mother to serve him.

Paulette removed the ceramic plates from the shelves, resisting the urge to smash them to the tiled floor in frustration.

Much like her gooey pastries, Antonio's mother, Reina, had the bad habit of lingering around longer than she should and leaving a nasty taste behind. Since Paulette and Antonio had arrived back from their honeymoon, Reina had come to their new home almost daily to add her own knickknacks and finishing touches, to cook a few meals, and to generally make sure that "her boy" was being taken care of.

Paulette had known that Antonio was a bit of a mama's boy. When they had started dating, she had found it charming that he had such a close relationship with his mother. A man who respects his mama is bound to respect the woman he loves, as the saying goes. But as time wore on, the connection between Antonio and Reina began to make Paulette more and more . . . uncomfortable.

Reina's name meant "queen" in Spanish, and obviously, the three-hundred-and-fifty-pound woman seemed to take that title literally. She had tried to flex her muscles with Paulette early on, making critical comments about how she wore her hair, what clothes she wore, and how she should properly show Antonio affection. Paulette had tried to be nice and accommodate her at first, but after a while she'd started to chafe under Reina's constant criticisms.

Paulette had grown up with a father who had lorded over her and the rest of her family. Once she'd moved out of the Murdoch estate and become an adult, she'd had no desire to return to those days. She didn't want to be like her mother, who had sat by quietly while being taken advantage of. She wouldn't bow down and kiss Reina's ring, no matter how much the woman wanted.

Paulette set two plates on the table. "Actually, I think I'll save my sticky buns for later, Reina. I'm not hungry."

"You should be hungry," Reina said as she walked to the table. She used a metal spatula to scoop out a sticky bun onto Antonio's plate. "Tony tells me you didn't cook any breakfast this morning—not even for him!"

Paulette glanced at her husband, who looked down sheepishly as he grabbed his fork and dug into his sticky dessert.

Thanks a lot, honey, she thought.

"I didn't have a chance to cook anything," she explained, leaning against the kitchen island. "We both had a busy morning."

"Uh-huh," Reina grunted, eyeing her. "Well, Tony's a boy who needs three meals a day. He's always been a big eater."

"Oh, I'm sure. But Tony knows how to use an oven just like I do, don't you, baby?"

At that, even through all those layers of fat, Paulette could see Reina's shoulders and back stiffen. She wasn't accustomed to being talked back to, but it was something she would just have to get used to from now on, Paulette resolved.

Antonio loudly cleared his throat. "So, uh, baby, think you can take a break from our wedding gifts?" he asked, trying desperately to change the subject. He knew how she felt about his mother, but he hated to see the two argue. "Mama wondered if maybe you could go to church with her and help out."

"The deaconesses are gathering goods for our food drive," Reina said proudly while Antonio helped himself to yet another sticky bun. "Lots of good Christian folk donated canned food and other things for the homeless. We could use some extra volunteers."

"Sorry, Reina, I would love to," she lied, "but I already have other plans for today. I was going to visit someone. I haven't seen her since the wedding and I really didn't get to talk to her that day anyway with all the stuff that was going on."

Reina frowned. "What *friend*?"

As if asking, *"What person could possibly be more important than me?"*

"Leila Hawkins. You don't know her, but she used to be a close friend of the family. She was good buddies with my brother Evan."

Very good . . . then it all fell apart, Paulette thought sadly. She had never gotten a straight answer from Evan for why he was no longer friends with Leila.

"She's bad news. Just keep your distance from her. Okay? Trust me," Evan would say without any further explanation. But Paulette wasn't sure she believed that, even if for years she had respected her big brother's wishes and had not attempted to contact Leila on her own. But after hearing that Leila was going through a painful divorce and Evan had ignored Paulette's wishes and had kicked Leila out of the wedding, Paulette felt she had to break ranks. Evan was acting like an unreasonable bully. She owed Leila a chance to explain her side of the story.

Especially after what she did for me way back when.

Paulette would be forever indebted to Leila. That was reason enough to pay her old friend a visit.

Chapter 5
LEILA

Leila glared down at the scratched laminate top of the restaurant's table and eyed the tip her customers had left behind.

"*Seventy-five cents?* Come on!" she griped under her breath.

It had been a forty-five-dollar tab. They couldn't spare four bucks? The family of five had had her jumping like a kangaroo from the kitchen and service station to their table with their requests for more sodas, more napkins, and new forks. Then the mom had complained that she had wanted French fries, not onion rings. The father had said he wanted his burger "medium well" instead of "well done." Leila had met all their ever-changing demands. A ten percent tip was at least warranted. She thought she had done a good job.

Despite her outrage, Leila dropped the change into her apron pocket. She was too broke to turn down anything. She sighed dejectedly and began to clear the restaurant table of dishes and glasses. They were short-handed today so the waitstaff had to do their own table busing.

Her mother, Diane, had done waitressing jobs like this one most of Leila's childhood, slaving away for meager tips from rude customers.

"I work my fingers to the bone so you won't have to do the same when you get older, honey," her mother had tiredly confessed to her one evening when Leila was a teenager. "I want better for you."

And here I am doing the same damn thing, Leila thought as she continued to clear the table, disappointed in life and herself.

She should have been more self-reliant. Before she married Brad, she had had dreams of becoming a graphic artist, of maybe owning her own stationery and graphic arts studio. Instead, she had dropped out of school one semester shy of graduation to get married. She had quit her job when Isabel was born and had let Brad become the sole breadwinner of the family. She had put all her trust in him.

And look where that got me!

Now she was waitressing at Dean's Big Burger and working part-time as an office assistant for a local law firm. Together, the jobs made for a decent wage that allowed her to pay everyday bills and her debts, but it was still a struggle to survive, especially now that Leila knew she would soon have the added burden of covering rent on just her salary once the bank foreclosed on Diane's home. They'd have to find somewhere else to live.

"Remind me to never have kids," murmured one of the other waitresses, Hannah, as she walked past Leila, breaking into Leila's weighty thoughts.

"Why?" Leila carried her plastic tray of dirty dishes to the restaurant's kitchen, trailing behind Hannah. "I happen to like mine."

"Yeah, because Isabel's a cutie pie, but not that pint-sized jerk at table six who pegged me with his ice cream sundae!" the tall blonde exclaimed over her shoulder. She then pointed at the vanilla ice cream and chocolate syrup on her uniform, showing Leila the oozing evidence. "I swear he waited until I leaned over before throwing it at me."

Despite her earlier melancholy, Leila couldn't help but laugh at Hannah's outrage and the oozing ice cream. She handed off her dirty dishes to one of the restaurant's dishwashers. "I'm sure it was an accident," she said between giggles.

"No, it wasn't! That little demon had it in for me ever since I told him we ran out of crayons for the children's table mats."

Leila laughed again. "Well, at least the lunch rush is ending. No more little demons for another few hours."

Hannah nodded. "Thank God for small favors." She looked down at her chest. "I'm going to try to get some of this off." She then strode toward the women's bathroom.

Watching Hannah walk off in a huff, Leila decided that life could be worse. At least she wasn't broke *and* covered in ice cream.

Leila returned to the front of the house a few seconds later with a wet rag in hand. She leaned over and started to wipe the crumbs and spilled ketchup from the tabletop and then the pleather seat cushions.

"Leila?"

At the sound of her name, she looked up to find Paulette Murdoch smiling down at her. The young woman seemed out of place in the low-end burger joint with its bad fluorescent lighting and bubble-gum-encrusted rugs. Paulette looked like the embodiment of youth and wealth with her expensive-looking pink sundress and heels. A Gucci handbag was on her arm. Leila watched as Paulette pushed her purple-tinted sunglasses to the crown of her head.

"Sorry, I . . . I didn't mean to interrupt you," Paulette said quickly. "I just wanted to—"

"No!" Leila assured. "You're not interrupting. I'm just cleaning up." She held up the dirty rag in her hand. "So what brings you here? I didn't take you for a cheeseburger kind of girl."

Paulette shrugged. "I heard that you worked here now and I . . . well, I didn't get the chance to talk to you at the wedding. Antonio and I got back from our honeymoon a couple of weeks ago. We've been so busy settling into our new home, but I finally got a break. I thought I'd stop by to say hi. You know . . . pay you a visit. Talk for a bit."

Leila inclined her head. Why had Paulette come all the way to Dean's Big Burger to talk? Paulette could have just as easily picked up the phone and called her. Her mother's number was listed.

"What did you wanna talk about?"

"Oh, just . . . stuff."

Stuff? God, I hope this doesn't have anything to do with my dust-up with Evan at her wedding, Leila thought. She hadn't meant for it to be done so publicly and certainly hadn't meant to shame Paulette.

Whatever Paulette wanted, she seemed eager to talk about it. Leila had always liked her and was willing to oblige her.

"Okay, let's talk then," Leila said, making Paulette's smile widen. "Let me tell the floor manager that I'm taking a break. I'll meet you by the front door."

Paulette nodded.

Minutes later, the two women walked out of the restaurant. It was sunny outside and humid, causing the red polo shirt Leila was wearing to instantly stick to her skin. Leila fanned herself and glanced at Paulette. The young woman didn't seem at all fazed by the heat. She looked as if she could have just strolled off some sandy beach or yacht with the airy vibe she was giving off. Leila wished she could look that tranquil.

"How about the little park across the street?" Leila said, pointing to a few wooden benches and a playground on the other side of the sleepy roadway. "We can sit there and talk if you'd like."

"That sounds nice," Paulette murmured, adjusting her purse.

They settled on a bench near the monkey bars. A few children played on the swing set and slides several feet away.

Leila waited for Paulette to start the conversation since she was the one who had said she wanted to talk. But Paulette continued to stare at the children in front of them.

"I hope I have kids one day," Paulette whispered, her words barely audible above the squeals and laughter surrounding them.

"I'm sure you will."

Paulette suddenly turned to her, looking surprised. "You think so? *Really?*"

"Sure. Why not?"

At that, Paulette shrugged. She fell into a quiet reverie again.

"Paulette, is something wrong?"

Paulette's brown eyes shifted toward her. The young woman pursed her lips. A pained expression suddenly crossed her pretty face. "Well, I'm not sure how to broach the topic with you. It's a little delicate."

"Delicate? Delicate in what way?"

"Well . . ." She hesitated again.

"Just say it, Paulette. Please. The suspense is killing me."

"Why . . . why did you come to my wedding, Leila?"

Leila was caught off guard by that question. She struggled to come up with a plausible lie. "I, uh . . . I hadn't seen you in a while and I heard you were getting married. I watched you grow up. I thought it would be nice to see you walk down the aisle."

Paulette eyed her. "So you came to see me, not to talk to Evan?"

Leila broke Paulette's gaze. Her eyes drifted to the packed dirt and grass beneath her feet. "Look," she began, "I know that I—"

"I mean it's okay if you did!" Paulette rushed. "It makes sense. You want him to help you, right? With your money issues?"

Leila raised her eyes. "What money issues?"

"Well, everyone knows about your divorce, Leila. I know that you're . . . that you're broke now."

"So *that's* why Ev thought I was there? *To beg him for money?* Is that what he told you?" she asked angrily.

"Evan didn't tell me anything! I just assumed—"

"That I came there begging for cash? Yeah," Leila said ruefully, "I bet you did. I bet everyone else in town assumed that too. So what else is everyone saying? That Bradley dumped me and left me penniless? That I was in cahoots with his pyramid scheme?"

"No one's gossiping about you, Leila," Paulette insisted though Leila could tell from the look on her face that she wasn't being honest. "Some of us are really worried about you! We all know you're struggling. If you need money—"

"I don't need money! I came to the wedding to ask Ev for help. My mom's house is being foreclosed on and Murdoch Bank owns the mortgage. I was . . ." She sighed. Her shoulders slumped. "I was hoping that Ev could say something on her behalf. I wanted him to talk to the bank manager and get them to work something out with mama . . . lower the interest rate . . . maybe, lengthen the terms by a few years." She threw up her hands. "Hell, I don't know. I just wanted his help!"

"And he refused?"

Leila closed her eyes and nodded. "He wouldn't listen to me."

"Well, maybe I can help."

Leila opened her eyes and narrowed them at Paulette. "What do you mean by 'help'?"

"I don't know if I can talk to bank management about your mom's mortgage, but I can give you money to help get a new place," Paulette answered, making Leila quickly shake her head. "I'll give it to you outright. You don't even have to pay it back!"

"No," Leila said firmly. "I'm not going to take money from you, Paulette."

She had her pride. There was a reason why she hadn't declared bankruptcy and why she hadn't borrowed money from anyone, though some friends had offered. She wanted to prove she could handle this and take care of it herself.

She had borrowed money once in her life—from Evan—and to this day, she still regretted it. She wasn't going to do it again.

"But you *have* to take the money, Lee! I feel like . . . I feel like I owe you so much."

"You don't owe me anything."

"Yes, I do! I'm still grateful for what you did for me. Everyone thinks I'm this spoiled little rich girl who hasn't had to go through things, but you know differently."

Leila fell silent. Her eyes drifted to the grass beneath her feet again.

"We've both made our share of bad choices when it comes to men," Paulette continued. Her long lashes suddenly began to dampen with tears. "You were there for me . . . and I'll never forget that, Leila."

"I told you it's what anyone would have done, honey."

Paulette wiped at her eyes with the backs of her hands. She then opened her handbag and pulled out a few tissues. "No, it wasn't what anyone would have done. You went above and beyond."

Leila remembered. She had been the only one to figure out that sixteen-year-old Paulette was sneaking around with a boy that Paulette's father never would have approved of. The boy was poor and rough around the edges. He also came with a level of danger and spice that the sheltered Paulette craved.

Leila had tried to warn her off of him. She had grown up around guys like that in her neighborhood: wannabe thugs with pretty faces who only knew how to get a girl in trouble. Unfortunately, Paulette hadn't listened. Her walk on the wild side had come with a big price in the end.

"You went to the clinic with me when he wouldn't even come," Paulette whispered. She sniffed and wiped her nose with one of her tissues. "You held my hand in the waiting room and drove me home after the abortion was over. If my father had found out that I had gotten knocked up, Leila, he would have disowned me. He would have kicked me out of the house! I don't know what I would have done!"

Leila reached out and placed a hand over Paulette's. "We all make mistakes. You were young and you needed someone. I'm glad I was there to help."

"I'm glad you were there too," Paulette said as she sniffed again. "You know, I still haven't told anyone about that. Not even Antonio."

"I haven't told anyone either," Leila whispered.

She hadn't even told Evan. She knew how he idealized his little sister. Besides, when she'd promised Paulette that it was their secret, she'd intended to keep that promise—until the day she died.

"I'm still so embarrassed, Leila. How could I have been so gullible and so stupid? I'm so ashamed that I—"

"You have nothing to be ashamed about, honey. *Nothing,*" she assured firmly, squeezing Paulette's hand. She watched as Paulette took a shaky breath, then finally nodded. "Look, no matter what happened back then, you don't owe me anything. You certainly don't have to repay me for what I did. You don't have to give me money for it."

"But it would be me helping you this time! That's all. Just tell me how much you need!"

Leila shook her head.

"If you and Ev weren't fighting, he'd give it to you. What's the difference?"

"It doesn't matter because I would never ask him for it. If there's anyone I don't want another penny from, it's Evan Murdoch."

She had borrowed money from Evan ten years ago to help Brad, though she had lied and told Evan the money wasn't for her then fiancé. Leila thought she'd be able to quickly repay Evan because Bradley told her she'd get the investment back within a month or two. She'd get him the money back before Evan figured out she had lied. Needless to say, the money never came. Guilt ridden, she sent Evan a check a year later with an apology for the long delay. She got a terse reply in the mail from him a week later.

Keep the money. Just don't ever ask me for another damn dime again, his note had read, with her check also enclosed.

She should have expected as much from him.

It was a shame that their relationship had come to this. Watching him from a distance at Paulette's wedding and reception, she had wondered why she hadn't fallen in love with him back then. He was attractive and definitely had qualities that most women looked for in a man—intelligence, charm, and wealth. Why hadn't she seen that back then?

But that didn't matter now. Evan was married and he had made it abundantly clear that he wasn't interested in having a friendship with her. She was done with being rejected by him. She'd rather crawl on broken glass than go to him again for help. She would have to figure this out on her own.

"Whatever happened between you two?" Paulette asked in bewilderment. "You used to be so close. Now it seems like Ev wants nothing to do with you . . . and you want nothing to do with him."

Leila sighed and shifted her gaze to the now-deserted monkey bars. The kids had run off screaming when an ice cream truck drove by. They now stood several feet away on the curb, all shouting their orders, trying to be heard over the tinkling sound of *Pop Goes the Weasel*, which played on the truck's loud speaker.

"It's complicated," Leila finally confessed.

"Is it because he was in love with you and you weren't in love with him?"

Leila's eyes snapped back to Paulette. "How did you know that?"

"*How did I know that?* Leila, I may have seemed like a ditzy teenager, but I wasn't. I wasn't blind either! Everyone could see how Ev felt about you!"

Everyone but me, Leila thought forlornly.

"Did you do something to him?"

Leila considered Paulette's question. She struggled to remember what she had done to make Evan so bitter and angry.

"I lied to him once. It upset him . . . disappointed him too."

Paulette's frown deepened. "That's it? *One lie?*"

"I honestly don't know, Paulette. He's never told me the real reason why. I guess one day he will, and maybe then, we'll be able to be friends again," Leila conceded, though she doubted it. "I guess it's just going to take more time."

"Well, even if you guys don't come around, I hope *we* can stay in touch, especially now that you've moved back to Chesterton. I feel bad for not reaching out to you all these years. I hope we can start over again."

Leila wrapped an arm around the younger woman's shoulders and gave her a hug. "Of course, we can, honey."

The two women stood from the park bench and walked back across the street.

"Here's my number," Leila said, scribbling her phone number on her order pad. She ripped off a sheet of paper. "Give me a call and we'll meet up soon. Maybe we can go to lunch." She glanced at the smiley face on Dean's Big Burger's glass door. "It'll be a nicer place than this one though . . . and we won't eat burgers. We'll have something more sophisticated."

Paulette laughed as she took the sheet of paper from Leila and tucked it in her purse. "I'd like that." She sighed. "Well, I guess I should say good-bye now. I'll let you get back to work. And I'm sorry I couldn't help you."

"You don't need to be sorry," Leila assured. "I told you, don't worry about it."

Paulette nodded and waved good-bye. Leila watched as Paulette walked back toward a sleek sports car that was parked along the curb at the end of the block.

It warmed her heart that Paulette had been willing to write a check to erase all her problems. But Paulette couldn't. Leila would have to dig herself and her family out of this hole.

Chapter 6
LEILA

Hours later, Leila arrived at her mother's pale yellow bungalow, which sat at the end of a cul-de-sac bordered by grand old oaks and maples. A tire swing hung in front of the house, swaying faintly in the evening wind. Isabel's tricycle was turned on its side on the front lawn.

The night barely cloaked the drabness of the neighborhood. Most of the houses had been built in the late sixties and early seventies with exteriors that could use a fresh layer of paint. There were more chain-link fences than white picket ones. Front lawns were dotted with chipped garden gnomes and Mother Marys instead of manicured rose bushes. It was definitely one of the less glamorous enclaves in Chesterton, but the neighbors were kind, quiet, and humble people. Leila and her small family were happy to call it home.

Leila parallel parked her hatchback along the curb. When she killed the engine, the sound of crickets filled the night. She saw Isabel silhouetted by the kitchen light shining through the screen door. The little girl eagerly bounced on the balls of her feet as Leila walked up the concrete walkway with heavy plastic bags in her hands. Diane stood behind Isabel.

"We were wondering when you would get home," Diane called out as she pushed open the screen door. Isabel rushed toward her mother in her pale yellow pajamas, squealing with excitement. Her black pigtails went flying behind her. She instantly leaped at Leila and wrapped her in a hug around the waist, making Leila laugh with joy and almost teeter backward to the walkway. All her sadness from earlier that day instantly dissolved.

"Hey, baby!" she cried, leaning down to kiss her daughter on the crown. "What are you doing up this late? It's nine-thirty—well past your bedtime! I thought you'd be asleep by now."

"I tried more than once to put that child to bed, but she wouldn't hear of it until you got home," her mother said, stepping aside to let Leila and Isabel through the front door. "See, Izzy! Mama's home. Now you can finally go to sleep, girl!"

Leila lowered her grocery bags to her mother's WELCOME mat and eased her way through the crowded entryway that, thanks to her pack-rat mama, was bordered by potted plants, a metal stand filled with umbrellas, stacks of newspapers and magazines that had yet to be recycled, and a few of Isabel's discarded toys.

Leila playfully swatted Isabel on the behind, making the little girl giggle. "Okay, off to bed with you. I'll be in your room in a minute."

Leila watched as Isabel ran down the hall to her

bedroom. Leila then turned to her mother when the door closed. "Mama, can you take these into the kitchen for me? I stopped by the store to pick up a few things."

Diane nodded before leaning down to grab the bags. "Sure. Tell me how your day went after you kiss Izzy good-night."

Seconds later, Leila strolled into her daughter's bedroom only to find Isabel screaming and bouncing up and down on the bed, making the bedsprings squeak rhythmically.

"Get down!" Leila shouted, holding back a smile, trying her best to play the role of the stern mother but failing miserably. Her daughter let out one last squeal before flopping back onto her double bed.

The ten-by-ten-foot room was painted a pastel pink and decorated with stickers and figurines of unicorns and rainbows. A few posters of teen pop princesses were on the walls. It used to be the only guest room in the house, but it had become the little girl's bedroom once Isabel and Leila moved in with Diane. To give Isabel privacy, Leila slept on the living room's fold-out sofa.

"Did you brush your teeth?" Leila asked, perching on the bed beside her daughter.

Isabel crawled to her knees and emphatically nodded, though Leila was skeptical.

"Uh-huh. Let me smell your breath so I can know for sure."

Isabel melodramatically rolled her brown eyes and leaned toward her mother's face. "Ahhh!" she shouted, making Leila laugh again.

"Okay, you're minty fresh. I guess you're good." She pulled back the tie-dyed comforter and thumped the mattress. "Time for bed. Climb in and say your prayers."

Isabel scrambled to the head of the bed and lay back against the pillows that were propped against the headboard. Leila placed butterfly kisses on her button nose, making the little girl giggle again. She entwined her fingers, closed her eyes, and bowed her head. Isabel dutifully did the same.

"God bless Mommy and Grandmommy," Isabel began, lisping a little thanks to her missing front teeth. "Bless my teacher Miss Abrams, even though she tells me I talk too much in class. Bless our janitor at school, Mr. Dudley. Bless my best friends Tisha and Miranda. Bless the doggie I saw on the street on the way home, God. He looked really hungry. That's why I gave him the rest of the nasty sandwich Grandmommy made me for lunch."

At that, Leila cracked open one eye and choked back her laughter.

"Bless the goldfish in the tank at school. It looks really bored. I hope it makes friends with the other fishies in there. Bless the turtles in Miss Whitley's class. Bless the—"

"All right, Izzy. This list is getting kinda long, baby. Do you think we can wrap it up now?"

"All right, Mommy," Isabel said before letting out a dramatic sigh and pausing for a bit. "Bless all the kittens in the world. I hope I get one of them for my birthday in August. Oh, *oh!* Before I forget . . . *please* bless my daddy too, God. I miss him."

Leila tried not to flinch at that one. She knew Brad would always be Isabel's father and Isabel would probably always love him.

Even if he is a son of a bitch, she thought.

"Amen," Isabel whispered.

"Amen," Leila chimed before kissing her daughter

again and pulling the sheets up to Isabel's chin. "Good night, baby."

She then walked to Isabel's dresser and turned off the only lamp in the room. She leaned down and turned on a nearby unicorn nightlight before creeping to the bedroom door.

"Mommy?" Isabel called out just as Leila stepped into the hallway.

"Yeah?"

"When are we gonna live with Daddy again?"

Leila paused, taken aback by the question. "What do you mean? We live here with Grandma Diane. Your daddy lives back in California."

"I know," Isabel answered quietly. The little girl then began to pick at a loose thread in her comforter. "But when I talked to Daddy tonight, and asked him when I would see him again, he said that we'd all be together soon. He said we'd be coming back home soon too."

Leila clenched her jaw and silently cursed under her breath. She had gotten used to the mind games Brad would play on her during the course of their relationship, but it pissed her off that he was still playing those same games now that they were separated. This time, he was doing it through their daughter.

"Honey," she said, stepping back into the darkened room. She sat on the edge of the bed again and gazed into her daughter's eyes. She could see faintly by the light in the hallway. "We aren't going back to California to be with Daddy. *This* is our home. Here in Virginia. This is where we live now."

"But Daddy said—"

"I don't care what Daddy said!" Leila answered firmly, cutting her off.

Leila inwardly kicked herself when Isabel's eyes went downcast. The little girl bit down hard on her bottom lip and sniffed. Sadness washed over her face.

"I'm sorry, baby," Leila whispered, rubbing her shoulders. "I just don't want you to get confused. I'm sorry if what Daddy said confused you, but we aren't going back to live with him."

Isabel sniffed again, no longer meeting Leila's gaze.

"But maybe you can go to visit your daddy in a few weeks when summer vacation starts. Maybe then you can spend some time with him. Huh? Wouldn't that be nice?"

She watched as Isabel hesitated and nodded.

Leila hoped Isabel and Brad would get to spend some time together. Who knew when father and daughter would see each other again if Brad got sentenced to jail time for his fraud and money-laundering charges? It could be years—maybe even decades.

"Try to get some sleep, honey. You need your beauty rest."

A smile finally crept to Isabel's lips. "Okay, Mommy."

"Night, night, Izzy," Leila said, walking back to the bedroom door. "Love you, baby."

"Night, night, Mommy. Love you too," Isabel whispered just as Leila closed the door behind her.

When the lock clicked, Leila stood alone in the empty hall for several seconds. She took a few deep breaths, feeling as if the weight of the world were on her shoulders. This was too much. It was all just too much—between the divorce, her back-breaking debt, her mother's foreclosure, and now Brad wreaking his own brand of havoc from as far away as California. Thinking about it all, Leila's lashes started to dampen with tears. How was she going to stand this? How was she not going to crumble even though every day it was a struggle not to sit in a corner, crawl into the fetal position, and weep?

"Lee?" her mother suddenly called from the kitchen.

Leila straightened her shoulders and quickly wiped her eyes with the backs of her hands. "Coming, Mama!"

Leila took her final deep breath and strode down the hall and into the dinette kitchen, where she found her mother putting a carton of apple juice Leila had just purchased onto one of the refrigerator's metal shelves.

"I didn't know you were going to stop at the grocery store," Diane said as she balled up the empty grocery bag.

"We needed the food," Leila answered, reaching for one of the bags. "I thought I'd just get it on the way home after work."

"But you've got to be tired, Lee! Didn't you pull a double shift?" Her mother sat down at their metal kitchen table. When the older woman fell back into the chair, she let out a groan and kicked off her canvas shoes. "I know I'm tired just thinking about it," she muttered before flexing her toes.

"I'm all right. Don't worry about me." Leila removed a loaf of bread from one of the bags and placed it on the counter.

"I can't help but worry about you," her mother muttered.

Leila pretended like she hadn't heard that. She chose to change the subject instead. "So you'll never guess who stopped by Dean's Big Burger today."

"You better watch out, Lee, or you'll end up with feet like mine! Damn my corns," Diane mumbled before looking up at Leila, taking a break from rubbing the ball of her right foot. "I'm sorry, baby—what were you saying? Who came to visit?"

"Paulette Murdoch."

Diane did a double take. She slowly lowered her foot back to the floor. *"Paulette Murdoch?* You mean Evan's sister?"

Leila nodded as she put a bottle of dishwashing liquid near the sink.

"I didn't even know you were talking to the Murdochs again! Why'd she come to see you?"

"She wanted to reach out to me since we didn't get to talk at her wedding."

"Wait a minute! You went to her wedding?"

Leila paused. She forgot that she hadn't told her mother about crashing the wedding last month. She shrugged. "Uh, yeah. She invited me so I went," Leila lied.

"What did she want to talk to you about?"

"About Evan and the way he's been treating me. I think she feels bad about it."

"As she should!" Diane obstinately crossed her arms over her chest and poked out her chin. She had known Evan since he was a young man, back when he would ride home with Leila after school in his father's chauffeured Lincoln Town Car, looking every bit like a pre-teen African prince. Diane also knew a little about the drama now between Evan and Leila. "I've got no idea what crawled up that boy's hind parts when it comes to you, but he better dig it out! It wasn't your fault you didn't want to marry him!"

Leila rolled her eyes as she placed the last of the groceries in the fridge. "Don't exaggerate, Mama. Evan never asked me to marry him."

Diane looked at her knowingly. "Only cuz you didn't give him the chance to ask."

At that, Leila's face flushed with heat. She turned away from her mother and closed the refrigerator door. She always became unnerved when someone brought up the topic of Evan's unrequited feelings for her. It made her embarrassed that she had ignored for years what seemed to be plainly visible to the rest of the world. But it had obviously been a bad case of puppy love that Evan didn't feel anymore. She didn't understand why everyone kept bringing it up.

Leila busied herself with putting the discarded grocery bags into the recycling bin under the sink.

"Well, anyway, Paulette didn't just want to talk about Evan. She wanted to give me money too."

"What?" her mother exclaimed. Her eyes widened.

"I know, right? She said she knew about my divorce from Brad. She heard I had hit hard times so she offered me money to help out."

Diane eagerly sat forward in her chair. "And what did you say?"

"I turned her down, of course." Leila turned back to her mother to find the older woman gazing at her in disbelief. "What?"

"You turned her down? *Are you crazy?* Why in the world did you do that?" Diane shouted.

"What do you mean, 'Am I crazy?' Mama, there is no way I could accept money from Paulette! I couldn't take advantage of her like that."

"You wouldn't be taking advantage! Those M&Ms have more money than they know what to do with. If they wanted to give you some of it, you should have just said thank you and told them who to make the check out to!"

Leila shook her head, now bewildered. She'd thought her mother would take her to task for humbling herself and begging Evan for help, which was why she hadn't told her about going to Paulette's wedding. Instead, her mother was now chastising her for not accepting his sister's money.

"I can*not* believe I'm hearing this! I mean . . . from you of all people, Mama! You're the one who taught me about working hard and not accepting handouts! You're the one who taught me about being proud and self-reliant and—"

"And look where all that pride and self-reliance got me," Diane said, sweeping her hand around the room with flourish. "Look where it got *us!* With the situation we are in, Lee, you can't be too proud to take a hand-out, honey."

"Well, it's too late anyway," Leila grumbled. "I told her no, and I'm not going back to bring it up with her again."

The kitchen fell silent. Leila turned on the faucet and grabbed a sponge. She began to take out her frustrations on the pile of pans in the kitchen sink.

"I'm heading to bed," Diane murmured before rising from the metal table. "Don't stay up too late. You need your rest." She stretched, winced at the cracking sound in her back, and shuffled across the room. When she reached the kitchen entryway, she turned to stare at Leila. "If you're going to do this on your own, you need all the strength you can get, honey. Trust me. I speak from experience."

She then turned back around and headed to her bedroom, leaving Leila alone with her burdens and her thoughts.

Chapter 7

EVAN

"So he's trying to renege on our agreement?" Evan asked Joe Cannon, his director of operations.

Joe shook his snow-white head. "Not renege. He says he wants to '*renegotiate*.' He knows our contract is up for renewal next year and he's playing hardball. He wants to charge us more to lease those warehouses. He claims that he has another company that's interested and willing to pay more for the space. Greedy little bastard," Joe muttered.

Evan pursed his lips as he listened.

They were discussing a group of warehouses Murdoch Conglomerated used for its line of specialty food products. The guy who owned the storage facilities wanted to bump up the price of the lease he was charging the company by more than 50 percent. Joe considered the price outrageous. Evan considered it a personal affront to his sensibilities as a businessman.

"So what are our options?" Evan asked. "Can we just switch the inventory to another facility?"

"Maybe." Joe shrugged. "But it'll be a real pain in the rear to find one. He has the special refrigeration we need for storage that most facilities in the U.S. don't have."

"I see," Evan muttered. He reclined in his desk chair and sat silent for several seconds, contemplating a solution to their business dilemma.

Joe tried to do the same, to lean back and think, but he could only manage to shift awkwardly in his leather chair. It was all blunt angles and little padding. He grimaced as he tried his best to get in a comfortable position while Evan sat across from him, lost in thought.

The chairs were one of many additions and changes that Evan had made to the expansive CEO office on the twelfth floor of Murdoch Conglomerated. The room had once been occupied by George Murdoch and therefore reflected the old man's aesthetic, which leaned toward more traditional design and antique accents and furniture. In fact, George had modeled it after a study he had seen at an old estate in the Hudson Valley. He had wanted the office to have presence and gravitas.

"Let any man who steps through that door know not to underestimate me," George had instructed the designer.

But when Evan took over the office when he became CEO seven months ago, he'd wanted to show there was a new sheriff in town—in more ways than one. He got rid of the walnut paneling his father had so loved, gave away the rosewood desk, removed the French sconces, and ripped down the heavy curtains over the windows. He'd replaced it all with clean modern furniture that had steel frames, glass shelves, and a low profile. He'd had the walls painted a stark white and ordered simple solar shades. No sconces—just recessed lights. No expensive oriental rugs—just plain hardwood floors.

I am not my father, he wanted the room to say. *I am my own man.*

"All right, then let's do this," Evan finally said. "Have our people scour the country to find a space that's comparable. And this time we're not leasing it. We're buying the warehouses outright."

"Buying? Do we have the capital for that?"

"We'll find it," Evan said firmly. "We have no other option. I'm not going to allow our inventory to be held hostage by every guy who wants to make a buck and raise the rent on us whenever the hell he feels like it. I also want you to find out who's the vendor for his refrigeration system. We'll install it in our own facilities if we have to."

Joe sighed. "Okay, if you think this is best, Evan."

"I do."

Joe stood from his chair. "I'll have my people get right on it."

"Good."

Evan walked with Joe to his office door. He patted the older man on the back. Joe had been with the company for more than twenty years. Evan's father had personally hired him. Evan considered Joe a family friend and knew him well.

"Look, Joe, I know you don't like confrontation, but it has to be done this time. If this guy thinks he can play hardball with me, he has another think coming." His jaw tightened. "I don't respond well to threats and I'll be damned if I let that asshole push me around."

Joe paused in Evan's doorway. He turned and eyed the younger man. His bushy eyebrows knitted together. "You're sounding more and more like him every day."

"Huh? More and more like who?"

"Your father," Joe said quietly, nodding to an imposing portrait of the late George Murdoch that hung on Evan's wall. It was the only holdover from his father's old office.

Evan's eyes widened with amazement. He watched as Joe walked out the door and shut it behind him.

"*My father?*" Evan murmured aloud.

Evan found that hard to believe. George had been a stern businessman—in some cases, even ruthless. Through sheer drive and a predatory instinct, in thirty years, George had grown the Murdoch family's forgettable cookie shop on Main Street in Chesterton, which Evan's grandfather had given his grandma Lucille to "keep her occupied," to a chain of stores, and eventually to Murdoch Conglomerated, a two-hundred-million-dollar manufacturer of food consumer products and owner of several local food franchises.

Evan wasn't like his father. Though he had respected the old man's business acumen, he never wanted to be as cold or brutal as George had been. Hearing that he was starting to sound like George was unsettling.

Evan walked back to his desk and opened his calendar for the day on his computer screen to see what meeting he had next, but he was interrupted by the ringing of his cell phone. He picked it up and glanced at the number on his screen. When he saw who it was, he did a double take. It was his wife, Charisse. He was surprised she was up this early. Thanks to her hangovers, she didn't usually rouse out of bed until noon and was only capable of holding a conversation after she downed two mimosas with a handful of aspirin.

"Hey, Charisse, what's up?" he asked distractedly, scanning through his calendar. It looked like he had another meeting in an hour and more until 6 p.m. This was going to be a long ass day.

"Tell these people you'll pay for it!" she barked into the phone.

Evan frowned. "Pay for what?" He had no idea what she was talking about. "What people?"

There was a pause. He could hear frantic voices in the background and lots of shouting. "Just tell them you'll pay for the car, Evan. You know, this never would have happened if you would have just gotten me the convertible like I asked you to!"

He leaned forward in his chair, feeling the familiar coldness ease up his spine. Every time he got a call from his wife nowadays, it was bad news of some kind. Gone were the days that she called to say how much she loved him or that she couldn't wait for him to leave the office so that she could see him. Now he waited for the call when she was asking him to bail her out of jail for taking out a pedestrian or plowing into a school bus.

"Charisse, where are you? What the hell happened?"

"I'm at the Jaguar dealership in Tyson's Corner. I was trying to buy a new car and I had a little fender bender," she answered breezily. "It wasn't my fault, but they claim it is. Like they don't have insurance." She huffed. "Just tell them you'll pay for the car!"

Evan closed his eyes and took a deep breath. Her voice was slightly slurred. She had been drinking again. He could tell, and chances were, if there was an accident, Charisse had been at fault.

"Here! Talk to him yourself!" Charisse said.

"Hello!" a man shouted into the phone. "Hello!"

"Hello, this is Evan Murdoch," he answered resignedly. "To whom am I speaking?"

"This is Henry Franco. I am the manager at this dealership and this . . . this *woman* . . . your wife . . . she . . ." The man seemed at a loss for words. "Sir, she was test-driving one of our new Jaguar convertibles and *plowed* into several cars in our lot. She's totaled more than two-hundred-thousand dollars' worth of merchandise! We can't—"

"Have someone at your dealership calculate the total for all the damage and I'll write you a check."

"A check?"

"Yes, a check. I assume that's acceptable. You don't need a cash payment, do you?"

The manager seemed to hesitate. Evan knew how absurd it sounded. Who the hell wrote a check for that much money? But he would happily do it to make this go away.

And if there was anything the Murdochs did best, it was throw money at their problems.

"No, we don't need cash, but . . . sir, it . . . it isn't just about the money. Your wife"—the manager dropped his voice to a whisper—"your wife also seems to be intoxicated. I'm afraid we will have to call the police and report—"

"Come on now, is that really necessary, Mr. Franco? I'm sure my wife is very apologetic. I'm offering to pay for all the damage. You can have the check today. There's no need to get the police involved."

"B-b-but . . . but, sir, she's obviously—"

"Look, how about this? I write you a check for the damage with some additional funds for your time and frustration. I arrange to have a cab pick up my wife from your location so that she gets home safely. That way she's out of your hair. Or, we go with the alternative. You call the police and my offer to write you a check and pay for the damage in full is withdrawn,"

Evan said. The steel in his voice that had emerged earlier during his conversation with Joe Cannon now returned. "And not only do I not write you a check, but I
also sue you and your dealership for defamation. I will
pay the best lawyers in town to make sure I not only
own the car she drove and the ones she damaged, but
also every goddamn car you have on your lot. How
about that? Which of those two scenarios do you prefer?"

The manager cleared his throat. "The . . . the first
one . . . I suppose."

"Good. I'm glad we agree. Now please put my wife
back on the phone."

Evan heard some mumbling and then his wife's
voice. "So you're going to pay for it then? They're
going to leave me alone and let me get the hell out of
here?"

Evan sighed. "Yes, Charisse, I'm going to pay for it.
But damn it, you can't keep doing this," he said
through clenched teeth. "Your drinking has gotten way
out of hand."

"I'm not drunk!"

"Bullshit! You're lucky you were on a car lot and
you hit a couple of empty Jags. What if you had seriously hurt someone? You need to go to counseling,
maybe even rehab. We'll tell people you went on a
cruise vacation. Something! Just get this shit under
control and—"

"I don't need a fucking lecture from the likes of
you, Evan Murdoch! I like to have fun every once in a
while and I drink occasionally. *So what?* That doesn't
make me an alcoholic. I'm just not boring *like you!* I'm
not some anal-retentive workaholic who sleeps on a . . .
a . . . pull-out couch in his office three times a week!

Hell, if you could live in that goddamn office, you would!"

A vein started to bulge along his temple. "My work has nothing to do with—"

"Thank you for your help, Evan. If I run into another car, I'll be sure to call you again," she snapped before hanging up on him.

He gripped his cell phone in his fist, wanting to hurl it at the office wall. Instead, he closed his eyes again, took several deep breaths, and calmly laid the phone on his desk.

"You should have let that manager call the cops," a voice in his head insisted. "You should have let them arrest her. She could have gone to jail and some judge would have ordered her into detox. It probably could have helped her."

But he never would have done that. He never would have risked his or his family's reputation with such a public embarrassment. Charisse's face would be plastered on the front page of *The Chesterton Times*. He could only imagine the fallout from such a scandal. No, he would continue to clean up her mess, just like he continued to pretend to most of the people in town that he and Charisse were blissfully happy and he wasn't locked in an empty, sexless marriage.

Sex. He hadn't had it in more than a year.

Damn, has it really been that long? he thought with a cringe.

His crazy work schedule since his father's death had kept him so busy that he had been somewhat able to ignore that vital element that had disappeared from his life. But it was starting to get very old. His sexual frustration was building, scaling higher and higher like a pyramid. He could feel it.

He guessed he could break down and try to have sex with Charisse, but even if he could overlook her bitchiness, how sloppy drunk she could get sometimes (well, most of the time lately, quite frankly) was a major turnoff for him. She wasn't the alluring blonde he remembered from years ago. Instead, a cold, moody lush had taken her place.

"There are other ways to handle this," the voice in his head answered. "You could always have an affair."

And if he wanted to make it even simpler, some men of means would just make a few phone calls and have an escort delivered to them. A woman like that would come prepared and be willing to fulfill Evan's every desire. But Evan didn't believe in getting a call girl. And he didn't want to have an affair with a woman who wasn't paid for her company either. He'd seen the way his father's affairs had ravaged his parents' marriage and lives. He had wanted different: a happy, monogamous relationship with the woman he was madly in love with. He hadn't wanted to go down a path similar to his dad's.

But you can't go on like this forever, the voice in his head argued. *You're not a monk, Evan.*

Just then, Evan heard a soft knock at his door, snatching him from his thoughts. He looked up to find his sister, Paulette, peering around the edge of his door frame at him.

"Hey, big bro! You busy?"

Seeing her standing there, his heavy mood instantly lightened.

"When am I not?" he muttered with a chuckle. He then slid back from his desk and rose from his leather swivel chair. The day was already hectic, but he could spare a few minutes for Paulette.

She pushed his door further open and stepped inside his office. "I didn't want to just barge in on you, but your assistant wasn't at her desk. I couldn't ask her if you were occupied."

"That's because I am currently without an assistant, unfortunately." He gestured to one of the upholstered chairs in the center of the room, offering his sister a seat.

She sat down and adjusted the front of her skirt. "*Without an assistant?* Why?"

He shrugged and took the seat across from her. "She just wasn't working out. I'm looking for a new one though."

Paulette narrowed her eyes at him knowingly. "Did you scare her off with your type-A personality, Ev? She didn't have the patience for your color-coded systems?"

"Who knows!" He chuckled again. "So what brings you here today, Sweet Pea? I thought you were still busy settling into the house you and Antonio bought before you left for your honeymoon. I figured you'd be knee deep in swatches by now."

"Well, I . . . you know . . . just wanted to stop in and see how . . . you know . . . you're doing."

"I'm doing fine."

The two fell into an awkward silence.

"I also wanted to see how the business is, umm . . . is doing."

"*You* want to know how the business is doing?"

That didn't sound like Paulette. She had never expressed interest in the family business before. Hearing about stuff like sales figures and marketing plans had never been her thing. In fact, it always seemed to bore her to death.

"I don't know," she said, evading his penetrating

gaze. She waved her hands nervously. "I was just . . . I was just wondering about stuff."

"What stuff?"

"I had . . . I had read stuff in the local paper, you know, about Murdoch Bank and . . . and homes that are being foreclosed on. I just wanted to know . . . what's . . . what's happening with all that."

"Nothing's happening. They haven't paid their mortgages and we're foreclosing on their properties. It's that cut and dry. Of course, no one likes to be fore-closed on, hence them running to the newspapers."

She mumbled something, making Evan squint.

"What did you say? I can barely hear you, Sweet Pea."

"I said I don't think it's that 'cut and dry'!" she re-peated louder. "These are people, Evan. *Real* people. Some of them have lived in Chesterton for decades. The economy sucks and they've fallen on hard times. I don't understand why we're being so . . . so mean to them. It's not like we need their money. We have plenty! Why can't we cut them a deal?"

"Paulette, sweetheart, we run a bank, and a bank is still a business. No bank is in the business of lending to people and simply forgetting that they owe money simply because they're nice or they've 'fallen on hard times.' That would be a horrific business practice. We'd default within months."

"But if you'd . . . if you'd just give them a bit longer, if you'd just give them a *chance,* Ev, you'd—"

He held up his hand, stopping her. "Where is all this coming from?"

"What do you mean?"

He lowered his hand and leaned forward in his chair. "Why are we even talking about this? What brought this up?"

"I-I told you. I read about it . . . in the . . . you know, in the paper. That's all."

He could see her wavering. She was hiding something, but Paulette had never been a very good liar when she was put on the spot. He watched as his little sister gnawed her bottom lip and fidgeted. Finally, she threw up her hands in capitulation.

"Don't do it, Ev! Please don't kick Lee out of her house!"

"This is about Leila?" His face hardened. The bulging vein along his temple returned. "That's why you came today? Wait." He narrowed his eyes. "Did she put you up to this?"

"No, she didn't put me up to this! I-I wanted to do it." Paulette grimaced. "Please don't get mad. I didn't want to tell you who it was because I knew you'd react this way."

"How can I *not* get mad?" he shouted. He rose from his chair and fought to regain his calm, but it was a struggle. "I cannot believe Leila did this. It's completely out of line! What the hell was she thinking, coming to you about bank business? I already told her we were going forward with the foreclosure! So she thought she could go whining to you about it? She thought she could manipulate you?"

"She wasn't trying to manipulate me! She didn't ask me to do this! I'm doing it because *I* want to do it!" Paulette insisted, glaring up at him.

Evan didn't believe that for one second.

Leila couldn't get him to change his mind so she'd decided to target the kind-hearted, weaker one in their family—Paulette. Desperate times called for desperate measures and desperate Leila had decided to latch on to his naive little sister. How could she stoop so low?

"Well, I'll tell you this. Now that I know that she

went behind my back and approached you, I'm definitely not changing my mind," he declared. "Besides, it's out of my hands—*our* hands—as I had already explained to her."

"It's not out of our hands! Our last name is on that bank! If we said something, they would—"

"We aren't saying or doing anything! *We* are going to stay the hell out of it! Look, Sweet Pea—"

"Stop calling me that!" She fisted her hands in her lap. "Stop calling me that stupid fucking nickname! Stop talking to me like I'm some little girl, Evan! You sound just like Dad!"

At that, he flinched.

"Fine then, *Paulette.* Is that better?" he asked sarcastically, raising his brows. "Paulette, you've taken no interest in the family business, in any of the subsidiaries, until Leila Hawkins came crying to you! Stick to what you know. All right? Stay out of it!"

"Stick to what I know?" Paulette shot to her feet. "So I guess I should stick to shopping and getting my nails done! I should be like Mom and sit around, look pretty, and shut up? No, Ev! I own part of this company, just like you do! This is my legacy too! And Leila is my friend!"

"Your friend? You've barely spoken to her in ten goddamn years!"

"And why is that?" she yelled. "Why haven't any of us spoken her? Because you shut her out! You basically banned us from talking to her, and I'm not doing it anymore! Just because you're pissed off at Leila, doesn't mean all of us have to be! This has nothing to do with business! You're angry that she rejected you and married someone else! You just want to get back at her, and I wish you would grow up and—"

"The answer is still no," he said, his tone colder

than a sheet of ice. He silenced Paulette with his hardened gaze.

Paulette grabbed her purse. "Fine," she muttered before stomping to his office door. "You have a nice day, asshole!" She then slammed the door behind her, making the frame rattle.

Evan closed his eyes and tiredly ran his hand over his face, feeling a lot like Job. He also could feel the beginnings of a headache coming on.

This was turning out to be a horrendous day. First, there was the argument with Charisse, now the yelling match with his sister. He glanced at his wall clock. It was only 9:24 a.m. He hoped the day wouldn't get much worse. He didn't think he could take another ten hours of this.

He walked across his office to the floor-to-ceiling windows and loosened his neck tie. He glared at his scenic view. The midday sun refracted off the Potomac River in the distance, making it twinkle. A few sail boats cut through the water. Watching the picturesque scene, Evan became lost in thought.

What had gotten into Leila's head? First, she had crashed the wedding to ambush him; now she had decided to go to Paulette to beg about the foreclosure. It wasn't Paulette's job to clean up Leila's messes.

He sighed and rested his throbbing brow against the cool glass.

Where was the Leila of Evan's childhood—the sweet, honest Leila whom he had fallen in love with? Because he *had* loved her once, probably since the day when they met at nine years old at their small private school, where he had been a legacy student and she had been on a low-income scholarship. For all those years, he had only pretended to be just friends with her because he hadn't had the courage to tell her the truth.

But he should have told her he loved her. Maybe then she could have avoided falling for Bradley Hawkins.

Evan knew that slimy bastard was nothing but trouble, "a grade-A bullshitter," as Evan's father liked to say. Evan had noticed how the guy talked endlessly about himself and how Brad's gaze followed other women when Leila wasn't looking. Brad wasn't worthy of Leila. Evan had tried to tell her as much, but she and Brad had gotten engaged anyway. And Leila had done everything and anything for her man. She'd made excuses for him and, sometimes, outright lied for him. But one day, she'd taken it too far. Even Evan couldn't make excuses for her anymore.

The last straw had been when Evan's father, George, was beaten and robbed at gunpoint one night coming home late from "the office." (The truth was the old man had probably been leaving one of his mistresses' houses.) George said he hadn't seen the men who had robbed him because they'd been wearing ski masks, though he did say one of their voices sounded eerily familiar. But the identity of the woman who had driven the getaway car that the robbers hopped into after stealing his wallet was emblazoned in George's memory.

"It was that bitch!" he had shouted at Evan after stumbling home, bloodied and furious. "That cunt of yours—Leila! I'd know her from a mile away."

Evan had said it couldn't be Leila. His father had to be mistaken, though George insisted that he wasn't.

"It was her! I swear my life on it!" he had cried.

Evan couldn't say for sure that his father was right, but he hated to admit that the allegations made sense. Brad didn't seem above doing anything illegal to make a buck, based on the questionable "investments" he had tried to get Evan involved in more than once. And Leila had shown in the past that she was willing to lie to help Brad. Maybe she was willing to do a lot more than that to give her man a leg up.

It had taken lots of arguing, negotiating, and outright begging to get his father not to drive to the Sheriff's Office and press charges against Leila. Evan had known that if it was his father's word against hers, Leila didn't stand a chance. Evan had considered it his last favor to her, the last thing he owed her from their years of friendship. After that, he wanted nothing to do with her. He hadn't looked back since.

Leila had changed so much—on the inside, anyway. But on the outside she was still as beautiful and sexy as he remembered. When he closed his eyes, he could still see her smiling face, those bedroom eyes and her tempting curves. At the wedding reception, just a mere touch from her had sent his pulse racing.

Slowly, Evan opened his eyes again. A thought began to crystallize.

Leila faced a serious problem, but so did he. She wanted to halt foreclosure proceedings, and he needed and wanted the sexual comforts of a woman. Maybe she would be amenable to solving their problems together.

"So you're willing to have an affair, after all?" a voice in his head asked. "Would Leila be up for that though?"

The old Leila wouldn't, he argued in response, *but maybe the new Leila would.*

He wanted kinship from his wife. He wanted love and passion, but Charisse wasn't willing to give him that. She made that abundantly clear with the contempt she showed him daily. He couldn't see enduring such an empty existence year after year after year. He needed a respite, something to get him through the cold loneliness. But he couldn't risk his reputation with a messy divorce either. So if he had an affair he had to make sure it was with someone who could show some discretion, who had just as much to lose if their affair was made known. Leila was going through a divorce and she needed to keep up appearances of being a virtuous wife and respectful mother. She would have to be discreet.

Maybe she would be willing to "help" him. It would be a business deal, after all—no different from the hundred other contracts he handled day after day. Instead of agreeing to purchase an office space or acquire a subsidiary, he would be agreeing to purchase Leila's company for a few months. That's all. Well, more like an exchange of services. She would fulfill a need he had, and he would find a way to end her mother's foreclosure.

It wasn't like getting a call girl he had never met before. He knew Leila and she knew him. This would be two adults engaged in a mutually agreeable business relationship.

The more he thought about it, the more plausible the idea seemed.

If there was anything Evan had learned during the years under his father's tutelage, it was that sometimes, to get what you want, you had to think out of the box. You had to take a chance. This was as far out of the box as Evan could get—but he wanted to try it. Despite his growing distaste for Leila, he still wanted her.

"Joe Cannon was right," the voice in his head argued. "You are changing."

Maybe I am, he thought resignedly.

With his new plan in mind, he turned away from his office window and returned to his work for the day. Sometime this week, he would give Leila Hawkins a long-overdue call back.

Chapter 8
PAULETTE

Paulette adjusted the cups of her black balconette bra, then the lace bands of her thigh-high stockings and took one final look at herself in her full-length mirror's reflection. She turned to her right, then her left, wondering if she looked more alluring than she felt.

"Positive thoughts. Positive thoughts," she murmured to herself as she walked across the bedroom's plush carpet in her satin stilettos. She seemed to be repeating that phrase a lot these days. But she needed to say it now to take her mind off of the argument she'd had with Evan that morning.

Paulette wasn't sure what she found more infuriating, that Evan had told her what was going on at the company their father had founded was none of her business, or Evan's inability to realize just how unfair he was being to Leila. Her brother was so proud and pigheaded sometimes. It may serve him well in the business world, but it made for a shit job in his personal life.

But Leila had to push thoughts of Evan aside for now and focus on getting herself sexy and ready for her husband, who was coming home *on time* from the office in less than fifteen minutes. Antonio not working late was a rare occurrence these days. She had to take advantage of it.

Paulette gave one final glance at their darkened bedroom. She had drawn closed the new curtains that Antonio had hung only a couple weeks ago and lit scented candles around the room, setting a few on the dresser and armoire. A trail of red and pink rose petals led from the door to the foot of their four-poster bed. A few were sprinkled on the gray Dupioni silk bedspread.

She hoped her romantic gesture would surprise him. It didn't take much to get Antonio in the mood, but lately her man had been too distracted or tired to climb on top of her and get the job done—so to speak. Maybe this evening, they would finally . . . *finally* make the baby she was longing for.

Just as Paulette closed the bedroom door behind her, she heard Antonio pull his Mercedes into the driveway. She ran as fast as her heels would allow down the second-floor hall, then down the stairs. She raced into her spacious kitchen and grabbed a few important items, then raced back into the main foyer just as she heard Antonio inserting his key into the front door.

"Welcome home, baby," Paulette said in a throaty purr when he pushed open the door, giving no hint to the flurry of activity that had kept her occupied for the past hour and a half.

Antonio stepped inside the foyer and almost stumbled on the straw WELCOME mat when he saw his wife standing six feet in front of him in her lingerie with a can of whipped cream in one hand and bottle of chocolate syrup in the other. She strutted toward him and saw that familiar gleam in his eye that reminded her of the days when they'd first started dating. She saw the way he licked his lips and looked her up and down, like it took all his willpower not to throw her to the hardwood and make love to her right there.

"Either you're gonna make me a sundae or tonight is about to get real interesting," he murmured as he slowly lowered his briefcase to the floor.

Paulette wrinkled her nose. "Sorry, we're all out of ice cream." She then stood on the balls of her feet and nibbled his bottom lip before dragging it between her teeth. "But that doesn't mean we can't have dessert."

He laughed and wrapped his arms around her, drawing her close. She could already feel his erection poking through his pants, nudging her insistently. "I love it when you talk like a porn star," he whispered into her ear.

"Like it's my *talking* that you love." She kissed him again, grabbed his hand, and tugged him toward the staircase. "Come on."

It was a challenge to get Antonio to the second floor. Every few steps, he had his hands on her, sliding one up her thigh or cupping one of her breasts. She playfully tried to fend him off but couldn't while holding the chocolate bottle and the whipped cream can. Besides, the whole point was to entice him. By the time they reached the bedroom, whatever patience Antonio had had all but disappeared.

Good, she thought as they fell back onto their bed. *We're going to make a baby tonight if it kills us.*

And if it did kill them, at least they'd die blissfully.

The garters went first, then the thigh-high stockings, next the balconette bra, and finally her thong. She straddled him and shook the whipped cream can. She then sprayed a puff on her nipples, down the center of breasts, and along her navel.

"Better lick it off before it melts, Tony," she whispered, tossing her hair over her shoulder and setting the can aside on their duvet.

He instantly obliged, sucking the cream off her nipples until she moaned. When all of it was licked off, he grabbed the can and sprayed her again a little too eagerly, making a burst of whipped cream splatter their headboard. Some of it sprayed her in the eyes.

"Damn, baby, sorry," he muttered as he wiped the cream off her face and she giggled with delight.

Only her Antonio could turn such an erotic moment into slapstick comedy.

But her giggles quickly morphed into moans and yelling when he sprayed her in between her legs and licked off the rest of the whipped cream with a tantalizing deliberateness that made her toes curl. Each stroke of his tongue left her writhing in ecstasy. When the orgasm hit her, she fisted their bedsheets in her hands and breathlessly shouted out his name.

Later, she treated his body to the same carnal play, using the chocolate syrup instead of the whipped cream.

"Two of my favorite chocolates," she whispered before flicking her tongue over his left pec. She then followed the winding trail of chocolate lower until she reached his groin. She saw the abdominal muscles tighten as her tongue went lower and lower and lower.

"Stop torturing me, girl," he groaned before she finally took him into her mouth.

Antonio shoved his hands into her hair as she licked and sucked the chocolate off his shaft.

"Aww, shit! Shit!" he shouted after a few minutes. "Oh, God!"

That was her cue. She licked the last traces of chocolate off her lips and pulled her mouth away. She straddled him again and lowered herself on top of him, feeling him glide inside her with a smoothness and ease she had grown to love. He grabbed her hips to steady her as she rode him. He then cupped her bottom, all the while rocking underneath her. Paulette closed her eyes and braced her hands on his broad shoulders, increasing the tempo and enjoying herself as he met her thrust for thrust. It didn't take long for her to reach orgasm again or for him. After they both came, she fell on top of him, gasping for air.

They lay silently, both slick with sweat and sticky from the chocolate syrup and whipped cream. Paulette was content as well as optimistic.

We made a baby this time, she thought as she closed her eyes and gave a winsome smile. *I'm sure of it.*

A half an hour later, she roused awake in the dim light of their bedroom only to find Antonio still snoring beside her. She felt and heard her stomach rumble and realized that neither of them had eaten dinner. Paulette crawled off the bed, stretching and yawning as she went. She strolled out of the bedroom and down the hall to the floor below. As she walked down the staircase she considered making two club sandwiches and grabbing a bottle of wine when she halted in her steps. She caught the shadow of movement by the dining room.

Suddenly, her mother-in-law leaned her head around the door frame. "Oh, there you are?" Reina said, pursing her lips.

Paulette screamed before trying feebly to cover her nakedness. "Reina . . . what . . . what are you doing here?" she cried, clamping her hands over her breasts. "How did you get in?"

The older woman's lip curled. "What do you mean how did I get in? I used my key!"

Paulette blinked at Reina in shock. *"Your key?"*

"Yes, my key. I came to make y'all some dinner." Reina gestured down to the gingham apron she was wearing with the spatula in her hand. "You don't seem to think feeding my son is a priority so I thought I'd make sure he got some proper food." She looked Paulette up and down. Her nose wrinkled with disdain. "Judging from all that yelling you were doing, I guess you're more concerned with other things."

"Tony! Tony, get up, damn it!" Paulette screeched as she angrily swung open their bedroom door and slammed it closed behind her.

Antonio instantly startled awake. He rose from the bed in shock. "What? What's wrong?"

"I just walked downstairs to find your mother cooking in our kitchen! Why did you give her a key to our house?" she yelled, making him wince.

"What do you mean, why did I give her a key? She's my mama! It's my house! She had a key to my apartment back when—"

"This isn't your house, Tony! This is *our* house! *Me and you!* Not me, you, and Reina Williams! She can't just barge in here whenever the fuck she feels like it!" Paulette screamed as she stormed across the room. She turned on the overhead lights and began to blow out the candles she had so painstakingly arranged around their bedroom. "Damn it, I hate feeling like a guest in my own home! She's here more than you are!"

"So what? You want me to tell my own mama she can't come around anymore?"

"No! That's not what I'm saying! I'm just . . . she

just . . ." She stomped her foot in frustration. "Tony, she saw me naked! She heard us . . . us *fucking!*"

"She wouldn't have seen you naked if you wouldn't have walked around the house with no clothes on! Anybody could have seen you through the windows! Come on, Paulette! Use your damn head!"

At those words, she went rigid. She glared at him. "What did you just say?"

"I said to use your damn head! Think for once!"

Paulette's father had often yelled the same thing at her mother when the two would argue at night when they thought both the mansion staff and the children had gone to sleep. But at the distant sound of raised voices, Paulette would wake up, creep out of bed, sneak down a series of hallways, and ease her parents' bedroom door open. She would witness the arguments. Well, they couldn't really be called "arguments" since they were almost exclusively one-sided. Paulette's father would be bellowing at her mother, chastising her like some child, while Angela Murdoch sat silently and wept. Paulette had been so angry at her father back then and sad for her mother. She vowed that she would never let any man do the same to her.

"You enjoy whatever meal your mama wants to cook for you," she said quietly as she walked into the bathroom. "I'm going out."

She then slammed the bathroom door closed behind her.

Less than an hour later, Paulette pulled into the parking lot of her local gym, prepared to sweat out her frustrations on the treadmill and elliptical machine. She had changed into a sports bra, a no-nonsense tank top, and a pair of black stretch pants. She had scrubbed off all her makeup and pulled back her lustrous curls into a ponytail. With a resigned sigh, she climbed out of her cherry-red Mercedes Roadster and took out her small gym bag that had been sitting on the passenger seat. She pushed through the glass door of the gym seconds later and absently waved at her trainer, Daniel, who was leaning over another one of his clients—a plump woman who was grunting and huffing her way through lunges and squats.

"Hey! What are you doing here?" Daniel called out to Paulette as she passed him. "I'm not supposed to see you until Wednesday at 7 p.m.!"

"Just felt like doing a quick workout," she mumbled as she strode towards the ladies' locker room.

"Yeah! That's what I'm talking about! Get it in, girl!" he cheered with a fist pump before returning his attention to the woman beside him, who looked near collapsing. "Okay, just one more, June. You can do it!"

Paulette walked past the tiled shower stalls toward the line of metal lockers along the back wall. She opened one of the lockers and tossed her gym bag inside after removing her MP3 player and a towel. She then headed to the cardio equipment on the far side of the gym, near the wall-to-ceiling mirrors, taking her place on a treadmill between an elderly man in a sweatband who was doing a slow shuffle and a muscular type who sprinted like he was training for the Olympics. She decided to select a pace that was somewhere in between the two. As she pressed a few buttons and started jogging, her mind drifted back to her argument with Antonio.

Had she been too hard on him? Maybe. He had a right to invite his mother to his home. But when were she and Antonio going to get the chance to live like a real married couple instead of a real married couple *plus one?*

"You knew what you were getting into when you married him," a voice in her head admonished. "You knew he was a mama's boy!"

Yes, this was true. But she had hoped that with time he would cut the apron strings, that her desire for more independence would inspire him to be equally independent. So far, though, that didn't seem to be the case. Antonio seemed happy and content nestled against his mother's bosom and Reina seemed loath to open her arms and let him pull away.

"But you agreed to love Tony for better or for worse," the voice insisted. "Try to remember why you fell in love with him in the first place."

As Paulette shifted from a jog to a cool-down walk on the treadmill, she thought back to their first date. Antonio had been suave and hilarious. There hadn't been one awkward pause. She had laughed throughout their date, but her laughter had died when he'd swept her into his arms in front of the door of her apartment, and kissed her for the first time. It had been one of those kisses that made your toes curl and your lips tingle, that made your nipples hard and sent an electric current and up and down your spine.

How could she give up on a man like that, who made her laugh and made her tingle?

"For better or for worse," the voice in her head reiterated.

I've got to give it another try, she thought. *Maybe I can ask him to only let his mama visit once a week. . . . at least until we settle in completely.*

With that, she pressed a few buttons on the treadmill's digital screen and stepped off the belt as it slowed. She walked toward the weights on the other side of the gym, resolving that after she did a few arm curls, she'd run home and try to make up with her husband. She grabbed two ten-pound barbells and sat down on one of the benches.

"One . . . two . . ." she quietly counted off with each lift.

"What's up, cutie? Long time no see, baby!"

At the sound of the booming baritone voice behind her, Paulette almost dropped the barbells. She whipped around, pivoting slightly on the workout bench, to make sure she had indeed heard what she thought she heard. Maybe it was her mind playing tricks on her because she was so upset, so frazzled. Yes, maybe that was it!

But when she did turn and look up, she saw a familiar face grinning down at her. He wiped the sweat from his brow and from along the collar of the red muscle T-shirt that showed his glistening brown pecs.

"What you been up to, girl?" he asked, taking another step toward her.

Oh, God, she thought, now staring at him, aghast.

It wasn't a trick of the ear or mind. He really was standing there!

"Marques?" she whispered. "Is that you?"

It had been almost a decade since she had last seen him. Now his cornrows were gone. He looked like he had put on about twenty pounds of muscle and he sported a beard, but he still looked the same for the most part.

The last time Paulette had spoken to Marques, she had been weeping quietly as they sat in the booth at a local pizza joint just outside of Chesterton—their secret meeting place. She had told him that she was pregnant and scared. Instead of him climbing out of his seat to go to the other side of the booth to sit beside her and reassure her, instead of him reaching across the table and squeezing her hand, he had dropped his half-eaten pepperoni pizza back to his plate and sneered at her in disgust.

"I know you ain't trying to say that baby is mine! Cuz I always pulled out! I handled my shit!"

She lowered her tissue from her nose and narrowed her reddened eyes at him. "Of course, it's yours! Pulling out doesn't mean anything!"

He drank the rest of his soda until a slurping sound emanated from his straw, making her cringe. He then shoved his empty glass aside. "It always worked before. I've never gotten a chick pregnant! Never!"

"You mean you've never gotten someone pregnant *until now,*" she insisted, making him shake his head in denial.

"Nope, it ain't mine! I ain't hearing that shit!"

"Then who else would it be? I've never been with another guy! You're the only one, Marques!"

He slouched back against the pleather cushion and shrugged. "Hell if I know! When you find the dude, let me know."

He then stood up and walked off, leaving her with the lunch bill and the prospect of a baby she had no idea how to raise on her own.

She had tried calling Marques a few times after that, hoping that maybe he was just as scared as she was and that was the reason why he had behaved so coldly toward her. But he had never returned her messages. Finally, she'd just stopped calling. After a few crying jags, she'd realized that Marques didn't love her and probably never had. Oh, he had loved the gifts she had given him: the gold chains, the new expensive sneakers, the video game console, and every other thing her rich-girl allowance could buy for him. And he had loved the sex, even if she was inexperienced. At least she had been eager to do whatever he wanted, whenever he wanted. But he didn't love *her*. He had used her and now she was no longer useful. She was deadweight.

Paulette had booked the appointment at the women's clinic. Leila had driven her there and taken her home after the abortion, vowing to keep her secret.

Paulette had never expected to see Marques again. She guessed she was wrong.

"Yeah, it's me, girl!" he said, reaching down to her as if he was going to embrace her in a hug. When she shied away from his touch, he stepped back. "Oh, it's like that?"

"I-I have to go," she murmured while rising from the bench, feeling shaky on her feet. She lowered the barbells to the floor.

"So you're married now?" Marques said as she started to walk away.

Paulette paused and turned to face him. "What?"

He pointed at her left hand. "I see that big-ass rock on your finger. Your dude got bank, huh?" He chuckled. "Yeah, I figured a rich girl like you wouldn't settle for less. Not Paulette Murdoch."

She didn't respond, but instead continued on her path through the maze of weights and workout equipment. She accidentally bumped into another woman, who was striding to one of the treadmills.

"I'm . . . I'm sorry," she mumbled, then raced to the women's locker room.

"I'll see you around, baby!" Marques called after her.

She certainly hoped not.

* * *

Paulette returned home soon after. As she set her gym bag on the foyer floor and removed her hoodie, she could feel her hands trembling. She was that shaken up. What had Marques been doing there? Why had he suddenly shown up now? She hadn't seen him in years, and now he suddenly—

"Baby?" Antonio called out, making her jump in surprise.

She turned to find a shadowy figure standing in the alcove leading to their living room. Her husband stepped forward into the dim light coming through the windows of their French doors. His hands were tucked in his jean pockets. Concern marred his face.

"Baby, can we talk?" he asked softly, taking a hesitant step toward her.

Paulette assumed his mother had left already. She couldn't hear Reina banging and clanging her way around their kitchen. But even though Paulette and Antonio were finally home alone, she wasn't equipped to have any deep discussions with him now. Not with the horrendous day she had been having. Her mind was lurching and bumping along like it was on a failing battery.

"I'm really tired, Tony," she said as she hung her hoodie on the coat rack behind her. "Can we do this some other day?"

He took another step toward her. "But we need to—" He paused, then eyed her. "Are you all right, baby? You look like . . . like you've seen a ghost or somethin'."

The worst ghost imaginable, she thought.

"I'm *fine*," she said tightly. "I told you, I'm just . . . I'm just tired, that's all! I don't want to talk about it right now!"

She hadn't meant to shout that last part, but the emotional fatigue of the day really was getting to her. She watched as her husband sucked his teeth, then nodded.

"Yeah, sure. All right," he muttered as he walked past her.

She sighed and placed a consoling hand on his shoulder. "Tony, I—"

He shoved her hand off and kept walking to the door that led to their basement, seeking the solace of his man cave, she could only assume. She heard the door to the entertainment room slam shut behind him less than a minute later.

Chapter 9

DANTE

It looked like the seventh annual Wilson Medical Center fundraiser was off to a running start. The throng of rich, drunk suburbanites was bidding on the luxury items up for auction tonight and enjoying themselves mightily while doing it. They danced, laughed, and shouted to one another across the crowded ballroom where everything from a ten-carat diamond pendant necklace to certificates for a private charter jet was on display.

The chatter around Dante was loud, almost to the point of deafening. He winced as a man at the banquet table next to his barked out a laugh that was so hard the man started coughing.

"Enjoying yourself?" Charisse asked as she leaned toward Dante, snapping him out of his malaise.

Dante lowered his champagne glass. "I was about to ask you the same thing."

"Do you really have to ask?" she murmured dryly

before rolling her eyes at her husband, who was taking a business call on his BlackBerry.

Charisse wasn't the only one of the Murdochs who seemed to be in a less than jovial mood. In fact, Dante would venture to say that the atmosphere at their family table was a bit strained. Evan and Charisse sat together but ignored each other, which wasn't unusual. But it also seemed like Evan and Paulette were making an effort to pretend like the other wasn't sitting only a few feet away.

Paulette's husband, Antonio, had come to the fundraiser with her. Considering that couple had only been married a little more than a month ago, Dante had expected them to be still firmly in the honeymoon phase and all over each other. But they weren't kissing or holding hands. Instead, Paulette sat stoically in her chair, looking like a little black Barbie doll in her blue sequined gown—and just as plastic. Antonio kept his eyes focused on his dinner plate like it was the most important meal he had ever had.

The Yukon potatoes are good, Dante thought as he watched him, *but they ain't that damn good!*

The only person who seemed to be in a talkative mood was Terrence, who would not shut up about some basketball game he watched last night. If Terrence could come down with whatever voice box illness that seemed to have struck the rest of the family, that would suit Dante just fine.

Dante needed to concentrate. He could sense an opportunity here. There was dissension among the ranks and he had to use this to his advantage.

"So how's married life, you two?" Dante suddenly piped up, cutting into Terrence's retelling of an epic four-point shot. "Enjoying your days as man and wife?"

Antonio finally looked up from his plate. He set

down his fork and knife, stopped chewing, and glanced at Paulette. "Sure, it's . . . uh . . . it's fine."

"Uh-huh, perfectly fine," Paulette concurred, then sipped from her champagne glass. She looked away.

Fine, my ass, Dante thought with a saccharine smile as he gazed at the couple. He wondered what drama was going on between them behind closed doors. He wondered who would file for divorce first and when he or she would do it.

"You remember those days, Ev?" Dante shouted to Evan over the ballroom revelry. Evan had just ended his call and was back to scanning emails on his Black-Berry.

As Dante spoke, Charisse, who was sitting in between the two brothers, began rubbing her hand up and down Dante's inner thigh underneath the linen table-cloth. Dante wasn't sure if he should be amused or pissed that she was being so blatant. Anyone could look down at any moment and see what she was doing, but thankfully, everyone else at the table was too pre-occupied.

Evan looked up from his phone after typing a few more buttons. He tucked his BlackBerry into the inside pocket of his tuxedo and then gazed at Dante quizzi-cally. "Remember what days?"

"When you and Charisse were newlyweds," Dante elaborated. "I bet those were some crazy days, huh? I bet you two were . . ."

He paused. Charisse had shifted her hand even higher, so that she was practically cupping his balls. He could feel her fiddling with his pants zipper.

Evan raised his brows expectantly. "You bet I was what?"

Dante's smile tightened just as Charisse's slender hand slipped inside the now lowered zipper. She wrapped around his dick and gently squeezed, making him emit a barely audible grunt.

"Yes, what were you saying, Dante?" she asked, gazing at him with mock innocence. Her blue eyes twinkled merrily.

Dante set down his glass and swallowed as she began to massage him through the fabric of his boxers. What the hell was this drunken bitch doing? Giving him a hand job in the middle of the damn ballroom?

"I bet you two were all over each other," he said as he reached under the table, grabbed Charisse's wrist mid-stroke, and shoved her hand away. He gave himself points for keeping his smile locked in place the entire time. "You've been married for what? Five years now, Ev? Any advice for the newlyweds?"

"Never lose your sense of spontaneity," Charisse interjected over the lip of her wineglass, then winked.

Paulette suddenly rose from the table. "Excuse me, everyone. I'll . . . I'll be back in a sec," she mumbled.

Dante viewed the young woman with fascination as she grabbed her pearl clutch and nearly fled through the crowded ballroom to the entrance.

Terrence frowned as he watched his sister's retreating back. "Is Sweet Pea all right?"

"It's Paulette now," Evan said dryly. "She doesn't want us to call her Sweet Pea anymore."

"She doesn't want a lot of things lately," Antonio mumbled as he pushed his chair back from the table. He removed his napkin from his lap and slapped it near his plate, looking aggravated. "I'll go check on her."

"No," Dante said as he quickly raised his zipper, "finish your meal. *I'll* check on her. I'm sure she's fine though. Probably just had to go the ladies' room."

"Aww, you're always so helpful, Dante," Charisse

said as he stood from his chair. He paused and glanced down at her. He found her smirking up at him.

No worries, Dante thought as he turned to follow Paulette. He'd knock that smug expression off Charisse's face later in the bedroom.

She won't be talking so much shit then!

After pushing his way through the ballroom throng, Dante entered an adjacent salon only to find Paulette fleeing that room too. He grumbled to himself. There were a lot of rooms at Glen Dale, the recently restored antebellum mansion on the outskirts of Chesterton where the fundraising banquet was taking place. He certainly hoped he wouldn't be chasing her around this damn place all night.

At least the crowd was lighter in the salon. It didn't take him long to make his way across the room and find Paulette in the central gallery, where she pushed open a French door and stepped onto a brick terrace that led to the lush gardens at the back of Glen Dale. He found her standing at one of the railings, partially hidden in the shadows of the terrace. The smell of roses and gardenias was heavy in the humid air. A few couples strolled along the moss-covered brick pathways of the gardens below.

"Paulette?" he called out, making her jump in surprise and turn to him.

He could see even in the dim light of the half moon that there were tears in her eyes. She sniffed and quickly dabbed at them with a tissue before tucking the now makeup-stained tissue back into her purse.

"Oh, h-hi, Dante. What . . . what are you doing out here?"

"I was going to ask you the same thing," he said as he drew closer. "Are you all right? We were worried about you."

"Oh, I'm . . . I'm fine." She sniffed again and tucked a lock of hair of hair behind her ear that had escaped from her artfully coifed updo. "It was getting hot in there. I-I just needed some air. That's . . . that's all." She didn't meet his gaze. Instead she looked down at her fidgeting hands.

"You know, if anything's wrong, you can talk to me." He placed a hand on her shoulder. "We're family now. I'm here to listen."

"Nothing's wrong! Nothing's wrong at all! It's just . . ."

"Just what?"

She closed her eyes. "Well, there . . . there's a lot going on right now. Antonio and I just moved into our new home, but . . ."

She hesitated and began to gnaw her bottom lip. Dante continued to gaze at her, his facial expression now conveying his best impression of kindness and empathy. He knew from experience, as a lawyer who had conducted many cross-examinations, that sometimes silence was the best way to get a witness to talk. People hated the long pauses and felt the need to fill them with words. He just had to sit back and let them hang themselves with a verbal slip or two.

"But we're still getting used to one another, I guess," she continued predictably over the sound of music from inside and whirring of crickets in a pond near the gardens. "It's an adjustment for any married couple. I want to make things right with him. I just want for us to be happy, for us to have our happily ever after. You know? It's not his fault that his mom is so domineering." She laughed, but the laugh was a little too loud. It sounded almost shrill with nervousness. "I knew what I was getting into when I married him. He and his mama are a package deal."

Dante inclined his head as he rubbed her shoulder

soothingly. "That's true. Though anyone could understand why you'd be frustrated by it."

"I'm not frustrated. I'm just . . . I'm just tired of being bossed around, you know? Of being told what to do . . . of being discounted!" He could tell she was getting angry now. Not only had her tone picked up ferocity, but her chest was heaving visibly over her strapless gown. "I'm a grown woman. I hate being treated like some . . . some child or worse, an idiot! Even Evan acts sometimes like my opinions and my feelings don't matter."

At the mention of Evan's name, Dante's ears instantly perked up.

"How could he say that the family business isn't my business?" she asked indignantly, pointing at her chest. "George Murdoch was my dad too! I may not be the big CEO like Evan, but I own shares of that company just like he does—we all own our fifteen percent. My opinion and my vote matters just as much as Evan's at Murdoch Conglomerated!"

There it was. That was what Dante had been waiting to hear. He knew when he had followed Paulette out here, there would be a payoff in the end. That little nugget was what he needed to set his plan into motion.

"You're absolutely right, Paulette. Murdoch Conglomerated *is* your business and Evan has no right to tell you that it isn't." He began rubbing her shoulder again. "And if you ever need anyone to back you up on that, I'm here."

She smiled again. This time, it was genuine. "Thank you."

"After all, you have *three* big brothers now," he said, making her do a double take. "Don't forget that—ever. We're family."

"Of . . . of course not," she said, sniffing again. She

glanced over his shoulder. "We should head back inside. I bet everyone is wondering where we went."

"You go without me." He felt the wheels spinning rapidly in his head. His new plan was still fresh. He wanted to contemplate it for a bit longer alone and not have to deal with the clamor inside in the ballroom—or with Charisse manhandling him underneath the banquet table. "Tell everyone I'll be back in a bit."

She nodded before sauntering back inside the mansion. Dante lingered outside near the gardens a bit longer before opening the French door that led back to the gallery.

Chapter 10

LEILA

Leila nervously gnawed her bottom lip as she walked through the revolving doors and across the marble-tiled floor of the two-story atrium. As she passed a small reflecting pool, then a wall filled with video screens where commercials from a few of Murdoch Conglomerated franchises now played, she glanced at the balconies and a glass-enclosed catwalk above her. Office workers lingered on benches, leaned against brass railings, or walked swiftly to their sundry destinations.

So all these folks work for Evan now, huh?

It was hard to believe that her former friend commanded so many people. In their youth, he had been unassuming, almost soft-spoken. Now he was the big-time CEO of a multimillion-dollar company.

She lowered her gaze and strode swiftly toward the bank of elevators in front of her, but paused when a woman behind the receptionist desk began to call to her.

"Excuse me. *Excuse me!* Are you a visitor, ma'am?" the security guard drawled, tilting back her billed cap, which was perched atop a nest of fire-engine-red spiral curls. A metal sign emblazoned with the words MUR-DOCH CONGLOMERATED sat on the granite wall several feet behind her.

"All visitors have to sign in," she ordered, then picked up a pen and tapped it on the clipboard that sat on the lac-quered ledge of the receptionist desk.

Leila nodded then walked toward the desk. She picked up the clipboard and grabbed the pen.

"You gotta wear a name tag too—*at all times!*" the guard informed Leila, leaning on her elbow. "We don't let just anybody walk around here."

Leila pursed her lips. This wasn't exactly the NSA she was walking through. She doubted the security of Murdoch Conglomerated had to be quite that tight.

A few seconds later, she handed the woman back the sign-in sheet and pen. "I know the name of the person I'm supposed to be visiting today, but I don't know his office number. I left that part blank."

The guard stared down at the sheet, then looked up at Leila. She cocked an eyebrow.

"You wanna visit Mr. Murdoch?"

Leila nodded.

"You mean Evan Murdoch? *The company presi-dent?*"

Leila nodded again.

The woman slowly looked her up and down then burst into laughter, startling Leila and making her glance down at herself.

Okay, so maybe she wasn't exactly appropriately dressed for someone who was supposed to be meeting a CEO. She was wearing white linen shorts, a lavender sleeveless blouse, and canvas platform sandals as opposed to a power suit. But she and Evan were having lunch, not a business meeting—or at least she thought that's what they were doing.

He had invited her out to lunch earlier that week. She had been shocked to receive a call from him after all this time—so shocked, in fact, that she couldn't work up more of a response than a vague "Uh, yeah, sure." Evan *finally* seemed to be willing to hear her out, to give her a chance! Maybe Paulette had talked some sense into him.

But a few hours ago Evan called and said instead of meeting him for lunch at Le Bayou Bleu, an upscale Creole/ Cajun restaurant in Chesterton, to meet him at Murdoch Conglomerated headquarters in Arlington. They would make lunch plans from there.

She was somewhat put off by the sudden change in itinerary. She had told her boss at Dean's Big Burger that she would need an hour-long lunch break—one and a half hour, tops! But now that she was driving to and from Arlington, it would take much longer than that. The D.C. suburb wasn't exactly a hop, skip, and a jump away from Chesterton. It meant a half-an-hour to an hour drive in infamous beltway traffic that could test one's nerves and stomach even on a good day! But she guessed she could make this allowance and meet Evan halfway. She owed her mother that.

Leila nodded at the guard, now more than slightly perturbed. "Yes, I'm here to see Mr. Murdoch. Is that a problem?"

"You got an appointment?"

"Yes, in fact, I do."

"Uh-huh," the guard murmured incredulously. "Well, I'm gonna have to call upstairs and double-check on this one. You're gonna have to wait."

Leila pursed her lips and nodded again while the

guard picked up a phone at the receptionist desk and dialed a series of numbers.

"Hello? . . . Yeah, I'm sorry to be bothering y'all," she began, "but there is some lady down here who's come to speak to Mr. Murdoch. She says she has an appointment." The guard paused to glance down at the clipboard. "Her name is Leila Hawkins. . . . Yeah. Yeah, I know. I ain't heard nothin' about no VIP guests coming in today either, but she says she's here to see him." She turned to Leila, pulling the phone receiver away from her ear. "Are you sure it was Mr. Murdoch you were supposed to meet and not some other Evan or Ethan in the building?"

"I'm sure," Leila answered tightly.

The guard let out a deep breath and returned her attention to her phone conversation. "She swears it's him, but I'm looking at her and I don't think she—*Oh? Uh-huh.* . . . *Uh-huh.*" She anxiously glanced up at Leila. "Well, no one told me that. Hell, I didn't know either! . . . Yeah, I'll . . . I'll tell her."

She hung up the phone and gazed sheepishly at Leila. "Um, someone will be down shortly to show you upstairs, Miss Hawkins."

Leila glanced at her watch. She was now running late thanks to Shaniqua, Queen of the Front Desk.

"I'm sorry, ma'am," the guard whispered. "I didn't know. I mean . . . We usually have, you know . . . procedures for this type of thing. I—"

"Miss Hawkins?" someone boomed.

The guard had been cut off by a blond man in a charcoal pinstriped suit who looked to be in his late twenties. He strode across the atrium toward Leila and adjusted the wire-framed glasses perched on his aquiline nose. He extended his hand to her and she shook it.

"Yes, that's me."

"It's a pleasure to meet you, Miss Hawkins. My name is Carl McIntosh. I'll be escorting you to Mr. Murdoch's office."

As the younger man guided her to the elevators then out to the top floor, then down a series of corridors that led to the CEO office, he prattled on and on, leaving only a few gaps in the conversation for her to utter a quick "yes," "no," or "oh, really?" She found out that he was serving as Evan's temporary assistant, though he was really the assistant of the COO. She knew that he was happy that the rain had finally stopped so he could go to the local golf course and play a few holes. She knew that he planned to eat lunch at a small bistro up the street, which he highly recommended and suggested she patronize. By the time he knocked on Evan's office door and guided her inside, all the nervousness she had felt when she walked into the building had disappeared and was replaced with relief that she was finally getting to see Evan.

"Mr. Murdoch," Carl said with a broad grin. "Miss Leila Hawkins is here to see you."

Evan sat behind a glass-topped desk in a white button-down shirt with the collar undone and his paisley tie loosened. His brows were furrowed. His mouth was set. He looked intensely focused on whatever he was doing at the moment.

Evan had a commanding presence sitting there—dare she say, he even looked a bit sexy. A lot of power emanated from him. Evan glanced up from his computer screen at Leila and Carl, and nodded briefly before returning his attention to the screen.

"Thanks, Carl," he muttered.

Carl nodded then turned to Leila. "It was nice meeting you, Miss Hawkins."

"Same here."

She watched as Carl silently backed out of the room, closing the office door behind him.

"Just a sec, Lee," Evan said as he continued to type on his computer keys. "I'd like to finish this email while I still have my thoughts together."

"Oh, yeah. Sure! Go right ahead."

As he continued to type, she stood uneasily in the center of his office, twisting the strap of her purse, not quite sure what to do next since he hadn't offered her a seat. She looked around her.

The office was massive. It was probably half the size of first floor of her mother's bungalow. Evan's desk sat at the center, but behind him and to his right were a series of bookshelves and a wall-mounted flat screen. There was also a conference table, where six chairs sat. To his left was what looked like a wet bar, along with a large leather sofa, two armchairs, and a glass coffee table. Both sides of the office had floor-to-ceiling windows with views of the Potomac River and Reagan National Airport.

The design was neat, clean, and modern—an aesthetic Leila usually liked—but as she looked around her, she couldn't ignore the feeling that the room came off as incredibly sterile, almost cold. When her eyes settled on the imposing portrait of George Murdoch over her shoulder, the temperature in the room seemed to drop even further.

"And . . . *done!*" Evan suddenly proclaimed, making her snap her eyes away from the portrait. "Just wanted to send that out." He pushed away from his desk. "Didn't intend to make you wait."

"It's fine. I was . . . I was the one who was late. My apologies."

Evan stood up from his chair and walked around the desk toward her. As he did, his eyes scanned over her, like he was seeing her for the first time. His gaze lingered on long bare legs, making her cheeks warm with embarrassment.

"I'm sorry. I didn't know that I was going to be meeting you at your office today. If I had, I wouldn't have worn this." She gestured to her outfit.

His eyes instantly snapped back to her face. "Why?"

"Well, I would have worn something . . . something more business appropriate. I definitely wouldn't have worn shorts."

A gleam came to his dark eyes. A smile crossed his full lips. "What fun would that be?"

Her cheeks grew even warmer, but this time for a very different reason.

"Look," he said, turning away from her and gesturing toward the sofa across the room, "I had to change our plans at the last minute because something came up. I can only spare about thirty minutes for lunch." He glanced at the wall clock behind him. "Make that *fifteen* minutes. So I hope we can do this quickly."

She had been about to sit down but paused, mid-air, and blinked in surprise.

Fifteen minutes? How could they possibly have a meal—let alone a serious conversation—in a mere fifteen minutes?

"If this is a bad time, Ev, we can do it another—"

"No, this is a good time," he assured her, lowering himself into the armchair facing her. He gestured again for her to sit down. "I have no idea when my schedule will come open again this week and I want to get this done."

Get this done? She stared at him in confusion as she plopped on the sofa. Why was Evan talking like this?

A second later, there was a knock at his office door.

"Come in," Evan called out.

Carl pushed the door open and stepped inside, carrying two clear plastic trays of food, along with a stack of linen napkins and silverware. Leila gazed in amazement as Carl set the trays, napkins, and utensils on the coffee table between Evan and Leila.

"Let me know if you need anything else, Mr. Murdoch," Carl said eagerly before heading back toward the door. He closed it behind him.

"I hope you don't mind me making your order for you," Evan said as he rose from the armchair and walked to the wet bar. He leaned down and opened the door to a built-in refrigerator. "Time was of the essence so I couldn't wait around for you. I didn't know what you'd like to drink though. I've got—"

"Actually, I do mind," she said angrily.

First he was rushing her through lunch. Now he was telling her that he had ordered her food for her. *What the hell?*

"How do you even know what I want . . . what I like? You can't—"

"Lemon-flavored grilled chicken breast with sun-dried tomatoes and capers with a side Caesar salad. Hold the croutons," he said, cutting her off.

Leila's words faded. She stared at Evan, dumbfounded. He had remembered her favorite dish—*after all these years?*

He raised his brows. "I got it right, didn't I?"

Leila hesitated before nodding. "Most of it—except hold the croutons *and* the dressing. I'm not in my twenties anymore," she mumbled, running her hands over her thighs, which weren't quite as thin as they had been a decade ago.

A few minutes later, they both began eating lunch in awkward silence. This wasn't quite how Leila had envisioned her first meal with Evan in ten years. It wasn't easy conversation, ribbing and laughing over pizza slices like the old days. Now it was like eating with a stranger.

"So I guess you're wondering why I invited you here," Evan said, setting aside his salmon BLT after a few bites, leaning forward in his chair.

Leila paused mid-chew. She wiped her mouth with her napkin. "I was . . . I was hoping it was because you wanted to talk," she garbled, trying not to spit food onto her lap.

"I did. I want to offer you a business proposal."

She stopped chewing. "A business proposal?"

"I'll just get straight to the point. Paulette told me that you came to her about the mortgage situation."

What?

Leila swallowed the rest of her chicken, feeling it lodge in her throat. "She didn't say that, did she? Ev, I didn't . . . I didn't go to her about the mortgage! She came to visit me at work and I happened to mention that—"

He waved a hand dismissively. "Whatever! Either way, Paulette has nothing to do with what happens at Murdoch Bank. She can't help you, but we both know that *I* can."

Leila's heartbeat began to pick up its pace. Was Evan finally going to speak to the management at Murdoch Bank on her mother's behalf? That would be great—absolutely wonderful! So why did her stomach start to lurch in anticipation of what he was about to say next? There was a catch somewhere. She could sense it.

"I'll help you out, but only under a few conditions," he continued. His stare didn't waver. "I'll *strongly advise* Murdoch Bank to review your mother's mortgage. Coming from me—the CEO of their parent company—that carries a lot of weight. But I'll only do it in exchange for something you can do for me."

Leila frowned. "What . . . what do you want me to do?"

"There's no point in beating around the bush." He reached out and placed a warm hand on her bare knee, making the skin tingle, catching her by surprise. "You and I may have our differences, but I'll admit that even after all this time and all our bullshit . . . I'm still very attracted to you, Lee."

Leila stared down at his hand, gazing at the brown fingers that were splayed over her skin. Why was Evan saying this? Why was he doing this? He was married. She was still married too, damn it, at least on paper!

"Because he's attracted to you. Because he's always been! Didn't you hear what he said?" the voice in her head ridiculed. "And don't pretend like you don't feel it too, girl!"

Okay, so maybe, despite their differences, she was starting to find herself very attracted to him as well, and knowing that was unnerving. She had never considered Evan in that way in the past. He had always been like a sibling to her. Now he was morphing into something else in her eyes and she didn't know what to do about it.

"I'm a very busy man in a very shitty marriage, Lee. I've put sex on the back burner way too long. I'm not ready to divorce Charisse. When I said 'I do' to her, I meant it for the long haul but"—he sighed and absently rubbed Leila's knee, making the tingle she'd felt earlier radiate up and down her leg—"I accept that I'm no saint. I have needs just like any other man—needs that must be met. So I'm offering to help you in exchange for you meeting those needs."

"*In exchange for meeting your needs?*" The blood drained from her face. "Evan, what . . . are you asking me?"

"What does it sound like I'm asking?"

"It sounds like you're asking me to have sex with you!"

He paused. "Well . . . yeah. Yes, I am."

Leila stared at him, struck speechless.

He removed his hand from her knee and sat back in his chair, looking annoyed. "I can tell from your reaction that it wasn't what you expected me to ask. But before you say no outright, seriously consider my offer. I should add that I'm willing to sweeten the pot a bit if my terms aren't suitable. In addition to talking to the bank, I'll offer you one hundred thousand dollars outright for your time and effort."

Time and effort? Why, you smug son of a bitch, she thought. He was propositioning her, actually propositioning her like some two-dollar ho! Make that *one-hundred-thousand*-dollar ho!

"So this is what you thought you could get done in fifteen minutes or less? You thought you could get me to agree to be your mistress? You thought you could . . . you could buy me like some . . ." She sputtered helplessly. "How the hell could you even ask me something like this, Evan?"

"Oh, please!" He rolled his eyes. "Don't get on your moral high horse! You've done a lot more for the people you love, haven't you? Compared to that, this is a small price. Besides, at least with this deal, we *both* get something out of it. I've let you use me one time too many without getting something in return."

"Fuck you!" she barked, jumping up from the sofa in outrage, letting her napkin fall to the floor.

Is that how he saw their relationship? She had thought it was a mutual friendship. All this time, he had thought she was using him?

"Whatever," he replied, also rising from his chair. "Play the drama queen if you want. Either way, my offer still stands. You can say yes, or you can say no. It's up to you. But it's the only way you're getting me to talk to that bank. Those are my terms."

"Terms? *Terms?* Ev, would you listen to yourself! You've been stuck in this office for too damn long if you honestly think you can bargain sex like some . . . some contract! I don't care how shitty of a marriage you have or how horny you are. . . . Stuff like this between a man and a woman can't . . . it can't be worked out like 'Terms of Use'!"

He squinted. "Why not? People do it every day."

"With prostitutes! But I'm not a goddamn prostitute! I'm not gonna spread my legs for a man just because he offers to do me a favor or shakes a hundred grand in front of my face!"

"So what would you do it for?"

"What?"

"What else would you need to agree to something like this?"

She was struck speechless again. What had Evan changed into in the ten years that she hadn't spoken to him? She didn't recognize this man anymore.

"Come on, Lee. I already told you that I want you. I'm a businessman. I'm always open to negotiation . . . within reasonable boundaries." He took a step toward her, making her take a step back and almost bump into his coffee table. He gazed into her eyes. "Tell me your terms."

"I told you, I don't have any goddamn 'terms'! I only have sex with someone I care about. I only have sex with someone I'm attracted to and have passion for. I'm not a professional. I can't fake something like that, Evan! I can't—"

He suddenly closed the divide between them. She didn't have the chance to pull away before Evan abruptly lowered his mouth to hers.

The kiss caught her off guard, but the enticing feel of his full lips against her own sent her heart racing, even when she thought it couldn't possibly beat any faster. When her lips parted, he slid his tongue inside her mouth and lowered his hands to her waist, drawing her even closer to him. She momentarily forgot about his "business proposal." Instead, she focused on the feel of him: his powerful arms around her and his lean body pressed against her own, the warmness of his touch and the searing heat of his kiss. Evan—the man whom she had once considered a brother—now sent her senses whirling.

She closed her eyes and linked her arms around his neck. She stood on the balls of her feet and tilted back her head to deepen the kiss, meeting his tongue with her own. Her nipples hardened against the silk fabric of her blouse. The blood in her veins pounded wildly in her ears. His hands lowered from her waist to her bottom. She grinded against his pelvis and felt him harden. The junction between her thighs started to dampen in primal response.

When Evan drew back a minute later, they were both panting.

"Either you're a better fake than you thought," he whispered with a mischievous grin as he ran his thumb over her kiss-swollen lips, "or you're just as attracted to me as I am to you, Leila. I think we'll do just fine."

Leila grimaced. She stepped out of his embrace, re-coiling at the realization of what they had done. What had gotten into her? She had been trying to prove a point to Evan that he couldn't treat her this way. She wasn't some high-priced hooker. Her body wasn't up for negotiation, no matter what spark he ignited.

Leila grabbed her purse and shoved past him. She strode toward his office door.

"You've got until the end of next week," he called after her, making her pause as she gripped the door handle. "If you don't let me know by then, I'll assume your answer is no."

She whipped around and faced him, blinking back tears of anger. "You know, Evan, when I heard your father had died and that you were the head of your family now, I'd hoped that Paulette and Terrence were in good hands. Your father was a cynical, manipulative asshole who tried to make all of you his puppets. I'd hoped they'd have a better chance with you. But now I know I was wrong! You're a bigger son of a bitch than George Murdoch ever was! Because unlike him, you know better! I thought you were better than this!"

"Next week, Leila. That's your deadline," he said coldly before she opened his office door and slammed it closed behind her.

Chapter 11
EVAN

Evan killed the boat's engine, adjusted his Ray-Bans and walked a short distance. He then flopped down on the leather padded seat beside his brother, Terrence, who was currently examining his reflection in the chrome panel beside him. "Would you take a break from staring at yourself, pretty boy, and hand me a soda?"

Terrence instantly leaned down and reached into the boat's cooler. He handed Evan a chilled can of cola before grabbing a beer for himself.

"All right," Terrence said, adjusting the brim of his baseball cap. "What's on your mind?"

It was one of Evan's rare afternoons off and he had decided to enjoy the warm summer day by driving to Baltimore and taking his twenty-five-foot power boat on the Chesapeake Bay. The family owned a schooner they kept docked in the Virgin Islands that sat empty most of the year. They owned a yacht called the *Black Pearl* that they docked in Annapolis, Maryland. But the Murdoch boys had always preferred boating on something smaller that didn't require staff, that they could handle themselves.

Evan had invited Terrence to come along on this day trip under the guise of enjoying a scenic boat ride, then some steamed Maryland crab at Fell's Point, but the real reason he had invited Terrence was because he wanted to talk. He had considered inviting their half brother, Dante, along for some brotherly bonding, but bearing in mind the nature of this conversation, he wasn't sure if he wanted Dante around.

Evan had been replaying his "lunch" with Leila over and over again in his mind, and every time he thought back to the last thing she had said to him, he was flooded with anger and frustration. She had compared him to George, even claiming that Evan was worse than his old man, which was a joke. Evan had at least treated her like an adult, like an equal partner in this. His father never would have done the same. But still, her words nagged at him. This was the third time in the past week someone had compared him to his father and he didn't like it at all. He needed to talk to someone who had known their father just as well as he had. What better person than Terrence?

"Do you remember Dad's mistresses?" Evan asked suddenly after taking a drink.

Terrence's caramel eyes widened. "Whoa, it's like that, huh? This is a mighty heavy way to start a Saturday afternoon!"

"I'm serious, Terry."

Terrence sighed, turned the brim of baseball cap to the back, and nodded. "Yeah, I remember them—vaguely. I remember Mom wasn't too happy about them either."

"She died of a broken heart," Evan said quietly, gazing at the water that lapped along the side of the boat.

His mother had died five years before his father at an age that many would consider young—a mere fifty-seven.

"No, she died of a pulmonary embolism. That's a big damn difference!" Terrence slowly shook his head. "Ev, where are you going with this? Why are we talking about Dad's mistresses and Mom?"

"Did I tell you one of them came to my office?" Evan took another sip from his soda, still lost in his own thoughts.

"One of *who* came to your office?"

"One of his mistresses. She came about a month after he died—some chick who was way too young for him. She couldn't have been more than thirty ... maybe even twenty-five. She just showed up out of the blue one day asking to speak with me. The receptionist had seen her go to the C-suite a few times when Dad was alive, so they let her in."

"Why the hell did she want to speak with you?"

"She said that Dad had promised he would take care of her." Evan took off his sunglasses and lowered his eyes. "He had been taking care of her for the past five years. She knew I was the executor of his estate and she wanted to know who was going to pay her rent. Would I continue to pay the car note for her BMW?"

"Damn," Terrence said in a slow exhale. "That took a lot of gall."

"I guess she didn't have many options. She said she didn't have a job and she had quit school years ago because she thought Dad was always going to handle her bills for her. She wanted to know if he had included her in the will. But he didn't. He didn't mention any of them. I had to break the news to her that she was one of many, and he didn't set money aside for her or any of his other mistresses." Evan took a deep breath. "She broke down in tears right in my office, Terry. I felt bad for her. Even though I know how women like her made Mom's life so fucking miserable."

"So what did you do?"

"I wrote her a check for twenty grand. I told her that was all I could give her. I haven't heard from her since." He paused. "But why would Dad do that? Why would he make these women believe something that wasn't true? He had no intention of taking care of them for the rest of their lives. Why keep telling them those lies?"

"Hey," Terrence said, raising his free hand, "I'm not one to defend Dad, Ev, but these chicks weren't exactly babes in the woods either. They should have known nothing was promised to them when they hooked up with an old married man, no matter what he may have said." Terrence took a sip of Corona. "So what's with this trip down memory lane? That woman showed up to your office months ago. Why are we talking about it now?"

Evan closed his eyes. "I guess because I made a similar offer to Leila a few days ago, and I'm trying to convince myself that, despite doing that, I'm nothing like Dad."

Terrence stared at him. "Wait! Wait! Back up! When did you talk to Leila?"

"I told you . . . a few days ago when I invited her to my office. I asked her out to lunch."

"Why the hell did you invite her to lunch? I thought you hated her guts! You damn near lost your mind when you thought you had to share a reception room with her."

"I . . . well, I . . ." Evan took a deep breath. "I found out that Leila needed help with her mother's mortgage.

She wanted me to talk to Murdoch Bank, to see if maybe I could get them to stop her mother's foreclosure. So I invited her to lunch to talk about it. I told her that I would discuss it with the bank and help them out with a hundred grand in exchange for her giving me . . ." He paused. "If she would give me something I wanted."

Terrence gazed at his brother as if he was the dumbest man in the world. "And that something you wanted was her, right?"

Evan hesitated again then nodded.

Terrence chuckled. "Shit, Ev, you don't do anything halfway, do you? You couldn't just have an affair with some cute honey you met on a business trip. Instead you had to hit up your ex-best friend of twenty years and offer to buy her!"

"I didn't offer to buy her! Don't say it like that! It's not like she was up on the auction block."

"Fine, you offered to *lease* her then." Terrence shook his head again. "And I can only imagine what she said, knowing Leila. Did she tell you to go to hell and how to get there?"

"Pretty much. But, Terry, I was just being honest with her! I didn't lie to her like Dad lied to those women. I'm a man of my word. I was going to talk to the bank and give her the money. She just wouldn't hear me out! She acted offended . . . like she's some angel, when I know for a fact that she isn't! She got all sanctimonious about it and—"

"Ev," Terrence said tiredly, holding up his hand, "just stop. Rewind the tape. Play it back, man. You're trying to rationalize how it was okay to offer Leila a check to fuck you! You went all Robert Redford on her, making this indecent proposal, and you wonder why she got pissed?"

Evan leaned forward, crushing the now empty soda can in his hand. He angrily tossed it to the deck. "You're making me sound like an asshole!"

"Not an asshole . . . just really, *really* misguided." He clapped his brother's shoulder. "Ev, your marriage is messing with your head and making you miserable. You tried your best to make it work."

"Terry," Evan said tightly, the warning in his voice.

"Come on, man! Why don't you just end it already?"

Terrence was one of the few people who knew about the real state of Evan's marriage. He knew not only that Charisse had a drinking problem, but also that Charisse and Evan hadn't shared a bed in more than a year. He knew about the four miscarriages that had led the couple to give up trying to have a baby. He knew about the arguments and that Evan suspected his wife may be cheating on him. But he also knew that Evan would never, ever walk away from his marriage because he wouldn't sully his reputation or the Murdoch name.

If their parents had managed to stay married for more than thirty years despite all their drama and misery, why couldn't Evan do the same? But his brother kept bringing up divorcing Charisse, annoying him.

"I won't end it because I stand a lot to lose in a divorce: money, property, and maybe even our company. I won't end it because don't have the same approach to marriage that you have to all your relationships," he snapped, shrugging off Terrence's hand. "I don't throw in the towel after a month or two when I get bored with a woman."

Terrence narrowed his eyes. "No, you just try to make a hundred-thousand-dollar down payment on a side piece so you can *pretend* you've got a happy marriage!"

Evan's lips tightened. He turned away and glared at a boat sailing in the distance.

"Okay, fine," Terrence muttered. "Forget about Charisse. Forget I mentioned divorce. Let's focus on Leila instead. She's who you wanted to talk about, right?"

Evan nodded, finally turning back to his brother.

"Judging from her response, I don't think she's going to have an affair with you, big bro. You're gonna have to let that dream die."

Evan had come to that conclusion already. That fantasy had gone up in smoke when he'd watched her slam his office door behind her.

"Would you be willing to help Leila anyway . . . with no strings attached?"

Evan contemplated his brother's question. He didn't want Leila and her family kicked out of their house and tossed onto the street. Leila had done stupid, reckless things for love in the past. She had hurt him long ago, but should he hold that over her head forever?

"I guess I want to help her," he answered softly. "I'd at least do it for the sake of our old friendship, but there's so much shit that's gone down between us. I can't just shrug my shoulders and move on. We've got a lot of stuff to hash out."

"So hash it out. Don't yell at her. Don't try to seduce her. Just talk to her."

For once, Terrence was right. Evan had been clinging to his anger for almost a decade, never confronting her directly, never telling her just how much she had disappointed him. Maybe he should finally do that.

"Maybe I will," Evan said.

"Good!" His brother clapped him on the shoulder again. "Now enough with this heavy shit! Get the engine started again. I'm ready to eat some damn crabs!"

Chapter 12
PAULETTE

Paulette looked around the crowded pizzeria while drumming her fingernails on the Formica tabletop as she waited. She couldn't believe she was in *this* place again. She couldn't believe it was still here, seemingly frozen in time. Along the wall sat an ancient glowing glass jukebox that offered a selection of mid-nineties hits that had already been out of style by the time she had been a teenager. Fake Tiffany pendant lamps still hung from the water-stained, drop-panel ceiling, though now the lamps were covered with considerably more dust than she last remembered. The booths hadn't changed either—dark wood paneling with green leather cushions. Paulette sipped her Diet Coke as she checked the time on her cell phone. The drinks were served in the same clear plastic beer mugs and the sodas were just as watered down as she remembered.

None of these things ignited in her a sense of nostalgia or longing. What she longed to be was far away from this place, but that was impossible thanks to the note she had received in the women's locker room at her gym earlier that day.

"Hey," a woman wearing yellow stretch pants and covered with a fine layer of sweat had said as Paulette stepped out of the sauna. "Hey, is your name Paulette?"

Paulette had nodded, tightening her towel around her. "Yes, it is."

"One of the trainers asked me to give you this." The woman had held out a folded sheet of paper to her.

"One of the trainers?"

The woman had nodded.

Paulette instantly had an idea of who that trainer might be. Her ex, Marques, had cornered her again on the gym floor, this time while she was on the treadmill. She had tried to ignore him, to pretend like she couldn't hear him over the sound of the music in her headphones but he'd kept talking, getting louder and louder. Finally, her personal trainer, Daniel, had to intervene.

"Bra'," Daniel had said, clapping Marques on the shoulder. "My client is trying to do her workout. If you could let her do her thing, I'd appreciate it."

Marques had laughed, nodded, and walked off but not before giving one final look over his shoulder at Paulette. The look had given her the sinking feeling that it wasn't the last she had heard or seen of Marques.

Then the folded note had shown up and her heart had sunk even further.

"Thanks," she had murmured to the woman before taking the sheet of paper from her. She'd flipped it open and quickly read it.

So I'm guessing from how shady you're acting, your new man don't know about me or our baby, the note read. *You'd be smart to stop avoiding me, girl. Meet me at our old spot at 3 p.m.*

That was how she now found herself in the old

pizzeria in a town just outside of Chesterton. She was nervously waiting for Marques to show up. He was already fifteen minutes late, which she remembered from the old days wasn't unusual for him. But if the man was going to try to blackmail her, he could at least have the decency to show up on time.

"Ma'am, did you want to order something else?" the heavyset waitress asked with a cocked brow as she stepped toward the table. She dropped her hand to her ample hip. "That's all you want? *A soda?*"

Paulette glanced at the plastic-encased menu, squinting under the dim pendant light. Nothing among the listed selections looked remotely appetizing. But the waitress probably lived on her tips and Paulette was taking up valuable, money-making real estate by sitting in one of the booths as opposed to the small bistro tables toward the front of the pizzeria. Paulette didn't want to sit at one of those tables though. It was too far out in the open, near the windows, raising the chance that someone she might know would see her in here. That someone might wonder why the newly married Paulette Williams was having lunch with a man who wasn't her husband. Chesterton loved its gossip and she would imagine something like that would travel fast, especially when it involved one of the "Marvelous Murdochs," as she knew people around town liked to call her family.

No, Paulette would stay in the booth and she would order something—even if it sat on her plate untouched until it got cold.

"Uh, I'll . . ." She looked up from the menu. "I guess I'll have some breadsticks and . . . and, uh—"

"We want the medium pepperoni, extra cheese," Marques suddenly boomed as he walked toward her table.

When she heard his voice, she flinched. He grinned and plopped in the cushioned seat across from her.

"I'll have a Michelob too," Marques said, lowering the zipper of his track suit jacket, which had TRAINER written in white, large letters across the front and back. "Don't bother with the glass, baby. Just bring the bottle."

"I'll need to see your license for that," the waitress said.

"Awww, damn! You trying to card me?" He pulled out his wallet and winked at her. "I know I'm a nice-looking dude, but I didn't know I looked young too."

The waitress laughed, examined his license, and handed it back to him. "I'll be right back with your order—cutie."

Paulette watched as the waitress walked off. She shook her head in exasperation. Even after all these years, Marques could still work his charm on the ladies. But Paulette knew from experience that it was all smoke and mirrors. He was a liar, a hustler, and a user. Unfortunately, she had discovered all that way too late.

"So," Marques said, interlocking his fingers and leaning forward so that he stared into her eyes, "I see you showed up."

"Well, it's not like you gave me much of a choice," she answered sullenly, jabbing her straw into her mug.

He chuckled. "That's because you were trying to act brand new, like you didn't know a nigga . . . when we both know you know me, Paulette. You know me *really* damn well."

She ignored the insinuation in his voice, in his smirk. She gnawed her bottom lip.

"Your husband know I'm the baby daddy? Did you have a boy or a—"

"Just tell me what you want, Marques! Why did you call me here?"

He leaned back in his seat. "I wanted to talk business with you."

"Business? What business?"

"Well, being a trainer ain't exactly bringing in the big bucks, if you really wanna know. I've been running a few side hustles to bring in some extra money. The clients who wanna go the extra mile, who want to get their body extra tight, come to me because they know I can get them the goods. I can do what no other trainer at that damn gym can do. I can take them from a couch potato to Arnold Schwarzenegger. I call it the Marques Effect."

To illustrate, he reached into his wallet and pulled out a business card. On the laminated cardboard, she saw the words, *The Marques Effect. Go from fat to phat! RESULTS GUARANTEED.*

"Results guaranteed, huh?" She squinted at him in disbelief. "I don't see how you could do that without waving a magic wand. Unless you're selling them steroids in addition to your *training*," she said, using air quotes.

"Performance enhancement supplements," he answered tightly, narrowing his dark eyes. "And it's legit."

"Yeah, I bet," she muttered, pushing her drink aside.

This wasn't the first time Marques had sold drugs. When they were teenagers, Marques had sold weed—mostly to college students. It was part of the bad-boy image that she had found so appealing back then, but not anymore.

"Okay, so you said you wanted to talk business. So what are you asking?"

"I want you to invest in my company. Invest in the Marques Effect. I need twenty thousand to—"

"Twenty thousand?" she choked. "Twenty thousand dollars?"

Once a user, always a user, but Marques's expectations of her had definitely increased over the years.

"I don't mean pesos, baby! Don't act so shocked. We both know that twenty grand is chump change to a ballin' girl like you, but for a dude like me who got to work every day—*it ain't!*"

She was still in shock and shaking her head as he spoke. *Twenty thousand dollars? Is he serious?*

"Look, the supplements I get ain't cheap, and I don't always have a steady flow of cash to keep them coming. I need the money or my supplier is gonna cut me off. I already owe him."

"You're . . . you're asking me for drug money?" she whispered.

"No, I'm asking you for a business investment! You'll make your money back . . . eventually." He shrugged. "Hey, you ain't got to do it, but you best believe I'm gonna make sure that husband of yours knows all about us, that the child he's raising is mine and—"

"There is no child," she finally blurted out. "I didn't have the baby!"

Marques cocked an eyebrow. "You had an abortion?" He sighed. "Damn, I never would have guessed you were that type."

"What type? The type who didn't want to get disowned and kicked out of her home?" she asked angrily. "The type that didn't want to have to raise a baby alone at seventeen because you refused to believe the child was yours? Is *that* the type you're referring to?"

"Whatever, man! Don't try to turn this shit around on me. Your body, your choice, right? I ain't have nothin' to do with it!"

Paulette's lips tightened just as Marques started to smile again.

"I saw your husband's picture in the paper. It was an old one from your engagement. He looks like a pretty uptight dude. How he gonna feel about you and me? How he gonna feel about you killing our baby?"

Tears started to well in Paulette's eyes. For years, she had pushed aside the thought that she had killed her baby by having an abortion. She had rationalized it, explained to herself that her choices had been limited and raising a child alone as a teenager without her parents' support, wouldn't have done the baby any favors. She'd had no choice. She had done the noble and proper thing. But now it didn't seem so noble and proper anymore, and she doubted Antonio would see it that way either. Their new marriage seemed to be hanging on by a thread as it was. Something like this could make that thread snap.

"When do you . . ." Paulette sniffed and blinked back her tears. She'd be damned if she cried in front of someone like Marques. She loudly cleared her throat. "When do you need your money?"

"By the end of next week. And make it cash, no checks or money orders. That shit can't be traceable."

"All right! Here's your beer and breadsticks," said their waitress, walking toward the table with a tray. She set the bottle in front of Marques and the breadsticks basket in between them. "Your pizza will be out in a few minutes."

"I'm not hungry," Paulette mumbled, grabbing her purse and sliding out of the booth.

Marques rubbed his hands together eagerly. "More for me then!"

Feeling faint and lightheaded, Paulette shakily rose to her feet and ran toward the pizzeria door.

Chapter 13
LEILA

"Well, that was, um . . . nice," Leila said minutes after she pulled out of the apartment building parking lot. She glanced at her mother, who sat in the passenger seat beside her. "Wasn't it nice, Mama?"

A pained expression crossed the older woman's face. She fidgeted in her seat, not meeting Leila's eyes. "I suppose," Diane mumbled. "Though it did need a little work, Lee."

"It smelled like cat pee-pee!" Isabel suddenly piped up from the backseat.

Okay, maybe they have a point, Leila thought grudgingly. Perhaps the apartment at Buena Vista Terrace wasn't exactly what she had envisioned when she'd read the ad for a "spacious three bedroom, one bath with eat-in kitchen and scenic panoramic views." Not only had it looked dingy and smelled funky, but the bedrooms also were so tiny that the jail cells at the Chesterton Sheriff's Office probably had more square footage. She wasn't sure how that was supposed to be an eat-in kitchen when it seemed impossible for more than one person to enjoy a meal at the same time in the kitchen without bumping elbows. And she didn't think anyone could consider windows facing a parking lot and brick wall "scenic panoramic views."

But even with those downsides, Leila was still willing to consider the apartment and any other viable alternatives for a place to live if the price and location were right—short of moving back to California to live with Brad again. Her little family was coming down to the wire, drawing closer and closer to Diane's foreclosure date. They were running out of options.

Only a few days ago, Leila had come home from work to find deputies escorting their neighbors, Melanie and Randy Tillman, off their foreclosed property. A notice was taped to the Tillmans' door. Melanie had been in tears as deputies helped her husband carry what he could out of their house and load it into the back of his Ford pickup truck. A few neighbors had tried to help with the move. The rest had stood, gawking, as they watched the scene unfold, inwardly cringing at the idea that one day they could be in the Tillmans' shoes. Leila had resolved that evening that it was time to get serious about finding a new place to live. She refused to stand by as deputies set her mother's treasured curio cabinet on the front lawn, as they carried out Isabel's stuffed toys in garbage bags.

"It wasn't *that* bad, Izzy," Leila argued as she drove. "Right, Mama?" She nodded in agreement with herself when her mother didn't respond. "Yep, not bad at all! A little paint, nice drapes, and some cleaning and it could work. It could be really nice!"

"If you think so, baby," Diane said.

"I don't think so, Mama. I *know* so!" Leila smiled, even though the bleakness inside her reflected the expressions on the faces of both her mother and her daughter. "Come on, we could make it work if we had to! Plus, it would only be temporary. One year . . . maybe two years, tops, until we got back on our feet."

"Maybe I'll just get used to the smell of cat pee-pee," Isabel muttered as Leila made the turn to pull onto her mother's block.

"You won't have to get used to it. Pine-Sol will take care of it," Leila insisted.

"*Who* in the world is that?" Diane exclaimed, pointing at a car that was parked near the curb in front of their house.

Leila's smile disappeared. Her stomach lurched as she slowed her hatchback to a stop.

She instantly recognized the black Lincoln Town Car a few feet in front of her and watched in dismay as the driver stepped out and walked to the rear of the vehicle.

"It's the president, Grandma! It's the president!" Isabel shouted gleefully as she bounced up and down in the backseat and clapped her hands.

"It's not the president," Leila said as the driver opened the Lincoln Town Car's back door. Her hold on the steering wheel tightened. "It's Evan."

She hadn't seen or spoken to him since his infamous offer almost a week ago and she was still furious. She had come to him for help, had been willing to humble herself for the sake of her family, and what had he done in return? He had treated her like some common hooker! He had offered a quid pro quo of money and a favor in exchange for sex. For some insane reason, he had expected her to take him up on his absurd offer, but Evan had been sorely mistaken!

"Or had he?" the voice in her head asked. The truth was, in her weaker moments, Leila had considered his offer with more seriousness than she would have liked to admit. Evan was right about at least one thing: Despite how much she now detested him, she had felt a passion erupt between them when they kissed. It had been burning hot and had left her wanting more. The sex might even be pleasurable if she could divorce her emotions from the whole situation and let her body take the lead, but she wasn't made that way.

There were many things she was willing to do to clean up the mess Brad had created. There were many ways she had been willing to humble herself, but prostitution wasn't one of them. Evan may have changed a lot over the years, but she hadn't. Leila Hawkins wasn't that type of girl.

"Evan?" her mother asked, now wide eyed. They all watched as Evan stepped out of his car, adjusted his suit jacket, and walked toward the hatchback. "What is he doing here? You think he finally came to apologize?"

"I doubt it," Leila muttered. She hadn't told her mother about her visit to Evan's office or his "business proposal." If she had, she knew her mother would have stomped her way to Murdoch Conglomerated headquarters, ready to kick Evan's ass. "He probably wants to talk about something else."

Her mother frowned. "What else?"

"Nothing. Please just take Isabel inside the house with you. I need to talk to Evan alone."

Her mother's frown deepened. She turned and fixed her daughter with a questioning look but quickly deciphered from the expression on Leila's face that it was a bad time to ask any more questions. She nodded. "All right. Come on, Izzy. Help Grandma start dinner."

They all climbed out of the car. Leila angrily strode toward Evan with Diane and Isabel trailing behind her.

"Hi, Miss White," Evan said with a wave to Leila's mother as she passed him. The older woman had bee-lined for the walkway leading to the house.

Diane paused and briefly nodded. "Hello, Evan. Long time, no see." She then placed her hands on Is-abel's shoulders, steering the little girl back toward their bungalow. "Come on, Izzy."

"You must be Isabel," Evan suddenly said, drop-ping to one knee on the front lawn. He knelt in front of Leila's daughter, dirtying what Leila could only sur-mise was an eight-hundred to a thousand-dollar suit. He held out his hand for a shake. "I'm Evan Murdoch. It's a pleasure to finally meet you."

The little girl stared down at his hand. "I'm not sup-posed to talk to strangers."

Evan pulled his hand back and nodded. "You're right. You shouldn't do that, but I'm not a stranger." He glanced up at Leila, who was now glaring at him with her arms crossed over her chest. "I'm . . . well, I *used to be* close friends with your mother. We've known each other since we were about your age."

"Friends with Mommy?" Isabel looked up at her mother, turned back to Evan, and stared at him doubt-fully. "I know all my mommy's friends. Why haven't I seen you before?"

"Izzy," Diane began, looking embarrassed, "what did I tell you about being r—"

"It's okay, Miss White," Evan said as he held up his hand, silencing Diane. "Izzy, you haven't heard of me because . . . well, because of many reasons, most of which were my fault. But"—he looked up at Leila again, meeting her gaze—"maybe I can change that today."

What the hell is that supposed to mean?

Rightly sensing that something intense and long

overdue was going on, Diane loudly cleared her throat. "Let's go, Izzy." She nodded to Evan again. "It was nice seeing you, Evan." She then quickly walked toward the house, holding Isabel firmly in front of her despite the fact that the little girl was dragging her feet and peering over her shoulder at Evan and Leila the entire way.

Leila watched her mother and daughter until the front door closed behind them. When it did, she whipped around and faced Evan.

"What are you doing here?" she snapped.

He slowly rose to his feet. "I wanted to talk to you."

"Hi, Leila!" one of her neighbors shouted from the lowered window of a Toyota Civic as she rolled by the couple.

Leila waved. "Hey!"

The nosy neighbor stared at her, Evan, and the Town Car with interest a bit longer before finally pulling off. When the car disappeared, Leila whipped around to face Evan again.

"Look, I know your deadline is today, but you told me that if I didn't contact you by now then you'd take my answer as no. So why the hell are you here? Would you like me to say no to your face?" She took a step toward him. "Is that it? Well, then no! No, Evan, I don't accept your offer!"

"I came to apologize."

That knocked the wind out of her sails. "To . . . *to apologize?*"

He nodded, looking solemn.

She hadn't expected that. When she'd walked out of his office a week ago, an apology was the last thing she'd thought she would hear from Evan. He had seemed so sure of himself, so cocky.

"Why are you apologizing?"

"Because I was wrong, and I can admit when I'm wrong. I messed up when I made you that offer." He took a deep breath. "I still want to help you, if you'll let me, but there are some things we still have to hash out, Leila. I've carried around this anger toward you for too damn long."

"What anger? *Why?* Is it because I lied to you about the money . . . because I said it was going to my mom and I gave it to Brad?" She shook her head in frustration. "Look, Ev, I know what I did was wrong. I—"

"It's not just that!" He stared at her in disbelief. "You honestly think I wouldn't talk to you for *ten years* because you lied to me about loaning Brad money?"

"Well, if it's not that, then what the hell is it?"

He sighed and closed his eyes. "Did you help Brad and his friends rob my dad? Did you know they were going to pull guns on him and rough him up that night, or was that some dumb shit they decided to do without telling you?"

Leila blinked in amazement. She was struck speechless for a few seconds but finally regained her words. "Rob your dad? When the hell did Brad rob your dad?"

Evan opened his eyes then sighed gruffly. "Leila, please don't play stupid. You know what I'm talking about! Dad saw you drive the getaway car. I just want to know if—"

"Your dad said he saw me there?" She brought her hand to her mouth. "Is that why you've refused to talk to me for all these years? You thought I was involved in that? You *really* thought it was me?"

He didn't answer her, which was all the answer she needed.

"Jesus, Evan," she breathed.

Had things really gotten that bad between them that

Evan thought she was capable of doing something so horrific?

We're worse off than I thought!

"Ev, I wasn't fond of your father—by a long shot, but I would never, *ever* rob him, let alone hold him at gunpoint! What do you take me for?"

He pursed his lips then shrugged. "I didn't know who you were, Lee. I didn't recognize you anymore."

"Obviously," she muttered, now more than hurt.

"So I guess you're saying you didn't do it. Dad was mistaken?"

"Of course, I didn't do it! That's not even something I'm capable of doing!"

"But Dad *swore* he saw you at—"

"Then your dad was wrong! Either that or he was lying, Evan!"

And she wouldn't put it past Evan's father to make up a lie like that. George Murdoch had despised her and had barely masked his loathing. George had hated that she and Evan were friends, even back when they were kids. She couldn't understand why at the time. Was it because he didn't want Evan associating with a poor girl like her? Was it because her parents were divorced? It wasn't until she and Evan were much older that she'd figured it out. Leila realized that George had wrongly assumed she was trying to maneuver her way into the Murdoch family. He thought, like many in Chesterton, that Leila was only friends with Evan to move up the social ladder. He had thought her goal was to get Evan to marry her, when that couldn't have been further from the truth!

Evan now narrowed his eyes, scrutinizing her. Slowly, his features softened. "I believe you. Shit, I believe you!" He leaned back his head and groaned. "My

father played me like he always did. And I fell for it—
hook, line, and sinker. Shit!" he shouted, balling his
fists.

"I wished you would have told me this years ago,
Ev. Why are you just confronting me about it now?"

"Honestly?" He paused and thought for a bit. "I
guess it was easier to believe the lie. It was easier staying angry at you. That way I had an excuse to cut off
all contact. I wouldn't have to . . ." His words drifted
off. He looked over her shoulder at her neighbor's
lawn, breaking their mutual gaze.

"You wouldn't have to what?"

His dark eyes drifted back to hers. "I wouldn't have
to see you with Brad. I wouldn't have to let the jealousy eat me up anymore."

Her heart sank. An ache welled inside her chest.
"Oh, Ev. Evan, I am so—"

"Don't," he said, holding up his hand, cutting her
off. "That's old news. We can put it in the past now that
we've hashed it out. Let's focus instead on the real reason why I'm here."

She squinted. "Which is?"

"I want to offer you a job, Lee. A legitimate job . . .
if you're willing to take it."

Well, Evan was just full of surprises today! That
certainly wasn't what she had expected. "What . . .
what kind of a job?"

"Before I go into too much detail," he began, "I
guess I should start by saying that if you take this job,
you'll be working for me directly." He cocked an eyebrow. "Would that be an issue?"

Leila hesitated. Sure, they had "hashed things out,"
but considering he had tried to pay her for sex a week
ago, maybe working for Evan wasn't the greatest idea.

It was obvious their relationship as employer and employee would be starting off on very awkward footing—to put it lightly.

If it was any other guy, Leila would say "no" outright. But this was Evan. She had known him since she was nine years old, and for many of those years she had trusted him without question. Maybe what he'd done a week ago had been a momentary lapse in judgment. Maybe he did legitimately want to offer her a job.

Who knows? she thought. But at this point, she was willing to hear him out. She was willing to trust him again.

"No, working for you wouldn't be an issue," she finally answered. "What's the job?"

"My executive assistant. And I'm going to be honest with you, Lee. I've had a hard time keeping the position filled. I'm a hard boss to work for. I can have pretty exacting standards."

"I know. I remember you in sixth grade . . . how you had to have your pencils lined up just so. You even had a certain way you liked the housekeeper to stack your food in your lunch box. Didn't you have an order system for your locker in high school too?"

Evan pursed his lips, looking annoyed at being prodded about his OCD tendencies. "Well, anyway, if you agreed to take the job, you might find it a little challenging, but you would get a good wage and benefits. Do you have any office experience?"

She eagerly nodded. "Sure, I had a few office jobs in college and now I'm doing part-time office work for a law firm."

"Good! Good, so you won't raise any red flags with HR." He licked his lips. "Well, email me your resume. I'll have my human resources director set up an interview with you. We'll schedule it first thing next week. It's a given that I'll hire you, but for legal reasons we still have to go through the formal hiring process."

She nodded again, feeling elated. It was like the sun was starting to finally break through the storm clouds that had been her life lately. "I understand. That makes sense."

"Well, then, I guess I'll see you in my office next week for the interview." He turned like he was heading back to his car, but then suddenly halted. "Oh," he said, holding up a finger, "before I forget . . . there was also the issue of your mom's mortgage."

Had he managed to take care of that too? Judging from his facial expression, Leila surmised that he hadn't.

"It seems that I don't wield quite as much power as I thought," Evan began. "I tried calling the bank president, but it looks like the wheels of bureaucracy can't be stopped once they're set into motion. He was very apologetic, but he basically said that your mom's house will go into foreclosure. I heard that they want you guys out—"

"In three weeks," she said, finishing for him. They had gotten the final letter already. "I'm sorry, Lee. There's nothing I could do to stop it."

She sighed. Her shoulders slumped. "I understand. Thank you for trying anyway."

"But what I *can* do is offer you one of my rental properties. I've owned a few condominiums and town houses since college. Most have been good investments. You should be able to afford the rent on one of them with the new salary you'll be getting."

Leila's throat tightened. Tears welled in her eyes. So they wouldn't have to live in an apartment that smelled like cat pee, after all!

"Thank you, Evan."

"Don't mention it."

"No, I mean it! Thank you so much. I hadn't . . . I hadn't expected any of this."

"I'm not sure you want to thank me yet. You haven't started working for me. Being my executive assistant could be your worst nightmare."

"But it's a real opportunity. It's what I've been hoping for . . . hell, *praying* for! You have no idea what all this means to me!"

"Well, glad to help . . . and glad to have you on board."

They both stood in silence for a long time. She could feel that electric charge erupting again. It was the same feeling she'd had before he'd kissed her. It was building with each second, making the hairs on the back of her neck stand on end.

"See you next week," he said abruptly, ending the tense moment. "We'll work out the details about your lease then too."

He turned to head back to his car again, and she got the distinct feeling that he was fleeing. She wondered if he had felt the electric charge too. Was he getting goose bumps? Had his pulse also quickened?

The driver instantly stepped out of the car and rushed to beat Evan to the rear door.

"Bye! Thanks for everything, Magoo!" she called after him. She clapped her hand over her mouth in embarrassment when she realized she had accidentally called him by his old nickname.

Evan paused just as the driver opened his door. "Leila, I'm your employer now," he said grimly, fixing her with a steely glare. "If you're going to work for me, you have to have some decorum. All right?"

Oh, shit. Here was the exacting boss he had mentioned, the one who had caused his other executive assistants to quit. What had she gotten herself into?

"That's *Mister* Magoo to you," he said with a wink, before climbing inside the Lincoln Town Car, making her sigh with relief.

She grinned as the driver shut the car door behind Evan. Less than a minute later, the Town Car pulled off.

Leila turned and strolled up the walkway, relieved to have a new job, to have a place to live, and to finally have her best friend back.

Chapter 14

EVAN

"Charisse!" Evan called as he stood in the middle of their immense foyer. He glanced at his wristwatch and sighed. "Charisse, we're going to be late!" His voice echoed off the coffered ceilings and plaster walls.

"All right! All right! I'm coming!" she exclaimed as she stomped down the staircase leading to the east and west wings. "Just . . . keep it down. No need to shout the roof off."

Evan looked up to find his wife wearing dark-tinted sunglasses—definitely a sign she was recovering from the latest hangover. But at least she wasn't stumbling down the stairs. She looked presentable, wearing grey capri pants, a white halter top, and a lavender cashmere sweater draped around her shoulders. Her hair was in a chic chignon at the nape of her neck. Her look was befitting the wife of a CEO and co-hostess of the golf tournament fundraiser being held today. Whether she remained in such an immaculate state was the question.

"You look nice," he said.

Charisse waved away his compliment. "Let's just do this, Ev," she muttered before striding toward their French doors. "I've got an exfoliation treatment scheduled for five-thirty. I need to be back by then."

He sighed. So much for his halfhearted attempt at politeness.

A half an hour later, they pulled up in Evan's Maserati at the entrance of the Chesterton Country Club, where the Murdoch family had been members for decades. Evan had foregone using his driver today, giving the father of four the Saturday off so that he could spend it at home with his family.

The sports car's engine rumbled, then quieted to a soft growl when he drew to a stop on the country club's asphalt driveway between two orange cones designating the valet station. Evan quickly spotted Leila standing in the shadow of the country club's green and white striped awning. She waved.

At the sight of Leila, he smiled. From the safety of the tinted sports car window, he let his eyes trail over her—those long, sculpted legs, the curvy bust, and the tiny waist. Then he reminded himself for the umpteenth time that he was a married man with his wife sitting only a few feet away, no less. He also was now Leila's boss, which came with its own list of rules of conduct. But it was hard having a daily reminder of his lack of a sex life walking through his office door.

On any given day, he would see Leila stride toward his desk in her black pencil skirt, silk blouse, and high heels or a formfitting wrap dress and have to force himself not to stare. She would lean over his shoulder, pointing out something on his computer screen, filling his nose with her alluring scent, and his mouth would literally water. When they had to work late and she sat across from him with a carryout container and chopsticks in her hands, with her feet propped up and her head thrown back, laughing at one of his jokes, he would have to fight the urge to take her in his arms and kiss her senseless. It was like he was sixteen all over again. He remembered this slow agony well, and he had no idea why he was putting himself through it all over again almost twenty years later.

Because you want to help her, he silently told himself. *Because she's doing a good job and you need an assistant and she needs the money.*

Letting her go wasn't an option. Not only would he have no justification for doing so, but he couldn't bring himself to hurt Leila in that way, to turn his back on her again. So he pushed down his desires and focused on being as professional as possible around her, but it wasn't getting any easier.

Evan watched as his wife lowered her Chanel shades and glared at Leila over the plastic rims.

"Who's that?" she asked with a curl in her lip as Leila strode from the entrance and walked toward their car.

He threw the Maserati into park and removed the car keys. "My new assistant, Leila Hawkins."

Charisse turned to her husband and squinted her bloodshot eyes at him. *"New assistant?* What happened to the old one?"

"She quit. Couldn't hack it. Leila filled her position. She's turned out to be a good fit."

Charisse raised her sunglasses, pushed them back up the bridge of her nose, and pursed her lips. "You don't say."

Just then, the valet opened Charisse's car door. She stepped onto the brick walkway and Leila instantly rushed forward and extended her hand in greeting while Evan got his valet ticket.

"Hi, Mrs. Murdoch, it's a pleasure to finally meet you! Evan has told me so much about you."

That was a lie. Evan preferred not to talk about Charisse, especially to Leila, for fear of blurting out some sad detail about his marriage like the fact that his wife openly loathed him or that they slept in separate bedrooms.

Charisse glanced at Leila's hand but didn't shake it. Instead, she turned back to Evan. "So what's the agenda for today? Who are we schmoozing?"

Leila pulled back her hand and loudly cleared her throat. "You're going to meet fellow sponsors of today's fundraiser. We have representatives from some companies and a few foundations. Some of them brought their wives and they're all mingling in the clubhouse right now. We're serving hors d'oeuvres and cocktails."

Evan inwardly cringed. *Cocktails? Jesus Christ*, he thought.

Maybe, if Charisse kept it to just one or two mimosas, she wouldn't get too bad, but once she started moving on to the Bloody Marys and martinis, it would only go downhill from there.

"Please follow me," Leila said with the smoothness and professionalism she regularly showed back at the office.

"We know where the clubhouse is," Charisse said curtly, making Leila halt in her steps. "We *are* members of this country club, you know. Or did your new boss neglect to mention that?"

Leila's smile faltered. "Of . . . of course, Mrs. Murdoch. I didn't mean to . . . I mean . . . I hope I didn't offend you."

"I wasn't offended." She paused to look Leila up and down. "Evan was telling me how you're such a great assistant. May I ask, where did you work prior to taking this job?"

"Well, uh . . . I did freelance secretarial work for a law firm and um . . . I was a waitress."

"A freelance secretary and a waitress?" Charisse tilted her head. "And now you're the personal assistant to a CEO at a major corporation. That's quite a climb up the ladder!"

"I guess it is."

"A woman like you must have some *interesting* skills to make it up all those rungs."

"Charisse," Evan said warningly. He had no idea why his wife was acting so hostile to Leila, but he wasn't going to stand there and let her abuse his assistant and his friend.

Leila shrugged, now looking uncomfortable. "I'm a hard worker. Even though I may not look qualified on paper, I've tried my best to meet Evan's expectations."

Charisse chuckled. "Oh, I bet you do."

"Mrs. Murdoch, again . . . I didn't mean to offend you."

"I said I wasn't offended," Charisse muttered through clenched teeth.

"But I think we've started off on the wrong foot. I just wanted to introduce you to everyone at the clubhouse—that's all."

"It's fine, Leila," Evan said, hoping to put an end to this. "Thank you for being so helpful."

"Yes, thank you, Leila," Charisse said icily before walking off, leaving Evan and Leila standing near the entrance.

Leila slowly turned to him. "Damn, that sucked," she whispered, looking shaken. "I can't believe I put my foot in my mouth within five minutes of meeting your wife!"

He shook his head. "No, you didn't. You simply got the full Arctic blast known as Charisse Murdoch. She turns it on everyone at some point—even me. You just got it sooner than most."

"I guess I'll tread carefully then so she doesn't freeze me out again," Leila said with a forced laugh before licking her lips.

Evan's eyes drifted to those full lips, then followed the path of her pink tongue.

Leila wasn't the only one who would need to tread carefully.

"Ev," Leila said, though he was barely paying attention, still focused on that delectable mouth. "Evan!"

His focus returned to her face. "Yes?"

"I asked if we should follow her inside now."

"Oh, yeah. Sure. Of course."

She nodded and turned toward the country club's glass doors. Evan's eyes instantly rested on her ass and he inwardly chided himself and raised it to the back of her head.

Get it together, boy, he told himself as they strode into the air-conditioned foyer.

By the time they arrived at the clubhouse reception, the golf tournament was already in full swing. Evan and Charisse did their duty and acted as gracious hosts, though Evan's attention was mutually torn between keeping an eye on his wife to make sure she didn't become drunk and unruly, and trying *not* to keep an eye on Leila who lingered in the background, making sure everything ran smoothly. As the afternoon wore on, his smile became tighter and tighter. The muscles in his back and shoulders were rigid. The noise and clamor in the clubhouse were starting to give him a headache.

"Too bad you don't drink," Terrence suddenly said behind him. "You look like you can use one."

Evan turned to find Terrence smiling at him while holding a bottle of some expensive craft beer, judging from the label. Terrence was wearing a red polo shirt and black khakis with golf gloves tucked in his waistband. He vaguely resembled a caramel-eyed Tiger Woods, though Evan knew his brother rarely played golf. Terrence had no problem looking the part of a wealthy golfer though. That was the one trait besides the eyes that Terrence had picked up from their father, George: He was all about looking the part, hence his huge double walk-in closet. He had a bigger wardrobe than most of the women he dated.

"So you finally showed up? Where the hell have you been? I was wondering if you were going to make it."

Terrence shrugged and glanced around the crowded clubhouse room. "I was busy."

"On a Saturday afternoon?"

Though, frankly, Terrence's weekdays were often free too. He hadn't held down a job since his modeling days back in New York.

"What can I say? The life of a player can be a busy one," Terrence muttered. He then clapped his older brother on the shoulder. "Come on. Let's step out and get some air. All these old dudes smell like Bengay and mothballs."

Evan glanced across the room at Charisse, who was huddled with several other women and held a glass in her hand. He couldn't tell at this distance what she was drinking, but just seeing her sip from the glass made him nervous.

"No, I really shouldn't leave our guests. It wouldn't look good, you know?"

"You can't babysit her all the time, Ev," Terrence whispered, following the path of his brother's worried gaze. "We'll be gone ten minutes`. . . fifteen, at the most. How much trouble can she get into?"

A lot, Evan thought, but his brother had a point. He couldn't always keep an eye on Charisse—even if he wanted to.

He sighed. "All right. Let's just make it quick. So . . . you know . . . the guests won't notice I'm gone."

Terrence nodded and they strolled toward the doors that led to the outside deck that overlooked the golf course. Evan gave one final glance at Charisse before stepping through the doors. He and Terrence walked in silence until they reached the end of the terra cotta deck. They both leaned against the wrought-iron deck railing and stared at the eighteen-hole golf course, squinting against the bright afternoon sun. The rolling hills of the golf green were dotted with sundry clusters of spectators who observed the players competing in today's tournament. From this height, Evan could barely make out their faces. He caught the faint sound of the reception still going on inside the clubhouse, the rhythmic *thawk* of the golf clubs hitting balls, and the polite claps from the spectators.

"The turnout today looks pretty good," Terrence said, taking another drink from his bottle.

"Yeah, we had a lot of entries and sponsors. We should bring in plenty of money for the charity."

"I never understand going through all this fundraising stuff when the company could just write a big-ass check and call it a day."

"We *do* write a big-ass check. It's just better public relations to do it this way. It makes the company—and by extension, *our family*—look good."

"And we all know how important it is to look good," Terrence muttered dryly.

"I don't know. You tell me. You're the one with the six-figure tailor bill!"

"You got me there," Terrence said with a laugh. "But I wasn't always the big spender. That title used to belong to Paulette—until she up and married Bob the Builder."

"I don't know. She's working her way back up to her big-spending days."

In fact, one of the vice presidents at Murdoch Bank had given Evan a call earlier that week to apologize for the bank declining a withdrawal that Paulette had attempted to make on Tuesday.

"The teller didn't know any better, sir," the VP had said nervously into the phone. "She didn't know that your sister was a Murdoch. When I was alerted to the error, we promptly contacted Ms. Williams to let her know she could still withdraw the amount she wanted."

Evan had frowned as he listened to the VP's explanation. "Why wasn't she allowed to withdraw from her account in the first place?"

"Well," the VP had said, clearing his throat, "you see, it was a considerable amount of money, Mr. Murdoch. Your sister has withdrawn a great deal in the past few weeks. It is bank policy that when an account reaches a certain quantity of withdrawals in that short of a time period, the teller has to alert the branch manager. A hold had been placed on the account. But again, I wanted to personally give my sincere apologies for—"

"How much has she withdrawn?"

"Uh . . . well . . . sir, that's . . . that's privileged information that I can't—"

"How much?" Evan had repeated firmly.

"F-fifty-five thousand dollars."

"Fifty-five thousand dollars? In a matter of weeks, you said?"

"Y-y-yes, sir."

Evan had cursed under his breath before quickly regaining his composure. "Uh, thank you for your apology and relating this information to me."

"No problem, Mr. Murdoch. I hope that—"

The VP didn't get a chance to finish. Evan had hung up and sat at his desk, gazing out the floor-to-ceiling windows for quite a long while after that, deep in thought.

Now, as he recalled the phone conversation, he tried to understand it. What was going on with their little sister? It was her money and her business; he knew that. She had already chided Evan for treating her like a child, but he wondered why she was taking out so much cash. Did any of this have to do with what was going on between her and Antonio? Those two had been acting pretty strange lately. There seemed to be a growing tension between them that was starting to make Evan worry. Something was wrong with Paulette. He could sense it. But he couldn't talk to her about it without coming off as the meddling or overbearing older brother, or alienating her even more than he already had.

"Evan? Earth to Evan!" Terrence shouted through hands that were cupped around his mouth.

Evan blinked and turned to him. "Huh?"

"I asked you how things were at work. You still pulling sixty-hour weeks?"

"I do what I've gotta do," Evan answered blandly with a shrug.

"Yeah, well, I bet it's not that much of a burden now that she's around."

"Who's around?"

"You *know* who," Terrence said, while focusing his eyes on a spot at the other end of the balcony.

Evan looked in the direction that Terrence was gazing and saw Leila closing the balcony door behind her. She was whispering into her cell phone and had her back turned toward them. The instant he saw her, longing surged through him.

"Oh, damn," Terrence said with a wince. "I saw that look. I thought it would be easier with her at the office now, having your buddy on the premises, and all. Is it really that bad?"

It was on the tip of Evan's tongue to deny it, to say that he wasn't being tortured on a daily basis by the sight of Leila, but he wasn't up to lying to his brother today.

"I do what I've gotta do," he mumbled again, still staring at her as she talked on the phone.

"No more indecent proposals though?"

"No," Evan said through gritted teeth. "We're . . ." He deeply exhaled. "We're strictly professional."

Just then, the door opened again. Evan watched as Dante stepped onto the balcony. He was one of the competitors in today's tournament, which seemed to be winding to a close. From what Evan had heard, Dante had been one of the better golfers on the course. He watched as Dante walked toward Leila with his hand extended. She quickly ended her phone conversation and shook his hand. The two started to talk.

"Uh-oh," Terrence whispered, "looks like Dante is working his voodoo on Lee."

"No, he's not," Evan insisted, even as he frowned while he observed them laughing and talking. "He's just . . . just introducing himself."

"Yeah, I bet! A player knows a player, Ev. That guy isn't just shooting the breeze over there. I know a hook-up when I see it."

At that, Evan's nostrils flared in anger. Oh, he'd be damned if he'd stand idly by and let any man, let alone his own brother, try to make a move on Leila! Not while *he* was there.

Evan turned away from Terrence and instantly started to walk in Leila and Dante's direction until he was stopped by a firm hand on his shoulder.

"Wait," Terrence said. "What do you think you're doing?"

"I'm going to talk to them, to say hi to Dante."

"Uh-huh," Terrence said incredulously. "You know damn well you were going there to cock block. Ev, she's not yours."

Evan shook off his brother's hand. "I know that." But every fiber in him at that moment said the opposite.

He continued in their direction and heard Terrence grumble behind him. His brother followed him reluctantly.

As they drew closer, Dante looked up and noticed them. He grinned, and Evan got the illogical urge to punch him squarely in the face.

"Hey! I was wondering where you guys were," Dante said. "Ev, I was just talking to your lovely assistant, Leila, here about the tournament."

"I'm glad you enjoyed it," she said. "We hope to put it on again next year."

"Absolutely. Absolutely," Evan said, feeling the strain

of the fake smile on his face. "Dante, you wouldn't mind me borrowing my 'lovely assistant' for a second?"

"Oh," Dante said, looking a little thrown off. "Oh, yeah! Of . . . of course not! Go right ahead."

Evan took Leila's elbow and steered her away. Terrence took his cue and instantly engaged Dante in a conversation about the tournament.

"Is everything all right, Ev?" Leila asked. Her face was now clouded with concern.

"Everything's fine. Perfect. Nothing to worry about." He reluctantly let go of her. "I just wanted to tell you that our day is going to be a little longer than I initially thought. I got a call earlier about one of our new contracts. I have to head back to the office to review a few issues that've been outlined by our legal counsel. We have a conference call scheduled at five and I hoped you could—"

"Sure." She nodded. "I was planning to head back to the office after the tournament anyway. I had a few things to finish up from Friday that I didn't get to because of last-minute errands for today's event. I'd just called mom to tell her to come get me a little later than expected. She has my car today."

"I can give you a ride to the office and back home if you'd like," he quickly volunteered.

"That's okay. You don't—"

"No, we're going the same place. It's just . . . easier."

"Really? But what about Charisse?"

"She can . . . she can get a ride with one of my brothers."

Leila cocked an eyebrow. "Are you sure she'd be all right with that?"

"Trust me. She'll be fine."

Leila seemed to contemplate his offer while gnawing her plump lower lip. Again, he fought not to stare at her mouth. Finally, she nodded. "Okay, thanks. I guess I'll ride with you then."

"Great! We'll meet at the valet desk at four."

"Four, it is," she said before stepping away from him. "I should get back to work. Gotta wrap this stuff up."

"Go right ahead. And Leila . . ."

She paused and turned back around to face him. "Yes?"

"Thanks for being so . . . so . . ." His words faded, making her laugh.

"So what, Ev?"

Beautiful. Sexy. Intelligent. Funny. For filling my days with a warmth that had disappeared for a very long time, he thought. But instead he said, "Thanks for being so dedicated. I appreciate all your hard work."

She nodded again. "That's my job! See you at four."

She then turned around and walked through one of the open balcony doors.

Chapter 15

EVAN

As it turned out, Charisse didn't take the news that Evan wasn't driving her back to their mansion quite as well as he'd thought she would.

"What do you mean you aren't driving me back?" she asked shrilly, yanking off her sunglasses as they walked out of the country club.

"Terry said he'd take you." Evan inclined his head toward his younger brother, who was retrieving his Porsche from the valet. "He can even have you back in enough time for your exfoliation treatment."

"But I don't want to go with him! Why aren't you taking me?"

"I have something to do back at the office. What difference does it make?"

Just then, Leila stepped through the door with her purse on her shoulder. "Ready to go whenever you are, Ev!" she announced perkily.

Charisse narrowed her eyes at Leila then glared at her

husband. "Something to do at the office? By 'something,' do you mean *her?*" she asked while jabbing her thumb over her shoulder, gesturing to Leila.

Evan took a step toward Charisse. "That question was out of line."

"Oh, go to hell! Don't you dare lecture me, Evan Murdoch!" she snapped, drawing the valet and Terrence's attention, as well as the gazes of a few people who were exiting the country club. Meanwhile, Leila was watching the whole scene unfold and had undoubtedly heard what Charisse had said. Leila's cheeks were inflamed with embarrassment. She lowered her eyes. She looked like she wanted to melt into the floor.

Evan wrapped his arm around Charisse's waist, a gesture that would look affectionate to any casual passerby. But those who looked more closely would notice how tight Evan's hold was around her and that Charisse squirmed in his arms. He steered his wife several feet away, to a secluded spot near a row of hedges. He then loosened his hold and Charisse shoved away from him.

"Now *you* are out of line! What kind of a fucking question was that? Are you drunk again?" he whispered.

"No, I'm not drunk! I'm perfectly sober and can see quite clearly, thank you very much!" She laughed coldly. Her blue eyes twinkled with malice. "I thought you were all about your work, that you had your head shoved so far up your ass that you didn't have time for things that we normal human beings want—like passion or sex. I guess I was wrong. It seems you'd rather show your attention to a fat-ass waitress pretending to be your assistant than your own goddamn wife!"

"Pretending? *You're* the one who's been pretending, Charisse! You've been pretending to be my damn wife for the past five years!" he snarled before striding off.

When he returned, the valet already had the car waiting. Leila stood at the curb with Terrence at her side.

"Let's go," Evan muttered before climbing into his Maserati. Leila didn't respond but instead silently climbed into the passenger seat.

Terrence rolled his eyes. "Fine! I guess I'll handle Charisse then!" he shouted over the rumble of the engine as the car pulled off. "You're welcome!"

Evan and Leila rode in uncomfortable silence for several miles with him staring out the windshield and her pretending to read a pile of notes in her lap. After a while, she loudly cleared her throat.

"The . . . the event went well," she said. "We haven't gotten the final tally yet on how much money was raised, but Loni said the numbers look good. We got lots of compliments from the sponsors too, as well as the tournament participants. They all seemed to have a great time."

"That's good," Evan mumbled.

"Look, Ev, I'm . . . I'm sorry about what happened with Charisse back at—"

"Please don't apologize. It's not your fault. She and I would have had drama with or without you being there."

"I know, but I remember you telling me that you were in a shitty marriage. I just didn't realize how . . . well, how bad it was."

He turned to her. There was sympathy in her big brown eyes.

"I remember what it's like . . . to be in a shitty marriage, I mean," she continued. "Hell, I still am! I'm . . . I'm sorry to see things ended up the same way for you. I'd hoped you would be happier than . . . than I was."

Evan shrugged. "Yeah, well, I had hoped the same, but shit happens. That's the way the cookie crumbles, right?"

He chuckled, but she didn't join him in his laughter. Instead, she placed a warm hand on his shoulder. "It still sucks, Ev," she said softly.

He swore he could feel the warmth of her fingers through his polo shirt. His eyes drifted to her mouth, then settled on the swell of cleavage peaking over the top of her satin blouse and suddenly it felt a lot hotter inside the car.

"We both got the short end of the stick," she said, drawing his attention away from her cleavage and back to her face.

Evan remembered doing this skipping eye dance a lot when they were younger. How many times had he reminded himself not to stare at her? He had one vivid memory of Leila climbing out of the Murdoch family's Olympic swimming pool in her bathing suit when they were thirteen. That old blue suit had been baggy one year, but a year later, it barely contained her pubescent curves, which seemed to have sprouted overnight. It took all of Evan's willpower not to ogle her as she splashed around his pool and then stretched on one of their club chairs next to him.

He had dreamed about her that night—her in that blue bathing suit. He remembered it being one of the first wet dreams he ever had.

If Leila knew all the fantasies he had had about her when they were kids, it would have made her blush. If she knew the fantasies that were starting to float through his mind now as he looked at her, she'd be blushing all over again.

"Marriage can be a pain in the ass. Kind of makes you envy the singles out there," Evan said, trying to drag his thoughts out of the gutter. He returned his attention to the road. "Guys like Terry and Dante have it made . . . no commitment . . . jumping from woman to woman. They—"

"Do you really think Dante's like that? He seemed a lot more sincere to me."

"What do you mean?"

"You know . . . as in, he didn't seem like a player. He seemed very sincere, even kind of sweet. I thought he was very . . . well, charming."

Evan's hands tightened around the steering wheel. "Charming, huh?" Evan asked, trying his best to sound relaxed.

He reminded himself for the umpteenth time that he was Leila's boss, that he was married, and that he had absolutely no right to be angry. "I guess you've got a point there. He's a good guy all around. I'm surprised at how quickly he's bonded with everyone in the family."

Though, truth be told, Evan always got the nagging feeling that Dante was too nice, that there was no way possible for a man to be that affable twenty-four hours a day. Nothing seemed to faze Dante. He never seemed to get angry, let alone aggravated. Didn't he ever get pissed? Didn't he ever have jealousy or resentment surge through his veins, much like what was surging through Evan now?

"The only reason why you're questioning him at all is because Leila likes him," a voice in his head chided.

Maybe, Evan thought. But it still didn't change the

fact that Dante seemed to have the emotional depth of a puddle.

"You'll probably run into Dante at a few more events we have coming up," Evan said. "I bet he'll show up to the fundraiser we're having next month."

"I might see him sooner than that," she whispered cryptically.

"What do you mean?"

"Well . . ." She took a deep breath and turned away from the window. She finally turned to him. "Dante asked me out."

At that little announcement, Evan's heart dropped from his chest straight to his shoes. He suddenly whipped the steering wheel, causing the car to almost veer into the right lane. Leila grabbed the dashboard and screamed as he turned the wheel again, narrowly averting disaster. He missed sideswiping a Ford Explorer by mere inches. The driver of the Explorer swerved then blared his horn at Evan before accelerating and driving off.

"Ev!" Leila shouted in alarm. "What the hell are you doing? Are you trying to kill us?"

"I'm sorry! I just . . . I thought the car in front of me was braking," he lied. "I-I didn't want to rear-end him."

She collapsed back into the passenger seat and brought a hand to her chest. "Just be careful, okay? I have no desire to die on the beltway!"

He nodded and they fell into a strained silence. The soft murmur of the car's eight-cylinder engine filled the compartment. After a few minutes, he glanced at her again.

"So Dante asked you out on a date? When did he find the time to do that?"

She adjusted her seat belt. "Right before I was heading out to meet you. He stopped me in the lobby."

Of course Dante had pounced on Leila during the rare minute that she was out of Evan's sight. *That sneaky son of a bitch*, Evan thought, then silently corrected himself again.

She's not yours, he could hear Terrence repeat in his head. And she never would be.

"Did you say yes?" he asked, hoping to God that she hadn't. He held his breath.

"No, I told him that I had to talk to you first."

Evan exhaled with relief. His death grip on the steering wheel finally loosened. At least this time she had afforded him the courtesy of asking for his approval. When she had decided to date Brad almost a decade ago, she hadn't wanted to listen to anything Evan had to say.

"I wasn't sure if it was appropriate," she explained. "Me going out with Dante, I mean. With you being my boss and Dante being your brother. You get what I'm saying. Right?"

"Sure, I understand. Absolutely."

They fell silent again.

"Well?" she asked, looking at him expectantly.

"Well, what, Lee?"

She pursed her lips. "Would you be okay with me dating him, Evan? I want . . . I really want your blessing on this."

Evan swallowed the lump that had lodged in his throat. She wanted his blessing? She wanted his blessing to go on a date with another man, to hold his hand, laugh over dinner, take a moonlight stroll, and then probably end the night with a kiss. Did Leila realize what she was really asking him? He was supposed to put aside all his longing, lust, bitterness, anger, feelings of rejection, and regret and condone her having dinner with his brother. Was she *insane?*

"What about your divorce?" he asked, hoping to stall and direct the conversation away from himself. He would do anything he had to do in order to prevent himself from shouting at her, *"No, you don't have my blessing. Hell no!"*

"What about my divorce?"

"Is it going to look good for you to be dating someone while you're still going through a divorce? That's what I mean."

"Honestly? Probably not. I wouldn't have considered going on a date with anyone a week ago, but Brad let it slip to Izzy that he has a new girlfriend." She shrugged. "I figure what's good for the goose is good for the gander at this point. If I look bad for dating while I'm still married, so would Brad."

Well, shit, Evan thought. Once again, Brad proved himself to be completely useless when needed.

"So do I have your blessing?"

"Are you asking me this as your boss or in . . . in some other capacity?"

He was shamelessly stalling again, but he didn't care.

"I'm asking you as Evan Murdoch. I'm asking you as my boss, my friend, and everything else that it entails, Ev."

It was on the tip of his tongue to tell her, "Well, if that's the case, then you should already know my goddamn answer," but then she took a deep breath, closed her eyes, and said, "I just want to know that you're okay with it this time around. I don't want any misunderstanding, no hostility. I mean . . . if you have any misgivings about this or him, please, let me know now. I trust your opinion, Ev."

That's when he knew he couldn't do it. He couldn't let his jealousy and selfishness get the better of him. She had been stuck in a miserable marriage for almost a decade. Evan knew what that felt like. If Dante could offer her a distraction, an inkling of happiness, he couldn't take that prospect away from her.

"You . . ." He cleared his throat. "You have my blessing."

She raised her brows. *"Really?"*

"Yeah," he said, then smirked. "Why do you sound so surprised?"

"I just . . . I didn't know if . . ." She quickly shook her head and waved a hand. "Never mind. Thank you, Ev. I really appreciate it!"

He nodded and ignored the ache he felt spreading across his chest.

Chapter 16

DANTE

"Ladies first," Dante said while gallantly holding open the door to the restaurant for his date.

"Why thank you," Leila murmured then bashfully dipped her head.

As she stepped in front of him and removed her shawl from around her shoulders, Dante let his eyes travel languidly over the length of her. He resisted the urge to hungrily lick his lips though the desire that flowed through him was strong. On a scale of one to ten, it hovered at about an eight—and had been steadily climbing since their first date a few weeks ago.

Tonight Leila was wearing a red sundress with spaghetti straps and a belt at the waist that accentuated her womanly curves. He wondered what she would look like with that dress pooled on his bedroom floor and her bent over the side of his mattress, just wearing those red lips and red high heels. He hoped that tonight he would *finally* get to see her that way. She certainly was drawing this out. After three dates, the most he had gotten was a quick kiss in the car before he dropped her off at her door. Nothing hot and heavy, not even a dick rub through his slacks! Dante didn't know why Leila was playing so hard to get. She had a seven-year-old, for God's sake! It wasn't like she was some virgin. She'd better drop those panties soon or he'd start to get pissed.

But, until then, Dante was biding his time. After all, he wasn't dating Leila Hawkins solely to get a piece of ass, though he hoped to get it eventually . . . well, maybe sooner rather than later. He was really dating her because she was yet another step in his grand plan to take his rightful place as the head of the Murdoch family and Murdoch Conglomerated.

To do that, he needed access and more information about Evan. What better way to get that info and access than through the woman who handled his day-to-day tasks, who served as his go-between? Who else spent more time with Evan Murdoch than Leila, his personal assistant?

He had tried to explain as much to Charisse—that he had an ulterior motive in dating Leila—but she wouldn't hear any of it.

"She's not even pretty!" Charisse had exclaimed two nights ago while they were in bed together. *"And she's fat."*

"She's not fat," he had said just before swiping his tongue across Charisse's breast, making her close her eyes and moan just before she opened her eyes again and angrily shoved his head away.

"Don't try to distract me!" she ordered peevishly.

At that, he had chuckled and wrapped an arm around her before roughly tugging her toward him. "I thought distraction was exactly what we were here for."

"Honestly, Dante, what is so goddamn special about Leila Hawkins anyway? I don't get the appeal! Do men have such low standards? First Evan goes after her—*then you!*"

That gave Dante pause. He had leaned back on his elbow and peered up at her. "What do you mean 'first Evan . . . '? You don't really think they're fucking, do you?"

She'd snorted before taking a sip from her glass. "You don't keep women like that on the payroll for their office skills. If she isn't Evan's whore now, then she soon will be. You can bet on that." Charisse had given him a cold smile. "So you go on and enjoy Evan's sloppy seconds!"

Dante now watched Leila as they walked across the high-end Italian restaurant, wondering if what Charisse had said was true. Leila was so sweet and wholesome, like a black Maria from the *Sound of Music*. She certainly seemed as chaste as a Benedictine nun. He didn't think that Evan was fucking her. But at the golf tournament, Dante had definitely picked up territorial vibes from Evan. He wasn't sure if Evan was protective of her because she was his secretary or if something more was going on there. If Leila was Evan's side piece, that would explain why she and Dante had yet to get past polite kisses. Maybe she was saving up all her loving for her boss at the end of night.

Dante didn't know how he felt about that. He certainly didn't want any man's "sloppy seconds," as Charisse had put it.

He watched as Leila nodded and whispered her thanks when the waiter pulled out her chair. After they both sat down and were handed their leather-bound menus, Leila leaned across the bistro table.

"Thank you for bringing me here. I know this place

has a wait list so I've been dying to eat here for months!"

"It's my pleasure! I hope you enjoy it."

"I'm sure I will," she murmured before returning her attention to her menu.

"So how was work today?" Dante asked, deciding to do some fact-finding.

Leila glanced up from her menu. "Oh, fine. It was busy, but that's normal."

"Is Evan working you hard?" *In more ways than one*, he wanted to add, but held back from doing so.

"Yeah, but I expected as much. It comes with the job." She laughed and shrugged. "How was your day? Any exciting cases you're working on?"

"Not really. Civil law can be pretty boring. Lots of paperwork mostly." He leaned back in his chair. "I'm sure what you do every day with Evan at Murdoch Conglomerated is a lot more fascinating."

"That would require a very liberal interpretation of 'fascinating.' Like your job, my job involves lots of paperwork. It also involves plenty of meetings where I sit off to the side, nod my head, and pretend like I have a clue what everyone is talking about." She pushed aside her menu and gazed at him intently. She reached across the table and held his hand. "But let's not talk about work. Tell me more about *you*. Besides the basic details, I don't know much else. Where'd you grow up? Where'd you go to school? What are you favorite movies . . . your favorite books?"

Is she fucking serious?

Dante resisted the urge to roll his eyes. There was nothing he hated more than the boring small talk that came with dating. This was why he kept most of his relationships with women purely sexual. He didn't give a shit about Leila's favorite TV shows or the name of her boyfriend back in high school. What he cared about was whether she was good in bed and whether she was sleeping with her boss.

Luckily, the waiter appeared again to take their orders, saving Dante from the dating ritual he hated so much. When the waiter left, he tried to distract Leila with flattery; he told her how beautiful she was, how much he loved her dress, and how her fragrance was intoxicating. It usually worked when he did this. It certainly worked with Charisse. But Leila wasn't having any of it.

"So tell me about your childhood. What was your family like growing up?" she asked as the waiter set a platter of calamari between them.

"There isn't much to tell," he began slowly, carefully weighing his words. "It was just me and my mom."

"Same here."

"We didn't have a lot of money. We lived in a small apartment in a bad neighborhood."

"Also, same here," she said with a nod, raising her wineglass to her lips and taking a sip.

Dante raised an eyebrow. He'd had no idea he and Leila had so much in common. "I didn't know who my real father was," he said, feeling more emboldened. "My mom told me he was one of her boyfriends, but I found out the truth much later."

"Now that is where our stories diverge. I knew who my dad was, but he walked out on us when I was nine years old. I heard from him every now and then. But by the time I was twelve, he basically disappeared. After that, I wanted nothing to do with him."

"I always . . . always wanted to know who my father was," he said, reaching for the calamari. He popped a morsel into his mouth. "And when I found it was George Murdoch, I knew I had hit the jackpot."

She lowered her wineglass. "Why?"

"What do you mean, 'why?' Because it was George Murdoch—one of the wealthiest black men on the East Coast! I mean . . . I don't follow business news that closely and even *I* knew who he was! I was shocked." He winked. "My mama wasn't the smartest woman in the world, but she had damn good taste, if I do say so myself."

"Wait. So you were excited to find out he was your father because . . . because he had a lot of money?"

"Yeah, and what's wrong with that?" This time, Dante did roll his eyes. "Come on, Leila! Don't give me some speech about how money isn't important. No one's really naïve enough to believe that!"

"Of course money is important. It keeps a roof over your head and puts food in your belly. But it isn't everything!"

He laughed coldly. "So I suppose you're working for Evan for peanuts. He's hardly paying you anything, right? You don't need a big salary because money isn't important."

"He pays me enough," she answered tightly. "Besides, my salary has nothing to do with this conversation."

"Or maybe Evan is offering a few perks that can't be quantified. A rich guy like him—"

"Why are you so concerned about Evan?" she asked, narrowing her eyes. "You've bought him up twice already. You always bring him up during our dates."

Dante paused. "I don't always bring him up."

"Yes, you do—obsessively. 'What's it like working

with Evan? What do you and Evan do all day?' I mean . . . if you're so concerned about Evan, maybe he's the one you should have asked out instead of me."

"Don't be a smart-ass, Leila."

"I'm not being a smart-ass! I'm being truthful. Do you have some issue with him? Is that what this is about?"

He was tempted to lie, to tell her that he loved his half brother and was embarrassed if he had given her any impression otherwise. But her self-righteous indignation infuriated him. Whatever lust he felt for her had evaporated. Whatever filter he had preserved now disappeared.

"Yes, I have an issue with Evan," he began. "I have an issue with any asshole who runs a two-hundred-million-dollar company simply because his daddy gave him the job. This is the same daddy . . . mind you . . . who wouldn't even let me stop by his office—like he was ashamed of me. I have an issue with any thoughtless, entitled, pompous, dickless boy who isn't worth the dirt on my shoes!" he spat. "But everyone goes out of their way to kiss his ass while he walks around town like he's God's fucking gift!"

When he finished his tirade, Leila stared at him in shock. "What the hell did Evan do to make you hate him so much?"

"What the hell did he do to make you *like* him so much?"

"He's my boss and my friend."

"Really?" Dante inclined his head. "Is that all?"

"What does that mean? Are you asking if I'm having an affair with Evan?"

"Well, are you?"

Her beautiful face contorted with outrage. "No, I'm not! And I'm insulted that you would even ask!"

"Your entrees will be out shortly," the waiter said as he walked toward their table. "Would either of you like your wine refilled? Can I get you anything?"

Leila shook her head, removing her linen napkin from her lap and slapping it on the table. "No," she said to the waiter. "No refills. Please just . . . just bring the check."

Dante sighed gruffly. "Leila, come on! I'm—"

"We're done," she said, holding up her hand, silencing him.

They didn't speak after that. As they walked out of the restaurant, as he drove her home, Dante inwardly kicked himself. He had royally screwed up and messed up a prize opportunity because he had allowed his anger at Evan to make him lose control.

As he pulled to a stop in front of her town home, he turned to her.

"Look, Leila, I—"

She didn't give him a chance to finish. She opened the car door and slammed it closed behind her before striding to her front door.

Chapter 17

PAULETTE

Paulette lowered her head and adjusted her dark-tinted sunglasses as she stepped onto the sidewalk.

"Excuse me," she murmured to the three young men who stood in front of her, blocking her path. One lounged back against the wrought-iron fence in front of the apartment complex. The other two stood in front of him, barking with laughter. As they fell silent and stepped aside to let Paulette pass, she felt their dark gazes on her like groping fingers. Their eyes landed on her pretty face, which was now stony and withdrawn, her Chanel handbag, her plump rear end, and finally the Manolo Blahnik pumps she wore.

"Damn, ma!" one of the young men shouted, pushing back the brim of his cap as he licked his lips and leered at Paulette. "Who you rollin' with that got you ballin' like that?"

She didn't answer him. Instead she pulled the up-turned collar of her blazer tighter around her face and made a quick dash to the courtyard leading to the apartment building where Marques lived. The sooner she got in there, the sooner she could leave.

"And get the hell out of here," she mumbled to herself as she climbed the short flight of concrete stairs and glanced at the metal plaque near the door. She pressed the buzzer next to Marques's apartment number and took a deep breath, feeling almost queasy with unease.

She didn't know why he had asked her to come here today for the exchange. For the past few weeks, she had been surreptitiously giving him envelopes of money for "The Marques Effect" at the gym. She'd hand it off to him near the locker rooms or as she passed him in the parking lot. But this morning, he had called her and told her to come to his home instead.

Situation's changed. Bring it to my house, he had texted her before sending her the address.

The instant she read those words, she wanted to shout in frustration. It was bad enough that he was blackmailing her into giving him money—now she had to come to his home?

"Just tell Tony the truth," a voice in her head had urged. "Just tell him the truth and end all this."

But what would her husband think about her if she told him about that part of her past? Antonio had a well-defined idea of who his wife was. What if she told him that image wasn't true? They were already fighting. Would this just make things worse?

No, she would continue to give Marques money until her relationship with Antonio got on better footing. She didn't want this secret, and now the bribery, to be the two things to push her marriage over the edge.

Paulette pressed the intercom button again when no one answered.

"Yeah? Who is it?" a bass voice finally boomed through the dented metal speaker.

"Who else would it be, Marques? Buzz me in!"

She heard him chuckle. It was followed by a buzzing sound, then a click, as the building's front door unlocked. Paulette took another fortifying breath, pushed the door open, and stepped inside the lobby.

She hadn't been in an apartment building this lowbrow in quite a while. In fact that last time she could remember being in a place like this, it had been when she had gone to visit Marques at his home almost a decade ago. It was while his mother was at work at the local fast food joint. He'd shove his two younger twin brothers, DeShan and DeQuan, out of the bedroom they shared—to his brothers' great outrage. He'd shut the door and pat the mattress that was covered with Spider-Man bedsheets, urging Paulette to sit down. They'd sit there for hours and talk, make out. Eventually, she'd ended up losing her virginity on those sheets.

This apartment building had the same look as the old one: dingy tile floors, musky-smelling carpets, and paint that looked like it should have been retouched years ago. The apartment doors were all in the same drab brown and the light fixtures looked like something from the 1970s.

But how the apartment building looked was irrelevant. Paulette reminded herself yet again that she wouldn't be here long. She walked swiftly to his door and knocked before digging inside her purse to retrieve the folded manila envelope containing two thousand dollars. By the time Marques opened the door wearing a tank top, doo-rag, and low-slung sweatpants, she was already shoving the envelope at his chest.

"Here's your money," she said angrily.

"Whoa! Hey!" Marques said, laughing again. "What's the rush?"

She whipped off her sunglasses to glare up at him. *"What's the rush?"* she exclaimed. "I can't believe you would call me and tell at the last minute to come here! You think you can just—"

"Girl, calm down! Look, I called you at the last minute because I had to think fast. We couldn't do this at the gym anymore. I think the owner was catching on to my . . . well, my business situation. He told me he didn't want any shady shit going on at his gym. I told him 'Fuck you! I'll train my clients somewhere else. I don't need this shit! I do fine on my own.'" Marques shrugged. "So that's why we had to meet here."

"You do fine on your own?" She glanced over his shoulder at his apartment, looking incredulous. Her eyes scanned the cheap imitation-leather furniture, the shag rug, and the bare walls. The most expensive thing in there was his big flat-screen TV. "I wouldn't exactly call this living in the lap of luxury."

"I'ma pretend like I didn't hear that." He pushed the door open further and inclined his head. "Come in. Let's talk. I got a proposition for you."

Paulette quickly shook her head and took a step back from the doorway. She tugged her purse strap further up her shoulder. "No thanks. I think I've had enough of your 'propositions.' I just came to give you your money. I have to be getting home anyway. I—"

"It wasn't a question," he said tightly. His eyes darkened. "Come inside. We need to talk, girl."

Paulette glanced inside his apartment again. She was reluctant to go in there. What did he need to say to her that he had to say behind the closed door of his apartment, that he couldn't just tell her over the phone or now as she stood in front of him? Everything inside her screamed to just turn around and run as fast as her high heels would allow down that hall and out of that building. She took another step back.

"Or I can give your man, Antonio, a call." He shrugged again. "It's up to you."

She paused. Her grip around her purse strap tightened. At the mention of her husband's name, she instantly felt trapped.

You son of a bitch, she thought.

"Fine," she said, then shoved past him and stepped inside his apartment.

She stood awkwardly in the center of his living room while he shut the door behind her. He walked around her and reached down to his glass coffee table to grab one of a half dozen remotes. A music video was blaring on the TV screen. A rapper was kneeling on the marble floor, pointing up to the gyrating rear end of the long-haired dancer beside him. Marques raised the remote, pressed a button, and lowered the sound so that it was now background noise. Paulette watched as another half-naked woman came on screen to take the other's place.

"Want to sit down?" He gestured toward his sofa.

"Are you asking me or telling me?" she grumbled, crossing her arms petulantly over her chest.

He laughed. "You hilarious, girl. I'm asking. But you can stand there looking stupid if you want."

She rolled her eyes and stomped toward the sofa, then flopped down, making the fake leather burp beneath her. She watched as he strolled toward his small eat-in kitchen. He opened his refrigerator and peered inside.

"Considering how much money I've given you, I'm shocked that you don't live in a much nicer place," she muttered, surveying the apartment again. "You couldn't afford a decent condo?"

"Now you know that money is meant for my business. I gotta be smart with my investments. Besides, I don't care where I live." He winked. "Now my ride is pretty tight though. That's what the clients see. That's how they know you're a baller! I bought a BMW just last week. I paid for that shit in cash."

"Yeah, with *my* money," she mumbled under her breath.

"You want something to eat?" he asked over his shoulder, and she had to fight the urge to scream at him, "Why are you dragging this out? Just tell me what you want! Why am I here?"

"No, I don't want anything to eat."

"Come on!" He stepped back from the refrigerator and closed it. He walked toward her with a serving plate. "I got crackers and cheese—the expensive kind with the French-sounding name. I know how rich people like that shit."

He set down the plate in front of her.

"I'm not hungry," she said flatly.

He then walked back into the kitchen to open a cabinet. As he rifled around, her gaze gravitated to the television again. She stared, bemused, at the newest music video, featuring a girl in a bikini who was now doing splits on the hood of a Rolls Royce. Paulette looked up to find Marques setting down two glass cups next to the serving plate. They were filled with red wine.

Or a really dark Kool-Aid, she thought dryly.

"What's all this for, Marques?" she asked.

He sat down in the reclining chair facing her. "Damn, can't a nigga be hospitable?"

She narrowed her eyes at him.

"Okay! Okay! Look, I just wanted to celebrate," he said, grabbing one of the glasses. "So drink up!"

"Celebrate what?"

"Drink some wine and have some cheese first!"

"If I eat and drink something, will you tell me what you want to tell me so I can get the hell out of here?"

He nodded and grinned.

She sampled one of the crackers and then the red wine. The crackers tasted as bland as corrugated cardboard and were equally appetizing. The wine tasted overly sweet. Maybe it was Kool-Aid after all. She finished the glass halfway then tried the cheese. "So talk," she said between chews.

"I just wanted to celebrate us taking The Marques Effect to the next level."

"To the next level? What does that mean?"

"Well, now that my supplier is happy, he's keeping me flush with the supplements I need to give to all my clients. He wants to sell me more, but I don't have enough clientele for that yet." He pointed at his tattooed chest. "Luckily, I'm the type of nigga that can see opportunity for potential. I was thinking about it, Paulette, and I thought, instead of me just offering training to one or two clients at a time, why don't I open my own place . . . my own gym where I could help *hundreds?*"

She frowned. "You really think that's a good idea? If you attracted attention to yourself at my gym, what type of attention are you going to get opening your own establishment? The cops would figure it out."

"No, they wouldn't. Everything would be on the down low. We'd only offer supplements to the clients who wanted it and knew how to keep their mouths shut."

"We?"

"I've got some boys who are ready to come on board as soon as I open my own place. A few of them are already my clients and have had good results with The Marques Effect."

She closed her eyes and sighed, feeling tired all of a sudden. "Okay, so how do you plan to get the money to open and start this new business?"

He inclined his head and glared at her. "How you think?"

"Right. Of course. Me . . . I'm the investor." She sucked her teeth. "And how much money are we talking about?"

He casually shrugged and leaned back in his recliner. "I don't know . . . another fifty grand to put a down payment on the property. It's this hot spot not far from Chesterton. It's all glass and chrome—super turnt up! Then about another twenty to thirty grand to buy equipment. Then maybe—"

"Wait!" She held up her hand. "You're already at eighty-thousand dollars and you haven't even talked about hiring staff. Marques, I don't have that kind of money that I can just keep giving it to you!"

"Girl, don't fake! I know you rich as hell!"

"If you think you've been attracting attention, what about me? I've been going to the damn bank every week withdrawing five to ten grand at a time. What's going to happen if I ask for *fifty-thousand dollars?*"

"I don't care! Do what you gotta do. I need the money!"

"Why are you doing this?" the sane voice in her head questioned. "Why are you putting yourself through all of this?"

Because she didn't want her husband to know about the abortion she'd had nearly a decade ago? Because she was ashamed of the poor choices she had made as a naïve sixteen-year-old girl?

It's not worth it, she thought. She didn't want to ruin her marriage, but handing over a seemingly endless stream of money to Marques and responding to his every ridiculous whim would only lead to her financial ruin and Antonio would definitely figure out something was going on with her. She was doomed either way. Better to bite the bullet and end this now.

"No," she said firmly. "No, I'm not going to invest in this, Marques. I can't!"

He reached for the cell phone. "Then I guess I better give a call to ol' boy and tell him everything about what happened between you and me!"

More threats? God, she was so tired of this! She was just plain exhausted—in every sense of the word. She suddenly felt the urge to take a nap.

"Then do it," she barked, grabbing her purse.

"Oh, don't get it twisted, girl! I know his number at KDR Associates!"

She paused and squinted her tired eyes at him. "What did you say?"

"You heard me!" He gave her a lupine grin—all teeth and nastiness. "I looked it up! I know where he works! I'll put all this shit on blast if I have to!"

She gritted her teeth, fighting the bile that rose in her throat. But she wouldn't back down. He would threaten her again and again, and how far would she have to go to finally make him happy? Marques was a user. He would always want more.

"Then do it," she repeated, shooting to her feet.

As Paulette did, she was suddenly hit by a dizzy spell. She tried to walk toward the front door, but wobbled slightly in her high heels. The living room went topsy-turvy. She felt like she was on an unstable amusement park ride.

"What . . . w-what's . . . ?" she slurred.

She wanted to say, "What's happening to me?" but the words wouldn't come out right. Her mouth felt heavy and so did her head, which lolled from side to side. Her purse slid off her shoulder and went crashing to the floor, its contents spilling out onto the shag rug.

Paulette reached out, flailing at the air, trying to grab hold to something to help stable herself. Marques didn't offer her any assistance. He stood staring at her, still grinning like an ass as she stumbled around his living room. Her rolling gaze drifted from him and fell on the half-empty glass on the coffee table.

Oh, God, was the last coherent thought she had when she realized that he had spiked her drink, spiked the wine. No wonder it had tasted so sweet! He had probably done that to mask the taste of whatever he had put in there.

She reached again for the front door, but it felt further away than before, like it was on the other end of a long tunnel.

"Oh, no! Where you think you're going? You can't drive, girl!"

She felt Marques loop an arm around her waist. She tried to shove it away but to no avail.

"Don't worry. I'll take care of you," was the last thing she heard when the room grew dim. Then everything went black.

When Paulette awakened, she was lying in bed, but she could tell instantly that she wasn't in her own bedroom despite the fact that everything around her was one big blur. There wasn't the faint hint of jasmine and vanilla wafting from the scented candle she kept near her bed side. There wasn't the smooth feel of the Egyptian cotton sheets she and Antonio had been given as a wedding gift or the filtered morning light streaming through her honey oak window blinds. Instead she saw a flimsy bedsheet taped over the window, heard the blare of a television where a football game now played, and felt the mattress dip as Marques plopped on the bed beside her wearing nothing but his boxers and the same wolfish grin he had given when she fainted. She guessed he had dragged her into here. She was shocked he hadn't left her sprawled on the living room floor and just poked her with a stick until she woke up.

Paulette slowly pushed herself up to her elbows as her vision finally cleared. The bedsheet that was thrown over her tumbled down to her lap and she looked down and realized in horror that she was naked.

"Where the hell are my clothes?" she yelled, springing up from the bed. She felt dizzy all over again and panicked that she was about to collapse. She grabbed the headboard, closed her eyes, and waited until tilt-a-whirl settled.

"Where the hell do you think they are?" he laughed. *"You* took them off."

She started to shake her head then stopped when the dizziness came back. "No . . . no, I didn't!"

"Yes, you did." He turned to her. "You don't remember, baby?"

Her blood ran cold. She pulled the bedsheet tighter around her. "W-what are . . . what are you talking about?"

"Don't worry." He held up his cell phone and shoved it toward her. "I took videos in case you forgot."

He pressed the screen button and the video began. Paulette watched as she lay face down on the bed with Antonio laying on top of her, grunting and humping his hips. She cringed. It was obvious to her she was clearly unconscious, but a casual viewer may not come to a similar conclusion—and Marques knew that.

"We were having some fun, weren't we, baby?" he asked over the sound of his groans.

She gripped the headboard to keep from falling to her knees. Her eyes welled with tears.

"Why . . . why would you do this?"

"Do what?" He glanced at the phone screen. "You mean take a video of us making love?"

"Making love?" she screeched. "Making love? You raped me! You drugged me! How could you—"

"Prove it," he said. He glanced at the phone screen again. "I say we were making love and if you act up again and tell me no when I ask you for anything . . . and I mean *anything*, Paulette, I'll show this to your man and I'm posting this shit on YouTube. And I'm sure he and every other motherfucker in the world will think the same thing that I do."

Paulette closed her eyes feeling overwhelmed with both shame and anger. How could she had walked into yet another trap? How could she have let Marques do this to her?

He suddenly reached for her and wrapped his arms around her waist. He tugged down the bedsheet and grabbed a handful of one of her breasts. She quickly began to struggle in his grasp but stopped when he barked, "What did I just say?"

At the reminder of his threat, she stilled and glared down at him as he shoved her down on his lap. His fingers trailed over her nipple and she felt his burgeoning arousal through the thin cotton of his boxer briefs, making her tremble with fury and outrage, making her want to scream.

He stared up at her. "So when you gonna get me my fifty grand?"

Chapter 18

LEILA

"Good morning," Leila called as she walked through the revolving doors. She scampered across the atrium and past the stainless-steel receptionist desk of Murdoch Conglomerated, careful not to spill any coffee from the paper cup she carried.

"Oh! Uh, g-good morning, Ms. Hawkins!" said the security guard.

The guard didn't stop Leila this time to give her the third-degree or even make her sign her name on the clipboard that sat on the edge of the desk. *Everyone* knew that Leila Hawkins was Evan Murdoch's new executive assistant and to harass her was the same as harassing Mr. Murdoch, which just wasn't done.

Leila boarded the elevator that, thankfully, was empty, then zipped to the twelfth floor, where she passed yet another desk—this time manned by a plump receptionist whose hair was a very unexceptional shade of chestnut brown.

"Good morning, Emily!" Leila called out again.

"Morning, Leila!" Emily sang back, shifting her head-set aside.

"Did I beat him?"

The receptionist laughed. "Yeah, he's not in yet. You've got a few minutes."

"Thank God!" Leila cried before turning to head to her office.

"Wait! Wait!" The receptionist stood up and reached for a tall glass vase on the counter that was overflowing with red and pale pink roses. "I almost forgot. These are for you!"

Leila almost did a double take. "*For me?*"

"Oh, yeah!" Emily nodded and held the vase toward her. "And by the looks of those roses, you've got quite the admirer! They're gorgeous, Leila!"

Leila grabbed the bouquet and opened the small white envelope nestled in one of the rose petals. She flipped the envelope open and read the card inside it.

Beautiful flowers for a beautiful woman, the note read. *I'm sorry for the way I behaved. It was a bad day. I hope you'll give me a second chance. Love, Dante.*

"Gah, I'm so jealous!" Emily squealed as Leila read the note.

Leila pursed her lips. "Don't be," she said over her shoulder before racing the thirty yards to the other end of the corridor toward her desk, which sat directly in front of Evan's office.

She had no interest in the flowers or the person who had sent them. Ever since her last date with Dante, she planned to put as much distance between herself and him as possible.

She dropped her purse in her roll-away chair, before using her key to open Evan's office door. She placed the vase filled with roses on the center of his coffee table, quickly removing the ribbon and tucking Dante's card in her pocket. Evan's schedule for the day sat on her printer and she grabbed it. She then raced inside his office and turned on the overhead lights, placed the paper printout of his schedule on the center of his desk, and raised the window blinds. Leila went back to her desk to get the cup of gourmet coffee and toasted butter croissant she had purchased at the bakery downstairs that morning. She set them both next to his schedule. Finally, she did a quick scan of his desk again to make sure everything was as it should be, and raced back through the door to her desk.

By the time Evan arrived at his office eight minutes later, Leila already had listened to his voice messages as well as hers, made the necessary adjustments to his schedule due to one meeting cancellation, and confirmed his and her hotel reservations and chartered a private jet for a two-night stay in L.A. for a business trip next week.

As Evan strode toward her, Leila felt like she had been to Albuquerque and back, but she didn't show it. When he reached her desk, she looked calm and serene, prepared to commence the routine they seemed to reenact daily. If Evan was anything, he was a creature of habit.

"Morning, Leila," he said, glancing up from his BlackBerry.

"Good morning, Evan." She grinned and looked up from her computer screen. "How are you today?"

"Good, good." He cocked an eyebrow. "Any surprises I should know about?" he asked as he strolled into his office. It was the same question he asked every morning.

That was her cue. She stood up from her desk, quickly grabbed her notepad and pen, and followed him through his office doorway.

"Your one p.m. meeting was canceled, but you still have the meeting scheduled with Jim in fifteen minutes. He wanted to bring in the marketing team to make sure all you guys were in consensus," she said. "He told me to let you know so that there were no surprises."

Evan nodded absently as he continued to read the emails on his BlackBerry.

She stared down at her notes. "You have that interview with *Black Inc.* magazine scheduled for eleven."

Evan threw back his head and groaned. "Please don't remind me."

"I have to remind you, Ev. That's my job."

"I hate talking to the press. They always make me seem so . . ." He tossed his leather satchel into his chair and grabbed the cup of coffee she had left for him. He grimaced before taking a sip. ". . . so *stiff.*"

Leila stifled a laugh at that one. No one could make Evan seem any stiffer or more reserved than he actually was—which was stiffer than a starched shirt. In the old days, she'd had an arsenal of tricks to get him to loosen up and relax: bad knock-knock jokes, loudly singing R & B hits off key, and once even breaking into the robot.

But she couldn't do that now. She was his executive assistant and that required some decorum—the robot notwithstanding.

"You'll be fine, Ev," she assured instead. "I forwarded you their questions last week. They said they'll stick to those. No surprises. Just stay to your talking points."

"I'll try," he murmured, before dropping his Black-Berry onto his desk. He glanced at the vase on his coffee table. "What's that doing here?"

She followed his gaze. "You mean the roses? I thought some flowers might brighten up the place."

His office often seemed so lifeless, like a warehouse. Every time she stepped inside the space, she wanted to add color to the walls or a lush throw pillow to the sofa—*anything* to soften the room, to add a little warmth. Leila had no use for Dante's flowers, but maybe they could bring Evan's office a little bit of badly needed warmth.

He considered the flowers then shrugged. "If you say so. Just tell me how much they cost and I'll reimburse you."

"You don't need to reimburse me. They're just flowers!" She flipped her notepad closed. "Besides, I didn't pay for them. They were a gift."

"A gift?" He abruptly turned away from the roses. "It's not your birthday. What's the occasion? Who sent you flowers?"

"Oh . . . nobody you know," she lied.

He continued to gaze at her searchingly, and she felt like she was under a heat lamp, being forced into a confession.

Though Evan had said he condoned her dating Dante, she knew that he hadn't liked it one bit. For that reason, she had kept discussions about her dates with Dante, and her love life in general, to a minimum, to keep things from getting even more awkward between her and Evan. But it looked like she wouldn't be able to do that today.

"Okay, fine." She flapped her arms. "If you really want to know . . . Dante sent them."

"Dante?" At the mention of his brother's name, Evan tried his best to control his facial features, but he didn't succeed. His nostrils flared and his lips tightened before his expression went placid again. "So

Dante's sending you roses at the office now? You guys must really be getting serious then."

"Not . . . quite."

"Not quite? What does that mean?"

Leila sighed. "We're not dating anymore, Ev."

"Oh, really?" He smiled before he had a chance to hide that too. "What happened?"

"Nothing! Nothing happened. We're just . . . not a good match. After a few dates, it was pretty obvious. He's not a guy I can see in my life for the long term."

And one of the reasons why she didn't want him in her life was because he hated her best friend/boss with a passion that unnerved her. Dante also seemed bitter as hell. She didn't need that kind of bad energy in her life—she'd had enough of it when she was married to Brad.

Evan lowered his coffee cup back to his desk and took a step toward her. "Dante didn't do anything to you, did he? Because if he did, I swear I'll—"

"No! No, it was nothing like that. We just didn't . . . click. That's all. It didn't work out."

"Oh! Well, that's . . . that's good to hear."

"Thanks for being so protective though. It's sweet. But don't worry. I can take care of myself."

They gazed at one another for a long time after that. Finally, Evan nodded and cleared his throat. "Look, I have to make a few quick calls before my meeting so—"

"No problem!" She turned to head back to his opened door. "I was just leaving. Let me know if you need anything. I'll send Jim in when he arrives."

"Thanks, Lee. Oh, and Lee?"

She paused mid-stride and turned back to him. "Yeah?"

"I know you can take care of yourself, but . . . I can't help but be a little protective. If it's any consolation, Dante is missing out on a good thing."

Her cheeks warmed at his compliment and the intensity of his gaze. "Thanks, Ev," she whispered then swiftly exited his office, shutting the door behind her with a soft click.

When Leila got back to her desk, she slumped into her chair and took a deep breath, and not just because she felt exhausted.

Though she knew Evan tried his best to temper it, the tone of his voice and the look in his eyes sometimes told her his attraction for her was still there. They both tried their best to pretend that it wasn't, as if they were in silent agreement to continue the lie, but it was getting harder to pretend.

Evan still wanted Leila, and frankly, she loved him too—in her own way. How could she not? He had apologized for his past mistakes. He had offered her a home and a job to help her regain her footing. He had extended his friendship again.

She loved Evan and always would love him.

"But do you love him like a brother?" the nagging voice in her head asked. "Or are you starting to feel something more?

Leila faced her computer and began typing a memo, refusing to answer that question. It was too messy to consider anyway. Evan was married. He was her boss. They held no potential romantically.

An hour later, Leila looked up from her monitor screen to find a beautiful woman with dark shades, wearing a flowing yellow sundress, striding through the office entrance toward her. When she realized who the woman was, her face lit up.

"Paulette!" she exclaimed, rising from her chair. She quickly walked around her desk to embrace Evan's sister. "Ev didn't tell me you were visiting today!"

"He didn't tell you because he didn't know. I just . . .

well, I just decided to do an impromptu visit." Paulette tugged off her sunglasses, walked into Leila's out-stretched arms, and hugged her. "I can't believe I for-got that you're his assistant now. I hope that brother of mine is treating you well."

"Of course, he is!"

Paulette inclined her head and gazed at her know-ingly. "And working you hard, I'm assuming."

"Well, yeah. That too." Leila laughed.

Evan had warned her that working for him wouldn't be easy. After being his executive assistant for almost three months, she now knew what he meant. If she'd thought serving a burger joint full of customers could make her head spin, that was *nothing* compared to working for Evan Murdoch. The guy seemed to have ten things going on at once, and he had an energy level that left her in awe. As his assistant, Leila not only had to keep up with him, but anticipate what he needed and when he needed it. She felt like she was always on standby now, ready to jump up and get him something at a moment's notice. There was more than one occa-sion when she had jumped from her bed in the middle of the night to get him something from the printer or copier, only to realize she had been dreaming.

But Evan only asked as much of her as he asked of himself. He was definitely a hard worker. Plus, she was amply compensated for all the stuff she was doing. The salary he was giving her was more than three times what she had been making at Dean's Big Burger. Thanks to her new job, money was no longer as much of a worry for her. But Evan was definitely making her earn her pay. She had several cans of caffeinated booster drinks in her desk to prove it.

She watched as Paulette glanced over Leila's shoul-der at Evan's closed office door, looking anxious.

"Speaking of my brother . . . is he busy? Can I see him?"

"He's in a meeting right now."

She watched as Paulette's face fell.

"But the meeting should be done soon!" Leila quickly added, holding up her hand. "If you wouldn't mind waiting for ten or fifteen minutes . . ."

"Of course not. I've got time. Plus I . . . I really need to talk to him."

"I'll make sure that you do. In the meantime, it'll give us some time to catch up since we never got to have that lunch." She pointed at the small sofa opposite her desk. "Have a seat. Can I get you anything to drink? Some coffee or tea maybe?"

"Earl Grey tea would be nice. Thanks."

"I'll be right back." Leila sauntered off to the nearby lunch room and got the cup of Earl Grey. She returned to her desk five minutes later, carrying a small tray holding a ceramic cup, a few paper packets, and some creamer.

"I wasn't sure if you wanted real sugar or an artificial sweetener," Leila began as she walked toward the sofa, "so I just brought—"

"I know. I *know,*" Paulette said tightly into her cell phone. "I'm working on it now."

Leila instantly fell silent, embarrassed to realize that she'd almost interrupted Paulette's phone conversation. She stood silently behind the sofa, unsure of what to do next.

"I'll get you your money. . . . I'll get it! . . . Look, don't threaten me, Marques," Paulette whispered fiercely.

Leila frowned at the mention of the name Marques. Why did it sound familiar?

"I said I was going to do it and I'm going to fucking

do it. So *stop* calling me!" Paulette spat. "Fine! . . . Fine!"

She then pressed a button on the phone screen and tossed her cell phone onto one of the cushions. She dropped her head into her hands.

Leila finally walked around the sofa and set the tray on the ebony wood coffee table in front of Paulette. Paulette instantly gathered herself together. She sat upright and plastered on a smile though her face looked weary, though her eyes were glistening with tears.

"Here's your Earl Grey," Leila said softly.

"Thanks, Lee," Paulette said in reply, reaching for her cup.

"Is . . . is everything okay?"

"Everything's fine," Paulette answered quickly. A little too quickly, in Leila's opinion. She watched as Paulette reached for a sugar packet, ripped it open, and sniffed.

"Are you sure?"

"Yeah, I'm . . . I'm sure." A solitary tear spilled onto Paulette's cheek and she wiped it away with the back of her hand. She poured the sugar into her tea, grabbed a straw, and began to stir.

Leila sat down on the sofa beside her. "You know you can talk to me. I know we're not as close as we were back when you were a teenager, but I'm here for you now like I was back then. That hasn't changed."

Paulette sniffed again and turned away from her. She murmured something in reply that Leila couldn't hear.

"What did you say?" she asked, placing a consoling hand on Paulette's shoulder.

"I said that I *can't*, Lee! I just can't. I'm too humiliated. I can't believe I did this shit to myself all over again! I'm so fucking stupid!"

She was crying more now and Leila quickly rose from the sofa to grab some tissues from a box on the edge of her desk. She glanced at the rest of the office, where a few passersby stared at Paulette curiously through the glass enclosure that surrounded Leila's office. Leila handed a few tissues to Paulette and watched as the younger woman wiped her eyes.

"Let's go somewhere else," she whispered to Paulette, feeling several eyes now watching them. "We should talk about this in private."

Leila could have closed the blinds, but it still didn't seem private enough, not with Evan only a few feet away.

Paulette nodded weakly and lowered her tea cup back to the table.

A minute later, Leila guided the younger woman into an empty conference room and shut the door behind them. She pulled out one of the twelve leather roll-away chairs from the table in the center of the room and gestured for Paulette to sit down. She then took the chair adjacent to her.

"Now tell me what's wrong," Leila said.

"I've ruined my marriage," Paulette began, now sobbing. "I've ruined everything! I let some asshole blackmail me into cheating on my husband. And if Antonio finds out, I don't know what I'm going to do!"

Leila gazed at Paulette in shock. "What are you talking about? Why are you cheating on Antonio? With *who?*"

"Marques," Paulette whispered. She twisted the tissue in her hands. "My ex . . . the one who got me pregnant."

Leila closed her eyes. Now she knew why that name sounded so familiar.

"He said that he was going to tell Antonio about the baby . . . about the abortion, I mean, if I didn't give him money. I was so afraid, Lee! Antonio thinks of me as this perfect little wife. Sometimes, he even calls me his black Barbie. We were already fighting. I didn't want to make things worse so I-I-I just gave Marques the money, but . . . but it got to be too much! He asked for money *constantly*. When I tried to tell him no more, he drugged me."

Lee's eyes flashed open. She gaped in horror.

"He raped me, Lee!" Paulette said between sobs. "And he took a video of it. He said he would send the video to Antonio and that's how he blackmailed me into having this . . . this affair. And now he still wants more money. But I don't have it. My trust fund limits how much money I can get each year and I'm already at my limit." She shook her head. "I'm an idiot, right? I'm a moron for getting myself into this."

"No, you're not," Leila answered quietly. She reached out and placed her hands over Paulette's trembling ones. "You didn't want to hurt or disappoint Antonio and Marques took advantage of that." She gazed into the younger woman's eyes. "But you can't let him do it to you anymore. You have to go to the police."

Paulette furiously shook her head. "I can't! I can't, Lee!"

"Yes, you can! That son of a bitch should go to jail for what he's done to you!"

"Didn't you hear what I said? I don't want Antonio to find out. If I went to the police, I'd have to press charges. If I did that, there's no way Antonio wouldn't discover what's been going on. What if the story gets leaked to the local newspapers? Antonio would be humiliated. My entire family would—"

"Damn it, none of that matters, Paulette!"

"Jesus, what is it with the Murdochs?" Leila thought with exasperation. They were obsessed with maintaining their reputations, with keeping up appearances, and the only thing it did was make them miserable.

"Look, you said yourself that you don't have any more money to give him," Leila argued. "What other choice do you have but to go to the police?"

"You're wrong. I do have another choice. That's why I'm here today. I was going to ask Ev to give me a loan of about a hundred grand or so. That should be more than enough. Maybe then, Marques will finally leave me alone!"

"Paulette, you can't honestly think Marques is going to stop after you give him even *more* money. You weren't being stupid before, but if you do this, you're a fool!"

Paulette angrily yanked her hands away. She glared at Leila. Her expression became stony. "I'm a fool?"

"Or a smart woman who's lying to herself!"

"So what if I am, Lee? I wouldn't be the first person to lie to myself, would I? My mother did it for the thirty-plus years that she was married to my dad, telling herself that she could make him love her. Evan does it every day that he stays married to his wife, pretending like no one notices that those two can barely stand each other. And I bet you do it too, pretending that you and Evan can carry on this little charade . . . that things aren't going to come to a head and he's not going to be angry, hurt, and rejected all over again! We *all* lie to ourselves!"

Leila winced. That last jab particularly stung. She opened her mouth to reply just as the meeting room door opened.

"Oh! I'm sorry," said the young man who stood in the doorway. He held a laptop in his hands. "I didn't know anyone was in here. I thought this room was reserved for ten o'clock IT review. I can come back if—"

"No, you can have the room," Paulette said while shoving herself away from the table and rising to her feet. "We were just leaving."

Five minutes later, Evan's meeting ended and he was surprised to see that his sister had paid him a visit.

"I didn't know you'd be here today," he said, looking genuinely elated at seeing Paulette there. He embraced his sister as Leila sat quietly at her desk.

By now, all of Paulette's tears had dried. She had artfully reapplied her makeup in the women's room so that she looked as beautiful as she had when she'd walked into the building. Evan had no idea about the little meltdown his baby sister had had only minutes ago. He had no idea about the upheaval now going on in her life either.

"Lee, will you hold my calls?" Evan asked as he ushered Paulette into his office.

Leila nodded. "Sure," she said just as he closed the door behind him.

When she heard the lock click, Leila closed her eyes and lowered her head, saying a little prayer for Paulette. She hoped everything would be okay. She hoped that things would turn out all right for the younger woman, but a part of her—the one that was now cold and hollow—knew it wasn't likely. It wasn't likely at all.

Chapter 19

LEILA

Leila lowered the tinted window of the Lincoln Town Car, held her hand over her eyes to shield against the sun glare, and peered at the pedestrians wandering through downtown L.A. It was a gentrified area that had been once known as seedy, but now only a few homeless people bothered to tread the streets of San Figueroa and West Olympic.

While the driver dodged through L.A. traffic, Leila took in the sights. She beamed, feeling like an absolute tourist, when they passed the Grammy Museum, the Staples Center, and L.A. Live. She and Evan were on their way to the Ritz-Carlton, where they would be staying for their brief business trip.

"So how does it feel to be back on the West Coast?" Evan asked from beside her.

Leila sat back in her seat after slowly rolling back up the window. She turned to Evan and grinned. "It feels a hell of a lot better than when I left! It feels damn near wonderful!"

He chuckled. "You're in a good mood."

"How could I *not* be?"

She had been traveling like a queen and treated like a high-level celebrity all day.

I could get used to this, she thought as she slumped back into the plush leather seat. Classical music played over the car speakers. A small television in the headrest in front of her showed stock and business news.

This is the life!

She had flown on her first private jet—a Gulfstream G550—that took them from Dulles to LAX. While Evan had scanned his BlackBerry and reviewed documents from his briefcase during the flight, Leila had been giddy with excitement as she peered out the jet's windows, barely able to stay in her seat. She had sampled the complimentary champagne and the wine and cheese the charter service had offered for the flight. She had dumped a few complimentary mints in her purse, along with the soap from the women's room, as keepsakes.

Then, when they arrived in L.A., a driver had greeted them as soon as they stepped out of the gate and quickly ushered them to the waiting car. A fleet of airport personnel had been there to take their bags, which were being shuttled in a separate car even though it was only two suitcases. Now they were pulling up to the VIP entrance of one of the best hotels in town.

"Welcome to the Ritz-Carlton," the doorman said as he held open their car door.

"Thank you," Leila murmured in reply.

The driver of the other Town Car unloaded their luggage, which a hotel bellhop placed on a luggage cart.

A woman wearing a black skirt and crisp white

blouse stood near the revolving door, smiling. "Mr. Murdoch? Ms. Hawkins?"

They nodded.

"My name is Ingrid. I'm with the concierge staff. I'm here to show you to your suites." She gestured to the door. "Please come with me."

They stepped through the revolving doors and Leila gazed in awe at the hotel's foyer: the high ceilings, the marble floors, the sumptuous topiaries in stone vases. As they neared the elevator that would take them to one of the penthouse suites, where Evan would be staying (Leila would stay at one of the slightly cheaper, though still outrageously lavish, suites on another floor), she shook her head in amazement.

"What?" Evan asked, finally glancing up from his BlackBerry. The whole time she had been gawking, he had been checking his email and prattling on the phone.

"How *do* you do this every day?"

"Do what?"

"Take all this luxury as a given," she said as she gestured to the sumptuous lobby. "You're so blasé about it."

He shrugged while Ingrid pressed the up button for them. "I don't know. I guess because . . . I grew up with it."

Having everything at your fingertips and having people fawn over you were definitely things Leila Hawkins hadn't experienced. She remembered her childhood as being tough. She remembered her mother working multiple jobs just to pay the bills. She knew that Evan had grown up very differently. She hadn't been blind. She had visited his home enough back when they were younger, but seeing all this and experiencing it firsthand were reminders of just how different their lives were.

Damn, he's rich!

The elevator doors opened, and Ingrid turned to them and continued to smile her beatific smile. "This will take you to the top floor, where another hotel staffer will be waiting for you at your suite. Thank you again for staying with us, Mr. Murdoch and Ms. Hawkins."

Evan nodded and Leila followed suit, afraid if she spoke out loud she would start gushing again and embarrass herself by showing how gauche she was.

They boarded the elevator and she slumped back against the wall, watching the numbers overhead as they ascended to the top floor.

"'Must be nice' . . . I remember thinking that back in high school."

"Thinking what?"

"That it must be nice to be a Murdoch. I mean . . . you guys get everything! You—"

"We don't 'get everything,' Lee. Not by a long shot. Money can buy you a lot of things, but it can't buy you happiness." He paused to tuck his cell phone into his breast pocket. "I was just saying that to Paulette the other day, but I'm not sure if the message got through to her."

Leila fell silent at the mention of Paulette's name.

"Have you spoken with her, by the way?" he asked, turning his penetrating gaze on Leila. "Has she . . . has she mentioned anything to you?"

Leila's eyes widened. She cleared her throat. "Umm, no," she lied. "W-w-why?"

"That day Paulette came to my office, she asked me for something. I didn't want to give it to her at first, but she sounded so . . . so desperate, Lee. I couldn't turn her down."

"What was she so desperate about? Did she tell you what was wrong?"

"No! That's the problem. She wouldn't tell me any details. She said she couldn't tell me. But I don't like it, Lee. What she asked me to do . . . all the secrecy . . . I'm really starting to worry about her."

Leila felt the overwhelming urge to tell Evan the truth. She wanted to tell him that he should be worried about his sister because Paulette was in a lot of trouble. But how could she betray Paulette like that? If Paulette hadn't told Evan the truth, then it wasn't Leila's job to do it.

"But Paulette's digging herself into an even deeper hole," a voice in her head argued. "Maybe if you told Evan what's going on, he could talk some sense into her. He could help her!"

Leila bit the inside of her cheek, now facing a dilemma. She didn't want to break Paulette's trust, but she hated keeping a secret like this. This wasn't like the secret she'd kept for Paulette more than a decade ago. This was much, *much* bigger, and the price Paulette could pay for continuing to be blackmailed by her ex could be immeasurable.

"Ev . . ." Leila took a deep breath. "Ev, I have to—"

Just then the elevator doors opened, causing Leila to stop mid-sentence. They were greeted by a young man in a dark suit with a gold name tag with the Ritz-Carlton emblem pinned near his lapel.

"Hello, I'm Kevin! Welcome to the Ritz Carlton!"

Leila instantly fell silent as Kevin ushered them down the hall to Evan's suite, where she checked every detail to make sure the accommodations were as Evan had requested.

As she followed the hotel staffer from room to room, asking questions that a competent assistant should ask, she got the gnawing feeling that she'd missed a golden opportunity in the elevator that she might regret later.

I should have said something, she thought as she glanced at Evan, who had returned to talking on his BlackBerry.

But the topic of Paulette would never come up again, not while they finished checking into their hotel rooms, took a chauffeured car ride to a downtown office building, or ran to a flurry of business meetings that would last well into the evening. By the time they returned to the Ritz-Carlton, they were both exhausted and in no mood to talk at all. They walked through the lobby, which was teeming with even more people than when they first arrived. All the patrons looked as if they were preparing for a night on the town. Meanwhile, Leila and Evan planned to spend the night in their respective hotel rooms, recovering from the jam-packed day and jet lag.

"I'm going to take a hot bubble bath, then sleep forever!" Leila groaned as they boarded the elevator.

"Not forever. We have more meetings tomorrow starting at 9 a.m."

She nodded and sighed, before glancing down at her business phone, which was buzzing. She dug her phone out of her purse and raised it to her ear.

"Hello, Leila Hawkins speaking."

"Hi, Leila! Glad I finally caught you!" said Carl, the assistant to Murdoch Conglomerated's COO.

"Carl? What's wrong?" She glanced down at her watch. It was a little past 7 p.m. West Coast time, and after 10 p.m. on the East Coast, where the headquarters were located. If Carlton was calling at this late hour, something was definitely amiss.

"We have a little emergency on our hands over here," he said, confirming her worst fears.

"What emergency?"

Overhearing her conversation, now even Evan was frowning.

"I emailed you earlier, but I guess you didn't get it," Carl explained. "Joe tried to contact Mr. Murdoch too, but had no luck. We figured you guys were busy. It's about the new warehouses the company is purchasing."

As Leila listened to Carl talk on the other end of the line, her shoulders fell. The details were above her head, but it all sounded like she and Evan weren't going to get any rest any time soon.

There goes that bubble bath, she thought sadly.

"Okay, I'll have Mr. Murdoch call Mr. O'Brien as soon as he can, Carl. Will do . . . bye," she murmured before hanging up.

"What was that about?" Evan asked.

"I'm not quite sure." She dropped her phone back into her purse. "Something involving warehouses and a refrigeration system, I think. Joe say he has to talk to you about it immediately."

"Shit," Evan said as the elevator doors opened.

"Shit indeed," she mumbled.

An hour later, Leila was gathering printouts of documents corporate had emailed from the printer in Evan's hotel suite. Evan sat in an armchair with his laptop open on the ottoman in front of him, making the suite's living room his makeshift office.

"Yes, I'm looking at it now, Joe," he said into his cell phone as she walked into the living room and placed the neatly stacked sheets on the ottoman cushion beside his laptop. "I'll review the docs tonight and tomorrow when I get the chance. I'll be ready to discuss it with you Tuesday." He shook his head. "No apologies necessary. We'll figure this out. . . . Now get some sleep. Talk to you tomorrow, Joe."

She watched as he hung up and set his BlackBerry on a nearby end table. He then tiredly ran his hands over his face before glancing at her.

"Lee, I can take it from here. You go ahead back to your room and I'll see you in the morning."

She shook her head before flopping back onto the sofa and cuing up her iPad. "Nope, I'll stay."

"Lee, really, I'm fine. You can go."

"I don't think so, *capitán!* If you're still going strong, so am I. That's what I get paid to do, right?"

He raised his hands in surrender. "Okay, have it your way. I'll admit . . . it certainly makes the long nights a lot less lonely having someone burning the midnight oil with you. I'm usually by myself. Nothing like arriving home when everyone from your wife to your house-keeper is snoring."

"Charisse never waited up for you?" Leila asked quietly.

"She did . . . in the beginning. But I guess it got old waiting for me to come home or . . ." His words drifted off.

"Or what?"

"She got tired of pretending to care," he answered honestly. He then returned his attention to his laptop.

"I used to wait up for Brad a lot too," she began with her eyes downcast. She set her iPad aside. "After a few years, I stopped waiting, but not because I got tired of it. I found out he came home so late because of the women he was seeing, not because of work. After a while I just felt stupid, you know? Here I was spending night after night alone, staring at the clock, waiting for my man to come home. Meanwhile, he was spending those hours in someone else's bed." She leaned back on the sofa. "Later, I would spend those hours alone thinking about what my life would be like if I had made different decisions. What would have happened if I had divorced Brad years ago or if I had never married him at all?"

Evan nodded, not looking up from his computer keys as he typed. "I know what you mean. I've had those contemplative moments too. Solitude tends to do that."

"Have you ever wondered what life would have been like if we would have ended up together?" she suddenly asked and then immediately regretted it.

Evan's eyes darted up from his laptop. His fingers paused mid-motion. He stared at her as if she had just announced she was a reincarnation of Houdini.

Why did I ask that? This was not an appropriate conversation to have with her boss, let alone a married man, but the question was already out there. She couldn't take it back.

His look of astonishment gradually faded. It was replaced by irritation.

"I make it a habit not to wallow in things that are in the past or things that were never a possibility," Evan muttered before returning his attention back to his work.

"Why do you think it was never a possibility?"

"Because you didn't think of me that way. You made that pretty damn clear, remember? You just saw me as a friend, almost a brother."

"That's what you think? That I just saw you as a brother?"

He looked up again and held her gaze. "Are you about to tell me that you saw me as more than that?"

She thought about it, considering his question before she answered. Had there ever been a time when they were younger when she'd felt more for Evan than just friendship or a sisterly love? Leila could recall a few fleeting moments when she'd admire the way his strong arms had looked in a T-shirt or how his butt looked in a pair of jeans. That certainly wasn't sisterly. She could also remember moments when she would inexplicably lash out at some girl he was dating or wanted to date, when she would roll her eyes whenever he would rave about how beautiful, smart, or funny some other woman was. That wasn't very sisterly either. She could even remember one night when he had driven her home after a party and she'd wondered, just before she'd climbed out of his car, whether she should just lean over the armrest and kiss him. But of course, she hadn't. She'd waved good-bye, made some joke, and told him she'd see him in class the next day.

So why had she held back? Why had she never let those fleeting moments and feelings develop into something more?

"It's not . . . it's not that I never thought of you in that way, Ev. I just couldn't let us be more than what we were."

"Why?"

"I don't know." She shrugged helplessly. "Maybe it was because I hated how everyone assumed that we would end up together. Everyone in Chesterton acted like it was inevitable that we'd hook up and get married. They didn't treat us like we were friends, but like we were a couple. It didn't matter how many times I said there was nothing going on between us. It annoyed the shit out of me to have my life scripted out like that!"

"But what we had was a good thing, Leila. We were close. That was something people admired. There was nothing to be annoyed about."

"I was a codependent mess and you were lost in puppy love, Ev. Admit it!"

"I wish you would stop calling it that. It only pisses me off when you do."

"But it's the truth! It *was* puppy love because it didn't have any potential. Be honest. And even if it did, your father would have nipped it in the bud. He hated my guts."

"He didn't *hate* you."

"He didn't want me around you!"

She could see from the uncomfortable look on Evan's face that he agreed with her, even if he didn't want to admit it.

"Look, you tried your best to hide it . . . to shield me from him, but I know how your father felt about me. He never would have named you as his will executor or made you the head of his company if we had ended up together."

"You don't think I knew that?" he shouted, his exasperation now morphing to anger. "But I didn't care!"

She stared at him, now dumbstruck.

"So what if I wasn't CEO! So what if he disinherited me! I wanted you, Lee! I loved you . . . like a grown man loves a woman. It wasn't puppy love. I knew the risk, but I would've married you anyway. I would've made the sacrifice. That's how badly I wanted to be with you." He sighed gruffly. "But that doesn't matter now, does it?" He returned his attention to his computer screen and the stack of papers in front of him. "It's all ancient history. Like I said, I prefer not to wallow in the past."

The hotel suite fell into silence.

He had been willing to sacrifice all that for her? Leila had had no idea.

"Of course, you didn't," a voice in her head chided. "Just call you Miss Oblivious."

Leila felt like a knife was being twisted in her chest.

"I'm sorry, Ev."

"Huh?" he answered distractedly after typing a few computer keys, now engrossed again in his work.

"I said that I'm sorry."

He looked up at her.

"If I could go back ten years and do it all over again, I would do things differently." She shook her head. "I wouldn't have been so blind and naive."

He tiredly ran his hand over his face again. "Lee, we can't—"

"No, Ev, please let me finish! Let me get this off my chest. I should have . . . I should have chosen you," she whispered, knowing in her heart that she meant those words. "I would have been happier with you than I ever would have been with Brad. You did love me. You always made me feel special. No one else has ever made me feel that way."

Evan lowered his gaze and didn't say anything for several seconds. Finally, he looked up at her. "Lee, I've learned to let it go. All we have is the here and now, right? It's better to focus on the present."

She didn't reply.

"Come on. Let's get through this stuff so that we can both get to bed before midnight." He tossed aside a folder before picking up another. "So much for this business trip being like a vacation, huh? Sun, sand, and relaxation, my ass," he murmured as he pulled up a spreadsheet on his screen.

She watched him work, but she could tell something had changed. He no longer seemed focused on what was in front of him. He looked unnerved, and frankly, so was she.

He's married. He's my boss, she silently reminded herself. *But he's also Evan, the man who's loved me and wanted me for . . . for forever. And I . . . I want him too.*

Leila let that realization settle into her. She wanted Evan. She couldn't deny it anymore.

She hesitated only briefly before rising from the love seat and crossing the hotel suite's living room. She sat on the edge of the ottoman in front of him and he looked up at her again.

"What?" he asked.

She tugged the papers out of his hands and set them on the end table. She removed his laptop and set it beside the papers.

He furrowed his brows in confusion. "What are you doing?"

"What do you think I'm doing?" She cupped his clean-shaven cheeks and closed her eyes. "I'm kissing you, Ev," she said, before bringing her lips to his. Their lips melded together perfectly, as if sculpted from the same flesh.

Leila had caught Evan off guard with the kiss, but it didn't take long for him to return it or for it to deepen. This had been building up between them for months, maybe even *years*. Now that they had started, there was no going back.

He pulled her onto his lap and wrapped his arms around her possessively. She could feel the heat of his searing touch through the fabric of her blouse. Their tongues delved inside one another's mouths and they savored the tastes and smell of both the new and the familiar. Evan tasted like the chocolate he had been nibbling on earlier and smelled just as good.

He tugged her bottom lip between his teeth and she moaned against his lips. His mouth shifted to her neck and then her collarbone, leaving a trail of kisses. When he began to undo each pearl button of her blouse and his mouth descended, she arched her back, inviting his licks, nips, and kisses, enjoying the thrill of his lips and tongue on her skin.

To give him better access, she shifted, swinging one leg to the other side of the armchair so that she was straddling him. Her skirt shimmied higher up her thighs, giving him a tantalizing peek at the black silk panties she wore underneath. He grabbed her bottom and eased her forward on his lap and she felt his erection press urgently against the zipper of his pants and into her groin.

"Lee?"

"Yeah?" she murmured breathlessly as they kissed.

"I've wanted this for a *looooong* damn time," he said as he tugged off her blouse, leaving her in nothing but her black lace bra and her skirt.

Instantly, she was happy she had decided to forego wearing panty hose that day. One less article of clothing he'd have to remove.

His fingers skimmed the lace edging of her bra, then the tops of her breasts, reverently, and her skin started to tingle and gooseflesh all over again.

"If I could tell you how many times I'd fantasized about doing this, about seeing you topless, you'd think I was the biggest damn pervert in the world," he said.

He lowered the straps off her shoulders, pushed down the front of one of the cups, then the other. In the cool air of the hotel room, her brown nipples hardened.

"Damn," he said, licking his lips. "They're just as beautiful as I imagined."

He eagerly lowered his mouth to one of the nipples

and she breathed in sharply. She closed her eyes. When he tugged the brown nub between his teeth, she moaned again.

One breast wasn't enough. Evan hurriedly removed the entire bra, tossing it onto the hotel floor. She tugged off his tie and was just as fast at getting off his shirt.

He cupped her bottom again and showed equal attention to each breast, suckling them and licking them until she arched her back again, dug her nails into his shoulders, and bit down hard on her bottom lip to stifle her moans.

She felt the hem of her skirt being pushed up even higher, up to her waist. Then she felt him roughly pull down the waistband of her underwear.

"Let me show you what love from a grown man feels like," he whispered just as she felt his fingers tease the slick wetness between her thighs. Leila cried out and lowered her head into the crook of his shoulder. She moaned as he massaged her clit, alternating between slow and fast. The hand between her legs and the mouth on her breasts cast a wicked spell on her body, making her slowly lose control.

Evan shifted from massaging her clit to plunging two fingers inside her over and over again. Her hips met those fingers stroke for tormenting stroke, until she was almost bucking on top of him. The tingle that had started along her skin now sank deeper and coasted all over her and she whimpered and moaned yet again. Her vision started to blur. When the orgasm rocked her, she threw back her head and shouted into the quiet hotel room.

He eased her off of his lap and back onto the ottoman soon after. He rose to his feet. She was still dazed and trembling when he returned to the living room less than a minute later with condom packet in hand. She had no idea where he had gotten it and wasn't about to ask as he pushed her back so that she lay flat against the ottoman cushion. He tugged her panties down her hips, then her legs, and let them fall to the floor. He then knelt between her thighs and spread them wide. She watched as Evan lowered the zipper of his pants and put on the condom, now eager to enjoy what she just had. Her body was more than ready for him, even if her mind was still catching up to all of this. But Evan abruptly paused.

"Lee, you know I still love you, right?" he asked, as he hovered over her. "The years and everything that's happened haven't changed a thing. I still—"

He stopped midsentence when she raised a finger to his lips and shook her head.

"Less talking, more loving, Ev," she said as she wrapped her legs around his waist. "We've talked enough."

She raised her lips and kissed him again. She was sucking on his tongue when he joined their bodies with one thrust that almost sent them both flying off the ottoman. She cried out again. The second thrust was more controlled but just as deep. She felt him ease himself inside her, filling her body and her heart. Leila gazed into the soulful dark eyes she had always admired as they slowly rocked and grinded. They hungrily kissed again, devouring one another. Just their moans and whispers broke the silence of the room. It was like the rest of the world outside of the room had disappeared.

Leila's heart pounded like a steam engine. The tingle she had felt earlier was now a raging fire that sent her nerve endings into overdrive so that his every touch sent her purring. She wanted this moment to last forever, but she could tell from the pressure that was building up inside her again that it wouldn't and couldn't.

The deliciously slow rocking suddenly picked up in tempo. Evan's hands shifted from her back to her hips and bottom, as he plunged harder. He bit down hard on his bottom lip—so hard that the pink skin now was virtually white. He closed his eyes.

Leila started to tremble again. She gripped his broad shoulders to steady herself, but it was of little use. She was quaking all over, feeling her legs and her arms rapidly turn into putty. When the shockwave finally crested over her, she closed her eyes and shouted his name. Her back arched. The muscles in her legs and arms clinched. She bucked her hips with each spasm.

Evan came soon after. She felt him swell inside her then he cried out. He tightened his hold around her back and her hips. He collapsed against her chest and took gulping breaths. He shuddered and his body convulsed with each tremor. Leila cradled him in her arms until the shudders subsided.

When he peered down at her seconds later, he was smiling. At that moment, Evan looked like the happiest man in the world.

Chapter 20

EVAN

Evan sailed through the doors of Murdoch Conglomerated with a grin on his lips and a hop in his step.

"Good morning," he almost sang to the security guard at the front desk. He then strode toward the elevators.

"Uh, g-good morning, Mr. Murdoch!" she cried belatedly as he pressed the up button. He was foregoing his private elevator today to be one with the people. An eager smile was on the guard's bright pink lips. "Y-y-you have a good day, sir!"

He nodded and boarded the elevator, which was already crowded with people from the lower parking garage.

"Good morning," he said to everyone as the doors closed. Several mumbled their replies, though the elevator fell into an uncomfortable silence as it ascended floors. He was used to it. No one wanted to make small talk when the company CEO was around. Now he remembered yet another reason why he used his private elevator.

When the elevator finally hit the twelfth floor, the others in the compartment all stepped back or shifted aside to let him out first.

He chuckled. "You all have a nice day."

"You too, sir," a few murmured.

He said, "Good morning," a few more times as he made his way to his office, drawing a mix of greetings and panicked expressions as he passed. Finally, he saw her through her opened doorway.

Leila sat at her desk, typing away on her computer. Her delicate brows were drawn together in concentration.

He tried his best to play it cool and to look casual for the sake of office appearances, even as the world around him seemed to go into slow motion. The symphony in his head started to play, building up momentum as it reached its crescendo. As he neared her office, she looked up at him and the face he had seen in his dreams all last night, greeted him in the light of day. His heart and his dick swelled simultaneously. He felt like a giddy teenager.

Look casual! Look casual, damn it, he silently told himself as he stepped into her office.

"Morning, Leila," he said, glancing down at the BlackBerry he held in his hand.

"Good morning, Evan. Happy Hump Day!"

He almost dropped his phone. He stopped midstride and stared at her in amazement. Had she actually said that at the office? "What?"

She chuckled. "Happy Hump Day . . . Happy *Wednesday,* Evan. How are you today?"

Shit. That's what she meant by "Hump Day." For a second there, he thought she was talking about . . .

"Good. I'm good," he said, regaining his poise. "Any surprises I should know about on the schedule?" He then pushed open his office door and strolled inside.

She stood up from her desk, quickly grabbed her notepad and pen, and followed him through the doorway. "Well, the meeting you had with Mr. Stuart from Antwerp Inc. that was scheduled for two p.m. was canceled. But he wants to try to reschedule it for next week, if that's possible. I told his assistant that I'd get back to her later today with a few possible dates and times." She glanced at the words scribbled on her notepad. "The contract you had the company lawyers review came back yesterday. I forwarded their changes to you. It's in your email inbox."

"Yes, I saw," he murmured, gazing down at his phone screen again. He tossed his leather satchel onto one of the chairs near the sofa.

"Your flight and hotel reservations for later this month are confirmed," she continued.

"Did you give them my suite specifications?" he asked as he turned on his computer.

She was going on another business trip with him, this time to Chicago. They had booked separate rooms for cover though he had specifically requested a California king in his room along with a Jacuzzi tub. He was getting hard again just thinking about what they could do in that tub.

"Yes, they have all that information," Leila said with an efficient nod. "The concierge desk even called to confirm a few things. It's all taken care of."

"Good job, Leila."

She lowered her notepad. "Thanks."

"Just a few more questions and I'll let you get back to work." He pulled out his chair, took off his suit jacket, and tossed it over the back of the chair. "Could you shut the door though?"

She glanced at the opened doorway. "Oh, yeah, sure."

He watched her as she walked. She was wearing a dress today—a sweet, floral light blue wrap dress with quarter-length sleeves.

A dress. Good, he thought as his eyes scanned her long legs then settled on her ass, which swayed back and forth as she walked. Dresses and skirts always made things easier.

She shut the door and started to turn to him. "I wasn't sure if—"

She didn't get a chance to finish. He already had crossed the room, wrapped her in his arms, and her back pressed against the door, which he had locked with a click, before he lowered his mouth to hers.

"You have a meeting in a half an hour," she breathed against his lips as his hands slid up the backs of her thighs then gripped her bottom.

"Plenty of time," he said as his lips shifted to her neck and he licked the skin, making her shiver.

He loved how she smelled. It was a zesty fragrance today—a mix of vanilla, orange, and some flowery scent he couldn't quite place. He longed to bury his face in another smell right now, to dive between her legs and get a taste of her if she would let him.

"Evan," she whispered warningly as he began to tug at her underwear, easing the lace fabric down her hips. "Evan!"

He could do it on his office desk. They had had sex there at least three times this month. Or they could try his conference table. That offered a little more support and there were fewer things he had to push aside. Or they could try old faithful—the office sofa. That would certainly be more comfortable for her.

"It is 8 a.m., Ev! *Everyone* is in the office. They're going to hear us!"

He shook his head. "We can be quiet."

Since they had started their affair a little more than a month ago, they had kept their dalliances to after hours, when the offices were deserted. On rare occasions he would meet Leila at her place whenever her mother had one of her bingo nights or was out with friends. Isabel was visiting her father in California so there were no worries about the seven-year-old running in on them.

Leila preferred those arrangements. She said there were less chances of them getting caught, but Evan didn't always want to wait until the end of the day to touch her, kiss her, or plunge himself inside her. He didn't want to be a good little boy and wait for his dessert. He had waited for twenty years for this! He had gone without sex for almost a year! Enough waiting. He wanted his cake—*now!*

"Evan," she said again, though fainter this time as one hand slid to the front of her thighs and began to massage her between her legs. The other hand cupped her breast. He rolled his thumb over her nipple, feeling it harden through the fabric of her dress and her bra.

Her breath caught in her throat as he pushed the crotch of her panties aside, and teased the wetness between her thighs. She closed her eyes, bit down hard on her bottom lip, and arched her hips, meeting his touch even as he felt her push against his chest to ease him away. "Evan, come on. Stop! Please," she whimpered.

Despite her protests, he knew he could have her anyway right here in his office. He knew which buttons to press now to make her tremble, to make her moan. But even though he wanted her—he loved her even more. If she really wasn't comfortable doing this, he wouldn't force her. She wanted the people in the office to respect her. They wouldn't if they all figured out she was Evan's mistress. He also had a facade he wanted to maintain, and he couldn't do that if he lost control, if he gave in to every little desire.

He sighed, gave her one final kiss, and eased away from her. "Fine."

She took a steadying breath, pushed down the hem of her dress, stepped away from the door, and walked further into his office. She picked up her notepad and pen, which had fallen to the hardwood floor. "I'll make it up to you this evening. Don't worry," she whispered, making him raise an eyebrow.

"You've got something in mind?"

"Mama has an overnight shopping trip to some outlet and pottery factory in Delaware. She's going with a friend. They leave this afternoon and won't be back until tomorrow afternoon."

He instantly perked up. "So we've got all night?"

"Until the wee hours of the morning, if you'd like," she said with a smirk, unlocking his door.

"Oh, I'd like." He nodded eagerly. "I'd like a lot!"

"Good, then I guess I'll see you tonight then," she said seductively over her shoulder before opening his door and stepping back into the main office. She closed his door behind her.

Evan slowly exhaled, then looked down at his erection. He hoped he could wait that long.

Until then, he had twenty-four minutes to get rid of this hard-on.

* * *

At exactly 7 p.m., Evan rang the doorbell to the town house that he was now renting to Leila. He was the owner so thankfully, his occasional visits at odd hours didn't raise too many eyebrows from the neighbors in the conservative, stately subdivision. At least, it didn't raise the eyebrows of the few neighbors who bothered to notice the comings and goings of Leila and her family.

He heard Leila undo the dead bolt and another lock. The door cracked open and she peeked around the edge of the frame. He got a glimpse of the neatly decorated foyer behind her.

"Right on time! I was wondering if you'd be able to get away from the office with all the work you had."

"Wild horses couldn't keep me away!" he replied, making her chuckle. But she didn't open the door further. He frowned. "Uh, can I come in?"

"Oh, sure! Of course," she said, easing the door open a little more, but he could barely squeeze through the opening.

When she shut the door behind him and he saw what she was wearing, he instantly realized why she had only cracked the door a smidge.

Definitely wouldn't want the neighbors to see this outfit, he thought.

She had on a red negligee with a halter top made of lace and some flimsy fabric that he ached to touch. He could see the thong beneath it, along with her dark areolas. She was wearing a garter belt and stockings. Towering red stilettos adorned her feet.

He let his gaze sweep over her appreciatively. "Well, damn! Is all this for me?"

She began to undo his belt then lower his zipper. "I

told you I'd make it up to you," she whispered against his lips.

"That you did."

Leila began to nibble at his lips. She kissed him and he kissed her back eagerly. He fisted his hands in her hair, tilting back her head and pulling her closer to him so that their bodies were almost plastered together. She lowered his boxer briefs, wrapped her hand around his dick and began to slowly stroke him right there in the foyer.

"Ah, God," Evan moaned just as she stepped back slightly. He watched as the beautiful woman he had adored and lusted after for years, slowly dropped to her knees in front of him.

"Good things come to those who wait, Ev," she said before taking him into her warm, wet mouth, making him groan.

I couldn't agree more, he thought as she sucked him to knee-buckling orgasm.

An hour later, Evan and Leila lay naked in her bed, wrapped in each other's arms, taking a badly needed breather. They had made love twice already and probably would a few more times before the night was done—body and spirit willing! But, in the morning, he would take a shower, shave, and put on the change of clothes he'd brought with him. He would walk into the office thirty minutes after she had arrived (as planned), see her at her desk, exchange polite greetings, and the pretense would start all over again. Day after day, they would have to play these roles, and there seemed to be something sad and profoundly unfair about it all. Evan *finally* had the woman who completed him, and yet he had to pretend like she was just his assistant. He wanted the world to know that he was in love and finally happy for once in his damn life, and he couldn't tell a soul. The only person he had told was Terrence, and even then, he had gotten a lecture.

"I don't know why you keep doing this to yourself, bruh," Terrence had said with a shake of the head. "If you just got a divorce, you wouldn't have to do all this sneaking around."

Why can't I just get a divorce? he thought, trailing his fingers down Leila's shoulders while gazing at the ceiling. *Why can't I ask Lee to move in with me and give our relationship a real try?*

"Because you've got too much to lose," a voice in his head quickly answered.

He would probably lose his shirt in a divorce. When he and Charisse got married, they had signed a prenuptial agreement with a clause saying that either party had to pay a hefty penalty if either committed infidelity. He suspected that Charisse was also having an affair, but he couldn't prove anything so far. If the truth about him and Leila came out, he'd have to pay Charisse a great deal of alimony and she would own half of his portion of Murdoch Conglomerated. Evan couldn't do that to his brother and sister, make them have to share their legacy with the likes of Charisse.

Terrence had already warned him about the huge chance he was taking. "You're walking a tightrope, Ev. Just hope you don't go tumbling over the side. That ground is going to hurt like hell when you fall."

Not to mention that Leila was still going through her own messy divorce. Even if Evan managed to make it out of his divorce with Charisse alive, who knew how long Leila's divorce from Brad could continue to drag on.

And even if they didn't face all these obstacles, he would still draw quite a few whispers if he decided to start dating his assistant. There was nothing triter than the big boss who decided to seduce his secretary. Leila needed this job. It wasn't like she could quit.

All of these things would open them both to derision and ridicule. A family name he had tried so hard to protect would get mud slung at it.

He couldn't do that.

"I can practically hear the wheels turning," Leila said. She lifted her head off his chest and gazed into his eyes. "What are you thinking about?"

He shook his head and started to say, "Nothing," then thought better of it. He slowly exhaled. "I was thinking about how I'll have to leave when dawn rolls around and there isn't a damn thing I can do about it," he answered honestly.

"What do you mean?" She propped up one of the pillows on the headboard and reclined against it. "I would ask you to stay longer, but I figured we both have to get ready for work. And with Mom on her way home—"

"I mean the sneaking around, Lee. I mean . . . how long are we going to do this? Weeks? Months? *Years?*"

She fixed him with a level gaze. "I don't know, Ev."

"So what? You never think about it? You never wonder how long this is going to last?"

"Of course I do! You think I *like* doing this? You think I like having to wait until the office is cleared out for the day for me to kiss you? You think I like being paranoid that someone is going to figure out the looks we give each other? Do you think I like . . . I like being the . . . the other woman?" she said ruefully then shook her head. "No, Ev, I can assure you that I don't. But I just try to remember what you told me the first night we were together. You said all we have is the here and now . . . that it's better to focus on the present." She reached out and held his hand. She squeezed it. "That's all I can do. That's all *we* can do."

"I hate it when you turn my words back on me."

"I'm just telling you the truth. I don't know what the future holds; neither of us do." She leaned toward him and lightly kissed his lips. "But just . . . just *be* with me. This could be our last night. This might have to end tomorrow. But just be with me . . . tonight, *please?* We'll figure out tomorrow when it comes, okay?"

She didn't have to ask him twice. He cupped her face and raised his mouth to hers again. The kiss was languid and deep and quickly developed into a lot more. They made love one more time before falling asleep in each other's arms.

The next morning, Evan awoke to the sound of the news broadcast and running water. He slowly lifted his head from his pillow and opened his eyes, only to squint at the rays of sunlight that streamed through the cracks of her bedroom blinds. When the sound of running water ended, he turned to find Leila striding out of the bathroom, toweling herself off. He admired her naked body, which was still covered with a few droplets from her shower. He could remember the feel of her warm skin against his fingertips, the taste of her mouth as she'd cried out his name against his lips in the dark.

Leila paused to wrap the towel around her and sit on the edge of the bed. She had grabbed a bottle of body lotion off of her night table and now absently began to rub some of the alluring scent onto her legs and arms as she watched a weather girl point to storm clouds in the Midwest.

"What time is it?" he asked with a yawn, rubbing his eyes.

"Six-thirty."

"Six-thirty? *Really?*" He glanced at her alarm clock. He had planned to get up at 6 a.m.

"Why didn't you wake me?"

Leila turned to him. "You seemed so content. I didn't want to disturb you. Plus"—she laughed—"you were snoring."

"I don't snore."

She smirked and rolled her eyes. "Of course, you don't." He watched as she stood from the bed and walked toward him. "Don't worry. You still have plenty of time to do whatever you need to do to make it to the office by 8 a.m. You'll have my bathroom all to yourself. I'll just put on my makeup and do my hair out here."

He slowly let his gaze trail over her. "Yeah, well, there were a few things I may have wanted more time to do that you didn't consider."

She set her lotion back on the night table. *"Oh?* Like what?"

Leila yelped with surprise when he suddenly reached up and wrapped his arms around her waist before dragging her on top of him. She landed, sprawled across his torso, and they soon became a tangle of limbs and twisted bedsheets. She started to protest but fell silent when he lowered his mouth to one of her breasts and began to stroke her between her thighs. She closed her eyes and twisted her hips to meet his touch. She arched her back so that her breasts molded against his hand.

Evan loved seeing Leila like this—in the throes of sexual delight. He loved to watch her pant and writhe, to feel her muscles clench and her to grow wetter against his fingertips. Eliciting such a response from a beautiful woman that he loved and damn near worshipped made him feel more powerful than winning any multimillion-dollar contract or buying any new sports car. This was a high he wished he could have forever.

"Oh, God! Don't stop, Evan," she whispered into one of the pillow cases. "Don't . . . ever . . . stop!"

He shifted from kissing her breasts to leaving a trail of kisses down the center of her stomach. The skin was still damp from her shower. She smelled like her bath gel—a tantalizing mix of milk and honey.

"Don't worry, baby. I won't," he promised.

He then eased her legs wider and switched his fingers for his mouth and tongue. He licked and sucked her clit and her body went into overdrive. Her breathing became shallower. The whimpers and moans morphed into yells that echoed off the bedroom ceiling. When the orgasm hit her, he felt her thighs tremble and her stomach clench. As the last tremors ebbed, her entire body went slack. She rolled onto her side and he rose from his crouch and stared down at her, wiping his mouth.

She looked tranquil, almost blissful with her arm thrown over her eyes and a smile on her face. She must have felt his gaze on her. She lowered her arm and turned to him, and her smile widened into a grin. She eased herself upright so that they were almost level eye to eye. Leila then reached out and wrapped her hand around him. She began to stroke him.

"Now you," she whispered against his lips before kissing him again.

He knelt between her thighs, gritting his teeth and moaning under her expert touch. He would have come right there in her hand, but he managed, with a great feat of willpower, to wrench her hand way. He fumbled for a condom on the night table and quickly sheathed himself. She spread her legs and braced herself with her back against the headboard. Seconds later, he plunged inside her and she shouted out his name. With each thrust, her grip tightened around his back and so did his grip on the headboard. He moaned and groaned against her lips, loving the feel of her breasts pressed against his chest, of her arms and her legs wrapped around him. There was no better moment than this.

"I love you, Lee," he whispered, closing his eyes.

Leila suddenly screamed in alarm. That wasn't quite the reaction a man expected when he told a woman he loved her.

"What's wrong?" he asked as she started twisting against him and shoving him away from her. She gave another hard shove and he fell back against the mattress in a sprawled heap.

"Lee, what the hell's wrong?" he repeated, watching bemused as Leila scrambled away from the headboard to the other side of the bed. She grabbed for one of the bedsheets, cloaking her nakedness.

What had gotten into her?

"Mama! What . . . what are you doing here?" Leila asked breathlessly, shoving her hair out of her eyes.

"Mama?" Evan turned to find Leila's mother, Diane, standing in the doorway.

"Shit!" he spat before grabbing for one of the bed pillows and holding it in front of his groin in a feeble attempt to cover himself. But it was obvious from the look on the older woman's face that she had seen enough already, that she had seen too much. She looked utterly stricken and worse—sickened—by the sight of them.

"Marsha got sick last night," Diane whispered, barely audible over the sound of the news broadcast. "We decided to head home early. I . . . I left you a message saying I was on my way."

Leila tightened the sheets around her and crawled

off the bed. She stood near her night table. "I-I didn't get the message."

Her mother's stricken expression disappeared. Her lips puckered like she had just tasted something sour. "I guess you were busy doing . . . other things." She then shifted her withering gaze to Evan. "Didn't expect to see you here."

Evan adjusted his pillow, unsure of what to say in response to that.

"Don't you have a home and wife you should be attending to?" Diane asked.

He blinked in shock. Was she none-too-subtly kicking him out of his own rental? Evan turned to Leila to see if she would come to his defense, but she kept her head bowed. She refused to look at him.

So it's like that, huh?

He slowly climbed off the bed and headed to the bathroom. "I guess I do," he mumbled before closing the bathroom door behind him.

Chapter 21

LEILA

Leila had just finished gathering the last of her dirty laundry, tossing her clothes and damp towels haphazardly into a plastic basket that she planned to drag down the stairs to their laundry room two floors below, when she heard a soft knock at her door. She paused, looked over her shoulder at the closed door, and took a deep breath. She knew who was knocking: it was her mother, and the older woman was probably tired of waiting to give the lecture she had undoubtedly been itching to give all day.

"Lee? *Lee?*" Diane said from the hallway, knocking again. "Lee, I know you hear me!"

Leila gnawed her bottom lip, wondering, if she stayed quiet long enough, whether her mother would go away.

She couldn't put into words how humiliated she had been to have her mother stumble upon her and Evan in bed together. Seeing the look of horror and disappointment on the older woman's face had caused whatever

feelings of joy and ecstasy Leila had had at that moment to evaporate. Instead, she had felt an overwhelming, almost crippling sense of shame.

After Evan put on his clothes and left, she had shut
her bedroom door and sat on the edge of the bed for almost an hour, staring at nothing. She didn't go to work
that day. She had barely left her room. She saw that
Evan had called her cell phone more than once, but she
didn't answer. She told herself that she needed to be
alone, that she needed to think things over, but the
truth was that she was hiding. She was hiding from
Evan and she was hiding from the woman on the other
side of her door who wouldn't take Leila's silence as a
cue to leave.

"I'll just keep knocking until you answer, Lee," her
mother called. "Open up!"

Leila sighed and finally trudged across the carpet to
her door. She slowly opened it and found her mother
standing in the hall with her arms crossed over her
chest.

"If you made me wait any longer, I would have to
beat that damn door down," Diane said.

"I know." Leila turned away and kicked her basket
aside and out of her mother's path. "Believe me—I
know."

"It's a little after one o'clock. You didn't come
down for breakfast or lunch. You gonna stay holed up
here forever?"

"If I have to," Leila muttered before tossing a
sweater into the laundry basket.

Diane raised a brow and walked further into the
bedroom. "You avoiding something?"

"Maybe."

"Like what?"

Leila pursed her lips, wondering why her mother

was drawing this out. "Oh, I don't know, Mama. Maybe, the lecture I have coming to me."

"You think I'm going to lecture you?"

"I don't think you are; I *know* you are. You're going to tell me that I shouldn't be having an affair with a married man. You're going to tell me that you raised me better than this. You're going to tell me that—"

Diane sucked her teeth. "I wasn't gonna say any of those things. Shows how much you know."

Leila paused, now confused. "What do you mean?"

"You're a grown woman, Lee. If you are happy with what you're doing with that man, nothing I can say can stop you. If this is what you really want, so be it."

Leila stared at her mother, now wondering if the older woman was trying to trick her into confessing something. "So you're . . . you're saying you're fine with what Ev and I are doing?"

"Oh no!" Diane quickly shook her head. "I didn't say that! I said the decision is yours. If you're okay with being what some folks in town always thought you would be, then"—Diane shrugged—"that's up to you."

Leila frowned. "What some folks thought I would be . . ."

"Uh-huh," Diane said, taking a step toward her daughter. "Since you and Evan were old enough to know what love is, Evan was in love with you, but some jealous folks out there didn't think you two stood a real chance of being together. I heard it myself once from a woman at church. You remember Miss Ida?"

Leila nodded, now even more confused by the direction this conversation was going. "Vaguely. She always wore those leopard-print hats, right?"

"That's the one! Miss Ida was supposed to be a Christian—or at least that's what she called herself even though she could say some mean and hateful things sometimes."

Diane walked to the foot stool at the end of Leila's bed and sat down. She crossed her legs primly at the ankles.

"One day, that woman showed her true colors, but she didn't know I was standing by listening. Miss Ida saw you and Evan walking down the aisle together at First Good Samaritan, collecting the donation baskets and whispering and laughing to one another. You two were no more than fourteen, maybe fifteen years old—just kids. That hateful woman turned to her friends and said, 'I wonder does that girl know that's the only time she's ever gonna walk down the aisle with a Murdoch. Leila White can smile up in that boy's face all she wants. The most she can ever hope for is being one of their whores.'"

At those words, Leila felt as if she had been punched in the gut.

"I wanted to slap the teeth out her mouth, Lee. I wanted to yank that leopard hat *and* that cheap wig right off her head, and probably would have if we weren't inside a church. I caught up with her later though, when she was handing out cake at one of the church picnics. I pulled that heffa aside and I pointed my finger right in her face and I said, 'How *dare* you? How dare you use my daughter's name and that word in the same sentence! My daughter would never, ever agree to be any man's whore, *even* a Murdoch's! And if I ever hear you talk about my child like that again, I'm going to yank you into the parking lot and its gonna be me and you battling it out, old woman!' She must've believed me because she never said it again."

Leila gazed at her mother in shock. She gaped. "I-I didn't know that."

"Of course, you didn't! Why would I tell you? I wanted to protect you from that hurt, that venom. You didn't deserve to be called a whore." Diane abruptly narrowed her eyes and twisted her mouth in disgust. "But I can't say that anymore. You made yourself into what that woman thought you would be. You made her right and you made me a liar, Lee."

Leila swallowed the lump that had formed in her throat. She shook her head. "I'm not . . . I'm not his whore, Mama."

"You could've fooled me from what I saw this morning."

"We're in love! Evan *cares* about me," Leila insisted, though her voice was trembling.

Diane jumped up from the footstool to glare at her daughter. "How much does he care? Does he care enough to tell the world how much he loves you? Does he care enough to leave his wife?"

"He can't do that. He has too much at stake! It's not that simple! He could—"

"Yes, it is! It's as simple as that. Any man who puts you on his payroll so that you're beholden to him—"

"It's not like that."

"—who asks you to sneak around so that you can't even tell your own mama what's going on—"

"I told you, it's not like that! He hasn't asked me to do anything!"

"—doesn't love you. Or at least, he doesn't love you like a man *should* love you, honey. He needs to stand up. He needs to be a man, a *real* man! And you need to be enough of a woman to say you don't deserve any less from him!"

Leila closed her eyes and dropped her face into her hands. She slumped back onto her bed, from which she had already removed the sheets that she and Evan had slept on only hours earlier.

"I can't ask him that. His family, his name, his reputation . . . it means so much to him. It's been drilled into him for . . . forever. I can't ask him to toss all that aside for me."

Diane gazed at Leila evenly. She walked toward her and pulled the younger woman's hands from her face so that they stared into one another's eyes.

"Then don't, Lee," Diane whispered. "But don't let him ask you to push aside everything that's important to you either. Don't forget the woman that you are just to make him happy."

At that, Leila's stomach clenched. Her mother was right. Dear God, she was right! All this time, Leila had been deluding herself into believing differently. She had told herself not to ask questions, to put off all misgivings and doubts and just go with the moment. But she couldn't do that anymore. She had to accept the truth: her affair with Evan had to end.

"Morning, Leila!" the perky younger woman called as Leila darted past the stainless-steel receptionist desk on the twelfth floor of Murdoch Conglomerated.

Leila almost tripped on the C-suite's plush carpet, startled by the sudden greeting.

"Oh, hi! G-g-good morning, Emily," she stuttered. She then adjusted her purse strap and shifted the empty cardboard box she held so that it was now mostly hidden behind her back.

"We missed you yesterday!" Emily gushed. "Were you out sick?"

"Uh, yeah." Leila did a fake cough and motioned to her throat. "I, uh . . . I had a little cold."

"Oh, that's a bummer." The receptionist shifted her headset aside. "Melanie had her retirement party. You missed an awesome cake! They got it from that nice shop downtown. It had three layers and one was tiramisu or something like that. Or was it hazelnut?" She tapped her cleft chin thoughtfully. "It had this weird flavor that—"

"You don't say," Leila muttered, glancing at her office door. "Look, I should get going."

Emily nodded and waved her hand. "Sorry. Listen to me jabber when you've probably got plenty of work to do," the young woman said with a laugh. "I won't keep you. Catch you later, Leila."

"See you later," Leila echoed, though that was a lie.

If it was up to her, she might never see Emily again—save for when she made her way back to the elevators to leave Murdoch Conglomerated for good. Leila hoped to have her desk packed and her letter of resignation waiting on Evan's desk in less than a half an hour. She hoped to be out of this building and driving away before his driver pulled into his reserved space in the parking garage.

"Morning, Lee!" the assistant director of marketing called.

"Hey, Leila!" someone else said as she passed.

Leila winced and lowered her eyes, waving awkwardly to the company staffers who called out their greetings, trying her best not to get sucked into any more conversations that could cost her time.

She glanced at her watch and felt perspiration form on her brow when she realized another minute had ticked by, another minute that drew her closer to Evan's arrival.

Gotta speed this up, she thought.

She knew she was handling this the cowardly way.

She was avoiding confrontation with Evan, slinking out the back door with her tail between her legs. But what was she supposed to do? What could she possibly say that wouldn't make him angry at her, that wouldn't seem like she was giving him an ultimatum?

It's either me or your marriage, Evan. It's either me or your precious reputation.

But she wouldn't tell him that. She couldn't. So rather than give him a choice, she was making the decision for them. She was walking away with that little part of her soul intact.

He would be hurt by her decision, maybe even furious—at first. But later, he would see the wisdom in it. He would know she had had only the best of intentions.

With that resolved, Leila's guilt abated a little. She decided to focus less on Evan and more on packing. She entered her office and quickly assessed her desk, determining at a glance what to trash, what to pack, and what to leave behind since it was rightfully company property. She sat aside the envelope containing her typed and signed resignation letter and placed the cardboard box in the seat of her rollaway chair. She quickly began to gather pictures—three of Isabel and one old photo of her mother—and placed them in the box. Next she dumped in a crystal paperweight and pen holder. Just as she grabbed her stapler, she heard the door open behind her. She turned, startled, to find Evan standing in his doorway.

Leila dropped the stapler to the floor with a clatter. She gaped. "Wh-what are you d-doing here?" she asked, whipping around to face him, bumping into her desk.

"What do you mean, what am I doing here? I came in early to prep for the eight o'clock meeting with Wendell Foods."

When she continued to stare at him blankly, he raised his brows. "You don't remember the meeting with Wendell Foods? The one *you* scheduled?"

"N-no, I don't."

I've been a little preoccupied lately, Ev.

"What are you doing anyway?"

She followed the path of his gaze to her half-filled cardboard box. "I . . . well, I . . ."

Her words faded. She couldn't say it. This wasn't how this was supposed to happen. He wasn't supposed to come in for another hour! He wasn't supposed to see this!

Leila watched as Evan stepped closer to her desk, leaned down, and picked up the fallen stapler. He placed it on her desktop beside the envelope that had his name scribbled on top. He picked up the envelope. "What's this?"

Standing before him, watching his confusion, all her resolve faltered. She helplessly shook her head. Her eyes began to water. "You weren't supposed to be here," she whispered softly.

And that's when he knew. She could see the realization of what she was doing dawning on him like a curtain on a window suddenly being drawn back, revealing the landscape on the other side of the glass. But this landscape was desolate and empty, sad and barren. That was what overwhelmed her as he raised his eyes from the envelope and stared at her. She saw a myriad of emotions flash across his face—shock, hurt, disappointment, and finally, anger.

His lips tightened. She watched as the muscles along his jaw rippled. "Come into my office," he said, clutching the envelope in his fist. He turned and shoved the door open.

"Ev, I—"

"Inside!" he barked and she winced. Even one of the other secretaries who happened to be walking by paused and stared at Evan, stunned. He didn't usually talk to anyone, let alone Leila, that way.

He stalked inside and toward his desk and Leila followed him reluctantly, feeling her heart thud wildly in her chest, feeling weak in the knees. She kept her eyes downcast, unable to meet his furious gaze any longer.

"Close the door," he ordered and she followed his command like she had so many times in the past. But unlike those other times, Evan wasn't about to rush across the room to hold her close or to steal a kiss. Right now, he radiated no warmth.

She had felt this coldness before when he refused to ever talk to her again during that phone call ten years ago. She wondered if that was about to happen all over again.

But what did she expect? For him to say, "*Sure, Lee, I understand if you want to break it off. Don't worry. We can still be besties!*"

No, he wouldn't let her off that easily. She realized the full scope of what was about to happen. She wasn't just ending an affair with her lover; she was also about to lose her best friend all over again.

Leila watched as he started to pace in front of his desk.

"I *knew* something was up! You didn't come into the office yesterday. You didn't return any of my phone calls. I figured with your mother walking in on us that you needed to work through some things, that you may need some time. But this . . ." He paused from his pacing, held up the envelope, and furiously shook his head. "I never expected any shit like this!"

"I'm so . . . so sorry. Really I am, but . . . I can't . . . I can't do this anymore, Ev."

"Do what?" He tossed the envelope onto his desk before turning to glare at her. "Do what, Lee? Work for me? Have sex with me? *What?*" he yelled.

"All of it! All of it, Ev!" She finally raised her eyes and took a step toward him. "I have to quit my job. I have to end this, *all* of this!" She pointed to the envelope. "In there is my letter of resignation and . . . and a check for the next two months of rent."

"You think I care about a fucking check?"

"Look, I know we're moving out with little notice, but I wanted to make sure that—"

"Do you really think I want your goddamn money?" he boomed.

She didn't respond. She didn't know what to say.

"Did your mom put you up to this? Did she give you some guilt trip and say what we were doing was wrong so that changed everything that you felt about us, about *me?*"

"She didn't put me up to anything! She reminded me of who I am . . . of who we used to be." Leila took a deep breath and shook her head again. "We're better than this. It's time to admit that we made a mistake."

"A mistake?" He looked hurt all over again. "So me being in love with you was a mistake?"

"You know that's not what I meant."

"So you just . . . you just want to wash your hands of all of it? You want to act like none of this ever happened. Act like you never loved me . . . *if* you ever loved me!"

"Damn it, Evan, I do love you! Don't you get it? That's why I'm doing this!"

The tears that had been pooling in her eyes finally spilled onto her cheeks. She wiped at them with the backs of her hands. "I want to be with you. I want it more than . . . than anything." She took another step toward him so that now he was within her reach. "I look at you sometimes and I think, 'He's mine and I'm his.' No one can tell me any different. We've been friends since we were kids. You know more about me than any other human being on this earth. We've shared a bed together. We've made love, told each other our deepest, darkest secrets. Except for Izzy, you're the most important person in this world to me."

She raised her hand to his cheek, preparing herself for him to pull away from her touch. But he didn't. Instead, he met her gaze and she ached because she saw so much pain in his eyes.

"But despite all that, the truth is that you aren't mine and I'm not yours. You're married to someone else. Charisse is your wife and I'm just . . ." The tears were falling more profusely now. They were coming too fast to wipe them away. "I'm just your mistress. And I can't be that anymore. I can't be one of your deep, dark secrets. It's not right," she said, dropping her hand from his face.

"So what are you asking me to do? To announce to everyone that we're having an affair, to divorce Charisse? You want me to bring ruin to my family, to the company?"

"No, that's not what I'm asking. I know how . . . how important those things are to you. I wouldn't ask you to do that."

And that was the part that hurt the most—that she knew not to even bother to ask Evan because it was totally out of the question. Despite how much he professed to love her, she knew she was a risk he would never take.

Leila turned away from him then and headed back toward his office door. She paused when her eyes fell on the portrait of George Murdoch less than ten fee away. The old man looked like he was watching her as she retreated. He seemed almost smug.

I knew you two would ever end up together, his arrogant stare said. *You were fools to ever think you would have your happily ever after.*

I guess you were right, you heartless son of a bitch, she thought.

"So if you're not asking me to get a divorce, then what are you asking, Lee?" Evan suddenly said as she wrapped her hand around the door handle. "Please tell me. Because I don't . . . I don't understand. What do you want from me? Tell me what you want!"

"I want you not to hate me . . . even after I walk away," she murmured before opening his door, walking out of his office, and out of his life.

Chapter 22

PAULETTE

Paulette sat in the driveway of her home with the engine running, gazing at darkened windows of the beautiful colonial she shared with her husband. She turned off the engine, removed the keys from the ignition, slumped back onto the leather seat, and closed her eyes. In the silence of the car's interior, she heard nothing but the thudding of her own heartbeat—by far the loneliest sound she had ever heard. Her lashes dampened with unshed tears. Her chin trembled as she bit down hard on her bottom lip, holding back her sobs.

She wished the ground would open up and swallow her whole.

Paulette had sworn to herself that she wouldn't grow up to be like her mother: a doormat who was ignored by the people she loved, and dominated by the men in her life—first and foremost, Paulette's father, George. But not only had Paulette grown up to be like her mother, she had managed to surpass the woman's legacy of servitude and misery.

Paulette felt like the world's biggest fool for falling into Marques's trap and allowing herself to be black-mailed. And now that he had nearly all the money he needed from her for his sham business, he used her al-most exclusively for sex. Every time she left his apart-ment after doing some sexual favor for him, she felt dirty—so dirty that a thousand showers wouldn't make her feel clean again. Whenever she closed her eyes, she'd see Marques looming and leering over her, feel his mouth on his skin, or the weight of his body on top of hers and she'd cringe at the flashbacks, nearly sick to her stomach.

She was locked in an invisible prison, and she had no idea when or how she would ever get out of it.

"You did this to yourself," she whispered. "It's a prison of your own making."

But knowing this didn't make her feel any better. It just made her want to scream. It made her want to slit her wrists.

"Don't think that way," the little voice in her head encouraged. "If you found your way in, you can find your way out. Think positive. Think positive!"

She wanted to think positive, but it felt more and more like a silly mantra. How could she be optimistic when her life was so bleak?

After taking a deep breath, Paulette finally climbed out of the car. A minute later, she was pushing open the front door to her home. She turned on the light near the door and gazed around their empty foyer. She sup-posed her husband was either in his office or in his man cave in the basement, where he often went nowa-days. She dropped her gym bag to the hardwood floor and started to hang up her jacket when she heard the sound of a throat being cleared. She turned to find An-tonio standing in the entryway of their living room.

"You're home late," he said, leaning against the door frame.

"I-I am?"

He nodded as he walked toward her. He was still in his work clothes. His silk tie was loosened. The sleeves of his lavender dress shirt were rolled up to his forearms.

"Yeah, it's nine o'clock. You're usually back home from the gym by eight at the latest."

"Oh? Well, uh . . . Daniel tried out this new routine tonight. It's really intense, but he says it gets good results. I guess it . . . it took longer than I thought." She laughed anxiously.

That wasn't true, of course. She hadn't worked out with her trainer Daniel tonight. She hadn't been to the gym in weeks. Instead, she had spent a good two hours in bed with Marques tonight until—satiated—he finally drifted off to sleep. When she'd heard his loud snores, she'd eased out of bed, grabbed her clothes, quickly dressed, and rushed out of his apartment before he could wake up and make another "demand" of her.

"Sorry, I'm so late. I-I hope you weren't waiting for me," she now whispered to Antonio.

"Actually, I was." He took another step toward her and shoved his hands into his pockets. "We need to talk, baby."

Paulette stilled. Her pulse quickened. So it was finally happening. Antonio was going to confront her about the distance that had grown between them and all the nights she'd arrived home late. He probably suspected that she was having an affair, but the truth was even worse than he imagined.

"S-sure," she stuttered nervously, trembling like a

leaf in a strong wind. "What did you . . . what did you want to talk about?"

His handsome face broke into a gentle smile. "I have something to show you first." He extended his hand to her and her anxiety instantly disappeared.

"Something to show me?"

He nodded. "Yeah, come on."

She took his hand and let him lead her through their living room and into their dining room. When she saw their dining room table, she breathed in audibly. It was covered with fine white linen, silver-lidded dishes, and two table settings that included crystal stemware and fine china. A bouquet of roses sat next to one of the settings. The lights in the glass chandelier were turned down low so the only light in the dining room came from two candelabras at each end of the table and one sitting on the sideboard.

"I know we've been going through some things lately," he said as he pulled out one of the table chairs. He then picked up the bouquet and handed it to her. "I admit that we've . . . well, we've had some issues. But I want to try to make things right, baby."

She gazed at him, now struck speechless.

"I thought a candlelight dinner might help. I didn't know for sure when you were getting home so I didn't schedule reservations somewhere. Mama said she would cook it for us." He began to walk around the table, removing lids from the dishes, revealing a Cornish hen, a platter of greens, red potatoes, and corn. "I let her pick the menu. My only rule was no sticky buns," he said, laughing awkwardly at his own joke. He gestured to the seat again. "So go ahead. Sit down."

Paulette took the flowers he handed to her and cradled them against her chest. She stared at the table and the chair he held out for her and slowly shook her head as her vision began to blur with tears. She couldn't hold them back anymore. The dam broke and the tears spilled onto her cheeks like a ceaseless river.

"I'm sorry," she whispered. "I'm so . . . *so* sorry, Tony."

"Sorry for what, baby?" He walked toward her and embraced her. In his loving arms, her sobs only got worse. "Honey, what's wrong?"

"I messed up. I messed up so bad!" she cried, wetting his shirt with her tears. "I'm sorry!"

He rubbed her back soothingly. "Listen to me. Listen to me, okay? You didn't mess up, baby! We just hit a bump. That's all. We're good! I swear we're good."

But they weren't "good." She knew that for a fact. If what they had previously been going through was "just a bump," their marriage was officially a five-car pileup now—and it was all because of her mistakes. She was giving Marques thousands upon thousands of dollars and having an affair with him. It wouldn't matter to Antonio that she was being blackmailed into doing it, or that she loathed Marques. It wouldn't matter that she closed her eyes, gritted her teeth, and prayed for it to be over whenever Marques climbed on top of her. It would only matter to her husband that she was sharing her body with another man, that she had broken her wedding vows.

Paulette had been afraid before about what Antonio would do if he found out about her decade-old abortion. She could only imagine what he would do if he found out what she had done only an hour ago. He'd scream at her. He'd hurl her bags out the door. He would hate her.

"Listen to me. Stop crying," Antonio urged, blissfully unaware of his wife's transgressions. He eased her away from him and gazed into her eyes. "So what if we argue? So what if we fight? I love you, baby! *Nothing* is going to change that!"

If only that were true, she thought sadly.

"I love you too," she whispered, closing her reddened eyes. "I love you so much."

His arms tightened around her again and he leaned down to kiss her. When their lips met, she shied away from him, unconsciously reminded of Marques's lips, of being wrapped in his embrace. Her eyes flashed open to find Antonio frowning down at her worriedly.

"What's wrong?" he asked.

"N-nothing. Nothing."

She stood on the balls of her feet and kissed her husband again, forcing herself not to pull away, reminding herself that she was with Antonio—not Marques. These were Antonio's arms, lips, and hands. She loved her husband. She wanted him to touch her and caress her. But it wasn't easy. Marques kept intruding on her thoughts like a malevolent phantom. And when the kiss deepened and she could feel Antonio's hand cradling one of her breasts, the flashbacks to Marques became even more vivid.

Could Antonio sense that she had been touched by another man? Did Marques's cologne still linger on her or some other manly smell that would give away her secret?

Antonio shifted her, easing her back onto an empty spot on the dining room table. He stood between her parted legs. As he tugged her tank top over her head, her mind flashed to Marques roughly tugging her bra straps off her shoulders. As he eased her yoga pants over her hips and down her legs, she remembered Marques yanking down the same pair of pants and shoving her back onto his mattress.

Antonio continued to kiss her, even as he eased the crotch of her panties aside and lowered the zipper of his slacks. When he entered her, she cried out. She tensed, her body going rigid with unease. She squirmed uncomfortably on the table and whimpered against his lips.

He abruptly pulled out of her. "Baby, what's wrong?" he asked again, this time sounding impatient. "Do you not want to do this?"

She was frustrating him. She could tell. And frankly, she was frustrating herself too.

"Nothing is wrong, Tony. I swear."

He looked doubtful so she cupped his face and kissed him. She wrapped her legs around his waist, drawing him back to her. "Everything is . . . is fine. Please . . . keep going. Don't stop."

He hesitated but finally kissed her again and she met his tongue with her own. She ran her hands along his back. She pressed her breasts against his chest, all the while silently repeating to herself, *Relax. It's Tony. Relax. It's just Tony!*

It worked. Within minutes, Antonio's fervor had returned and he became lost in the thrill of moment. Unfortunately, Paulette didn't share his zeal. Every impulse told her to shove her husband away, but she valiantly kept those impulses at bay. When he entered her again, her mind instantly shifted to its new default whenever she had sex. She closed her eyes, braced her hands on the edge of the table—and waited for it to be over. As he pumped and ground against her, her mind went blank. She wasn't there anymore.

Later, Paulette and Antonio lay in bed together under their crisp, newly washed linens. In the old days, after they had made love in the dining room, they would have done it again in the living room or even the kitchen and finally ended up in their bedroom, but not tonight. Paulette had no desire to make love again. Perhaps Antonio had sensed it and he hadn't bothered to ask.

Unable to sleep, Paulette now stared in the dark at the glowing number on her night table clock. Antonio cradled her from behind, breathing softly into her ear. Her mind was a riot of thoughts that refused to be quieted even though she was both physically and mentally exhausted.

"You can't go on like this," the loudest voice in her head said. "Something's got to give. You have to tell someone what's—"

"Are we good now?" Antonio suddenly whispered, interrupting her thoughts and startling her.

She thought he had fallen asleep more than an hour ago. She shifted slightly so she could turn to look at him. In the darkness of their bedroom, only the whites of his eyes were faintly visible.

She placed her hand on his shoulder and rubbed it. "Of course we're good now."

He paused. "Then why doesn't it feel like we are?"

"I-I don't know what you mean, Tony," she lied.

He waited another beat, shook his head, and murmured, "Never mind."

She watched helplessly as he turned over, turned his back to her, and finally went to sleep.

Chapter 23
EVAN

"Come in," Evan murmured at the sound of knocking. He barely looked up from his laptop screen and didn't quit furiously typing on his keyboard even when his brother peered around the edge of his office door.

"So he lives and breathes!" Terrence exclaimed, striding confidently into Evan's office. He shut the door behind him. "I was wondering if you were still alive! I haven't heard from your ass in more than a week. I was about to send a P.I. after you!"

Evan didn't seem to notice Terrence's playful chiding. He didn't even pause from his typing to glance up at his brother. "What do you want?"

"Damn! Is that how you're saying hi nowadays?" Terrence flopped back onto the sofa and propped up his long legs on the glass coffee table, a move that would have pissed off Evan in the past, but he ignored it today. Terrence leaned back against one of the leather cushions and laced his fingers behind his head. "No wonder you can't keep an assistant."

At that, Evan did stop typing. He looked up from his screen and glared at his brother. "Don't test me, Terry," he said with a subzero iciness. "Today is the wrong goddamn day."

Actually, the past several days had been the "wrong goddamn day"—make that the past few weeks!

Most on the twelfth floor of Murdoch Conglomerated knew not to bother the company's young CEO with their questions or concerns, to stay out of his way and even his periphery if they knew what was good for them. Because Evan Murdoch was in a bad mood—the *worst* mood that anyone had seen in quite a long time. Gone were the days where he said, "Good morning," as he passed. Gone were pleasant inquiries about someone's wife or new baby. He was all business now—short, cold, and straight to the point. It was like a dark spell had been cast over him, siphoning out all his kindness.

Even Charisse had noticed the change in him. "What the hell's gotten into you lately?" she had asked during one of the rare nights he ate dinner at home.

"Nothing," he had murmured before returning his attention to his halibut.

Few knew the source of his sudden chilliness. Some wondered if maybe a big contract Murdoch Conglomerated was banking on had fallen through. Others speculated that maybe one of the VPs had left the company and gone to work for the competition. Or maybe it was the fact that yet another one of his personal assistants had quit, leaving him high and dry. Yes, maybe that was the culprit of his bad mood.

But only Terrence knew the truth. He knew how much Evan missed Leila. Terrence knew that Evan had spent almost a week calling her, emailing her, and texting her—practically *begging* her to talk to him and take him back, but to no avail. All messages had gone unanswered. Finally, Evan had taken the hint and stopped calling.

She and her family had packed up their things and moved out of the rental two weeks ago. After that, the only communication Evan had received from Leila was an impersonal postcard with her forwarding address.

That's why Terrence's little comment about not being able to keep an assistant felt like the ultimate betrayal, a stab to the gut when Evan was already lying on the ground bleeding.

"If you just came here to be an asshole, Terry, you can leave now," Evan said, sliding back from his desk. "I don't need it."

"No, you *do* need it! You need someone to finally call you on your shit, Ev! Unlike everyone else around here who's scared to talk to you, I'm not scared. I'm going to tell you the truth. I don't give a damn. You want to hear it? Here it is: this misery is all of your own making. You're in the situation because of the decisions you made. That's the God's honest truth!"

"And what decisions would those be?" Evan asked as he rose from his chair.

It sounded like a challenge, but it really was an honest question that he would love to have someone answer. Could someone tell him how this had happened? How had things gone so wrong?

Evan had spent almost a month wondering why Leila had ended their affair. He'd thought they were in love. He'd thought they were happy. Their arrangement hadn't been the best, but even she had told him not to obsess over it, to focus on the here and now.

At first, Evan had placed the blame for their breakup squarely in Diane White's lap, faulting the older woman with Leila's sudden change of heart.

If that meddling old bitch would have just minded her own goddamn business Lee and I would still be together, he had thought in his darker moments.

But Evan knew better. Criticism from her mother wouldn't have been enough to lead Leila to do what she had done. She must have been thinking about this for a long time. She had to have been harboring doubts but never voiced them aloud. If she hadn't broken it off that day, she would have done it eventually.

Of course, none of this took away Evan's heartbreak. Knowing that their affair had been doomed from the start didn't take away the crippling disappointment that came with knowing that you had once had in your hands everything you had ever wanted, only to have it slip away.

"I've been telling you for months . . . hell, for *years*, to end it with Charisse, man." Terrence leaned forward. All traces of humor had left his handsome face. "If you want Lee back, you know what you have to do. All you have to do is—"

"Damn it, I can't! You know I can't! It's not that simple. Charisse would . . . she would *slaughter* me in divorce court!"

"You don't know that for sure," Terry argued, vehemently shaking his head. "You can get just as many high-priced lawyers as she can! You could—"

"Terry, come on!" Evan stepped around his desk and strode across his office to stand squarely in front of his brother. "Charisse thought I was fucking Leila even when nothing was going on between us," he said, dropping his voice down to almost a whisper. "What the hell do you think will happen if I start walking around in public with Lee on my arm, if people realize we're together? You honestly think Charisse wouldn't bring that shit up in court?"

"If she brings up Lee, then you bring up her screwing around on you!"

"But I don't know if Charisse is screwing around; I just *think* she is. I can't prove it! But my affair would be for the world to see! They'd just see me as some rich, philandering asshole who wants to offload his wife." He took a deep breath. His shoulders slumped. "If Charisse could get a judge to side with her, she could get half of everything, including my share of the company. Do you want that?"

"Of course I don't! But you can't keep using the company and the family as an excuse."

"It's not an excuse! It's—"

"Yes, it is! You've hidden behind this 'I'm the responsible one. I'm the one who meets my obligations,' way too long. Dad put that burden on you, and even though he's dead, you keep lugging it around like a sack of bricks. Let it go, Ev," Terrence pleaded as he gazed into his brother's eyes. "The company will survive. Paulette and I will survive, if the worst-case scenario happens. It won't be the end of the world. Trust me. We know you've wanted Lee for forever. Do what you gotta do to get her."

Evan stared at his brother, at a loss for words. He stepped back and watched as Terrence slowly rose to his feet.

"Look, I'm tired of talking about this. I'm tired of seeing you like this too. The 'Grinch who stole Christmas' routine is getting old," Terrence muttered. "Just make a fucking decision and stick with it. Make the sacrifice you need to make and go after her. Or stay married to Medusa and shut the fuck up about it. But don't act like you don't have a choice, because you do!"

He then stepped around Evan and headed to the office door.

Evan didn't watch his brother leave. Instead, he walked toward the floor-to-ceiling windows, shoved his hands into his pockets, and gazed at the view below. His eyes scanned the sparkling water of the Potomac River, the myriad sailboats and the occasional cruise ship that went by, and the power plant on the D.C. side of the river.

Could Terrence be right? Had Evan really wasted all this time keeping up pretenses and trying to avoid losing everything only to end up losing what he wanted the most—a life with Leila? His family name, his legacy had been so important to Evan for so long. Had he been dumb to put so much stock in them?

Evan sighed and pressed his forehead against the cool glass, hoping that it would quell his now-throbbing head.

Could he do it? Could he risk the scandal and the hit his reputation and livelihood could take if he decided to stop pretending and admit his marriage was a sham? Could he *finally* walk away? Years ago, he had been bold enough to take such risks. Of course that was before he got married, became the head of the family and company CEO, and became burdened with so many albatrosses around his neck he could barely hold his head up. But could he be bold like that again?

Evan raised his forehead from the glass. For a moment, he felt like the window in front of him had disappeared. Instead was the vastness of the river a thousand feet below him and the blue sky hundreds of thousands of feet above him. All he had to do was take one step forward and he would plunge into the unknown. And Evan felt finally ready to do just that.

*   *   *

The instant the driver pulled to a stop in the circular driveway in front of Evan's home, Evan took a deep, trembling breath. He fidgeted anxiously in the Town Car's backseat, telling himself that he was making the right decision, that telling Charisse he wanted a divorce was a bold and smart move. Of course, he could do all this and find out that Leila *still* wouldn't take him back, but that couldn't be his focus right now. He had to see this through, despite the aftermath.

He could have asked for a divorce by phone, but something like this seemed more appropriate to do in person. When he told Charisse that he wanted to end their mutual misery, he wanted to do it to her face—not hiding behind his BlackBerry.

He had left the office abruptly, canceling all his meetings for the rest of the day. He didn't want to save this for the evening. He wanted to do it as quickly as possible, before he lost his nerve. Because Charisse rarely roused before noon, it was a pretty safe bet she was at home. Evan glanced at his watch. She had probably just stumbled out of bed only a half hour ago. But if she had already left for the day, he'd wait for her to return. There seemed to be little alternative at this point.

"Sorry that I can't pull all the way up to the front door, Mr. Murdoch," the driver called over his shoulder from the front seat. "There seems to be a car blocking the entrance, sir."

Evan looked out the window and instantly recognized the car parallel parked in front of stone steps leading to the mansion's French doors. It was Dante's silver Jag.

"What's Dante doing here?" Evan muttered aloud as the driver climbed out and walked toward the back passenger door.

Five minutes later, Evan walked down the silent corridor that led to his wife's bedroom in the east wing. She had moved to this part of the mansion two years ago, when they officially started sleeping separately. Evan hadn't kicked her out of their bedroom; she had made the request to move out.

"If we aren't having sex, why bother sharing a bed?" she had spat before storming out one night in a huff.

Whenever he went to this part of the mansion, it felt like he was walking into a separate apartment.

Evan looked around him. He still hadn't spotted Dante, and as he neared the bedroom door he realized why.

"You want this? You want this?" he heard Dante bark.

"Yes! Oh, God, yes!" Charisse yelled in response, making Evan's hand pause near the brass door knob.

His heartbeat quickened. His eyes widened. He turned the knob—surprised to find the door wasn't locked—and stepped inside his wife's bedroom.

The lovers weren't in the four-poster bed, though it was obvious they had been at some point. The sheets were thrown back and the pillows were askew. Charisse's robe dangled over the headboard. Dante's pants lay crumpled on the floor near the foot of the bed. Evan walked silently across the room's plush carpet and glanced in the trash can near her night table. A knotted, used condom lay at the bottom along with a torn packet.

Well, at least they're using condoms, he thought dryly. *Better safe than sorry.*

He continued unhurried to Charisse's bathroom, where the moans and yelling were a lot louder. He slowly pushed open the door and found the couple in the shower stall. Charisse was pressed back against the tiled wall, screaming in ecstasy, closing her eyes as the rainfall showerhead poured water into her face. She was being held in the air by Dante, who was pounding into her and moaning and grunting like some water buffalo.

Evan inclined his head as he watched them. He had suspected Charisse was having an affair, but he'd had no idea with whom. Now he knew it was with his own brother.

Instead of being overtaken with rage that his wife was having an affair with Dante, instead of wanting to beat Dante into a pulp for the betrayal, he slowly smiled. He couldn't have arrived home at a more fortuitous time. Now he didn't have to worry about losing everything in a divorce. Charisse was the one who should be worried.

He reached into his suit jacket pocket and pulled out his BlackBerry. He held it up and snapped a few quick pictures of the couple for evidence before tucking the phone back into his pocket. Evan then raised his hand and loudly rapped his knuckles against the bathroom door. It sounded like a gun being fired in the echoing bathroom. "So I see Dante decided to pay a visit!" he called out.

At the sound of his voice, Charisse's eyes shot open. Evan almost laughed at the look of horror she gave him through the foggy shower glass. Dante abruptly whipped around, still holding Charisse. He lost his balance on the slippery, wet glass tile and dropped her before falling to his knees. They both cried out in pain.

Dante scrambled to his feet first, leaving Charisse sprawled on the shower floor.

"This . . . this isn't what it looks like," he said and Evan couldn't hold back his laughter any longer.

"Really? Because it looks like you were fucking my wife!"

"Oh, like you give a damn," Charisse grumbled, finally pushing herself from her knees to stand beside Dante. She pushed her tangled, wet hair out of her face. She reached beside her and turned off the faucet, then shoved the shower stall door open and groped for a towel hanging on a chrome rod. "So what if he's fucking me! It's not like you want to!"

"Shut up, Charisse," Dante whispered fiercely.

"No, Dante, it's the truth!" She wrapped the white towel around her, then turned her cool blue eyes on her husband. "So what? So what if you caught us? News flash, Evan! We've been having an affair for almost a year now!"

"Shut *up*, Charisse!" Dante said. He then turned to his brother. "Evan, she doesn't—"

"Don't worry. I know my husband. He's not going to do a damn thing. He's just going to turn around, shut the door behind him, and pretend like none of this ever happened."

Evan raised his brows. "You think so?"

"I know so! If I've been playing the role of your wife the last five years—as you claim, then you've also been playing the role of my husband. We keep pretending that everything is perfect, that we're a happy couple. But that's why you married me, right?" she asked, stepping out of the shower. She walked across the bathroom and glared up at Evan. "I'm willing to put on an act. I'm the perfect wife to have on your arm so everyone thinks Evan Murdoch is so goddamn wonderful." She sniffed and looked him up and down. "If they only knew . . ."

Evan gazed at his wife. How had he managed to stay

in the same room with this woman let alone married to her? She radiated so much contempt! She couldn't even pretend to be ashamed or apologetic about being caught screwing his brother.

Evan watched as she casually walked toward her vanity and grabbed a comb. The whole time, Dante stood awkwardly in the shower stall, like he was unsure of what to do next.

"Why are you home anyway?" she asked as she faced the mirror and began to tug at the tangles in her hair. "Ran out of supplies at the office? Had to come home to get your toothbrush?"

"No," Evan answered flatly, "I came home to tell you I wanted a divorce."

She stopped combing her hair, whipped around from the mirror, and faced him. He could tell from the expression on her face that of all things, she hadn't expected him to say this. "W-w-what?"

"I said I want a divorce. Unlike you, I'm tired of this charade. I had come here to tell you that you could have whatever you wanted just as long as we could make the divorce quick. I was willing to give you the house, alimony . . . anything just so that we could get out of each other's lives as soon as possible. But"—he paused to glance at Dante—"it looks like circumstances have changed." He glared at her again. "I'm not giving you a goddamn penny. I'm keeping everything. You hear that? Every-*fucking*-thing! And you'll be paying my legal fees."

Her face crumbled. Her plump lips twitched. The comb she held tumbled from her hands to the bathroom floor. "You . . . you can't do that!"

"Oh, yes, I can. Read our prenup! You signed on the dotted line just like I did. All the terms were clearly stated." He pointed to Dante. "You're a fucking law-yer. Explain it to her."

Evan then turned on his heel and walked toward the bathroom door.

"See you in court, Charisse!" he called over his shoulder before striding out of the bathroom.

"Evan, wait! Wait!" she yelled shrilly after him, but he didn't stop. Instead, his smile widened into a grin and he kept walking.

Leila stepped back from the cabinet underneath the kitchen sink, examining the contents of the plastic bucket she held. Between the Pine-Sol, heavy-duty anti-bacterial cleanser, Windex, sponges, and toilet brush, she would be able to attack any lingering dirt and grime that had been left behind by the former tenants of apartment 402 at Buena Vista Terrace. More importantly, she could hopefully finally eradicate the phantom smell of cat pee that seemed to be haunting their living room. But she wondered if she would have to buy a heavy-duty carpet scrubber for that one.

"You sure you don't want to come to the movies with us?" her mother asked, walking up behind her. "I heard Beyoncé is the voice of one of the platypuses."

Leila carried her cleaning bucket across the kitchen. She dropped the bucket to the floor to adjust the hand-kerchief on her head. "I don't think even Beyoncé can make me want to spend two hours watching animated platypuses sing, Mama. No, you and Izzy go ahead to the movies without me. Have fun."

"But it would get you out of the house, Lee!" Diane pleaded. "Is this really how you want to spend your weekend . . . scrubbing bathroom and kitchen floors?"

Leila tugged on her rubber gloves. "It needs to be done."

"But don't you want to take a break, honey? You worked hard all week. Get off your feet for once."

Diane was right. Leila had worked hard. She was waitressing again at Dean's Big Burger until she found a better position somewhere else. Her replacement hadn't worked out too well so the manager was elated that Leila wanted her old spot back. Hannah hadn't been as happy to see her old friend though.

"Why the hell are you back here?" Hannah had lamented while Leila tied on her apron. "I thought you had gotten out! You know . . . sailed off to that happy place where people tip you more than a quarter and you don't get varicose veins from standing on your feet all day. I thought you got an office job somewhere."

"It just didn't work out," Leila had whispered in explanation. She hadn't elaborated.

For the past week and a half, Leila had been pulling double shifts to make enough money to pay for rent, though she could pull double shifts and her salary still would come nowhere close to what she had been making while she worked for Evan.

She might have been able to get another job as an executive assistant somewhere else if Evan had written her a recommendation. In one of the many messages he left her, he had offered. He said he'd sign one for her if she would see him, if she would just *talk* to him. She hadn't taken the bait.

She didn't want to see Evan again. She knew if she did, her resolve to end their affair would fade. Hell, it had taken all her willpower, the moment she'd stepped out of his office almost a month ago, not to turn right around and tell him she took it all back.

"I didn't mean it, Ev!" she wanted to tell him. "Being a mistress isn't that bad. As long as we get to be together, what does it matter, right?"

But it did matter. She knew that in her heart. They couldn't continue the status quo. So, to protect herself, she had cut off all contact with Evan, much like he had cut off all contact with her to protect himself several years ago. But she still thought about him—a lot. She did it while she wrote down orders at Dean's Big Burger, while she brushed Isabel's hair before school, and while she lay awake in bed at night, staring at the ceiling because she couldn't sleep, because she wanted to be lying next to him.

"Mommy," Isabel shouted as she rushed into the kitchen, "you coming with us?"

Leila shook her head. "No, baby, Mommy is staying here. I have to clean up this place. But Grandma will take you." She leaned down and kissed her daughter on the brow. "So you make sure you behave yourself and be a good girl. Maybe if you are, Grandma will take you out for ice cream afterward."

Isabel's eyes widened. She jumped up and down on the balls of her feet. "Ice cream! Ice cream! Ice cream!" She instantly turned to her grandmother. "Can we get ice cream, Grandma? I want a strawberry sundae!"

"You heard your mama. We'll have to wait and see." Diane wrapped an arm around Isabel's shoulders and gazed at her daughter. "We better get going if we're gonna make the two o'clock show. Lee, you sure you don't—"

"I'll be fine here," Leila answered before her mother could finish. She made a shooing motion. "You guys go ahead before you miss the previews."

Diane gave her one last hesitant look before ushering Isabel out of the kitchen. Leila could hear them gathering their things as she grabbed a broom and started to sweep the linoleum tiled floor. She glanced over her shoulder just as they opened the front door.

"Bye, Lee!" Diane called out with a wave. "We should be home in a few hours."

"Bye, Mommy!"

"Bye!" Leila called back. Her eyes then zeroed in on an orange wool cardigan hanging on the back of one of the dinette table chairs. "Hey, Izzy, you forgot your . . ."

Her words faded when she heard the door slam shut behind them.

You forgot your sweater, she thought. It was early October and though an Indian summer had kept the temperatures in the mid seventies for the past couple of weeks, it had gotten a lot chillier since Tuesday. Isabel would need her sweater, especially for a cool theater.

Leila sighed. *Oh, well. Maybe they'll realize she needs it and turn around and come back.*

Ten minutes later, as Leila was scrubbing down the kitchen counter, she heard a frantic knock at the door. Leila halted mid swipe. She knew her daughter's knock from anywhere. Diane had probably realized Isabel had left her sweater behind and sent the seven-year-old upstairs to get it. Leila instantly dropped her sponge and ripped off her soapy, wet rubber gloves.

"Coming, honey!" she cried as she walked across

the kitchen and grabbed the sweater. She continued to the front door, unlocked it, and tugged it open. "I was wondering if you . . ."

She couldn't finish. Her heart and stomach plummeted simultaneously when she realized who was waiting for her in the apartment hallway. It wasn't Isabel.

"Hi, Lee," Evan said. He wasn't wearing one of his expensive suits today. Just a T-shirt and jeans, and he couldn't have looked more handsome.

She didn't respond to his greeting. She couldn't. Her tongue felt heavy. Her mouth went dry.

Why was he here? Why was he standing at her front door like it was the most normal thing in the world? Why was he doing this to her?

"Can I come in?" he asked softly.

She slowly nodded then blinked, stopped herself and shook her head. "Evan, y-you can't just . . . why are you—"

"Because I needed to talk to you. I needed to ask you something and I knew if I tried to call or email first, it would go right to voice mail or to your email trash can. I figured I'd be harder to avoid in person."

She wavered, feeling an overwhelming rush of emotions—elation at seeing him again, longing to touch him, and frustration at being so goddamn weak.

"Please, Lee," he said, barely above a whisper and she lost all her defenses. She instantly opened the door further and stepped aside to let him into her home. She wordlessly waved him forward.

He stepped past her into her living room and their shoulders brushed. It was like flicking a tuning fork. Her entire body seemed to vibrate with sexual tension. The longing she felt at seeing him instantly morphed into desire and she wanted to yell at herself, "Snap out of it, Lee!" But she couldn't snap out of it. She shut the door behind him.

"What did you want to ask?"

Leila watched as he turned in a circle. His gaze surveyed the room. His eyes finally settled on her.

"First, I want to tell you that I'm getting a divorce," he said and the instant he did, Leila raised her hand to her mouth in shock. "I've already contacted a lawyer and he filed the paperwork on Wednesday. I'm going to end my marriage, Lee. Charisse and I are done."

"She didn't . . . she didn't find out about us, did she?"

Leila hoped their affair wasn't the reason why he was getting a divorce. She hadn't wanted to put him in that position, for him to put everything at risk. That's why she had walked away in the first place.

"No, she didn't find out about us. Not that it would matter much, considering she's been having an affair with Dante for about a year now."

Leila gaped. *"Dante?* You don't mean your brother Dante, do you?"

Evan nodded. "The one and the same. I ran in on those two in the shower together."

"Oh, my God!"

She was stunned to hear that Charisse and Dante had been having an affair, but then part of her wasn't. Even when she had dated him, there had always seemed to be something off about Dante—like he was hiding something beneath the surface. She also didn't understand his hostility toward his brother Evan. It had seemed to come out of nowhere. Now she knew that hostility was deeper than she'd ever realized.

"But I'm not here to talk about Charisse and Dante. I'm here to talk about us." He cleared his throat and took a step toward her. "When I decided to end my marriage to Charisse, I knew there were no guarantees when it comes . . . well, when it comes to us. I know I asked a lot of you before. I know you're still married and—"

"No, I'm not," she said. This time, he looked surprised.

"What?"

"My divorce was finalized last week. I got the papers in the mail. Brad wants to marry his new girlfriend and I guess she put pressure on him to move things along. He finally signed everything. So I'm not . . . I'm not married. Not anymore."

He stared at her for a long time after that. "Well, that makes what I have to ask you a lot easier than I thought. It feels a little less crazy to ask it." He took a deep breath. "Lee, would you—"

"If you want to try again, the answer is yes," she blurted out, unable to hold in her joy. She couldn't even pretend that she had to think things over. She was well past that point. "I'm willing to give us a second chance if you want to, Ev."

He slowly shook his head. "That wasn't what I was going to ask."

Her breath caught in her throat.

Then what was Evan asking? She doubted he wanted her to work for him again. He wouldn't come all the way here just for that. She was a good assistant, but she wasn't *that* damn good. *No*, she thought. Or maybe he was only interested in just reigniting their friendship and nothing else. Maybe she had put him through too much over the years, yanking his emotions back and forth like a rag doll between dueling toddlers. Her shoulders fell. If that was case, she would just have to accept it.

She watched in confusion as he reached into one of

his jean pockets and suddenly fell to bended knee. From that point on, everything seemed to happen in slow motion. He took out the black velvet box and flipped open the lid. He held the solitaire diamond aloft, and she took a hesitant step back, feeling as if her knees were about to buckle.

"I know it seems like an empty gesture," he began, "with me still being married. But as soon as my divorce goes through, I want to do this, Lee. I'm tired of waiting for the life I wanted to finally begin. I've waited too damn long. Will you . . . will you marry me?"

Leila's heartbeat thudded in her ears. Her vision blurred with tears as she gazed at the ring he offered her. This wasn't really happening, was it?

She must have stayed silent way too long because Evan lowered the ring box. He rose from his kneel to stand in front of her. "Like I said, I knew nothing was guaranteed," he muttered.

"Yes!" she said, grabbing his arm. "Yes, Evan. Of course, I want to get married. Of course, I want to marry you! I . . . I . . ."

She didn't know what else to say so she dropped Isabel's cardigan, looped her arms around his neck, and kissed him. He wrapped his arms around her and kissed her back. They stood there in the living room, locked in each other's arms for a very long time. As they kissed, the vibrations started all over again, undulating over her body like ocean waves. If she wanted him before, that was nothing compared to how much she wanted him now.

Leila abruptly pulled back her head, stopping them mid-kiss, and shoved away from him.

"What's wrong?" he asked breathlessly.

Leila didn't answer him. Instead, she grabbed his hand and tugged him out of the living room and down the short hall that led to her bedroom. Several cardboard boxes still sat on the carpeted floor, waiting to be unpacked. A pile of clothes was tossed on the foot stool at the end of her bed, waiting to be hung in her closet. But Evan didn't give a second glance at the disarray surrounding them.

"How much time do we have?" he asked frantically as he started stripping her of her clothes and taking off his own.

"Two and a half hours," she answered against his lips. "Maybe three."

"Oh, that's plenty of time."

Within seconds, they were both naked and Leila fell back onto her bed, tugging Evan with her.

"Wait," Evan murmured against her lips just as she started to straddle him. He pushed her back onto the mattress and crawled off the bed.

"What are you doing?" she asked as he walked across her bedroom. He started fiddling with the door handle. "Seriously, Ev . . . what are you doing?"

"This damn thing doesn't lock?" he grumbled.

"No. Why?"

She watched in amazement as he yanked open the bedroom door and strode down the hall, buck naked.

"Ev, where are you going?" Leila shouted as she lay back on the bed, furrowing her brows with puzzlement. She instantly felt the chill of his absence and grabbed one of the sheets to cover herself. "Ev?"

He returned to the bedroom less than a minute later, holding one of the dinette chairs. She burst into laughter as she watched him close the bedroom door and wedge the chair underneath the door handle.

He turned around to face her and grinned. "I've had too many bad experiences with running in on someone or having someone run in on me. I'm not doing that shit again!"

"Come here," she said, hooking her finger at him.

She didn't have to tell him twice. In less than a second he was across the room and on top of her.

Chapter 25

DANTE

"Excuse me! Excuse me, ma'am!" Dante heard the office assistant shout on the other side of his door.

He looked up from his computer screen.

"Ma'am, you can't just barge into—"

"I will do whatever I damn well please!" he heard Charisse yell as his office door suddenly swung open. The door almost hit the sleek console table along the adjacent wall where he displayed his awards and photos of himself posing with various celebrities and dignitaries he had rubbed elbows with over the years.

Charisse stood in the doorway, a more bedraggled version of her usual self. He could tell from her lack of makeup, disheveled hair, and wrinkled clothes that she was on one of her drinking binges. He could also tell from the unfocused look of her red-rimmed eyes.

"So . . . so this is where you've been hiding?" she shouted, jabbing her finger at him. "Behind a fucking desk! You and Evan have more in common than I thought!"

The beleaguered-looking assistant leaned her head around the door frame. "I am so . . . so sorry, Mr. Turner. I tried to tell her that you were busy," the young woman said timidly, "but she wouldn't listen. She just—"

"He isn't fucking busy! He's a fucking *coward,* that's what he is!" Charisse glared at him. "Why haven't you returned any of my phone calls? Why are you avoiding me?"

Dante pasted on a charming smile and rose from his leather swivel chair. "I'll take it from here, Lindsey." He walked around his desk and buttoned his suit jacket. "You can go back to the front office."

Lindsey gave a worried glance at Charisse before nodding and turning back to the corridor, where other doors were now open. A few people leaned out of their offices to see the source of all the commotion. Dante watched as Lindsey began to walk toward the front of the law offices of Nutter, McElroy & Ailey, where Dante worked, where he had been trying for seven years to make partner.

And this bitch may have fucked up all my aspirations in one fell swoop, he thought as he angrily strode across his office, grabbed Charisse by the arm, dragged her farther into the room, and slammed the door shut. But that wasn't a surprise. Charisse had managed to mess up all his other plans too.

"Have you lost your damn mind?" he asked. "What the fuck were you thinking coming in here like that?"

"Why haven't you returned any of my calls?" Charisse repeated. Her cheeks were inflamed with indignation and the bourbon she probably had imbibed earlier that day.

He let go of her and contemplated coming up with

an excuse, but honestly couldn't think of one or work up the will to fabricate a conceivable lie.

"Because I didn't want to talk to you."

"Why?" she cried, looking so vulnerable at that moment, he almost laughed. "What did I do wrong?"

"What did you do wrong?" He couldn't hold in his laughter anymore. In light of his reaction, her anger was replaced with confusion.

"What's so funny?" she asked as he continued to laugh.

What did she do wrong? Where should I begin?

Maybe it was the fact that she had talked him into coming to her house the day that Evan had discovered they were having an affair. Dante hadn't wanted to come to the Murdoch mansion. He had meetings scheduled throughout that Wednesday with several of his clients, but she had argued, whined, and cajoled. Finally, she'd sent him sexy text messages accompanied by X-rated pics of herself wearing nothing but a thong and a smile. He had found it hard to resist and agreed to stop by and stay for an hour or two.

The worst goddamn decision I ever made, Dante now thought as he glared at Charisse.

And when Evan had stumbled upon them together, Charisse hadn't been smart enough to keep her mouth shut or act humble. She had instead been self-righteous and goaded Evan into bringing out the big guns. Now Evan was enforcing everything in their prenup, including the clause that said she forfeited all rights to his company shares if she committed adultery.

So there went Dante's plans to use Charisse as a way to finally get a part of the legacy that his father had denied him. She would have been the sword Dante wielded to help take down Evan, to claim his rightful place in the Murdoch family. Thanks to her big mouth, there went all those months Dante had spent wooing Charisse, sexing her, and putting up with her drunken bullshit!

What a waste of time, he thought.

"Go home." Dante waved her off, gesturing toward the door. "Just turn around and go back home, okay?"

"I *can't* go home! You obviously didn't listen to my messages. I tried to tell you that Evan is kicking me out!" She pouted her collagen-injected lips. "He . . . he told me to pack my things and move out by the end of the week. I know he just wants to get me out so he can move in his personal assistant, Leila! I knew when I saw her that she was nothing but a piece of trash! They're engaged, you know. I guess Evan forgot the little fact that he's still married to *me!*"

"He and Leila are engaged?" Dante asked, feeling a spark of anger rise at that revelation. Leila had insisted that nothing was going on between her and Evan.

That lying bitch, Dante thought, shaking his head ruefully. *I swear you can't trust anyone.*

But he would make her pay for deceiving him, just like he would finally figure out how to get to Evan. He would not give up on that one.

"He's putting me up in some rental property . . . some tiny condo!" Charisse scoffed. "I told him that he might as well toss me out on the street. He said if I didn't like it, then I could go live with my mother! *My mother,* Dante! Can you believe he said that to me? The fucking nerve . . ."

Dante loudly sighed. "And how is any of this my problem?"

"What do you mean, how is this any of it your problem? You can't let Evan do this to me! I thought you were in my corner. That I could turn to you if I—"

"Well, you thought wrong," he said coldly. "Look,

Charisse, we had some good times and good sex, but that's all it was. Don't try to make it sound like I promised you the world, because I didn't."

"That's *all* I was to you? *Good times and good sex?"* she screeched, balling her fists at her sides. "You . . . you asshole! You . . . you sorry excuse for a human being! You piece of—"

"And you're a drunken, entitled whore," he said, growing bored. "People in glass houses shouldn't throw stones, Charisse."

Charisse's chest heaved up and down as she trembled. This time, real tears pooled in her eyes, but he still wasn't moved. The tears spilled onto her reddened cheeks.

"You think you can just . . . just get rid of me like some . . . some piece of trash?" she whispered. "You think you can—"

She stopped when someone suddenly knocked on the door.

"I'm busy!" Dante yelled, but the door opened anyway.

A tall dark-skinned man stood in the doorway. He wore a red tracksuit jacket with the word TRAINER in white letters stitched across the front. His black sweatpants sat low on his hips.

He grinned and strode into the office like Dante had invited him into the room. "Wassup, man!" He extended his hand to Dante for a shake.

Dante glanced down at the hand, then slowly up at the man. He wondered why this guy was in his office and more importantly, why he was acting as if they were the best of friends.

"Who are you?" Dante asked, cocking his eyebrow.

"I'm Marques, man," he said as he pulled his hand

back. "Marques Whitney, and I need to talk to you right quick. I was wondering if I could contract your legal services."

"How did you get back here, Marques?"

Dante was going to have to have a little talk with Lindsey at the front desk. This was two instances of undesirables coming into his office. *Not acceptable*, Dante thought.

"Don't worry about that, bruh!" Marques's voice dropped down to a whisper. "Look, I got myself into a little situation with the cops. I got pulled over a few days ago and they found something in my . . . you know . . . vehicle."

Dante sighed while Charisse stood in the center of the office with her arms crossed over her chest. She was still crying.

"I had to stay in lockup until my friend came and bailed me out," Marques continued. "But the police are trying to pull me in for a hearing. They're trying to get my ass on felony charges! You see, cuz I'm already on probation so—"

Dante raised his hand. "Let me stop you there. I do civil litigation, not criminal and even if I did do criminal work"—he paused to look Marques up and down—"you couldn't afford my legal services."

"Yeah, I figured that." Marques's grin faltered slightly. "I figured you'd . . . you know . . . give me a discount."

"Right," Dante said dryly. "Look, as I said before, I'm very busy and I have no interest in giving you a discount or being your lawyer. So if you would let me get back to my work, I'd appreciate it."

"Oh, come on, man!" Marques exclaimed. "I need a lawyer!"

"So you're going to continue to pretend that I'm not standing here," Charisse said softly. "You're going to act like I don't exist?"

Dante tiredly walked to his desk and picked up his phone before dialing an extension code. "Lindsey? . . . Yeah, would you be so nice as to contact security? I'm going to need someone escorted from the building."

"Oh, so you're going to kick me out now, man?" Marques asked resentfully. "That's some bullshit!"

"I ruined my marriage," Charisse continued, slowly shaking her head and weeping. "I've given up everything!"

Dante fell back into his swivel chair and opened one of his desk drawers, pulling out a bottle of aspirin. He was starting to get a headache.

"How you gonna kick me out when we peeps? We almost family, bruh!"

"You are so heartless, Dante, so . . . so fucking cruel!"

"We tight, man! I know your sister! Paulette's my girl and you gonna treat me like this?"

"I have nothing and you're just going to abandon me?" Charisse cried.

At the mention of Paulette, Dante's ears perked up. He stopped chewing his aspirin tablets and raised his weary head. He stared at Marques. "You know Paulette?"

"Hell, yeah, I know her!" Marques's grin returned. "I know her *real* good."

From the look in Marques's eyes and the tone of his voice, Dante got a clue as to what "real good" meant. He was intrigued.

"We heard you needed someone escorted out?" a heavy baritone boomed, causing all of them to fall silent.

Dante looked up. Marques and Charisse turned.

Two burly-looking security guards in ill-fitting black uniforms stood behind them. The guards' broad shoulders and barrel chests took up the entire width of the doorway.

Dante nodded. "Yes, I do." He rose from his chair and gestured to Charisse. "This woman is harassing me."

Charisse stared at him, now staggered. She started to sputter with outrage.

"I asked her to leave and she declined. She is belligerent and obviously intoxicated. Would you please take her off the premises?"

The guards instantly stepped forward and grabbed both of Charisse's arms. As they tugged her back, her high-heeled feet were lifted off the floor.

"Let go of me!" she screamed as they dragged her toward the doorway. "Let . . . go of . . . me, goddamn it!"

The guards ignored her, even as she kicked and flailed. She swatted them with her expensive leather purse, sending a compact and mascara flying, but the guards continued with the task at hand.

"Dante! Dante, you . . . you son of a bitch!" she yelled as she was dragged down the hall. *"Daaaaaante!"*

Dante strode toward the door and closed it. It didn't shut out the sound of her screams entirely, but at least it muffled them.

"Damn," Marques muttered with a shake of the head as he turned his baseball cap to the back. He sucked his teeth. "That's one crazy bitch, bruh! That ain't your chick, is it?"

"Don't worry about her," Dante ordered, stepping closer to Marques. "Tell me how you know my sister. Tell me everything."

Chapter 26
PAULETTE

Paulette shoved open the door to her red BMW convertible—feeling as if she might rip the door off its hinges—and then slammed the door shut behind her as she stepped onto the asphalt driveway. She angrily strode up the steps toward the French doors of her brother's mansion and rang the doorbell. She paced back and forth under the vestibule as she waited for the housekeeper to answer. All the while, she quietly muttered to herself, cursing under her breath.

Paulette had been invited to Evan's home today to celebrate Evan and Leila's engagement. The small gathering was supposed to toast the couple and wish them many years of long overdue happiness, but Paulette was in no mood to raise a glass to anyone—especially to the likes of Leila Hawkins. Not after she had just found out how Leila had betrayed her.

"That bitch," she muttered as she continued to pace. "That back-stabbing bitch!"

How could Leila have done that? How could she

have told Paulette's most important secrets to someone like Dante?

Paulette had gotten a call from her eldest brother—or better put, she had been summoned by him earlier that day just as she was preparing to leave her home and head to Evan's place. When she'd seen Dante's number on her cell phone, she had initially ignored it. She'd had no desire to talk to that asshole, not after she'd heard about the affair he and Charisse had been having right under Evan's nose.

Our own brother, she had thought with a slow shake of the head when she heard the news, remembering how Dante had told her that they were family now. The Murdochs had their faults, but they believed in family loyalty, above all else. *A brother—flesh and blood—would never do that to someone!*

Granted, Paulette had suspected that Evan and Leila had been having their own secret affair for several months prior to getting engaged—but she'd been willing to be a little more forgiving in that situation. She knew those two had mitigating circumstances, and she, of all people, understood mitigating circumstances when it came to affairs.

Everyone in the family knew that Charisse and Evan had been married in name only for the past few years. She could sense that her brother was unhappy in his marriage though he had tried to put up a noble front. His wife had been, at best, apathetic toward him and, at worst, outright hostile sometimes. Maybe Evan had been wrong to cheat, but Paulette was happy to see that he might finally get a little bit of happiness with the woman he had always loved. But those well wishes went down the drain soon after she talked to Dante.

He had called her several times and she had let it go to voice mail. After he'd called for the fourth time, just as she had been grabbing her coat and heading toward the door, she'd finally dug her cell phone out of her purse. She'd picked it up on the third ring, now beyond irritated.

"What do you want, Dante?" she'd snapped.

He'd chuckled on the other end of the line. "Now is that any way to talk to your big brother?"

"My big brother is lucky I answered the phone at all, considering what a scumbag he is."

"Watch it," he'd ordered icily. "If I were you, I'd watch my tone and my words."

"Uh-huh." She'd rolled her eyes as she fished out her keys from the bottom of her snakeskin purse. "And why's that?"

"Because I know your little secret . . . or shall we say, your *secrets.*"

She'd paused and squinted. "What are you talking about?"

"You know what I'm talking about, Paulette. Don't play innocent, because we all know you aren't. At least, I and your friend Marques know the truth anyway."

At the mention of Marques's name, her keys had tumbled from her hand and landed on the foyer's tiled floor with a clatter. Her mouth had fallen open in shock.

"How . . . How d-do you know about Marques? What—?"

"Don't worry. All will be explained as soon as we have our chitchat, little sis. Meet me at Starbucks on the corner of Maple Leaf and Barnaby Road in . . . oh, ten minutes."

He'd then hung up and she'd stared at her cell phone in shock.

Paulette had hated how Dante assumed that she

would come running, like a show dog responding to his command. She could just as well not show up at the coffee shop, pretending like his veiled threat didn't matter. She could go straight to Evan's house instead. But something had told her that would be a foolish mistake to add to the long list of foolish mistakes that she had made lately. So Paulette had braced herself and opened her front door to head to Starbucks to meet Dante.

She'd arrived at the coffee shop eight minutes later, feeling as if her stilettos were made out of cinderblocks, feeling as if she were marching toward the guillotine. Here she was, being manipulated all over again. When would it end?

She'd pushed open the glass door and seen Dante sitting at one of the bistro tables not far from the counter. He'd been sipping from a paper cup and reading a newspaper. When she'd drawn near his table, he'd looked up from the broadsheet, lowered his cup, and grinned.

"Ah, so you made it!"

She'd slammed her purse on the table and pulled out a chair, dragging it across the floor so that it emitted a metal scraping sound that was even louder than the espresso machine where the barista behind the counter was blasting foam into a cup. The noise from Paulette's chair had made several of the coffee shop patrons look up and frown with annoyance. But she hadn't cared. She'd flopped into the chair, crossed her legs, and cut straight to the chase.

"How did you find out about Marques?"

She'd watched as Dante slowly folded his newspaper, looking bored. "How do you think I found out about him?"

"Look, I'm not up to playing games! I've been

blackmailed before. You could even say I'm an old pro at it," she'd admitted ruefully. "Just tell me who told you."

He'd continued to smile cryptically and drink his coffee.

"It wasn't . . . it wasn't Leila, was it?"

She'd known that he and Leila had dated briefly, but she couldn't believe someone she considered a friend and almost family, a woman she trusted, would do this.

She'd answered her own question by quickly shaking her head. "No, it wasn't her. That's not . . . that's not Leila. I know her."

"You said you've been blackmailed before. If you're really an old pro at this, I'm shocked that you could be so naïve, so trusting, Paulette." He'd set down his coffee cup, leaned forward, and gazed into her eyes. "What if I told you Leila did tell me . . . that she blurted it out in bed one night after I fucked her . . . that she started rambling all the Murdoch family secrets to me?"

Paulette had fallen silent.

"You probably still wouldn't believe me, would you? But let's be honest, Paulette. You don't know Leila as well as you think you do. You really don't know anybody for that matter. Not her, not me, not Evan—"

"What does Evan have to do with this?" she'd snarled. "Don't you dare bring him up!"

"Your precious big brother, Evan," he'd muttered dryly. "Oh, yes. How dare I say anything bad about *him*. Your brother is so perfect, so goddamn wonderful. That explains why he's been fucking his secretary, Leila, this whole time." He'd inclined his head. "I heard they're getting married. How nice! He might want to divorce his first wife though before he starts lining up the next one."

"One of the reasons why *our* brother is getting a divorce is because of you! You betrayed him!" she'd shouted, pointing at Dante. "And now you're trying to do the same to me. We accepted you as family, Dante. We trusted you! But we never should have—"

"Oh, wake up! Everybody turns on everybody. I've been around long enough to know that. You don't think Evan would turn on you if the chance came along, if he had to make a choice between you and something that he loves, that he covets? If the choice came between you and Leila, who would he choose?" He laughed again and shook his head. "I suggest you stop being so trusting and start looking out for yourself."

"I should start looking out for myself and be a two-faced asshole like you, you mean?"

"Two-faced asshole? I'm the one who knows your secret! I know about the abortion, Paulette," he'd said, lowering his voice, making her blood run cold. "I know about the little thing you and Marques have going on. Would a backstabbing asshole keep secrets like that?"

Paulette had pursed her lips. "He would . . . if he wanted to use that information to his advantage."

"Or maybe . . . just maybe, I want to use it to offer you an olive branch." He'd reached out to touch her hand and she'd instantly pulled away from him in disgust, like a snake had just slithered across her skin. He laughed even harder. "Paulette, don't you get it? I don't want to hurt you or ruin you! Frankly, you're small pickings to me, sweetheart. I'm willing to help you, to help neutralize your little problem, if you give me what I want."

"Which is?"

Dante had shifted his coffee aside. His smile had returned. "Give me your shares in Murdoch Conglomerated."

As Paulette continued to pace in front of Evan's
front door, she shook her head. She couldn't believe
that Leila had put her in this predicament. Dante had
offered to "take care of Marques," though he had given
no clue to how he would go about doing that, and he'd
said he would continue to keep Paulette's secrets—if
and only if she would sell him her share in the family
company.

"At a *deeply* discounted price, of course," he had
said.

He would own a portion of the company equal to
Terrence and Evan's portions. He also would have the
right to assert an equal voice at Murdoch Conglomerated, being one of the major shareholders.

Paulette didn't understand what was the point of all
this. Why did he care what went on at Murdoch Conglomerated? He was a lawyer, not a businessman.
What was Dante's end game? But Dante refused to tell
her.

"You don't need to know what all the wheels and
cogs are doing, sweetheart," Dante had muttered
smugly as he rose from the bistro table. "You just need
to know that the clock is ticking. Let me know your decision soon."

Paulette looked up just as one of the French doors
to Evan's mansion finally opened.

"Good afternoon, Miss Williams," the petite housekeeper said.

"Good afternoon," Paulette mumbled in return.
"Where're my brothers?"

She knew Terrence was here already. She had spotted his Porsche parked in the driveway.

"In one of the sitting rooms," the housekeeper said. "I'll take you there. They've been waiting for you."

Less than a minute later, Paulette stepped through the entryway of the grand sitting room to find Terrence sitting on the off-white, spacious sofa, reaching for a chilled bottle resting on the antique Chinese coffee table. Meanwhile Evan was smiling and laughing in front of his two-story limestone fireplace. Leila leaned back against Evan with her head perched on his chest. His arm was wrapped possessively around her waist.

The newly engaged couple looked so comfortable, so content. Seeing them that way only made Paulette angrier.

"There she is!" Evan exclaimed, releasing Leila so he could walk toward his sister. "We were wondering where you were. I thought you said you were going to be here an hour ago."

He strode across the sitting room, leaned down, and embraced her in a brotherly bear hug. She stiffly hugged him back, all the while glaring over his shoulder at Leila, who was blissfully unaware of Paulette's animosity toward her.

"I had to make a quick stop," she mumbled as he released her.

"Quick stop, huh? Well, we're glad you made it. Terry was just about the break open the bottle, but I told him to wait until you got here."

"Yeah, wouldn't want to spoil the sparkling cider by opening it early," Terrence said sarcastically, making Leila laugh.

Evan chuckled too. As he pulled back and looked more closely at his little sister, his smile faded. "Is everything okay? You look . . . off."

"I'm fine," Paulette answered flatly before walking

around him and falling into one of the English wing chairs near the sofa. "Just fine."

Terrence cocked a sardonic eyebrow at her. "Well, on that note . . ." He braced the heel of the bottle on his knee and released the cork with a loud "pop" that made them all jump in surprise. He then began pouring sparkling cider into the flutes lined along the coffee table. "Grab a glass! Grab a glass!"

Leila and Evan got their drinks first. Reluctantly, Paulette leaned forward and got a glass too.

Terrence rose from the sofa and held his flute aloft, grinning ear to ear. "I know we're here to toast Evan and Leila's engagement, but the truth is, Lee, you're the one I *really* want to toast. I don't know what voodoo you did. But *whatever* it was, you helped my brother escape from the clutches of that conniving, lying, Botoxed b—"

"Terry," Evan said warningly. "Stay on script."

Terrence rolled his eyes. "All right. All right! Well, anyway, congrats. This has been a long time coming— damn near twenty years! And I'm ecstatic that it's finally . . . *finally* happening! Cheers!" Terry suddenly turned to his sister. "Did you want to add anything, little sis?"

"Not really," she muttered before crossing her legs and sipping from her chilled glass.

Evan squinted. "Are you sure you're okay, Paulette?"

"What does it matter?" She laughed coldly. "You guys are finally getting your happy ending—like Terry said. Who gives a shit about the rest of us?"

"Whoa! What's with the attitude?" Terrence asked with a curl in his lip. "You're bringing the room down, Paulette. Why are you acting so pissed off?"

She raised her eyes to glare at her future sister-in-law. "Maybe you should ask Lee that question."

Leila lowered her glass to the fireplace mantle. "Why should they ask me? What did I do?"

"Nothing, Leila. You've done absolutely nothing," she said sarcastically before slumping back into her chair and finishing her glass. "You never do *anything* wrong. You're absolutely fucking perfect—or at least, that's what you would like everyone to believe, right?"

Leila walked toward Paulette. Instead of anger at Paulette's words, Leila's features were etched with so much concern that Paulette wanted to laugh.

Of course, she wants to pretend like she cares now, Paulette thought, feeling the venom of anger coursing through her veins. *Where was all that concern when she was betraying me?*

"Honey, what's wrong? You don't want Ev and I to get married?" Leila asked as she drew near her. "Is that what this is about?"

"I couldn't give a shit what you two do!" Paulette spat. "I don't care about you getting married. What I care about is that you put my marriage at risk, you . . . you backstabbing bitch! I trusted you, Lee! You said you wouldn't tell anybody!"

"Hold it right goddamn now!" Evan barked, striding across the sitting room. "I don't know what the hell is going on, but you can't talk to her that way! I won't—"

But he stopped mid-motion and fell silent when Leila held up her hand and shook her head warningly at him.

"Don't, Ev. Don't, all right?" she said calmly before turning back to Paulette. She reached out for her and placed a warm hand on her shoulder. "Let's not do this here. We should talk about this in private. Okay? We can go to another room and—"

"Oh, now you want to talk about this in private!"

Paulette screamed, feeling herself coming even further unhinged. She shoved off Leila's consoling hand. Tears were streaming down her cheeks. Even always unfazed Terrence was starting to look alarmed. "Now you want to pretend like secrecy means something to you? Why, Lee?" She shot up from her chair and glared into the other woman's eyes, feeling all her rage come bubbling to the surface. "You want to protect your image in front of your new fiancé? You don't want him to know what a liar and a schemer you are? How you ratted us out to Dante during your pillow talk? How you told him about Marques?"

"Who's Marques?" Terrence asked, bewildered.

"A guy I fucked!" Paulette yelled.

She saw the look on her brothers' faces change when she said those words. They morphed from outrage and confusion to total horror. She turned to stare at them both.

"That's right! Little Sweet Pea fucked another guy! In fact, several different guys before I got married! And I had an abortion too!" she shouted, making Evan grimace like she had struck him. "Never would have guessed, huh, Ev? Huh, Terry? Not your innocent little sis. Well, I have . . . and I've done a lot worse . . . more things that neither of you would ever believe I could do so just ruminate on that!"

"Paulette, please don't do this," Leila said. "Don't—"

"Don't do what? Tell the truth? You want me to keep lying? Sure! Why not? Let's keep pretending that we're the perfect family and we have perfect lives and everything is going to work out just fine! Antonio will still love me when he finds out everything I did. Charisse will just miraculously disappear and you guys will get married and live happily ever after." She clapped her hands and laughed again. "I'm sorry, Lee.

I don't believe in fairy tales. They don't exist and you of all people should know that. Because the world isn't perfect and people can't be trusted—*especially* you!"

"But you *can* trust me!" Leila cried. "I never told Dante. I promised you I would take that secret to my grave, and I meant it!"

"Then how does he know? Why would he lie?"

Leila fell silent and so did Paulette's brothers.

Leila closed her eyes and shook her head. "I don't . . . I don't know how he knows, but I swear I'm telling you the truth."

"Of course, you would," Paulette said.

"Paulette, sweetheart," Evan said softly. The anger that had flooded his face earlier had now disappeared. He looked sad and disappointed instead. "Look, I understand why you're angry, but are you really going to take Dante's word over Lee's? She's practically family! We've known each other since we were kids. She loves you like a sister! Why would she betray you?"

"I don't know, Ev," she answered honestly. "I don't know why she would betray me, but I know now that I can't trust her . . . and if you're smart, you won't either."

"Oh, come on!" Terrence shouted. "Damn it, this was supposed to be a happy occasion! This was supposed to be a good thing for once! Now we're fucking it up again with all this drama. Let's just sit down, have some of this weak-ass cider, eat some canapés, and cool off. Okay?" He turned to his sister. "Paulette, I have no idea what the hell you're talking about, but don't do this. I'm sure there's a good explanation for all of it if you would just—"

"I didn't do anything, Terry! I'm just pointing out what's been done to me by Leila and calling her on it! Besides, why are you defending her? You guys are supposed to be my brothers," she insisted, pointing at her chest, "not hers."

"Because you're not making sense!" Evan yelled. "You've been acting strange for months, Paulette, and now you flip out like this? What the hell did you expect us to do?"

She stared at her brothers. "I can't believe it. Dante was right! He warned me about this."

He told her, when it came down to it, everyone was alone. She should never assume her brothers would be in her corner. In the end, they—like everyone else—would turn on her.

"Since when did you get so chummy with Dante?" Terrence asked. A sneer was on his lips

"Since he was the only one willing to be honest with me," she muttered. "To hell with this. To hell with all of you."

With that, she grabbed her purse and walked out of the sitting room, leaving Leila, Evan, and Terrence completely stunned.

As she strode through the French doors and down the stone steps to her BMW, she pulled out her cell phone and dialed Dante's number. He picked up on the first ring.

"Hello?" he answered.

"Dante," she said before opening her car door, "how much are you offering for my shares?"

Chapter 27

EVAN

Evan was roused awake by the ringing of the phone on his night table. The instant he heard its shrill bleating in his dark bedroom, he cursed under his breath. He had only fallen asleep an hour and a half ago. He had lain awake staring at the ceiling, worried about Paulette, wondering when and why his relationship with his sister had gone so horribly wrong. Then, sometime around 2 a.m., the turbulent ocean that was his mind had finally, mercifully quelled long enough so that he drifted to sleep. But now Evan was awake again and annoyed.

"Who is that?" Leila asked drowsily as the phone continued to ring.

She was sleeping at his place tonight, a rare treat for them. Leila spent most of her nights at the apartment she shared with her mother and daughter, though he had been trying for a while now to convince her to move her family into his mansion.

"I have no idea," he muttered, wiping his eyes with the heels of his hands.

"Well . . ." She rolled onto her side and gazed at him in the dark. "Are you going to answer?"

Evan sighed and reached for the cordless phone. "Hello?" he grumbled.

"E-Evan?" a woman replied.

"Yes, who is this?"

"Evan, it's me . . . Charisse."

"Charisse?" He squinted in the confusion.

The voice on the other end of the line didn't sound like his wife—technically his soon-to-be *ex*-wife, now that he had filed for separation. She sounded timid and confused. She also sounded a little scared.

"Charisse, why are you calling me?"

At the mention of his wife's name, Leila frowned. She pushed herself up to her elbows and stared at him.

"Do you realize how late it is? I was—"

"Ev, I-I need your help. Please!" she sobbed. "Please help me!"

He instantly sat bolt upright in bed, pushing off the sheets and comforter. The cold air hit his bare torso and legs. His skin lit with goose bumps, though he wasn't sure if it was from the chill or because of how desperate Charisse sounded.

"What's wrong?" The haze of sleep had disappeared from his voice. His sluggish mind was clear now. "What happened?"

"I didn't mean to do it! I swear, Ev! It was an accident." She loudly sniffed. "They're going to put me in jail."

"Ev? Ev, what's going on?" Leila whispered behind him and he held up his hand, motioning her to stay quiet.

Dear God, he thought. *This is it.*

The call he had anticipated for years while his drunken wife took a chance with her life and everyone else's by insisting on driving. Had she finally hit the innocent pedestrian idly walking through a crosswalk?

"They want to charge me with . . . with all these things," Charisse continued on the phone. "They want to keep me here overnight. But I didn't hurt anybody! I didn't kill anybody! I just ran into a-a empty yard and hit a street sign!"

No people were involved. At least there's that, he thought, feeling some small parcel of relief. He fell silent as he listened to her weep on the other end.

"Evan, please . . . please help me," she whispered, sounding a lot like a lost little girl at that moment. "Please don't leave me alone here!"

He closed his eyes. "Where are you?"

"At the Chesterton Sheriff's Office. They had me in a holding cell, but I could make one phone call. I called my mother and she's not home . . . s-so I called you." She paused. "I didn't know. . . . I didn't know who else to call."

"Why didn't you call Dante? He's a lawyer. He could help you."

"Dante doesn't care. I-I know that now. He's made it pretty clear."

"Just hang up," a voice in his head urged. "Or better yet, laugh in her face and tell her that you don't give a damn if she rots in jail!"

Almost the entire time they had been married, she had acted like she had loathed him, like she would rather be married to any man *but* him. And she had cheated on him with his brother, for Christ's sake! Yet, as he listened to her cry, he couldn't work up enough anger or contempt to do what he had every right to do. He found himself feeling sorry for her.

"I'll be there in less than an hour," he said, his tongue heavy with reluctance.

"Oh, thank you! Thank you so much, Ev! I appr—"

He hung up, unable to listen to any more of her gushing. He sat on the edge of the bed with his head bowed.

"What happened to her?" Leila asked, startling him. For a minute there, he had forgotten she was in bed with him.

"Charisse had an accident. It sounds like she was driving drunk again. No one was hurt . . . or at least, she *claims* no one was hurt. She was arrested and now she's at the Sheriff's Office."

Leila sat up and reached for the lamp on the night table nearest to her. The immense bedroom suddenly flooded with light. Evan could see Leila clearly now, though her facial expression wasn't decipherable.

"You're going to bail her out?"

"Yeah, she said she had no one else to call. But I need to make a few phone calls first. It sounds like she'll need a lawyer."

Leila slowly nodded, pushing her hair out of her eyes.

"You don't . . . you don't mind, do you?"

"Don't mind what?"

"That I bail out Charisse."

"She needs help, Ev. I don't begrudge you for wanting to help her." He watched as Leila hesitated. "As long as . . . well, you're doing it for the right reasons."

"Right reasons?"

"I mean as long as you aren't doing it to protect the Murdoch name again. Or because you still . . ." Her words trailed off.

He turned around on the bed to face her. "Because I still what?"

"Because you . . . because you still have feelings for her." She lowered her eyes. "If that's the case, then I can leave."

"Leave? Why would you leave? I've tried everything imaginable to get you here, short of putting you in handcuffs and dragging you to my bed!"

She pursed her lips and stared down at the sheets. He watched as she absently began to fiddle with the engagement ring on her finger, twirling it around and around. "I told you before that I can't be the other woman again. I won't be, Ev. So if you want to try to make your marriage work with Charisse, don't let me—"

"Wait! Wait!" He reached for her hand. He held it and her ring firmly in place. He gazed into her eyes. "Let's stop for a second here. I have no intention whatsoever of trying to reunite with Charisse. There is no way you could be the other woman again, Lee. You're the *only* woman for me! You know that. Me posting bail for her and getting her a lawyer doesn't change that."

Leila stared at him a long time then finally nodded again. "Go ahead and make your phone calls." She pulled her hand away from him then tossed back the bedsheets and stood. "I'll get you some coffee. It sounds like you'll need it."

He watched as she grabbed a silk robe, put it on, and shuffled out of the bedroom, quietly shutting the door behind her.

"All right! So here's the situation, Ms. Murdoch," the lawyer said as he leaned forward on Charisse's sofa in her new condo. He spread out a series of documents on the coffee table and adjusted his tie. "You're being charged with DUI—obviously. The breathalyzer test placed your blood alcohol levels well above the legal limit." He glanced at a copy of the police report and let out a low whistle. "Wow! I haven't seen a level that high in quite a while!"

He guffawed, but neither Charisse nor Evan joined him in his laughter. He glanced at them both anxiously, then loudly cleared his throat.

"Uh, you're also facing property damage charges," the lawyer continued. "The homeowners say not only did you hit their fence and destroy a prized rosebush, but you also hit a Mercedes-Benz that was parked in the driveway." He looked up at Charisse. "Any questions so far?"

Charisse shook her head. "No, keep going," she murmured.

She sat with a bandage on her brow, nursing a cup of black coffee. She wasn't wearing a lick of makeup and her blond hair was pulled into a severe ponytail. Despite the monthly visits to a plastic surgeon for face peels and Botox injections, she looked like she had aged about ten years overnight.

"And finally, we have the disorderly conduct and resisting arrest charge. The homeowners said you yelled and cursed at them, I believe. The arresting officer claimed that you were combative when he tried to get you to perform a sobriety test. He said you slapped him and kicked him when he tried to place you in handcuffs. It took a second officer to subdue you."

Her brows furrowed. She winced. "I don't . . . I don't remember any of that."

The lawyer chuckled again. "Most people don't in these situations, Ms. Murdoch."

"Please . . . call me Charisse," she said, glancing sheepishly at Evan. "I don't think I'll be Ms. Murdoch for much longer."

The lawyer looked at Evan. "Oh."

Evan didn't say anything. He sat across from Charisse, looking grim. He was meeting with the lawyer to find out just how bad the charges Charisse was facing were. The more he heard, the dourer his mood and facial expression became.

The Chesterton Times had already run a story in the morning paper. They had somehow managed to get a copy of Charisse's mug shot. His wife had looked glassy eyed and out of it. A cut had been on her brow where her head had hit the steering wheel as she plowed thirty yards up the front lawn of a lovely Tudor on Pembroke Lane. She was lucky she had only hit the fence, rosebush, and Mercedes. She had nearly taken out the side of the house too.

"The bad news is," the lawyer continued, "a DUI in the state of Virginia comes with a minimum penalty. With your blood alcohol level, you will have to serve a minimum of ten days in jail."

"What?" Charisse yelled. "You mean I have to go back to that place?"

"That's the law unfortunately."

Evan closed his eyes, envisioning his wife in an orange jumpsuit, forced to share a cell and an open toilet with three other women. Charisse had thought the condo was a major step down. What the hell was she going to think about living in prison?

"You could also face up to a year of prison for all the combined charges—three years if the judge decides to run them consecutively."

Charisse let out a groan and raised her fist to her mouth and bit on her knuckle. "I couldn't! I'd die in there! I'd—"

"But," the lawyer said, holding up his hand, "the good news is that this is your first criminal charge . . .

your first DUI. I highly doubt the prosecutor would seek such a stiff penalty on a first offense. We can put in a guilty plea and offer the state's attorney's office a deal. Maybe you can get away with the ten days and that will be it."

Charisse lowered her knuckle from her mouth. "What . . . what kind of a deal?"

The lawyer leaned forward so that his forearms were resting on his knees. He looked at Charisse. "In exchange for them not seeking the maximum penalty, you agree to enroll in rehab. A thirty-day program at a nice facility that—"

"No!" Charisse emphatically shook her head, sending her ponytail flying. She slammed her cup on the coffee table. "No! I have to go to jail *and* rehab? Are you kidding? I got drunk and drove up a lawn! I'm not some . . . some drug addict, some *crackhead!*" She crossed her arms over her chest. "I'm not even an alcoholic! I just enjoy a drink every now and then, and . . . and I had too much that night. I refuse to go to a place like that. It's worse than prison. I outright refuse!"

The room fell silent. The lawyer leaned back, pursing his lips. "Well, if we have nothing to offer the prosecutor, I can't guarantee you the ten days, Miss . . ." He paused at glanced at Evan, who still hadn't said anything. "I mean, Charisse. This is our only option."

"W-what if I plead 'not guilty'? What if I let it go to trial?"

His eyes widened comically. "I would not suggest that."

"Why not? What do I have to lose?"

"Well, it's been my experience that someone of your stature with your background doesn't get a lot of sympathy from jurors. Frankly, they'll just see a rich, entitled blonde who got drunk and ran her car onto some-one's lawn. What do they care if you go to jail?"

Charisse lowered her eyes. She swallowed audibly.

"Look, I'll put in whatever plea you wish, Charisse, but my advice is to go with a guilty plea and a short stint at rehab. And keep in mind that your husband is paying me a *considerable* amount of money to offer you good advice." The lawyer gathered his files into a neat pile and dropped them into his tan leather brief-case. He then rose from his armchair, buttoning his suit jacket. "I'll give you some time to think about it, but please make your decision within the next few days, if you can."

Fifteen minutes later, Evan and Charisse sat alone in her living room, which was now so quiet that you could hear the ticking of the clock on her fireplace mantel. Charisse took a cautious glance at Evan, then sighed. She reached for the pack of cigarettes on her coffee table. "Go ahead and say it."

Evan looked up at her and inclined his head. "Say what?"

She lit the cigarette that dangled from the edge of her mouth. "Oh, come on, Ev! We both know you want to. Say 'I told you so.' Say 'I warned you that you had to get your drinking under control, Charisse. I said you needed to get your shit together and now look what's happened?'"

"That's what you think? I want to gloat?"

"Why not?" She laughed coldly and shook her head. She blew out a cloud of smoke. "You were right, weren't you? Evan Murdoch was right like he *always* is, and Charisse was the stupid idiot who dug herself into this hole."

He gazed at her in amazement. "We were married

for five years and you don't know me at all, do you? You really think I give a damn about being right?" He narrowed his eyes and glared at her. "Let me tell you something, Charisse. The last fucking thing I wanted was for my worst fear about you to come true! Why would I want this? Why would I want the humiliation of seeing my wife's mug shot plastered in the newspaper . . . of having to bail you out of jail?" he yelled, making her wince. "Why would I want my only relief to be that you didn't take out anyone while you were driving around Chesterton with enough alcohol in your system to kill a horse?" He lips tightened and he balled his fists. "It's not like I don't have enough on my fucking plate already! We're getting a divorce. Paulette has some drama going on in her life that is making her completely unpredictable. And Dante is making it worse by feeding her lies that's turning her against me, against Terry, against—"

Charisse squinted and lowered her cigarette into the glass ash tray in front of her. "What could Dante possibly say to turn your sister against you?"

"Nothing," Evan mumbled, rising from the sofa with irritation. He was at his limit and ready to leave. "Like you really care anyway."

She grabbed his hand, catching him by surprise, halting him in his steps. "No, I *do* care when it comes to Dante. I *hate* him."

"Oh, now you hate him! Funny, you were fucking him only a few weeks ago."

"Yeah, well, things change." She dropped his hand and slumped back onto the sofa. "So what did Dante say? Did it have anything to do with that guy who visited Dante at his office, the one who claimed to be Paulette's 'friend'?"

"Huh? What guy?"

"Some thug who came to his office last week," she said, sipping her coffee, then grimacing when she realized it was now cold. "He wanted Dante's help with a drug charge and said they were almost like family because the guy knew Paulette really well." She sniffed. "I knew when I saw him he was trouble. He and Dante looked like they could do some real damage together. His name was Marques something or other."

"Marques?"

"Yeah, you've heard of him?"

That name . . . Evan had heard that name before when Paulette had been ranting at Leila about the secrets she alleged Leila had revealed about her. So it turns out that Dante didn't learn the information about Paulette from Leila, as Evan had insisted all along. He had likely learned it from Marques—the man himself.

"Are you really grateful for me helping you out, Charisse?"

Charisse paused and looked a little confused by his abrupt subject change. "Y-yes," she began hesitantly. "I told you I was. Why?"

Evan slowly sat down next to his wife again. He gazed into her eyes.

"Good. Because I'm gonna need your help with something."

Chapter 28

PAULETTE

Paulette turned off the scalding-hot water and reached for a towel hanging on the rack near the shower stall. She slowly dried off herself and wrapped her gray plush towel around her. She reached for the body lotion on her counter just as the phone began to ring. She then quickly walked out of the bathroom and into her bedroom, where a cordless phone sat on her night table. She glanced at the name and number on the caller ID and instantly frowned.

"H-hello?" she answered uneasily.

"Hi, Paulette. It's Charisse. Are you busy?"

Paulette's frown deepened. She walked across the room and sat down on the edge of her bed. The last person she had expected to hear from was her sister-in-law. In the five years that Charisse had been married to Evan, she hadn't gone out of her way to interact with Paulette. She hadn't invited her on a girls' shopping day or out to lunch. She hadn't even asked her out for coffee. Yet she had called her out of the blue this morning. It instantly raised Paulette's suspicions.

"Umm, no. I'm not . . . I'm not busy. How can I help you?"

"It's not anything you can do for me. It's something I can do for you . . . or more specifically, something I agreed to do for you because your brother asked me to."

Paulette squinted. "What are you talking about?"

"Evan asked me to call you."

At that, Paulette loudly grumbled. She rolled her eyes and dropped her hand to her hip. "Look, Charisse, Evan and I aren't—"

"You two aren't speaking right now. Yes, he told me. But I wanted to let you know something."

"What?"

"That guy . . . your 'friend' Marques came to Dante's office a week ago."

Paulette instantly stilled at the mention of Marques's name.

"He tried to act all chummy. He made it sound like you and he had some . . . some *thing* going on, I suppose. When I left Dante's office, he and Marques were still in there talking. I can only imagine what they were talking about."

"Dante probably invited him there. They were—"

"He didn't invite him. He had no idea who he was. It was pretty obvious."

He didn't know who he was? Of course, he knew! *Leila told him*, Paulette thought indignantly.

"You must have been mistaken. They knew each other already."

"No, they did not unless they were putting on a master performance for my benefit, and I highly doubt that since Dante has made no bones about not giving a shit about me or what I think of him."

"Why . . . why are you telling me all of this?"

"I told you. Because I promised Evan that I would."

Paulette could feel the first wave of self-doubt flow over her. Had she been wrong to blame Leila? Had Marques blabbed her deep, dark secrets to Dante instead?

Paulette quickly shook her head. *No*, she inwardly insisted. *No, this is bullshit!*

"You're lying! Evan put you up to this, didn't he? He got you to say this just to protect Leila. He—"

"Do you really think," Charisse began frostily, "I would do anything to benefit Leila Hawkins? That bitch stole my husband! She's sleeping in *my* house! She's trying to fill *my* shoes! No, Paulette, I can assure you that I'm telling you this because it's the truth."

Paulette's heart raced.

"Look, do whatever you want with the information, but I did what your brother asked. Okay?"

"B-but you hate Evan. You cheated on him and—"

"I owe him. And I realize now that he . . . well, he wasn't quite as bad of a husband as I made him out to be. I thought Dante would be my savior, but I was badly, *badly* mistaken. I learned that too late. Just make sure you figure out which way is up before it's too late for you too. Dante has a habit of kicking you when you're down. I can speak from experience."

Charisse then abruptly hung up and Paulette was left staring at her beeping phone in confusion. She hung up her end of the line then set the phone in its charger. She stared into space at nothing in particular then lowered her head.

What if she had been wrong all along? What if she

had turned on her brother . . . on her family for no good reason?

Oh, God, she thought. She had made yet another mistake. She was about to sell her shares to a man who she could clearly see now was out to destroy her and her family.

"What did I do?" she murmured aloud.

She had to make this right.

"Take a deep breath," Evan urged as she fidgeted nervously in the metal chair beside him. He then reached out and grabbed her hand. He gave it a reassuring squeeze. "You'll be fine. We're here with you. Remember?"

Paulette took a deep, cleansing breath, then nodded.

She, Evan, and Terrence were at the local coffee shop in Chesterton. With the exception of the woman behind the counter who was rearranging bagels, scones, and pound cake on the glass-enclosed shelf, the Murdoch siblings were the only ones in the establishment and would be until Dante arrived in a few minutes. Evan had paid the owner a considerable amount of money to close down the shop for a few hours. He said he didn't want a big audience when they showed Dante they were a united front now and wouldn't put up with any more of his manipulations or shenanigans.

Dante was none the wiser, of course. He assumed he was coming here today to finalize the details about his shares purchase, as Paulette had told him over the phone earlier that week. He was completely unaware of their impending ambush.

Which is everything that asshole deserves, Paulette thought as she caught sight of him through the shop window.

He parked his Jaguar along the curb and whistled and twirled his car keys as he strolled toward the coffee shop door. Watching him, she felt a mix of fury and anxiousness. She wanted to do this. She wanted to confront him. But part of her was uneasy at how he would respond and what he would say when he was cornered by all his siblings.

When Dante swung open the coffee shop door, he immediately paused. His face fell. He stopped whistling. His eyes zeroed in on Paulette, Evan, and Terrence, who were sitting at a bistro table in the corner with Evan at the center. Dante cocked an eyebrow.

"Well," he said, smiling again, "this is a surprise. Paulette, I had no idea we would be having company at our meeting."

Evan kicked out the chair across from them. It slid loudly across the floor before coming to a halt only inches in front of Dante. "Sit."

Dante's jaw tightened. "I'm not a dog, Evan. I'm a man. And I'd rather stand."

Evan shrugged. "Have it your way. You can hear us just as clearly sitting or standing. We'll keep it short."

"We?" Dante turned to Paulette. His face was now clouded with barely masked rage. "So this is how it is? You can't talk to me like a grown-up, Paulette? Too scared, huh? You had to bring in your big brothers to—"

"Watch your mouth," Terrence said menacingly. "Watch how you talk to her."

It seemed that Dante wasn't the only angry man in the room.

"It's okay, Terry." She met Dante's gaze though her stomach was in knots. "I'm not afraid of you."

"Well, you should be . . . considering what I know about you, honey."

"You can save the threats," Evan said, his voice

heavy with authority. "She told us everything. She also told us that you tried to get her to sell all of her company shares to you. I had no idea you were so interested in Murdoch Conglomerated, Dante. I could've given you a prospectus."

"Yeah, well, there's a lot you don't know about me. That *none* of you know." He gave a caustic laugh. "Admit it. You all underestimated me. Why? Because you think you're so much fucking better than the rest of us. Fuck the Marvelous Murdochs! You think, with your money and your company and the Murdoch name, that you should have everything. When the truth is, without that money and that last name, you wouldn't be shit," he spat. "You've never had to hustle. You've never had to fight. I should be the head of Murdoch Conglomerated. Not you, Ev! I should be the one living in the mansion with four cars in my garage, not you, you prissy piece of shit!" he shouted, jabbing his finger at Evan. "There's no limit to what that company could be with someone like me guiding it. But I didn't get chosen, simply because my mother only fucked a Murdoch instead of fucking *and* marrying one!"

"So that's what this is all about? You think I'm the prince and you're the pauper. You slept with my wife . . . you tried to ruin our lives, for what? Not being born rich?" Evan chuckled and shook his head in exasperation. "You know what, Dante? If there are things I don't know about you, there's a helluva lot more you don't know about me. Because you'd know that none of us have it quite as good as you think. You'd also know that once we accepted you as family, you *were* family. If you wanted shares, if you wanted a position in the company, all you had to do was ask. All the subterfuge and tricks weren't necessary. But"—he raised his hand—"because you chose that route, we know

now that you aren't one of us . . . and there is no way
in hell you ever will be." His gaze went glacial. "So
you can take your 'poor me' routine and your chip on
your shoulder and get the fuck out."

Paulette turned and stared in awe at her big brother.
She couldn't have been more proud of him at that moment.

While Evan remained cool, calm, and collected,
Dante looked like his head was about to explode. The
veins bulged along his temples. The cords stood out
along his neck. His chest heaved up and down. His
hands formed into tight fists, and he took a menacing
step toward the table and raised his arm, like he was
about to take a swing at Evan. Paulette jumped back in
alarm. Terrence rose to his feet, ready to rumble.

"Oh, hell, no! Not in here!" Terrence barked.

Only Evan didn't move. He didn't flinch. Instead,
he gazed up at Dante, looking unfazed by their
brother's threatening gesture.

Dante stopped less than a foot away from the table
before staring at them for several seconds. He lowered
his arm, abruptly turned around, and silently strode to
the coffee shop door. He then slammed the door closed
behind him.

Chapter 29

LEILA

"How does my hair look?" Diane White asked as she lowered the car visor and gazed into the mirror at her reflection. She started to pat the curls on her head and wrinkled her nose. "Oh, Lord! I look like Bozo the clown! I told Yvette not to tease it too big!"

"You look fine, Mama," Leila reassured as she pulled to a stop in the driveway of the Murdoch mansion. "In fact, you look gorgeous. Don't worry."

"Don't worry?" Diane grunted before flipping up the visor. "When you dine with rich folks, you've got to look your best, Lee. I can't walk in there looking like just any ol' thing off the street."

"We're dining with rich folks?" Isabel piped from the backseat, leaning forward so that she could peer over her mother's shoulder at the immense home in front of them.

"No, we're having an early Thanksgiving dinner with friends. That's all," Leila clarified, giving her mother a silencing look. She then undid her seat belt and turned to face Isabel. "We're having dinner with a . . . a very important friend of mine and his family."

Isabel's brows knitted together in confusion. "What friend, Mommy?"

"You've met him before," Leila continued as she turned off her car and removed the key from the ignition. "Do you remember Mr. Murdoch?"

"Nuh-uh," Isabel said, shaking her head.

"Well, he's a . . . a very nice man. I know you'll like him. I *want* you to like him, Izzy."

It's important that you do, Leila thought desperately.

Leila still hadn't told her daughter that she and Evan were getting married. She had even gone so far as to not wear her ring whenever she was around Isabel to avoid having to talk about the engagement. It wasn't that she was ashamed of Evan. She loved him and wanted to marry him. She just was unsure of how to explain something like this to a seven-year-old, particularly a seven-year-old who still seemed to harbor fantasies that her mommy and daddy would get back together.

"We better head inside," Diane said quietly, knowing full well Leila's secret. "I bet they're waiting on us."

Leila nodded before opening her car door. Her stomach was filled with butterflies. She was so nervous that she felt jittery. She was worried that Isabel and Evan wouldn't click.

What if she doesn't like him? Leila thought dismally as she, Diane, and Isabel climbed the limestone steps to the massive French doors. She glanced over her shoulder at Isabel, who was wearing a navy-blue taffeta dress and black patent leather shoes that Leila had chosen for the occasion. The little girl was holding Diane's hand and hopping from step to step and giggling, blissfully unaware that she was about to have dinner with her future stepfather.

Could Leila really marry a man whom her daughter didn't like?

After they rang the doorbell, one of the French doors opened. Leila was shocked to find Evan standing in the doorway instead of his housekeeper. When he saw the trio, he grinned.

"You're here!" he exclaimed, pushing the door further open. He gestured for them all to step inside. "Come in! Come in! Welcome to my home!"

Diane nodded shyly and stepped through the doorway first. Isabel trailed in after her and stared around her in wonderment.

"Hey, I remember you now! You were the man who had a car like the president. Wow!" she shouted, looking up at the three-story ceiling of the center foyer. "Your friend *is* rich, Mommy! You live here all by yourself, Mr. Murdoch?"

"Izzy!" Leila exclaimed as she stood in the doorway, her cheeks warming with embarrassment.

Evan laughed. "Yes, I do, though I have a few people who stay here with me sometimes to help me take care of everything."

"Take care of everything?" Isabel repeated, now squinting with puzzlement. "You mean like a pet sitter?"

"He means he has servants, baby," Diane explained, rubbing the girl's shoulders. "Mr. Murdoch has people who clean up his house and cook for him."

"Like Mommy cleans up after people at the restaurant?"

"Umm, something like that," Leila muttered before finally stepping through the doorway. She met Evan's gaze, and her cheeks warmed again at the unrestrained heat and desire that lingered in his dark eyes. "Are . . . are we late?"

"No, you're right on time." He then leaned down to kiss her, but she suddenly turned her head so his lips landed on her cheek instead of her mouth. He pulled back from her, looking confused by her brush-off.

"Not in front of Izzy," she mouthed before turning to her daughter. "You know, if you ask nicely Mr. Murdoch might give us a tour of his home."

Evan glanced uneasily at Leila before turning his full attention to her family. He pasted on a smile again. "I'd be happy to give you a tour under one condition." He held up his finger. "You all call me Evan, not Mr. Murdoch. Mr. Murdoch's my dad and he's long gone."

For the next twenty minutes, Evan showed them from room to room, and both Diane and Isabel gawked at everything from the indoor basketball court to the lavish dining room that had been set up for Thanksgiving to the Olympic-sized swimming pool. When they toured the second floor of the east wing, Evan opened one of the doors, revealing a huge bedroom. It was painted a soft pink and decked out with everything a little girl's heart could desire: a pearl-grey armoire and dressing table; a corner with a toy box overflowing with stuffed animals and a wardrobe filled with costumes; and glass shelves along the walls covered with ballet figurines, unicorns, and Faberge eggs. Isabel ran toward the queen-sized bed that was decorated with a white silk canopy and had a gold crown over the headboard. She twirled in a circle as she gazed around the room.

"Wow! Who lives in here?"

"You can," Evan said as he casually leaned against the door frame, "whenever you and your mom move in."

Isabel stopped twirling. Her elation faded a little.

"Move in?" she repeated, visibly perplexed. "You mean live here . . . with you?"

Leila rushed into the bedroom. "What Evan means is—"

"Sure, you can live here whenever you want," he explained, oblivious to Leila's growing panic. "Before or after your mom and I get married. It doesn't matter to me."

When Evan blurted out those words, Leila grimaced.

Oh, God, she thought as she watched her daughter's face fall. *Oh, God, Evan, why did you say that?*

"You and . . . you and Mommy are getting married?" Isabel took a step back. She stared up at Leila with tears in her eyes. "But you're married to Daddy! You can't marry somebody else!"

"Honey, Daddy and I are divorced," she began softly. "I told you that. Mommy and Daddy can marry other people now. Your daddy wants to marry his girlfriend and I . . ." She swallowed the lump that had formed in her throat. "I want to marry Evan."

She watched as Isabel bit down hard on her bottom lip. Tears spilled onto Isabel's plump, brown cheeks. The little girl then pushed past Leila and ran out of the room, shoving Evan out of the way as she did.

"Izzy!" Leila yelled after her. "Izzy, honey!"

"I'll go get her," Diane said before following Isabel down the hall.

As she heard her daughter's sobs echo along the corridor, Leila closed her eyes. "Shit!" she shouted, stomping her foot on the plush rug. "Shit!"

"What?" Evan asked, striding toward her. "What did I say?"

"Why did you have to tell her we were getting married? I hadn't told her yet!"

"Well, that would explain this," he said, grabbing her left hand and showing an absent engagement ring.

She yanked her hand out of his grasp. "Don't start."

"Don't start? Don't start? Damn it, Lee, I gave you that ring to wear it! Not to hide it! And how was I supposed to know that you hadn't told Isabel we were engaged? We're supposed to get married next year! When the hell were you planning to tell her?"

"I don't know! Eventually!"

"Eventually? I thought you wanted to get married."

"I do, Ev." She raised her hand to her forehead, where a pounding headache was starting. "Of course, I do. And I was . . . I was going to tell Isabel soon. But she's a kid. I couldn't just drop it on her. I had to do it . . . delicately."

He sighed and ran his hand over his face. "Well, now it's done."

"I know," she mumbled before walking out of the bedroom to find her mother and daughter. "I know."

She found them a few minutes later, sitting on a bench in front of the floor-to-ceiling windows in the west wing. When they saw her approach, Diane looked up. She was cradling Isabel against her side. The little girl wasn't sobbing anymore, but she was sniffing, her eyes were red, and her lashes were still damp.

"Izzy, honey," Leila said, running a hand over the little girl's head, "I'm sorry that I upset you."

Isabel didn't raise her eyes so Leila knelt in front of her. Isabel finally looked at Leila from the crook of her grandmother's arm.

"I wanted to tell you sooner, but I didn't because I thought you might react this way. I thought it might make you cry. But, honey, just because Evan and I are getting married doesn't mean I love you any less. You'll always be my baby, my little girl. I—"

"He's not my daddy," Isabel whispered fiercely. Her watery eyes narrowed.

"Of course, Evan isn't! You have a daddy," Leila insisted. "But I want you to be all right with this. I won't . . ." She took a deep breath. "I won't get married if it hurts you that much."

Diane stared at her daughter with her brows knitted together, as if silently asking, "What are you saying?"

Leila looked away from her mother. What she had said, she meant. She didn't want her romantic relationship or her happiness to put a wedge between her and Isabel. The little girl had already gone through so much upheaval. If Isabel couldn't accept Evan, then Leila would break off the engagement. It was as simple as that.

She waited on bended knee, with bated breath, for her daughter's answer. Isabel finally loosened her grip around Diane's waist. She slowly raised her head. "Okay," she whispered.

"Okay, what?" Leila asked.

"Okay, you can get married and we can live here . . . only if Grandma can come with us too?"

"If she wants," Leila assured, smiling genuinely for the first time that night.

"Oh, there's no way I'd let y'all leave me behind! I want to live in a big mansion too, honey!"

Leila rose to her feet and held out her hand to her daughter. "Now let's go downstairs and get something to eat."

Chapter 30
PAULETTE

Paulette stood alone in her spacious bathroom, staring blankly at her reflection in the mirror. The water was running in the sink. She could hear the soft murmur of the sports channel on the other side of the bathroom door and Antonio opening and closing his bedroom closet as he finished getting dressed for tonight's Thanksgiving dinner at the Murdoch mansion. It was a dinner where the entire family would celebrate the end of bad times and what they had to be thankful for. Charisse was doing her stint of court-mandated rehab. Dante was out of their lives and would no longer be able to play his mind games and wreak havoc. Evan and Leila had officially set their wedding date, barring any problems with Evan's divorce. It was a time of renewal in the Murdoch family. The M&Ms were finally on the comeback! But Paulette didn't feel a bit like celebrating.

Her eyes lowered to the monogrammed hand towel that sat on her bathroom counter. She shifted the towel aside, revealing a pregnancy test.

"Hey, baby!" Antonio shouted through the bathroom door, making her jump in alarm. "You almost ready? We're already running late!"

"Yeah, I'm . . . I'm almost done," she called back.

She then grimaced when she saw the smiley face and the words PREGNANT in the digital window. She covered the plastic stick with her hand towel again and closed her eyes, willing the test to disappear.

This was some kind of a joke, some cruel twist of fate. She had wanted for so long to get pregnant again. She had wanted for her and Antonio to *finally* make a baby. And now she was pregnant and couldn't say for sure who the father was. She did the math in her head. She was seven, maybe eight weeks pregnant, and in that time she had slept with both Marques and her husband. At this point, figuring out the paternity would come down to a flip of a coin.

Heads, it's Marques's baby, Paulette thought gloomily. *Tails, it's Tony's.*

Paulette dropped her face into her hands, wondering how she would get out of this.

"You can get another abortion," a voice in her head whispered.

But what if the baby was Antonio's? She didn't want to get rid of their baby, their little one.

"But what if it isn't?" the voice countered.

Then she would be pregnant with another man's baby and Antonio would be the cuckold forced to raise another man's child.

Paulette slowly shook her head. She couldn't do that to Antonio. She had betrayed him in so many ways in the past few months. There was no way she could do that to him too.

Just then, her phone rang. She was never without it nowadays, always keeping it within arm's reach for fear of leaving it around and Antonio stumbling upon a text message from Marques. She grabbed it and glared down at the screen. She pressed the green button on the glass screen to answer.

"What do you want?" she asked.

"You coming over tonight?" Marques asked between munches.

"No, I . . . I can't." Paulette glanced over her shoulder at the closed door. She could hear Antonio laughing at something one of the sports commentators said on television. "I have something with my . . . my family tonight."

Marques sucked his teeth. "You ain't come over yesterday either! You always got some damn excuse!"

"I can't, okay? I just can't. Not tonight."

"Yeah, well, your ass better come over tomorrow night." He munched again. "I don't wanna hear no shit either. You better wear something nice, something sexy, and have that pussy nice and wet and ready for me," he growled, making her cringe, "or that man of yours is gonna get a call. *Understand?*"

Paulette hung up on him. She slammed her phone down on the counter, feeling tears sting her eyes. More threats . . . more blackmail . . . more bullshit. And now she was pregnant.

She finally realized she was postponing the inevitable. Eventually, Marques would get tired of threatening her and tell Antonio the truth. Or maybe Dante would tell Antonio to take out his revenge on her. She would always be looking over her shoulder, waiting for the day when all her secrets would get out.

This has to end, Paulette thought, gathering the pregnancy test, dumping it into a plastic bag and hiding it underneath the sink. *I can't do this anymore. This has to end. I'm telling Tony everything tonight. Everything!*

She had made things right with her family. Now she had to make things right with Antonio too. Before she could second-guess herself, she swung the bathroom door open to find her husband sitting on the edge of the bed, peering up at their flat-screen television.

"Tony, I have something to tell you," she said, catching him by surprise.

He turned to look up at her. He raised his brows. *"Ooookay,"* he said slowly and chuckled. "That doesn't sound good."

She took a deep breath, feeling her heart thud wildly in her chest and her stomach seize into knots. The rush of blood sang in her ears.

He narrowed his eyes at her. "What's wrong, baby? You look sick."

She had so much to tell Antonio about her history with Marques, his blackmailing her, the money, their affair, and finally the pregnancy. Where should she begin? What was the most gentle way to explain so many devastating things to the man she loved?

When Paulette didn't answer him but instead continued to take deep breaths as she stood in the bathroom doorway, he rose from the bed.

"If you don't feel well, we don't have to go to the party, honey. We'll just tell your brother we—"

"I cheated on you," she blurted out, saying the words with an exhalation of breath.

There, she thought. *It's out. It's finally done. I said it!*

Antonio blinked at her in amazement. "What did you say?" He chuckled again. "I don't think I heard you right because it . . . it sounded like . . . like you said you cheated."

"You heard me right, Tony." She swallowed and lowered her eyes. "I cheated on you."

His handsome face crumbled. His mouth fell open.

"And I'm so . . . *so* sorry," she said to the carpet, unable to meet his gaze. Her vision blurred with tears. "I never wanted to hurt you. I never wanted to have sex with him. I had no other choice!"

Antonio took several steps back until he bumped into the bed. He landed heavily on the mattress, like someone had shoved him back onto his butt. He grabbed the edge of the bed to stay upright.

"He blackmailed me, baby. He knew a . . . an old secret about me and blackmailed me into giving him money. I should have stopped it then. I should have told him to go fuck himself and . . . and let it end at that. But I was so ashamed, Tony! I thought giving him the money would make him go away, but . . . but it only made it worse! Then he blackmailed me into sleeping with him. He said he would tell you the truth, that he would tell you *everything*. He keeps calling me, Tony, and I can't tell him no! But I'm tired of it. I'm so tired of being scared and—"

"Wait!" Antonio barked, making her jump and finally raise her eyes to look at him. His dazed expression had disappeared and was now replaced with fury. "Wait just one goddamn minute! Are you . . . are you telling me this shit wasn't even a one-time deal! Are you still fucking this guy?"

Now Paulette was at a loss for words. That's all Antonio was concerned about? Whether she was still sleeping with Marques?

"No . . ." She paused and licked her lips. "Well, not really."

"Not really? *Not really?*" He shot to his feet. "What the fuck does that mean?"

She raised her hands. "Tony, I'm trying to explain to you the circumstances behind—"

"I don't give a shit about 'circumstances'!" he bellowed, making her clap her hands over her ears. "I just care that *my wife* . . . the woman who I trusted is fucking some other guy behind my back!" He shook his head and pulled at the knot in his tie, yanking at it like it was a noose around his throat. He ripped off his tie and tossed it onto the bed. He began to pace in front of her. "How long? How long has this been going on? How long have you been fucking him?"

"Baby, none of that—"

"Just tell me how long!" he shouted.

Veins bulged along his temples. The cords stood out along his neck. His dark eyes looked wild and bright with rage. He was starting to scare her.

"Three months," she said weakly, feeling fresh tears on her cheeks. She was starting to tremble. "Maybe four."

"Four goddamn months." He shook his head again. "That would explain all those late nights at the gym. I thought you were avoiding my mother or that you were trying to lose weight. That you had 'body issues.' But you were getting a workout, all right! Weren't you, Paulette?"

She pursed her lips and didn't respond to that jibe.

"Who is he? Is he your trainer . . . some guy you met at the gym? Do I know him?"

He was firing questions at her and still pacing, but all she wanted him to do was hold her and tell her that everything would be fine. She wanted him to tell her that the nightmare was over and that he forgave her, but it was obvious now that wasn't going to happen.

"Damn it, answer me, Paulette!" Antonio ordered, making her cringe.

"Y-y-you don't know him," she whispered, shaking her head and wrapping her arms around herself. "He's . . . he's an old boyfriend."

"What's his name?"

She squinted at Antonio. Why did he want to know that?

"What's his name?" he repeated again, glowering at her and taking a menacing step toward her. "What's that motherfucker's name?"

She was still gaping when he suddenly lunged for her, grabbing her shoulders and shaking her so hard that her bones rattled. "Tell me! Tell me, goddamn it!"

"Tony, you're hurting me!"

"Just tell me his name!" he ordered as he shoved her back against the wall.

"It's Marques!" she screamed and he finally released her. Paulette's teeth were chattering from how much she was shaking. "Marques W-w-whitney."

She watched helplessly as her husband stormed across their bedroom's plush carpet. He grabbed his car keys from his mahogany dresser, along with his cell phone. She took hesitant steps toward him.

"What . . . what are you doing?"

He turned and roughly shoved past her on his way to their bedroom door.

"W-where are you going, Tony? *Tony?*"

He didn't answer her. Instead, he strode through the bedroom doorway into their second-floor hall. She raced after him, running to catch up with him as he went down the hall and then the staircase. He took the steps two at a time.

"Tony, please don't leave! I'm sorry!" she yelled as he walked across their marble foyer, swung open the front door, and slammed it closed behind him. She stared at the closed front door in shock.

"I'm so sorry," she whispered before crumbling to the bottom step and bursting into sobs.

Later that night, Paulette called her husband's cell phone more than a dozen times. He never answered. Evan called her, along with Leila and Terrence.

"Just checking to see if you guys are on your way," Evan said in the voice mail message. "We don't want to start the dinner without you. Give me a call when you get this."

But Paulette never returned their phone calls. She just sat in the dark at the bottom of the staircase, crying softly and waiting for her husband to come home. She stared eagerly at the window when she caught sight of passing headlights, only to close her eyes, dejected when the headlights didn't turn into her driveway and, instead, continued down the road.

At 3 a.m., Antonio still had not returned. Heartbroken and exhausted, Paulette finally climbed the stairs, collapsed into her bed, and drifted off to sleep.

Paulette awoke a little before eight o'clock with puffy eyes and a hung-over feeling, like she had downed several bottles of wine. She pushed herself up to her elbows and looked to her left to find her husband's pillow still empty. Her shoulders fell.

So that's it, she thought as she pushed her hair out of her eyes and stared at the vacant spot on the bed beside her. Her marriage was over. She wondered whether she or her brother would get divorced first.

Paulette slowly climbed out of bed and went into her bathroom, removing her cocktail dress from the night before, which was now soiled with her sweat, tears, and makeup. She took a quick shower, brushed her teeth, and tamed the rat's nest that was her hair so that she could put it into a braid at the nape of her neck. By the time she walked down the stairs in a T-shirt and drawstring pants to the foyer below, she felt less groggy but still miserable. She also felt slightly nauseated, though she wasn't sure if that was the aftermath of the horrible night she had endured, or morning sickness starting to rear its ugly head. As she neared the kitchen, she paused. Her eyes widened in amazement. She halted in the entryway.

"Tony?"

He was standing near the granite counter with a laundry basket filled with folded clothes in one of his arms. A glass of orange juice was in his other hand. He was watching the small flat-screen TV on one of the kitchen counters. The volume was set on low, but she could see he had turned on the morning news where a digital map showed backups along the major arteries of Capital Beltway. It was such a benign scene—Antonio standing there in the kitchen with a laundry basket watching the news—that it caught her off guard. It was like she had pressed rewind and last night had never happened.

"Tony, what are you . . . when did you get in?" she asked, gazing at him in disbelief.

He glared at her. The look on his face alone—contempt mixed with barely contained anger—was a reminder that last night had indeed happened.

"Not too long ago," he mumbled.

She hesitated again before stepping into their kitchen. "Look, Tony, about . . . about what happened yesterday . . ."

"I don't want to talk about it."

"But . . . but Tony, I still have to—"

"I told you, I don't wanna fucking talk about it!" he exploded, slamming his glass back to the kitchen island, causing juice to splash over his hand and onto the granite.

She watched as he dropped the basket to the floor, grabbed the edge of the counter, leaned forward, and closed his eyes. She could see the muscles in his back and arms go rigid. He took several long breaths.

"I just . . . I just need some time, all right?" he rasped hoarsely. "I just need some time . . . to work through this."

She nodded. "Okay," she whispered. "Whatever . . . whatever you need."

He opened his eyes and looked at her. He then grabbed the basket from the floor and strode out of the room.

Paulette stood alone in the kitchen for several seconds, not moving and listening to the sound of the news broadcast playing in the background and Antonio's angry footsteps.

Her marriage wasn't over, but it was nowhere near to what it used to be. Antonio said he needed time, but how long would that be? Would he forgive her in enough time for her to tell him about the baby? Would he figure out that she was pregnant before she had the chance to explain everything to him?

Paulette sighed wearily and reached for a roll of paper towels and began to clean up the spilled orange juice. She looked at the glass that Antonio had held and saw that it was now cracked. She poured out the juice and tossed the glass into the trash, then grabbed the cold pitcher filled with OJ and carried it across the kitchen to the refrigerator.

Even though her life was falling apart, that didn't mean she also had to have a dirty kitchen.

As she placed the pitcher on the kitchen shelf, she noticed the news broadcast on television out of the corner of her eye. Police cruisers were parked in front of the wrought-iron fence of an apartment complex. The scene gave her pause. She turned and looked at the screen more closely. It was Marques's apartment complex with the bold words HOMICIDE underneath it.

Paulette quickly reached for the remote and turned up the volume, feeling her hand shake as she did it.

"Police are investigating the homicide of a long-time resident of Blue Arbor Towers," a female voice said as the camera zoomed in on the front door of Marques's apartment building, where several officers, in uniforms and plain clothes, streamed in and out. "The victim, Marques Whitney, was bludgeoned and strangled. Witnesses say that they heard noises coming from Whitney's apartment sometime in the early morning hours. Several report that they heard screaming, but no one saw the victim or anyone else leave the apartment."

A panicked voice started to scream in Paulette's head, "Where was Tony all last night when he wouldn't answer your phone calls? Where did he go? Did he use Marques's name to find him? Had Antonio tracked down her lover and strangled him to death?"

No, Paulette thought desperately as her shaking increased. *Tony wouldn't do that!*

The TV screen cut to the placid face of the Asian woman behind the news desk.

"Whitney was facing charges of drug possession and violation of parole at the time of his death. A confidential source said police speculate that his murder may be drug related. There are currently no suspects." The woman abruptly smiled. "In lighter news, a local track team is headed to—"

"I'm beat," Antonio suddenly said behind Paulette, making her whip around from the television and stare up at him. "I'm getting some sleep."

Paulette stared at Antonio, looking at his calm expression. She gaped.

"I'll be in the guest room. I'm moving my things in there," he said flatly.

"O-okay," she said softly, then watched her husband walk out of the kitchen and slowly up the stairs.

As she stared at Antonio's retreating back, she fought to control her breathing. She couldn't stop shaking. The vague nausea that she had felt before suddenly came over her like a superstorm. She turned, raced to the kitchen sink, and vomited until she felt completely empty.

Secrets and scandals are a way of life for the wealthy
Murdochs of Chesterton, Virginia. But the lies that
bind them may end up tearing them apart . . .

Don't miss the next thrilling novel in the
Chesterton Scandal series,

Lust & Loyalty

Available now

From Dafina Books

Wherever books are sold

Hospitals weren't usually happy places, especially the Wilson Medical Center ICU, where many of the patients hovered near death's door and a pall of sickness seemed to hang over every surface. But today the ICU staff at least *tried* to be festive in honor of the new nurse's birthday. Meredith, the plump nurse with the springy red curls and freckles, was turning thirty. The other nurses figured the big 3-0 deserved, at minimum, a small party in their break room. They had even brought a cake and candles for her. One of the nurses, Rhonda, had brought balloons and streamers that were left over from her nephew's birthday earlier that week. By the time they had finished decorating that sad-looking room, with its bare white walls, lone microwave, coffeemaker, and two tables, it looked like a completely different place. A small two-tiered cake sat at the center of one of the tables on a cotton bedsheet they used as a makeshift tablecloth.

They decided to hold the party midday when visiting hours were at a lull because many of the patients' families would leave to eat lunch and return in an hour or so to stand vigil at their loved ones' bedsides. The five nurses on that shift had agreed to take turns at the front desk and keep an ear out for buzzing from patients' rooms, though most of the patients were so sedated they wouldn't be buzzing anything. Not Mr. J. Hinkler in room 402, who was dying of cirrhosis of the liver, or Mrs. C. Reynolds in room 410, who had suffered multiple strokes and was now little more than a vegetable connected to a respirator, and certainly not Mr. D. Turner in room 406.

Turner was the youngest patient in the ICU, and if it weren't for the gunshot wound to the stomach that he had suffered a week ago, he probably wouldn't have found himself in the ward at all. He looked fit and handsome. The nurses had speculated that he had been quite the heartbreaker before the shooting. A few of them had even whispered about his six-pack abs and muscular arms, and admired and giggled about another appendage they had noticed while changing the dressing on his wound.

"No wonder his name is Dante," Rhonda had murmured ruefully as she pointed to his bare crotch. "A man *that* fine wielding *that* thing could certainly drag a girl through hell and back!"

But Mr. Turner wouldn't be putting any women through hell or breaking any hearts any time soon. He remained heavily sedated while his body repaired itself. And unlike the other patients, he'd had few to no visitors in his room.

Nurse Kelly took the first shift while the rest attended Meredith's birthday party. She glanced through the glass doors of each hospital room, including Mr.

Turner's, as she walked from the break room to the front desk, carrying her slice of carrot cake. She passed an old woman who gave her a wan smile before entering room 403.

"Hello, Mrs. O'Shea," Kelly said, giving her greeting from the doorway.

"Good afternoon," Mrs. O'Shea said as she dragged a chair toward the bed to sit next to her husband, who was dying of end-stage lung cancer.

A minute later, Kelly plopped into her rolling chair and dug into her carrot cake, finishing the entire slice in less than three minutes and licking the remaining icing off the plastic fork tongs and the tips of her fingers. She looked longingly at her empty paper plate. She could use a second slice.

A moment on the lips, a lifetime on the hips, she thought, glancing down at her wide hips that were encased in blue scrubs. She had been trying to lose her last ten pounds of baby weight for ages. Plus, she was supposed to be staffing the front desk while the other nurses were at the birthday party.

But then Kelly ran her tongue over her lips, tasting the remains of the cream cheese icing, and she almost shuddered in ecstasy. She remembered how fluffy the cake itself had been, how the bits of carrot had been so crisp.

"Just one more," she mumbled, rising from the chair. "I'll be quick."

With the exception of Mrs. O'Shea, it was dead as a doornail around the ward—no pun intended. None of the patients would miss her.

It was just seconds after Kelly walked out of the break room and plunged her fork into her second slice of carrot cake that she heard the alarm, a piercing beep to alert them at the nursing station that a patient was in distress. She rushed down the corridor, still holding her plate of cake in one hand and fork in the other, wondering if it was Mrs. Reynolds or poor Mr. O'Shea.

That's when she spotted something black jump out of room 406 and flash past her, like a wraith in a horror movie. She screamed and dropped her cake and fork to the floor. It was only after a few blinks that she realized it wasn't some ghost that had flown out the room, but a person—a living, breathing person dressed head-to-toe in black—hoodie, cap, and sweatpants—who was racing with breakneck speed down the hospital hallway.

"Hey!" she shouted after him—or her. She couldn't tell the sex of the person at this distance. "Hey, what were you—"

Her words died on her lips when the person slammed into the metal doors, shoving them open and disappearing into the adjoining hall. The door slammed shut behind them.

Kelly stared in shock at the closed door until the alarm shook her out of her daze. She turned back to room 406 and saw a pillow slumped on the linoleum floor. Her eyes raised and she saw Mr. Turner. His head was now tilted to the side instead of sitting forward and upright in its proper position, and it looked like his breathing tube had been partially removed. The white tape below his nose now flapped limply, revealing the peach fuzz above his lip. His mouth hung open like that of a catfish on a slab of ice.

"Oh, God," she whispered, feeling the carrot cake and bile rise in her throat as she realized what had happened. She rushed into the room and heard thunderous footsteps behind her as the other nurses and doctors came to assist.

It looked like someone had tried to kill Dante Turner—*again.*